Adrienne Chinn w[...]
up in Quebec, and [...]
after a career as a journalist. [...]
film researcher before embarking on a career as an interior
designer, lecturer, and writer. When not up a ladder or at the
computer, she can usually be found rummaging through flea
markets or haggling in the Marrakech souk.

www.adrienne-chinn.co.uk

X x.com/adriennechinn
f facebook.com/AdrienneChinnAuthor
○ instagram.com/adriennechinn

Also by Adrienne Chinn

The Lost Letter from Morocco

The English Wife

Love in a Time of War

The Paris Sister

IN THE SHADOW OF WAR

ADRIENNE CHINN

One More Chapter
a division of HarperCollins*Publishers*
1 London Bridge Street
London SE1 9GF
www.harpercollins.co.uk
HarperCollins*Publishers*
Macken House, 39/40 Mayor Street Upper,
Dublin 1, D01 C9W8, Ireland

This paperback edition 2024
1
First published in Great Britain in ebook format by
HarperCollins*Publishers* 2024

A catalogue record of this book is available from the British Library

ISBN: 978-0-00-850166-2

This novel is entirely a work of fiction. The names, characters and incidents
portrayed in it are the work of the author's imagination. Any resemblance to actual
persons, living or dead, events or localities is fictionalised or coincidental.

Printed and bound in the UK using 100% Renewable Electricity
by CPI Group (UK) Ltd

For my grandmother, Edith Adelaide Fry Chinn, and my grandfather, Frank Thomas Chinn, who, in 1922, made the journey from Britain to Alberta, Canada with my aunt Betty and my father Geoffrey to start a new life. Neither Edith nor Frank would ever see Britain again.

'Our paths may change as life goes along, but our bond as sisters will remain ever strong.'

Unknown

Cast of Characters

MAIN CHARACTERS

Cecelia (Celie) Fry Jeffries – *the eldest sister*
Dr Jessica (Jessie) Fry Khalid – *the elder fraternal twin of Etta*
Etta Fry Marinetti – *the younger fraternal twin of Jessie*
Christina Fry – *the sisters' mother*
Gerald Fry *(deceased)* – *the sisters' father*
Frank Jeffries – *Celie's husband*
Louisa (Lulu) Jeffries – *Celie and Frank's daughter*
Dr Aziz Khalid – *Jessie's husband*
Shani Khalid – *Jessie and Aziz's daughter*
Carlo Marinetti *(deceased)* – *Etta's husband*
Adriana Marinetti – *Etta and Carlo's daughter*

OTHER KEY PLAYERS

Harold (Harry) Grenville, the 6th Earl of Sherbrooke – *Christina's ex-lover, father of Celie*

Dorothy Adam – *Harold Grenville's ex-lover, mother of Christopher Adam*

Christopher Adam – *Harold Grenville's illegitimate son*

Max Fischer – *Celie's ex-fiancé*

Hans Brandt – *Max Fischer's stepbrother*

CJ Melton – *Etta's American lover*

Ruth Bellico – *American journalist, Jessie's friend*

Antonio Rey – *Republican freedom fighter, Barcelona, Spain*

Mavis and Fred Wheatley – *Celie's friends in Canada, parents of Ben Wheatley*

Ben Wheatley – *Lulu Jeffries' friend*

Robson McCrea – *American photojournalist*

Madame Layla Khalid – *Jessie's mother-in-law*

Zara Khalid – *Jessie's sister-in-law*

Isham Ali – *Zara's lover*

Stefania Albertini – *Christina's cousin, owner of Villa Serenissima in Capri*

Liliana Sabbatini – *Stefania's housekeeper and confidant*

Mario Sabbatini – *Liliana's grandson, Adriana's friend*

Paolo Marinetti – *Carlo's son from his first marriage*

Zelda Fitzgerald – *Etta's friend*

Hettie Richards – *Christina's housekeeper in London*

Ellen Jackson – *Christina's friend*

Marta Tadros – *the Khalids' cook and housekeeper in Egypt*

Kip – *Lulu's border collie dog*

Alice – *Adriana's ginger tom cat*

Part I

1932

Chapter One

Christina

Clover Bar, Hither Green, London - March 1932

Christina Fry pulls back the sheer curtain from her bedroom window and gazes out at the long green sliver of garden. The branches of the rowan and cherry trees bend under the assault of the pelting rain, and the path under the rose arch is littered with the blushing petals of the cherry, as the yellow heads of the daffodils weep over the flattened grass. Thunder rumbles and crashes and the sky lights up in a momentary flash. *Easter in England*, Christina muses. *Always best never to expect too much. Probably a good maxim for life.*

She releases the curtain and lets it fall back into place. She walks over to the large brass bed where the portrait Harry Grenville – now Lord Sherbrooke, of course – had painted of her on Capri when she was a young woman lies unrolled on the blue satin bedcover beside her old green diary. Sitting on the bed, she picks up the diary and opens it to the entry for August 6th, 1891.

He wishes to finish my portrait. I have agreed to meet him at the grotto on Sunday after lunch. Cousin Stefania always takes a long riposo – *nap – on Sunday afternoons, and the housekeeper, Liliana, and her husband, Angelo, who is the gardener here, have the afternoon off, so I shall be quite on my own. As long as I am back to the villa by five o'clock, no one will be the wiser.*

My heart, my heart. We will be alone together again. How I long to feel his kisses again.

How could it be over forty years since that summer that changed her life? She'd had such hopes for her future when she'd turned twenty that April – she was to start art classes in London that autumn, and she'd expected to meet her future husband – young, handsome and wealthy, of course – at one of the many balls she'd attend during the season. She'd been pretty and privileged, the beloved daughter of a respected architect and his beautiful Italian wife. The world was her oyster.

Then her mother and her baby brother had suddenly taken ill and had died of the Russian flu, and she'd been sent by her grieving father to stay with her mother's cousin, Stefania Albertini, on Capri to escape the flu raging through London. And there, one day when she'd been sent out by her aunt to buy lemons for her housekeeper, Liliana, she'd met Harry Grenville.

She runs her fingers over the smooth face of her youthful self. It had been the most wonderful and the most awful time of her life. She had loved – oh, she had loved! Every day of her love had been the high colour of an Italian summer, the scent of lemons and rosemary, and her heart skipping at the touch of his fingers, her body turning to honey under his kisses. And then it had all come crashing down around her when Harry had abandoned her, expecting his child, alone on Capri.

The long months of pregnancy and the difficult birth are little more than shadowy memories, and even these she suppresses when they threaten to infiltrate her mind. *At least Cecelia came from it all. I shall never regret that.*

What would she have done back in London if it weren't for Gerald Fry, the serious, self-effacing photographer who'd rescued her from her shame? Or had she entrapped him? She had woven a lie about the death of a fictitious Italian husband leaving her with a newborn baby, and that she'd thrown herself on the mercy of her English aunts. Gerald, bless him, had believed her, and she had done everything she could to ensure that he would fall in love with her. When he'd asked her to marry him, she did so without hesitation or expectation of the passion she'd experienced with Harry Grenville.

She'd never regretted her decision. Gerald had been a wonderful father to their daughters – Cecelia, and the fraternal twins Jessica and Etta – and a loving husband to herself. When she'd asked him to conceal the circumstances of Cecelia's birth and agree to the fallacy that Cecelia was their own daughter – for Cecelia's own good, of course – he'd agreed. In fact, Cecelia and Gerald had shared a special bond. They both had serious, conscientious and dutiful characters, and they had shared a passion for photography. Cecelia had been more like Gerald than his own daughters.

When Gerald had finally discovered the truth, she'd meant to make amends. It was only then, at the thought of losing him, that she'd realised how much she had come to love him. She loved him for his kindness, his thoughtfulness, his love and encouragement of their daughters, his hard-working determination to provide a good home for his family. Loved him for loving her, despite all her numerous faults. But he'd been killed by a German bomb before she could tell him this. She would take that regret to her grave.

There is a sharp rap on her bedroom door. 'Ma'am?' Hettie calls through the locked door. 'Taxi's outside.'

Christina rapidly rolls up the painting in its brown paper wrapping 'He's late.'

'Told 'im as much. 'E said, what do you expect with the rain pissin' down. Not my words. 'Is words.'

'Thank you, Hettie,' she says as she ties the string around the package. 'I shall be there directly. I mustn't keep Etta waiting. No doubt she is anxious to get home from the hospital after all this time.'

Chapter Two

Christina & Etta

Maudsley Hospital, Denmark Hill, London – March 1932

Etta Fry Marinetti, the youngest and, even at the age of thirty-seven, many would agree to be the loveliest of the three Fry sisters of Hither Green, London, with her bob of wavy honey- blonde hair, hazel eyes and skin as pale as milk, steps out through the blue doors of the psychiatric hospital into the spring sunshine, a large yellow-haired doll clutched in her hands. She pauses between the two towering Portland stone Doric columns that flank the modest concrete stoop and, raising her head to the sky, shuts her eyes and lets the rain wash over her face.

A hand closes around her left elbow. 'Etta, whatever are you doing? Come along, dear. The taxi's waiting. Hettie's prepared us a luncheon of ham and leek pie and has threatened to feed it to Adriana's hideous cat if we're late.'

Etta focuses her eyes on her mother. 'Mama? Of course, I forgot you were coming.' She blinks sleepily. 'Where are we going?'

Christina smiles stiffly and opens her umbrella. 'Home, dear.'

Etta's face brightens. 'Will Adriana be there? Matron's given me this lovely doll for her. Do you think she will like it? She has golden curls just like Adriana.'

Christina eyes the chubby-cheeked doll, feeling quite certain that her precocious sixteen-year-old granddaughter would look down her nose at the gift.

'Darling, I'm afraid Adriana won't be at home,' Christina says as she directs Etta toward the waiting taxi. 'She decided to stay at her school in Surrey during the Easter recess to study for her examinations.'

Etta frowns. 'That doesn't sound like Adriana.' She laughs. 'She's always getting into terrible scrapes with Mayor Esposito's daughter.'

Christina regards her daughter from beneath the brim of her stylish green felt slouch hat. Perhaps it was a mistake to agree to Etta's release from the psychiatric hospital, despite their assurances that she was ready to come home.

'Etta, darling, we're not in Capri. We're in England.'

Etta rubs her forehead. 'Yes, of course we are. I know that. They've given me something that's made me very sleepy. It's muddled my mind. I'm very much better, Mama. Really.'

'Good. Your doctor said you've made good progress, but that you must be careful not to become overstimulated. No more parties with your bohemian friends or jaunts to Paris to sell your late husband's paintings, I'm afraid. You can take up the piano again and come to WI meetings with me. I wouldn't wish to have to send you back here.'

Etta's eyes widen and her breath puffs from her mouth as if she's been hit. 'No, no, I wouldn't want that at all.'

'Neither do I, Etta.' Christina nods curtly at the taxi driver as he holds the door open for them.

Etta slides into the back of the taxi next to her mother. 'Don't talk about Carlo, Mama. It makes me sad.' She picks agitatedly at the worn leather seat. 'Paolo pushed Carlo, you know, Mama. He did, I swear it. Paolo pushed him off that cliff.'

Christina glances at her daughter, whose voice has risen and who is now clasping and unclasping her hands in her lap. It had been all Etta could talk about on that awful journey from Capri when Christina had gone there to bring Etta and Adriana back to London after Carlo's accident. *'Paolo did it! He pushed Carlo! He's a murderer! I saw it! I saw it!'*

Her poor Etta. Delusional, of course. Carlo's son Paolo had been nothing but solicitous and charming after the accident. Yes, he'd filed to replace Etta as Carlo's executor, but that had been entirely understandable given Etta's breakdown. And, yes, he had rather shockingly accused Etta of pushing Carlo from the cliff, but there was no evidence one way or the other, so the whole unfortunate incident had been ruled an accident by the inquest.

Etta had sunk back into a world of confusion and illusion. A world where Adriana was a baby and she a happy young mother awaiting the return of her beloved Carlo from the war. It was the same world Etta had succumbed to after the birth of Adriana back in 1915 when she'd rejected her baby daughter and had insisted that she was still an art student in London.

Then, after trusting Etta to the care of the Maudsley Hospital and Adriana to the nuns at Woldingham School, who would ensure the discipline and good Catholic education her granddaughter deserved, she'd received the letter from her cousin Stefania in Capri. Paolo was contesting Carlo's will, questioning the validity of Etta's marriage to Carlo, and Adriana's legitimacy. It had been a shock, to say the least, after Paolo's attentiveness following the accident. She'd taken that in hand, too, sending money to Stefania to pay for a lawyer to fight Etta's case. A fight that, after two years, appeared to have no end.

She glances at her daughter, who is watching the London

scenes pass by, transfixed like a child enjoying their first automobile ride. She will have to tell Etta about Paolo's lawsuit. Later. A taxi is no place to discuss such things.

She rests her hand on Etta's, noting the bitten fingernails. 'I've had Hettie set up easels for us in the new conservatory. I've been to Green & Stone to buy paints and brushes. My heavens, they're expensive.'

Etta's eyes widen. 'Paint?'

'Yes, dear.' Christina runs her fingers around her right ear and pats unconsciously at her silver-threaded auburn bob. 'I quite fancy the idea of painting again. It is obvious that you inherited your talent from me.'

Etta's fingers worry the doll's golden curls. 'I don't want to paint. I … I can't paint.'

'Whyever not? You always enjoyed it before, and your father spent a great deal of money funding your courses at the Slade School of Fine Art.'

'Please, Mama. You don't understand. I can't … I won't… Please don't make me—'

'All right, Etta. Fine. If you wish to waste all those years of training, I will respect your decision. I trust you have no objection to me painting?'

Etta shakes her head. 'No.'

Christina looks out the window at the frontages of the dull grey shops as the taxi speeds through the London suburbs. 'I was a free spirit like you once, Etta. In my experience it does no one any good. It's time to settle you down into a quiet life. Trust me, you will be so much happier.'

———

Hettie Richards, Christina's middle-aged housekeeper, sets a plate of homemade Bakewell tarts on the tea table in the sitting room's bay window and reaches for the teapot.

'More tea, Miss Etta?' she asks as she hovers the Royal Worcester floral teapot over Etta's teacup. 'Nuffing like Earl Grey, I always say. It's a proper English cuppa.'

'It's Mrs Marinetti, Hettie,' Christina reprimands. 'One must observe proper protocol.'

Etta smiles at Hettie's dour square face, relieved to feel the grogginess abating after a rest and tea. 'I'm simply Etta as I've always been, Hettie, and I'd love some more tea and one of your Bakewell tarts.'

Christina waves away Hettie's offer of tea. 'Where are the cannoli I had sent around from Terroni's yesterday? You haven't eaten them all, have you, Hettie?'

''Ow could I? You 'ad two wiff your cocoa last night and anovver two for breakfast. We've only an 'andful left. Why else do you fink I made the Bakewells? Couldn't 'ave Etta finking you 'ave a meagre tea table, could we? I 'ave to fink free steps ahead, and accusations of theft is the fanks I get.'

'Yes, well, do bring them in now, Hettie, if I can trouble you. Do help yourself to one, if you must. But not chocolate.'

Etta shakes her head as Hettie departs muttering under her breath. 'I'm amazed Hettie is still here after all these years, Mama. You do give her a hard time.'

Christina waves her hand dismissively. 'The fact of the matter is that I couldn't manage this house and the Chelsea flat without her, and she knows it. We have become two rather grumpy companions in our advancing years.'

She dabs at her lips with her napkin and sighs as she anticipates Etta's reaction to the news she is about to impart. 'Etta, I'm afraid I have some bad news.'

'What do you mean?'

Christina rises and retrieves a letter from the walnut secretary. 'Stefania sent me this two years ago, a few months after you entered the hospital. I'm afraid that while you were ill, Paolo contested Carlo's will—'

'He what?'

'I'm sorry, my dear.'

Etta presses her hand against her forehead. 'I remember … I remember Paolo and Carlo arguing at the grotto. Paolo said something about Carlo's will. He said…' She squints in concentration. 'He said that he'd ensure Adriana and I never saw a penny of Carlo's inheritance.' She looks over at her mother, her hazel green eyes wide. 'He said he'd see me and Adriana out on the street.'

'Etta—'

'What's he done, Mama? What's Paolo done?'

'Wait, please. Calm down. You need to know what happened while you were in the hospital. Let me read Stefania's letter.'

April 11th, 1930

My dear Christina,

I am so sorry to write you this letter. As you know, I have been fighting with Paolo Marinetti in the court on Etta and Adriana's behalf since he contested the will after Carlo's death last August. It has been a terrible battle. Paolo is well-connected through his late mother's family and has been able to call upon these connections to both fund and promote his claim on the entirety of Carlo's estate.

The circumstance of Adriana's birth out of wedlock while Carlo was still married to Marianna Ludovisi has unfortunately worked against Adriana, despite the fact that Carlo left half of his estate to her to be kept in trust until her twenty-first birthday. He has left the other half of his estate to be divided equally between Paolo and Etta, who was, at the time of his death, his legal wife. However, Carlo and Etta's marriage so quickly after Marianna's death, and Carlo's arrest for Marianna's murder that same day, has played into Paolo's favour.

Even so, we might have prevailed had it not been for Paolo's insistence that Etta had pushed Carlo to his death at the Grotta di Matermania that day. It is ridiculous, of course. I saw with my own eyes how happy Etta and Carlo were those last two years here at Villa

Serenissima with Adriana, and, of course, there is no proof. But Etta's breakdown and her rapid departure from Capri were seen, in some quarters, as an admission of her guilt. Christina, Paolo has won.

Carlo, despite his fame and his reputation as one of Italy's greatest modern artists, was not a rich man at the time of his death. Etta was very successful selling his paintings in Paris when he was in prison, but the money went to pay the lawyers and judges and any number of others in our fight to secure Carlo a retrial.

Carlo's death at the grotto has pushed him into the realm of the immortals. Paolo arranged for Carlo's remaining paintings to be sold by a leading art dealer in Rome. They sold for an incredible amount. This was before he contested the will, and I had thought the majority of this money would go to Etta and Adriana; but, as Carlo's now legally acknowledged heir, it has all gone to Paolo.

There is nothing left for Etta or Adriana. I am so sorry, Christina. I am old. I have been on this earth eighty-three years. I do not know how many more the Lord will give me. I have no children of my own, but I have this lovely home on Capri and a few modest investments left to me by my dear late husband. I am leaving these to Etta and Adriana in my will. They have been the family I never had. I wish only that I could do more.

I enclose a letter sent to me by Paolo's lawyer for Etta. I cannot imagine that it will be a pleasant read for her if and when she is well enough to read it. She is in my daily prayers. I know that you have arranged the best of care for her, and have taken Adriana in hand by enrolling her in a good school in England. Between the two of us, we shall ensure that they will not only survive, but thrive.

Your loving cousin,

Stefania

Christina folds the letter and lays it on the table. 'It is difficult to believe that the nice young man I met in Capri when I went to collect you and Adriana was capable of such a vendetta.'

'Paolo cares for no one but himself,' Etta says bitterly. 'It appears that a very great deal has happened since I went mad.'

'Etta, I do wish you wouldn't say things like that. You went through a terrible trauma that day at the grotto. Your doctor said it was similar to the soldiers coming back from the war with shellshock. You were ill, but I am assured that you are well now.' Christina scrutinises her daughter over her reading glasses. 'Do you feel up to reading Paolo's letter? It's been an active day. Perhaps it would be best to wait.'

Etta shakes her head. 'No. I'm fine, Mama. Give me the letter. I'd rather know everything now.'

Christina retrieves an envelope from a drawer in the secretary and hands it to Etta, who slices it open with her butter knife. She clears her throat and reads the letter aloud.

Etta,

There. I have won, as I knew I would. As fate would have it, because of the prices obtained by the recent sale of the last of my father's paintings, I am far closer to becoming the richest man in Italy than I imagined could be possible at the age of twenty-eight. For this I thank you with all my heart.

I do not know if you will ever read this, as I understand you have lost your mind, just as my mother lost hers. It seems my father had that effect on his wives!

Ha! Ha! I won't cry for either you nor my bastard half-sister. You were my father's problem, not mine. Now that I have what my father owed me, I am content.

I expect we shall never meet again.

Paolo Marinetti

Etta lays the letter down beside the plate of Bakewell tarts as she feels her spirit reawaken. *Those were* my *paintings that you sold for a fortune in Rome, Paolo! Every brushstroke came from* my *brushes.*

That was my *money. Mine and Adriana's. You won't get away with this, Paolo Marinetti. You haven't won. Not by a long chalk.*

'Etta? Are you quite well? You're flushed.'

Etta looks at her mother. 'I'm very well, Mama. I couldn't be better.'

Chapter Three

Celie

West Lake, Alberta, Canada - March 1932

Ol' Man Forbes rings open the till and counts out one dollar in coins. He hands them over to Celie Jeffries. 'Mighty sorry it can't be more, Mizz Jeffries,' he says, the drawl of his Georgia youth barely diminished despite thirty years in Canada. He slides his spectacles up his broad nose and scratches at the grey hair springing like wire from his head. 'Your pies are mighty popular, but everyone's pinchin' their pennies. Gotta keep prices low.'

Celie counts out the coins and frowns. 'I think...' She clears her throat. 'I'm sorry, Mr Forbes, but I seem to be fifty cents short.'

The old man sucks in his breath and shakes his head. 'Sorry, Mizz Jeffries. Times is tough. I've had to reduce my prices or they don't sell, good as they are.'

Celie tries to ignore the sinking sensation in her stomach. She smiles weakly and slides the coins into her change purse. She'd hoped to have enough to add it to the money she'd saved to buy a roll of camera film, but the film would just have to wait. 'That's all right, Mr Forbes. I understand. I'll bring you some strawberry tarts next week.'

Ol' Man Forbes glances up from writing in his ledger. He peers over the top of his spectacles at Celie. 'Oh, don't you be worryin' 'bout that. These here pies you brought in today will do me fine for a week or so. How 'bout we talk again end o' the month?'

'Oh. Yes, of course.' She wipes a bead of sweat off her forehead with her finger. 'I … uh … how about if I were to bring you some fresh eggs? We have more than we can possibly eat and they're terribly delicious—'

The old man smiles. 'Got plenty of eggs comin' in weekly from Mizz Majors.'

'Of course. Yes, well, what if I were to bring you some bread? I make a lovely crusty loaf. Even Frank says so, and you know how particular he is.'

'Oh, I don't know, Mizz Jeffries—'

'Mr Forbes,' a voice says from behind her, 'I've had the pleasure of eating Mrs Jeffries' rye and sourdough breads and they're better than any I've had even in Edmonton or Montréal. You must try them out.'

Celie jerks her head around. 'Hans? Hans Brandt? Good heavens!' She throws open her arms and embraces her former student. 'What are you doing in West Lake? Shouldn't you be in Montréal? Your Aunt Ursula said you'd got a job working as an engineer for Dominion Textile.'

Hans Brandt, tall, slim and blondly handsome in a tailored wool coat and navy cashmere scarf – far from the coltish boy she'd taught English with the other German immigrants back in the Twenties – takes off his fedora and laughs as he submits to Celie's effusive greeting. 'I was, but I'm here to visit my aunt and my uncle in Freedom for a week before I move to England.'

'England? What are you going to be doing in England?'

'I'm very pleased to say that I've secured a job at Vickers

Supermarine Aviation in Southampton,' he says in an accent as Canadian as the prairie wheatfields. His blue eyes light up. 'I'm finally going to be an aeronautical engineer just like I always dreamed of.'

'I'm so pleased for you, Hans!' Celie says, smiling. He's so much like his stepbrother Max was all those years ago when she'd met her new German tutor at the university in London. So full of enthusiasm and optimism. Has it been almost twenty years since that day? How could she be a girl of nineteen in love one day and an exhausted woman of almost thirty-nine the next?

She takes hold of Hans's arm. 'Let's go have some tea next door at the hotel.' She taps her handbag. 'My treat. You must bring me up to speed on everything.'

Hans opens the door, the bell tinkling above. 'Tea would be a pleasure, Mrs Jeffries. And cake, of course, but I insist on paying. It's the least I can do for the woman who taught me both English and how to believe in dreams.'

That evening, Celie is peeling potatoes for a rabbit stew when the door slams open and her husband Frank enters the kitchen. He pulls off his ice-crusted mittens and stuffs them into his woollen cap, which he tosses onto a chair.

Their daughter, Lulu, looks up from her notebook where she is working through her mathematics homework with her border collie, Kip, curled snoozing at her feet. 'Daddy!'

Frank lets his muddy boots clomp onto the floor as he shrugs out of his coat. 'Hello, sweetheart.' He hangs his coat on a hook and joins Lulu at the kitchen table, kissing her on her head. Looking over her shoulder, he taps at one of her calculations. 'Remember what I told you about your sums.'

Lulu huffs as only an almost-twelve-year-old can. 'I know. Please Excuse My Dear Aunt Sally.'

'And what's that stand for?'

'Parentheses, Exponents, Multiplication, Division, Addition and Subtraction.' She frowns at her sums and erases her solution. 'I made a mistake, but I'll fix it.'

'Good girl. We all make mistakes.' He glances at Celie. 'We just don't always manage to fix them.' He yawns and stretches. 'Supper's not ready?'

'I'm sorry, Frank. I bumped into Hans Brandt at Forbes's store and he treated me to tea and cake at the hotel. He's here to visit his Aunt Ursula and Uncle Klaus before he heads off to London for a new job. I'm afraid I lost track of time. Supper will be in half an hour.'

Frank sets the wash bowl into the ceramic sink and splashes water into it. 'I've been out trudging through the snow fixing fences all day. I shouldn't have to wait for supper just because you've been off gossiping with Hans Brandt.'

Celie presses her lips together and steels herself for the argument. *Here we go again.* Despite all the help Hans had given Frank on the farm before he went off to university in Edmonton, his patient yet fruitless efforts to teach Lulu violin, the apple strudels and plum cakes he'd bring them from his Aunt Ursula, and his gift of Kip to Lulu on her fifth birthday, the mention of Hans's name always set Frank on edge. *It's time to stop blaming every German for the war, Frank.* Even as she finishes that thought, she knows that Frank's intolerance has only a little to do with Hans's nationality. It's because Hans reminds him of Max, the man she had once loved and planned to marry. The man Frank knows she still loves.

She shakes a snaking potato peel off the knife and watches it drop into a curl like a question mark on the wooden cutting board. 'I couldn't very well not talk to him, could I? He's done awfully well for himself. He's off to design aeroplanes for Vickers Aviation in England.'

'Bully for him.'

'I gave him Mama's telephone number and made him promise he'd visit her when he's in London.'

Frank grabs the bar of yellow Sunlight soap and begins sudsing his hands. 'He's part of the family now, is he? You do like your Germans, Celie.'

Celie drops the paring knife onto the table. 'What is that supposed to mean?'

'You know what I mean.' He spies the camera tripod propped against a wall and her camera hanging from a coat hook as he shakes his hands over the washing bowl. 'Taking pictures again? When you had the job on the paper I understood it, but now it's nothing but a vanity project. Is that what you've spent your inheritance money on when we haven't had a decent cut of meat in a year and we still don't have our own truck? I'm a laughing stock getting around on old Betsy and a bike. We could get some money for your camera gear at the pawn shop.'

Celie picks up a potato and jabs the knife into the brown skin. 'Don't even think about that, Frank. Papa gave me that camera.'

'Offal and eggs, day in and day out.' His eyes narrow. 'Have you been skimming off the housekeeping money to buy film?'

'Frank—' Celie glances at Lulu, who is frowning over her slide rule. 'Let's discuss this later.'

'I want to know where my money is going, Celie.'

'*Your* money? The payments on the tractor and the mortgage ate up *my* inheritance, Frank. You know that as well as I do.'

He tugs the tea towel off the handle on the range and wipes his hands dry. 'You're my wife, Celie. Your money is *our* money.'

'Well, it's a moot point now.' Celie glares at Frank as he flops into his armchair and commences to tap tobacco into his pipe. 'I'm not going to stop taking photographs, Frank. It's the only thing I do for me. Rex Majors still pays me for pictures for the newspaper from time to time, even if he can't afford to have me write articles anymore.'

'Do you think I want to spend all the hours of the day working the fields only to have the wheat shrivel up and blow away in a dust storm, Celie? Do you think that's what I want to do for *me*?' Frank runs his hand through his thinning hair. 'I'm just about managing to keep food on the table and a roof over your head. I'm doing everything to keep my side of the bargain.'

Celie glances over at Lulu, who quickly looks back at her sums, frowning in mock concentration. 'Lulu, would you go get the laundry off the clothesline? We'll have supper when you come back.'

Lulu nods vigorously and pushes away from the table. 'Come on, Kip. Let's go play catch.'

The screen door slams behind them, and Celie turns to Frank, her jaw tight with anger. 'Is that what you think our marriage is? A bargain?'

'What would you call it? You still love *him*, don't you? *Max Fischer*. That's why you're friendly with all these bloody Germans. They all remind you of him and the life you might have had if you hadn't married me.' He thumps his hand against his chest. 'I'm what you've got, Celie, so get used to it.'

'Oh, I've gotten used to it, Frank. As long as you stay in your room and I stay in Lulu's, we'll manage. But I won't have you bossing me around. I'm sick to death of it.' She points the knife at her husband. 'Do you hear me, Frank? I know you spend money on moonshine and poker.'

'Is that right?' Frank says as he presses the tobacco into the pipe with his tobacco-stained fingertip.

'And the morphine.'

His head jerks up. 'What are you talking about?'

'I found your morphine tin years ago.'

Frank's face drains of colour. 'I've never touched morphine in my life.'

'I found the syringe, the vials, everything.'

Frank rises from the armchair and begins pacing the kitchen linoleum like the lion she had seen once at the Calgary Zoo.

'Are you accusing me of being a drug addict, because if you are ...' He shakes his head. 'How could you ... Why would you ... I would never—'

'Stop it, Frank.'

He turns to face her, his breath as shallow as a panting dog's. 'Celie ... I don't know what you want me to say.'

'You started taking morphine during the war, didn't you? Jessie told me that a lot of soldiers became addicted. Little morphine care packages sent from home courtesy of department stores like Harrods "to help ease the strain of battle".' She emphasises the quotation marks with her fingers. 'I remember seeing the advertisements in the newspaper.'

Frank's shoulders slump. He flops into the armchair and presses the fingers of his left hand against his eyes.

'I'm sorry, Celie,' he says, all the fight drained from him. 'I thought I could stop. I said to myself that as soon as we got to Alberta, I'd stop.' He drops his hand and peers up at her, his brown eyes those of a man near defeat.

The dark circles under his eyes have deepened, she notes, and a quiver of compassion shudders through her body. *How have we got to this point?* She had cared for him once, and he had loved her. She had tried so hard to love him, had convinced herself in the first few years after Lulu's birth that she did love him. Not like how she'd loved Max, of course. That had been special. Max had been the love of her life. No, her love for Frank had been a different kind of love. A mature love – that's what she'd told herself. It was the practical, dutiful love for someone whom she had chosen to travel with down the same path 'till death do us part'. But over the years of constant struggle to carve out a new life in this unforgiving prairie, the love had begun to wear away like a rock assaulted by waves until now there was nothing left but sand.

'I told myself I'd stop when Lulu was born, Celie. And then...'

Frank's voice cracks. 'Then I couldn't. It had me. It had me.' The long-hidden anguish rips out of Frank like an exorcised demon.

Celie observes him silently, then she picks up another potato and peels off the skin with the paring knife. She peels potatoes until Frank regains his composure.

'Do you want turnip in the stew?'

Frank wipes at his face with his handkerchief. Then he strikes a match and sucks at the pipe until the tobacco catches light. He exhales a puff of white smoke.

'Turnip would be good.'

Chapter Four

Jessie

Cairo, Egypt – March 1932

Kasr al-Ainy School of Medicine, Egyptian University

Jessie Khalid pushes her way through the mass of young male medical students in expensive grey suits and red *tarbouches* streaming into the large lecture amphitheatre, ignoring, as she always did, their *tsks* of disapprobation. She spies the cluster of black-gowned women students in *hijabs* in the seats against the left wall near the door to the toilets, their view of the visiting American professor's demonstration of the miraculous new iron lung machine for polio patients partially obscured by an ill-placed pillar.

Again? Seriously? The familiar feeling of injustice flares inside of her and she grits her teeth. Why are the women students always allocated the worst seats? Why do the men expect it and the women accept it? She was, of course, quite used to seating herself in the middle seats of the lecture halls, indifferent to the circle of empty seats that would suddenly appear around her as the male students shuffled away, as well as fielding the tediously predictable complaints in the registrar's office for her 'disrespect of protocol', but the cavalier injustice of the ongoing situation annoyed her no end. *It's 1932, for heaven's sake! This will not do.*

She stomps down the steps and taps a young woman on her black-clad shoulder. 'Fatima. What is everyone doing sitting here in Timbuktu behind this pillar? There's a row of empty seats down at the front.'

The young woman glances at the other women and back to Jessie, clearly unsure of how to respond. 'It is where we were told to sit, Jessica.' She smiles, her round face anxious to mollify Jessie's irritation, and gestures to an empty seat by the wall. 'There is a seat here for you. If you bend your neck, you will see well.'

Jessie grunts. 'There are only seven of us and a full row of empty seats right in front of the iron lung machine. Are they saving the seats for some special visitors?'

Fatima shakes her head. 'No one wishes to be noticed by the American professor and asked a question.'

Jessie ponders the empty seats and shifts her heavy leather schoolbag to her opposite hand. 'I've waited a long time to get into medical school and I am not afraid of being noticed by an American medical specialist who has been invited here to educate us on the latest innovations in polio care.'

'Yes, Jessica, but you are English. The English are used to getting their way. It is not the same thing to be an Egyptian woman. We must tread carefully or opportunities such as studying medicine can easily be taken away from us. There are many in Egypt who object to it' – Fatima glances around the room at the chattering men – 'as you know.'

Jessie shrugs. 'All right, I understand. But don't you think putting obstacles in our way' – she thumps the pillar – 'is meant to compromise our ability to learn? Then, when we do poorly, because we haven't been able to see the demonstration or hear the lecturer properly, they say it's because we're women, and, of course, anyone can see women have no place trying to become doctors?'

Fatima shakes her head vigorously. 'We mustn't call attention to ourselves. It would not be seemly.'

Jessie huffs. 'What has being seemly got to do with being able to actually see the demonstration today? Honestly, Fatima, we are being set up to fail at every turn.' Jessie heads down the steps. 'I'm going to sit down in the front.'

'Wait, Jessica.' The young Egyptian chews her lip, then she stands up abruptly and turns to the other women.

'Jessica is right. We have already been forced into the worst seats simply because we are women. We must not be silenced now that a door has been opened to us. Let us sit at the front where we cannot be ignored.' She collects her stack of notebooks and joins Jessie by the empty seats on the front row.

Jessie turns around to face the others. 'Well? What are you waiting for?'

Fatima beckons to the women. 'Come, sisters. These are our seats. It is only for us to claim them.'

Altumanina, Gezira Island, Cairo

Madame Layla Khalid looks up from the Louis XV settee and lays the copy of *L'Egyptienne* magazine she's been reading in her lap, her gold bracelets jangling like bells. She arches a black eyebrow below her gold silk turban and addresses Jessie like an imperious Egyptian queen.

'Ah, you have finally decided to grace us with your presence, Jessica. Dinner is long over and Marta has gone home.'

Jessie sets her schoolbag down on the marble floor and

unbuttons the jacket of her plain grey flannel suit. 'I'm sorry. We had a professor visiting us from the United States and—'

Layla waves her hand. 'I have no interest in the events of your day.' She rises from the settee, the folds of her black silk *jellabiya* glistening like oil in the lamplight. She picks up the magazine and thrusts it at Jessie.

'Did you give this rubbish to Zara? I found it in her room. It is all about Egyptian nationalism and the right for women to vote. I blame you for this. You and all your Western ideas. Who can possibly want shopkeepers and barbers in government? Everything was so much better when the Ottomans were in charge. Back then, people knew their place.'

Jessie smiles archly. 'Ah, yes, the rich in their villas and the poor in their slums. Everything was so much better then.'

'The poor have no business in government. When my uncle was the Khedive—'

'Yes, everything was so much better then, Layla, I know. For you, perhaps, but times move on. The world is changing.'

Layla huffs, her red-painted lips contorting into a sneer. 'The world is going to the dogs. The *English* dogs.'

Jessie ignores the insult as she slips out of her jacket and lays it over her arm. 'I had nothing to do with the magazine. Zara is a grown woman. She is quite capable of choosing her own reading material.'

Layla tosses the offending magazine onto the settee and strides over to a table where she removes a cigarette and a box of matches from a carved wooden box. She proceeds to light the cigarette.

'I didn't know you smoked, Layla.'

Layla blows out a puff of white smoke and focuses her kohl-rimmed amber gaze on her daughter-in-law. 'I have always smoked. My husband was fond of the cigarettes my uncle imported from Turkey and I picked up the habit from him, though of course I never smoked in front of him.' She draws her dark eyebrows together as she frowns at Jessie. 'You won't say anything to Aziz? He would not approve of his mother smoking.'

'Your smoking is none of my business.'

Layla taps grey cigarette ash into a brass cup. 'It seems we can agree on something.'

'Is Aziz home from his Wafd Party meeting yet?'

'No. It seems I am left to raise your daughter myself.'

Jessie shakes her head. *Again. Always the same thing. Layla the martyr.*

'That's not true. I see Shani off to school every morning and Marta collects her every afternoon and takes her to' – she counts the activities off on her fingers – 'Brownies on Mondays, swimming lessons at the Sporting Club on Tuesdays, her French lessons at the French Institute on Wednesday, her piano lesson with Mrs Bickersteth on Thursdays, and gives her a cookery lesson here on Fridays. I am usually home for supper and I help Shani with her homework, and Aziz and I spend the weekends with her whenever we can. When exactly do *you* raise Shani?'

Layla shrugs her slender shoulders. 'You work poor Marta to the bone. Her cooking is suffering for it. We had *koshari* twice this week. A peasants' dish.'

'Marta is well paid and she's told me how much she enjoys spending time with Shani, especially now that she and her husband have moved into the flat in the gatehouse above the clinic. As for the *koshari*, it's Aziz's favourite.'

'Aziz spoils that woman.'

'You would prefer to cook and manage the household staff yourself?'

Layla returns to the settee and settles down amidst the cushions. She taps ash into the brass cup. 'Certainly not. I wouldn't know how to boil water for tea if you asked me.'

'That's nothing to be proud of, Layla.'

The older woman scrutinises her daughter-in-law like a cat sizing up potential prey. 'You have become quite objectionable these past few years, Jessica. When Aziz first brought you to Altumanina, I thought you were a quiet little mouse. Quiet and plain.' She eyes Jessie's grey skirt, white blouse and sensible black shoes. 'You are no longer quiet, but you are still plain. I have always failed to understand what my son sees in you. It is certainly not beauty.'

Jessie smiles tightly. 'Well, they do say beauty is in the eye of the beholder.' She bends to pick up her schoolbag. 'Besides, I have other qualities. Qualities which, I assure you, Aziz very much appreciates.'

'Don't be vulgar, Jessica.'

'Let's just say that Aziz feels no desire to take a second wife, as much as you have tried to convince him of it. When I first met you, Layla, and in the early days of my marriage to Aziz, I attempted to be polite on his behalf. After you tried to force him into marrying a second wife because of my infertility issues, I no longer felt so obligated.' She heads toward the doors to the entrance hall.

'Jessica! Where are you going? I have something I wish to speak to you about.'

Jessie turns to face her mother-in-law. 'I am going to see my daughter, then I'm going to find something to eat. We have spoken quite enough for one night.'

'Mama! You missed supper. We had *koshari*.'

Jessie enters her daughter's bedroom and sits on the side of the bed. 'So I heard. Was it good?'

Shani nods, her dark curls falling over her shoulders. 'I helped Marta make it. I grated the onion and cooked the tomato sauce and boiled the pasta and the rice too.'

'That's an awful lot of things to have done.' Jessie brushes the errant curls off Shani's face. 'Shani, does it bother you that you have to spend so much time with Marta? You know I have to work and go to the university.'

Shani shrugs. 'It's okay. Marta takes care of me. Sometimes I call her Mama by mistake.'

Jessie's heart jolts with unexpected jealousy. 'Do you? Do you think of her like that?'

'I love Marta.' Shani pats Jessie's hand. 'It's okay, Mama. I love you, too. I'm lucky. I have two mamas.'

Jessie sits back and scrutinises her nine-year-old daughter as the guilt she tries so hard to suppress pushes into her conscience. Shani is so much like Aziz with her dark hair and eyes and warm brown skin. How did she ever create such a smart, beautiful girl?

'You know I love you as big as the moon, don't you, Shani?'

Shani smiles, her dark eyes shining. 'I know, Mama. I love you like the moon, too.'

Jessie leans over and hugs her daughter. 'I'm glad.'

'And I love Marta like the moon, too.'

Jessie sits up as the guilt and jealousy prick at her conscience. 'Yes. Yes, of course you do.'

'Nana Layla was cross you and Baba weren't home for supper. She told Mustapha to give yours to the street dogs, but I said no.'

'Did you, now? What did Nana Layla say to that?'

'She said I was impudent. What does that mean?'

'It means standing up for yourself even if other people object to it.'

Shani nods. 'Just like you, Mama. You're impudent.'

Jessie smiles. 'I suppose I am.'

She reaches for the copy of *Black Beauty* her mother had sent Shani for Christmas and opens to chapter ten. 'Now, where were we? Are you ready for another chapter?'

'Oh, yes!' Shani snuggles under the covers and pulls the sheet up to her chin. 'Mama?'

'Yes, darling?'

'I love you. Even bigger than the moon.'

Jessie smiles at her daughter. 'I love you, too, Shani. More than you can imagine.'

'I'm glad we're both impudent.'

'I'm glad we're both impudent, too.'

Jessie sits back in her desk chair at the table in the old nursery under the gables that she has converted into her study, and rubs at the throbbing callus on her right middle finger. Stretching out her arms, she yawns as she peers out the window at the yellow disc of the waxing moon.

She glances at her wristwatch. Just gone midnight and Aziz is still not home from the Wafd Party's meeting with the British High Commissioner. He worked far too hard and he was looking tired. His job as the head of surgery at the Anglo-American Hospital kept him more than busy. In her opinion, he didn't need to take on so much extra work on behalf of the nationalist Wafd Party now that it was in government. But, as he would tell her when she expressed any concern for the toll it was all taking on him – he smoked far too much now, and had developed a habitual cough – he was, above all else, an Egyptian, one who had been fortunate enough to have been born into a position of privilege, and as such he felt he owed a debt to his country and its citizens. She knows he will never give up the fight for a truly independent Egypt, free of British interference and the king's collusion with the hated interlopers.

She is only too aware, as she is sometimes reminded when she hears shopkeepers and random passersby mumble profanities at her in the Khan el-Khalili souk, that she is, and will always be, one of the interlopers, even though she has done her best to learn Arabic and slide into the rhythms of life in an Islamic country. She has no regrets. Her husband, her child, her home and her work are all in Egypt. She has found where she belongs, even if her mother-in-law would be the first to throw a party were she ever to leave.

She sits back in the chair and drops her fountain pen on the cluttered desk. That's not entirely true. She has one regret, and that's that she has left others to care for Shani while she pursues her own dreams. As much as Shani seems happy with the arrangement with Marta, the guilt is still there, buzzing around her like a pernicious mosquito. If only she'd been able to have another child, a sibling for Shani to share her life with, maybe then she wouldn't feel so guilty. Guilty for failing to give Aziz the son she'd known he wanted; guilty for making Shani an only child. Guilty for putting her own dreams and desires ahead of anyone else's.

She reaches across the stacks of notes and textbooks scattered over the table and picks up a framed black and white photograph. Behind the glass, the faces of three young women in white blouses and dark skirts gaze out at her, the white splashes of the waterfall in Yorkshire coursing down the glistening grey rocks behind them.

She runs her finger over the faces under the glass. *Weren't we all so hopeful and innocent back then?* Celie, a nineteen-year-old German student and earnest suffragette, she and Etta seventeen, with Etta dabbling at art and drama at the local college, and she herself, having just finished her first year of training as a nurse. It's almost thirteen years since she'd last seen Celie in London, and Etta … she hadn't laid eyes on her fraternal twin since Etta had eloped to Capri with Carlo back in 1914. Who's to say when they'd all be back together again, or if they ever would? Still, there were letters, and telegrams, and some day, when telephone connections between Cairo and North America improved, they may even be able to talk to each other.

She pulls out a sheet of writing paper from a stack on the table and picks up her fountain pen. She has just written 'Dear Celie' when she hears the thump of Aziz's feet on the stairs. The door opens and her husband, tall and dark, with threads of white in his thick black hair and moustache, enters.

'There you are, darling. Mustapha said that you were still up.'

Jessie smiles. 'There are no secrets in this house.'

'It appears not.' Aziz crosses over to Jessie and kisses her on her cheek. He takes hold of her hand and pulls her to her feet. He enfolds her in his arms and they stand silently for some time as their mutual fatigue envelopes them.

'You missed Shani's *koshari*,' Jessie says.

'I'm sorry for that. I am certain it was better than the kidney pie at the British Residency.'

'How was your meeting?'

Aziz stifles a yawn. 'The same as it ever is. The British play at being impartial observers here, but they are only concerned with maintaining their own interests, namely retaining control of foreign relations, communications, the military and the Sudan.'

'Do you suppose Britain will ever loosen its hold on Egypt?'

'I would like to think so, and this is what the Wafd Party is working towards, but I am afraid that the Suez Canal is too much of a jewel for the British to relinquish it easily. I can understand why younger Egyptians like Zara are impatient with the Party and get involved in all these anti-government demonstrations. The truth is we all want the same thing: a truly independent Egypt.'

Jessie sighs against Aziz's chest. 'Aziz?'

'Yes?'

'Do you ever regret marrying an Englishwoman?'

'It is the one thing in my life that I have never regretted.' He leans forward and whispers in her ear. 'Come to bed, *habibti*. I am tired and I miss you.'

Chapter Five

Christina & Etta

Clover Bar, Hither Green, London – March 1932

Hettie opens the front door. 'Miss Adriana! What the 'ell are you doing 'ere? I fought you was staying at Wolding'am for Easter.'

Sixteen-year-old Adriana Marinetti steps into the hallway and drops her leather suitcase on the encaustic floor tiles. 'I wrote my friend Mario in Capri to tell him I was staying at school for Easter and he telegrammed me and told me I was being selfish and I should come see Mama,' she says in vowels still lightly kissed by an Italian inflection. She tugs off her woollen scarf. 'So, I came.'

''Ere, then,' Hettie says, holding out her hands. ''And me your coat and 'at and I'll make some tea. They're in the conservatory 'aving words. I 'ad to turn up Mrs Webb's economical cookery programme on the radio as I couldn't 'ear myself fink. Mrs Webb's on about bones today.'

'Bones?' Adriana shudders. 'School dinners of liver and onions and tapioca pudding don't sound so bad.' She thrusts her coat and hat into Hettie's hands and shakes out her bobbed blonde curls. 'Is Mama … okay?'

'Right as rain. Go see for yourself.'

Adriana takes a breath and sets back her shoulders. 'All right. Here goes nothing.'

'Miss? You did the right fing coming.'

'I hope so.'

'Mama?'

Etta looks up from the copy of *The Joy of Cooking* that Christina has gifted her in the deluded hope of awakening a domestic impulse in her daughter and stares in confusion at the strange young woman.

'Mama, it's me. Adriana.'

'Adriana? My word, you're so … grown up!' Etta jumps out of her wicker chair and drops the book onto the cushion. She opens up her arms to her daughter. 'I thought you weren't coming home for Easter! Come, give me a hug!'

Christina wipes her paintbrush on a linseed oil-soaked cloth and stands it carefully in a glass jar with the other brushes as she watches the awkward reunion. 'You should have sent a telegram, Adriana. Hettie may not have bought enough to feed you Easter dinner tomorrow.'

Adriana rolls her dark eyes. 'Hettie always makes far too much food, *Nonna*. And you wouldn't see your favourite granddaughter starve, would you?'

'Favourite granddaughter?'

Adriana shrugs out of Etta's embrace. 'You don't know Shani or Lulu, do you? So, I have to be the favourite. It's logical.'

Christina unbuttons her smock and hangs it on a hook by the glass garden door. 'I'd best go speak to Hettie about tomorrow's menu. She'll be grumbling at me all week if we run out of anything, and that is something that will cause me no end of aggravation.'

Etta takes hold of her daughter's hand and pulls her over to the wicker settee where Alice the ginger tomcat is curled amongst the chintz cushions.

'Come, sit with me, darling. Tell me everything. How are you enjoying school?' The words tumble out of Etta's mouth like prisoners released from imprisonment. 'What's your favourite subject? Is it still art? I always loved receiving your drawings on my birthday. Why did you stop sending them? Has *Nonna* treated you all right on your holidays? She says you're going to Capri this summer to stay with Cousin Stefania for a month. Are you looking forward to that? I brought you a present. A doll. I can see how silly it is now. I thought … Adriana, you've gotten so big.'

Adriana picks up the cat and settles him in her lap. 'Everything's fine.'

Etta sits beside her and reaches out to brush a wayward curl away from Adriana's forehead.

Adriana flinches. 'Don't do that. I'm not a child.'

Etta folds her hands in her lap. 'Of course. I feel like I've missed so much.'

Adriana focuses a frosty look on her mother. 'Really? When I was growing up you spent more time in Paris than you did at Villa Serenissima. Cousin Steffi and Lili were more mothers to me than you ever were.'

'Adriana, I'm sorry. I had to sell Papa's paintings—'

'You could have let the art dealer do that. You didn't have to go to Paris. You were gone for months sometimes. You never thought about me or Papa. You never cared about us. You only cared about yourself.'

'Adriana! That's not true! I came back after Papa was freed from prison. We were a happy family then, weren't we? All of us together on Capri until Paolo—'

'You only came back to Capri because Papa dragged you back from Paris!'

'Adriana, it wasn't like that.'

Adriana cuddles the cat. 'I'm not stupid, Mama. I have eyes and I have ears. I heard Cousin Steffi and Lili talking about you. I knew you'd done something wrong. I saw how angry Papa was when he left for Paris to get you. And then Papa threw Mario out of the house because of you.'

'You were angry, Adriana. I understand, but that was a long time ago—'

'Mario was my only friend, Mama. *You* were the reason Papa made him leave. It's all *your* fault. Everything bad that has happened to me has been *your* fault.'

Adriana jumps up from the settee, holding the cat against her like a protective barrier. 'Did you push Papa off the cliff, Mama? Did you?'

Fragments of memories of that day spin in Etta's mind like playing cards flying through the air. She presses her hands against her forehead. 'Adriana, I ... I—'

'You don't even know, do you? You can't remember a thing. I feel sorry for you, Mama. You only ever think of yourself and when things go wrong, you simply forget how to think at all.'

The items on Hettie's tea tray jiggle as she enters the conservatory. ''Ere we go. Who's 'aving tea? I've made some fresh currant scones to go wiff it.'

Adriana drops the cat onto the floor and pushes past the housekeeper. 'Not for me. I've lost my appetite.'

Three days later

Christina sips her breakfast tea at the dining table, watching through the doorway as Etta shuffles into a raincoat, scarf and hat.

Alice weaves through her feet mewing until Etta picks him up and snuggles him against her cheek. Christina sets down her teacup with a loud rattle.

'It is beyond comprehension why you insist on going out to the pictures when it's pouring like Niagara Falls outside, Etta. And put down that cat. You'll get fur all over your new coat.'

Etta releases Alice onto the Persian runner. 'Are you sure you don't want to come out to the pictures with me, Mama? I'm meeting my old friend Violet at Woolworth's for lunch, then we're going to see *Dracula* with Bela Lugosi at the Prince of Wales Picture Playhouse.'

'*Dracula*? Are you certain that's a good choice, considering your … frame of mind?'

'My frame of mind is fine, Mama. I take my pills every morning. I'm fit as a fiddle.' She pulls on her leather gloves. 'I wanted to go with Adriana, but' – she shrugs – 'well, she had to get back to school to study for her exams.'

'Whatever happened between the two of you this weekend? You barely spoke a word to each other and Hettie was walking on eggshells. Did you say something to upset her? You must really watch yourself, Etta.'

Etta pulls on her leather gloves. 'It was nothing. Silly mother–daughter things.' She smiles weakly. 'I think she was upset about the doll.'

'Yes, the doll was rather a mistake.'

'You didn't need to show it to her. It only made things worse. It made Adriana feel like I didn't know who she was.'

'Don't be ridiculous, Etta. You're her mother. You now have the opportunity to act like one. This rift will heal.'

'I hope so.' Etta takes her felt hat off the coatstand and looks into the hallway mirror as she fixes it over her hair. 'I'll donate the doll to the WI's next flea market. Out of sight, out of mind. Are you sure you won't come to the pictures?'

'I have no intention of leaving this house when Noah is looking for his ark.'

Hettie appears in the hallway, solid and dour in her black dress and white cap and apron, drying a plate with a damp tea towel.

'Did I hear somefing about you being out for lunch, Miss Etta?'

'Listening at the kitchen door again, were you, Hettie?' Christina says. 'And it's Mrs Marinetti.'

Hettie turns her broad, impassive face toward Christina. ''Ow else am I supposed to know what goes on in this 'ouse?'

Etta smiles apologetically at the housekeeper. 'I'm sorry, Hettie. Did I forget to tell you? You know I'd forget my head if it wasn't screwed on properly.' She laughs. 'Oh, silly me,' she says, glancing at her mother. 'It isn't screwed on properly, is it?'

Hettie shrugs. 'Well, you'll just 'ave to make do with cold 'am and pota'oes for tea. I'll not be cooking up anovver 'ot meal today.'

'Cold ham and potatoes sound delicious.' Etta jabs a hatpin into her hat. 'I shall salivate all the way home.'

Hettie follows her out the door and collects the newspaper from the front stoop, oblivious to the chilly breeze that gusts into the house.

Christina looks up from the toast she is buttering to see Hettie hovering in the dining room doorway.

'What is it now, Hettie? Am I ever to eat my breakfast in peace?'

The housekeeper hands Christina the newspaper.

SHERBROOKE DEAD

Prime Ministerial hopeful, the Rt. Hon. Harold Grenville, 6th Lord Sherbrooke, 64, died shortly before midnight last night of a heart attack following a dinner at Quaglino's restaurant in Mayfair. He is survived by his wife, Rose, Countess of Sherbrooke, the former Rose McClellan, heiress to the McClellan soup fortune. There were no children. For a retrospective of Lord Sherbrooke's life, see page 6.

The butter knife slides out of Christina's fingers and clatters onto the wooden floor. Alice yowls and jumps into her lap. The cat's throat rumbles with a low purr as he kneads Christina's legs.

Hettie picks up the knife. 'For what it's worf, you were too good for the likes of 'im.'

Christina listens to the housekeeper's footsteps plod a retreat down the hallway toward the kitchen. She clutches the ginger cat against her and buries her face in Alice's soft, yielding fur.

Harry's dead? How can he be dead? Why do all the men she's loved die?

Chapter Six

Etta

Clover Bar, Hither Green, London – May 1932

Phipps Clinic,
Johns Hopkins Hospital,
Baltimore, Maryland USA

May 8th, 1932

Dearest Darling Etta,

How lovely to hear from you, darling! How clever of you to track me down through Scott's agent. I'm ecstatic that you're a free bird now, back in the land of sanity. Isn't it an odd thing that we both ended up in mental hospitals, darling? You don't suppose it was our punishment for having too much fun in Paris? Oh, but I would not have foregone all our lively times there for a dull little life in the suburbs, although it has certainly done something to my head. Even I can tell that!

I've been in ever so many hospitals since my first breakdown two years ago. I'm feeling much better now, and I've even managed to finish a novel! Yes, me! Can you believe it? Scott thought it was a terrible idea, of course, and insisted I cut out a whole section that he said I imitated from the novel he's been unable to finish for years. He blames me for that, of course. He says he has to spend all his time writing magazine stories to pay for my hospital treatment. Well, I say, can I help it that I've been ill? He's my husband and he has to take care of me, so there.

Anyway, I made the changes to appease him and now he's all for it. He's sorted out some deal with his publisher, and my dear little book 'Save Me the Waltz' will be published in October. I am beyond thrilled! I think it's every bit as good at Scott's 'The Great Gatsby' if I do say so myself!

Now, darling, what are you doing with yourself back in London? Are you painting? I saw you paint in Capri, do you remember? You are terribly talented. More than poor Carlo, to my mind. Have you heard from charming CJ? Is he still in Los Angeles? What are you doing for love, darling? Love is ever so important.

Do something, sweetie. You mustn't let your talents shrivel up and blow away in a puff of dust. Paint, dance, write, act … really, simply be the sparkling talent you are, darling. You are not meant for an average life, nor am I. It is perhaps our blessing and our curse.

Kisses, kisses, kisses.

Love always,

Zelda

PS: Buy my book when it's out! I want it to be a best-seller and show everyone that I'm as good a writer as Scott.

Etta folds Zelda Fitzgerald's letter and slides it into her vanity drawer. She'd read all about her friend's breakdowns and Scott's alcoholism in the old newspapers in the Lewisham library. Why had life played such a vile trick on them all? Carlo dead, Zelda mad, Scott a drunk, and herself … well, she didn't know what she was anymore.

At least Zelda had picked herself up and produced some art.

What does it matter if it's any good or not? Even banged up in a hospital, Zelda's done something. What has she done since her own breakdown after Carlo's death? Nothing. Not a stitch.

Etta frowns at her reflection in the mirror and rubs at a faint wrinkle on her forehead. She lifts her chin and rubs her fingers along her softening jawline. Three wasted years in hospital, her youth slowly fading like a flower fatigued by the effort of its bloom. She pulls out the glass stopper from her Penhaligon's perfume bottle and takes a drink of the honey-sweetened laudanum, eyeing herself as she swallows down the cloying liquid. She licks a drop off her lips and slides the stopper back into the bottle.

Zelda is right. She has to rescue herself from this life of tedious normality. She is bored and irritated with the unrelenting monotony of it all: the grocery-shopping, tea-drinking, church-going, polite conversation-making. She will surely end up back in the Maudsley Hospital if this is to be her life now.

Perhaps she could go back to Capri, though the prospect of returning to the site of Carlo's death fills her with dread. Besides, whatever would she do there, stuck in a house with her elderly cousin Stefania, and Stefania's housekeeper, Liliana? At least here she could escape to the pictures a couple of times a week, even if Hettie was often in tow now that Violet had gone back to Bristol. She huffs out a sigh. Oh, well. At least Hettie liked romances as much as she. And the cinema jaunts were a welcome respite from her mother's tedious prickliness.

She lifts her chin and examines her creamy complexion in the mirror. She could still pass for twenty-five. Certainly, no one would guess that she'd be turning thirty-eight on her next birthday. A touch of rouge on her cheeks, some cake mascara, a dash of her favourite Tangee lipstick, and some carefully pencilled eyebrows, and she'd give any Hollywood film star a run for their money.

She smiles into the mirror and pats at a wayward dark blonde curl. There is another possibility.

Sliding open the drawer, she takes out a piece of pristine cream paper. She unscrews the cap on her fountain pen and bends over the sheet.

Clover Bar,
   Hither Green Lane,
   Hither Green, London SE13

May 29th, 1932

Dearest CJ,
   It's me, Etta! How are you, darling? Do you miss me out there in Hollywoodland? Well, you needn't miss me any longer. Darling, I've been thinking…

Chapter Seven

Christina

Clover, Bar, London - May 1932

Christina sifts through the letters Hettie has set on the table beside her breakfast before leaving for the grocer's. The usual – utility bills, something from the WI, which she suspects is her annual membership renewal, the monthly newsletter from St Saviour's Church – then something unexpected addressed to "Mrs Frank Jeffries care of Mrs Gerald Fry". A return address is printed in elegant black lettering on the upper right-hand side of the envelope: Grenville, Montcrieff & Smith Solicitors, Pleasantview Chambers, 57 Lincoln's Inn Fields, London WC2A.

She studies the envelope. The address has been neatly inked by some poorly paid clerk who had rebelled against the restrictions of their position with a looping flourish on the final 's' of 'Jeffries'. Harry Grenville's legal chambers. She remembers the many days she would sit on a bench under a Judas Tree in Lincoln's Inn Fields, waiting for Harry to exit the glossy black door in the imposing Georgian building where he'd spend his days shuffling papers and plot his climb to leadership in the Conservative Party and its inevitable step to Prime Ministership of the United Kingdom.

She knows without opening the letter that it is to do with Cecelia's inheritance of the grand Bishop House in Marylebone, London. Cecelia *and* Christopher Adam's inheritance, of course. Harry's *two* illegitimate children.

The house means everything to her. It is the house that she grew up in and that her aunts Henrietta and Margaret Bishop had stolen from her upon her father's death. She'd persuaded Harry to buy the house before Henrietta's death, with the expectation of moving into it herself, only to be confronted on the doorstep by Harry's other mistress, Dorothy Adam, to whom Harry had rented the house for a penny! Oh, she'd been furious! And Dorothy's intransigent stance that her son Christopher, being male, outranked Cecelia's claim on the property had done nothing to dampen her ire over the past five years.

In the years that she'd known him, when the excitement of their youthful love affair and their later reconciliation had faded like a rose thirsting for water, Harry had shown himself to be self-centred, pompous, calculating and fickle. But he had promised her that he'd leave the house to both Cecelia and Christopher in his will so long as she and Dorothy swore never to reveal his identity as their children's father. Not only swear to it but also sign a legal document. She'd signed, of course, as had Dorothy. What choice did she have? It was the only way she'd get *her* house back, the house that should always have been hers.

She toys with the butter knife. She shouldn't open the letter. She should post it to Cecelia. But her daughter hasn't a clue about any of this. As far as Cecelia knows, she'd been born in London on May 3rd, 1893, the daughter of Gerald Fry and Christina Innocenti Bishop Fry, not one year earlier on Capri, the daughter of Harold James Grenville and Christina Innocenti Bishop. The only people left who know the secret are Christina, her cousin Stefania and

Stefania's housekeeper Liliana in Capri, and, quite unfortunately, Etta. She can trust everyone else to say silent, but Etta is a worry. Etta is a problem she has yet to solve.

No, she can't inflict this shock on her daughter. Cecelia must never know that the late Rt. Hon. Harold Grenville, the 6th Lord Sherbrooke, was her father. Christina runs her fingers around her ear as an idea takes hold.

She slips the butter knife under the envelope flap and slices through the paper. She scans the officious document. Harry has been as good as his word. He has left the house to both Cecelia and Christopher as an 'anonymous benefactor'. That is something, at least, but still strange enough to cause Cecelia to start asking awkward questions. No, there is only one solution that she can see.

She has her daughter's signature on any number of letters. It would not take too much effort to replicate it. Mrs Frank Jeffries, owing to her absence in Canada, will nominate her mother as her representative in the matter of Harry's bequest. She smiles at the simple elegance of the solution. No one will question it. She is Cecelia's mother, after all. She would have her daughter's best interests at heart. The only question left, now, will be how to deal with Dorothy and Christopher Adam, and Christopher's claim on half the property, but that is a problem for another day.

Chapter Eight

Celie

West Lake, Alberta, Canada – July 1st, 1932

Celie, her best friend, Mavis Wheatley, and Lulu shuffle across the back seat of Fred Wheatley's flatbed truck and step down into the dirt road in front of what was normally a stretch of patchy grass sandwiched between West Lake School and the town dump, which one of the early city fathers had, in a fit of optimism, misguidedly named Belleview Park. Today, however, to mark the national Dominion Day holiday, the park had been transformed into a fairground of games stalls and food vendors, and under a striped awning in the left corner of the park, in front of the dump, the local Lions Club brass band was screeching its way through an enthusiastic rendition of 'Just a Gigolo'.

Twelve-year-old Ben Wheatley, only a day older than Lulu but already a foot taller, leaps down from the back of the truck followed by his sixteen-year-old brother, Arthur, and Kip, who spins through the legs of the boys, barking in excitement.

'Secure the back well, boys!' Fred Wheatley shouts out his

window. 'I don't wanna lose the spare tyre like last week. Mrs Philby was *not* happy with it endin' up in her delphiniums.'

'Hold on, Fred,' Mavis says as she dabs at her perspiring forehead with the back of her hand. 'We need to get the picnic baskets and blanket out first.'

'Sure thing, Mave.'

Celie loops the handle of a wicker picnic basket around her arm and walks around to the front passenger window. 'Aren't you coming, Frank?'

'In a bit.' Fred Wheatley leans across Frank who is sitting in the passenger seat. 'Gotta go pick up Molly and her friends at the Majors' cottage up at the lake. They were up there for Lily Majors' seventeenth birthday party last night. I expect I'll find 'em splashin' around the lake screamin' like girls do when I get there.'

'Sure,' Celie says. 'Frank, you don't have to go. Why don't you come into the fair with the rest of us? Spend some time with your family?'

Frank's jaw tightens. 'Don't I have free will? Do I always have to do what you want, Celie? I might just want to spend some time with my friend. Is that permissible?'

Celie backs away from the window, her face colouring in embarrassment at this public display of discord. 'Of course, Frank. Enjoy your drive. I'll be here with Lulu.'

Mavis joins Celie as she watches the truck bump along the road in the direction of the lake. She loops her hand under Celie's and regards her with grey eyes clouded with concern. 'Everything okay?'

'Fine, Mavis. Everything's fine.'

'Good.' Mavis smiles at her friend. 'Do you suppose they have Hook a Duck? I haven't played that in ages and I'd quite like to have a go.'

Celie leans back on her elbow on the tartan wool picnic blanket and props her chin in her hand as she watches the townspeople enjoying the fair's entertainments. Frank and Fred have returned, and are now playing horseshoes with a group of local men, lubricated by what she suspects is some of Mavis's bathtub beer that Fred had hidden under the tarpaulin in the back of the truck.

She scans the milling crowd and sees Lulu and Ben laughing as they toss balls at the stack of cans in the Tin Pan Alley stall.

'Looks like Lulu and Ben aren't arguing for once.'

Mavis glances over at the pair from beneath the purple straw hat she'd bought from a hat hawker up from Edmonton. 'Ben has a terrible crush on her, you know.'

'I know. Poor Ben. I'm afraid Lulu's heart is already taken by Kip. And Hans, of course.'

Mavis laughs. 'Lulu isn't the only one who fancies Hans Brandt. Molly and Lily Majors used to swoon over him when he'd come to the house to teach Arthur and Ben knots for the Scouts. Poor Hans used to have to drink his body weight in the strawberry Kool-Aid Molly would make up for him.'

Celie sits up abruptly. 'Oh, no. It's Emma Philby. Oh, piddle. She's seen us.'

The tall, upright figure of the head of the school's board of governors and the Women's Christian Temperance Union steps through a group of children playing marbles, provoking squeals of indignation, and makes a beeline for their picnic blanket.

'Here we go,' Mavis says under her breath. She smiles broadly at the woman, who, despite the heat, is dressed in a high-necked, long-sleeved brown dress and brown felt hat. 'Hello, Emma. Enjoying the fair?'

'I wouldn't say "enjoying" exactly, Mavis. Why anyone thinks spending a holiday with crowds of inebriated men and screaming children is something to be enjoyed, I will never understand.'

'Times are hard, Emma,' Celie says. 'Everyone needs to let off a bit of steam. It was good of some of the town merchants to fund the fair this year with everything so tough.'

'The merchants can afford it, can't they? They're the ones making money off of us.'

Mavis clears her throat. 'My husband was one of the organisers of this fair. Is he one of the money-grabbing merchants you're referring to?'

Emma Philby swats away the question like a fly. 'Of course not, Mavis. Your husband is a fine, upstanding member of the St Andrew's Anglican Church council. He gives generously to the church.' She eyes Celie from under the brim of her hat. 'I haven't noticed your husband in church of late, Cecelia. You haven't converted him to Catholicism, have you?'

'Frank's been busy on the farm. He's had other priorities.'

'Priorities higher than attending church? Well, standards are certainly falling in this world.'

Mavis glances at Celie, then looks back up at the interloper. 'Was there something you wanted, Emma? You must be sweltering in that dress. Yes, in fact, you're getting awfully flushed. I'd head over to the lemonade stand if I were you.'

Emma graces Mavis with a withering look. 'I simply came over to ask Cecelia if she will be entering anything in the Women's Christian Temperance Union's baking contest this year. I didn't see anything from you in our stall, Cecelia, and everyone knows you sell your baking at Forbes's General Store.'

'I'm afraid not, Emma. Not this year.'

Emma harrumphs. 'Well, that is disappointing. I had expected as a member of the Women's Christian Temperance Union's board, you would have made an effort. We are rather thin on the ground with entries. I'm afraid Ursula Brandt's plum cake may yet again prevail.'

'It's very good cake.'

'It's *German* cake, Cecelia. We must speak to the Girl Guide leader about teaching our local girls to bake proper Canadian cakes and pies. I find it most embarrassing.'

'You could always bake something, Emma,' Mavis says. 'In fact, why haven't you?'

Emma smiles condescendingly at Mavis. 'My skills lie in organisation and leadership. I have little time to indulge in pie-making.'

A whistle blows and the band strikes up 'Minnie the Moocher'. Emma frowns. 'Someone needs to speak to the Lions Club about their music selection. In fact, I think I shall go and do that right now.'

Celie shakes her head as Emma Philby strides obliviously through the marbles game, knocking Cat's Eyes, Corkscrews and Benningtons through the fingers of the scrabbling children. 'There goes a woman who believes West Lake would become a den of iniquity without her stewardship.'

Mavis laughs. 'You mean she's full of herself.'

'That too.'

Mavis takes the thermos out of the picnic hamper and refills their cups with iced lemonade. She takes a sip and regards her friend. 'Is, um, is everything all right at home, Celie?'

Celie looks up from her cup. 'Yes. Of course.'

'It's just that, well, I know things have been tough for you both since the stock market crash in twenty-nine.' She reaches across the blanket and squeezes Celie's hand. 'You can talk to me anytime, Celie. It will never go any further. Not even to Fred.'

Celie nods. 'Thank you, Mavis.' She takes a sip of lemonade and looks out at the holidaymakers. 'I didn't bake anything for the stall this year because I couldn't afford to. I need the ingredients to make pies and things for Mr Forbes. Frank complains that he's the only person in town who never gets to eat his wife's desserts.' She sighs. 'I can't believe my life has degenerated to worrying about baked goods.'

'Celie, why don't you speak to Rex Majors about getting your old part-time job at the newspaper back? You should have brought your camera today. You could have taken pictures of the fair and written something about that. There are plenty of things happening around West Lake that people would love to read about in the paper. It doesn't all have to be doom and gloom.'

'I'm out of film, Mavis. I'm trying to save up for it, but, you know, there's always something else to pay for. Anyway, the last time I spoke to Rex, he said advertising is down and that means he has fewer pages he can print. And that means he can't afford me, except for a photo every once and awhile, which is hardly going to keep the wolf away from the door. I think my newspaper career is well and truly over.'

'Well, you need some money, and Rex Majors needs to sell newspapers. As Plato said, "Necessity is the mother of invention." We just need to think of a solution.'

Celie cocks an eyebrow at Mavis. 'Since when have you been reading Plato?'

'The travelling library. You wouldn't believe what you can get your hands on. I'm onto Kierkegaard next.'

Chapter Nine

Jessie

Altumanina Health Clinic, Cairo, Egypt – August 1932

Jessie slams the cab door and yawns as she fumbles in her handbag for the key to Altumanina's gate. She is about to turn the key in the lock when the gate creaks open. Her forehead wrinkles in irritation. She will have to speak to the gardener Mohammed about being more careful about locking up when he leaves at the end of the day. They can't afford to have the medical supplies in the health clinic taken, especially as supplies are getting harder to come by in Cairo with the economy in such a terrible state.

She shuts and locks the gate behind her and heads up the long drive toward the house, the white marble chips crunching under her feet. The sky is clear and moonless tonight, and stars twinkle like glitter on a black canvas. She is walking past the door to the health clinic when something causes her to stop abruptly. She turns her head to listen. What was it? A sound? She listens for a moment or so, but all she hears is the background buzz of cicadas.

She shifts her schoolbag to her opposite hand and is about to continue toward the house when she hears it again. Someone or something is in the health clinic.

She sets down her schoolbag and tiptoes over the marble chippings toward the clinic's door. Gripping the door handle, she slowly turns the knob. She pushes the door open and two dark figures freeze.

'Who's there?'

'It is me, Jessica. Zara.'

Jessie switches on the overhead light. 'Zara?' She looks over at the other figure, immediately recognising the man's fine-boned face. In his arms he carries a box laden with rolls of bandages and bottles of Dakin's Solution. 'Isham?'

Jessie's sister-in-law, Zara Khalid, shrouded in a black cloak and *hijab*, steps forward and clutches Jessie's arm. 'Please, Jessica. We need these. There was another demonstration today in the city. The police came and there were some injuries. Nothing serious, *alhamdulillah*, but we needed more supplies.'

'I thought you'd stopped doing this kind of thing, Zara. And, Isham, what are you doing here? If Aziz sees you, you'll be lucky to get out in one piece. He blames you for Zara's involvement in these protests.'

'It is not Isham's fault, Jessica. It is my choice. I am a proud Egyptian and I choose to fight for our independence.'

'The Wafd Party is doing that, Zara. Why don't you simply let the politicians and advisers like Aziz get on with things? You are all working toward the same goal.'

'They take too long,' Isham says. 'If we leave negotiations to them, we will always be under Britain's thumb.'

Jessie glares at Isham and turns back to Zara. 'What am I meant to do? Turn my back and ignore you? Let you and Isham swan in here whenever you wish, and take away supplies that you of all people, being the clinic manager, know the clinic needs? I turned a blind eye once and almost got both of you killed. Aziz saved your life when you were stabbed at the House of the Nation demonstration, Isham. You thank him by stealing our medical supplies?'

'It is not personal. It is simply a requirement.'

'It's personal to me!'

'Please, Jessica,' Zara pleads, 'let Isham go with this box and we will leave. We will not take supplies from here again.' She presses her hand against her breast. 'I promise with my heart and my honour.'

Jessica looks over at Isham and nods reluctantly. She digs into her handbag and takes out the key to the gate. 'You'll need this. I locked the gate. Slide it under the gate when you leave and I'll collect it before I go into the house.'

'There's no need for that, Jessica.' Zara indicates for Isham to leave. She shuts the door behind him and looks back at Jessie.

'What's going on, Zara?'

'I have a key. I am leaving with Isham.'

Jessie scrutinises her sister-in-law, noticing, for the first time, the smudges of fatigue under her eyes and the fine lines etching across Zara's forehead. 'Zara, I can't let you do that. What would your mother and Aziz say if they found out I let you leave with him? Your reputation—'

'Jessica, Isham and I are married.'

Jessie's mouth falls open. 'You're what? Does Aziz know?'

'No, of course not. Do you think he would have agreed to my marriage to a gardener's son? He is more modern than my mother, but not so modern as to accept such a rebellious act on his only sister's part.'

'Zara, I don't know what to say.'

'Say, "I wish you great happiness.". Say, "May Allah bless you with children." Say any of the things people say when a couple who love each other marry. You and Aziz married for love. You, above all people, should understand.'

Jessie pulls Zara into a hug. 'Zara, of course I wish you well. I love you like a sister. I only hope that you know what you're doing.'

'Can we ever know what the consequences of our choices will be, Jessica? Did you know when you married Aziz? We simply have to do what we believe is right, and for me, marrying Isham was right.'

Jessie releases Zara from her embrace. 'What am I to tell your mother and Aziz at breakfast tomorrow?'

'You need not worry, Jessica. I will be back by five o'clock and down for breakfast at the normal time. Marta lets me in the kitchen door.'

'Marta knows?'

Zara smiles. 'Marta knows everything. She has a romantic heart.'

Chapter Ten

Etta

Clover Bar, Hither Green, London – August 1932

Etta eyes the triple-layered Victoria sponge cake with thirty-eight blackened candles stuck in the powdered sugar like cactus spikes.

'Was it really necessary to deface a perfectly good cake with Woolworth's entire stock of birthday candles?' she says as Christina slices into the golden sponge.

Christina slides the slice onto one of her mother's Royal Worcester china plates and hands it to Adriana. 'Blame Hettie. I said one representative candle would be sufficient, but she insisted.' She brushes her forehead with the back of her hand. 'Why you and Jessie chose to be born in the middle of August, I'll never understand. It's as hot as Hades today and those candles don't help one jot.'

Adriana dabs at the strawberry jam oozing out the side of the cake and licks it off her finger. 'I'll bet Auntie Jessie's having a proper party with champagne and guests and dancing.'

Etta rolls her eyes. Adriana was still cross at having to leave her summer holiday on Capri to come back to London for her mother's inconvenient mid-August birthday.

Christina huffs. 'Not if her dreadful mother-in-law has anything to do with it. I've never met such a difficult woman.'

Adriana picks up Alice and sets the cat in her lap. 'I've been told that I'm difficult all my life. One Christmas I asked Father Izzo why Joseph didn't divorce Mary when he found out Jesus wasn't his son. I had to do fifty Hail Marys as punishment for my *insolenza*. I don't care. I have a mind and voice of my own and I intend to use them. If that makes me difficult' – she shrugs – 'then I'm difficult.'

Christina arches an auburn eyebrow. 'I wish you luck finding yourself a husband with that attitude, Adriana. Men don't like outspoken women. I know from experience.'

Etta eyes her mother across the table. Finally, a chink in her mother's armour. She'd been wondering how to broach the subject of the late Lord Sherbrooke with her mother. When she'd discovered Celie's Italian birth certificate in Villa Serenissima just before Carlo's death and written to her mother about it, she'd been told in no uncertain terms to keep out of it and not to mention anything to Celie. She'd done it, though it hadn't been easy.

But now that Lord Sherbrooke is dead, isn't it time for Celie to know who her real father is? The papers are saying that Lady Sherbrooke is contesting some 'issues' in the will. What if Lord Sherbrooke had left Celie money, or even his big estate up in the Scottish Borders? Imagine that! She and Adriana could move in there with Celie, Frank and Lulu. There would be plenty of room. Maybe she'd start painting again. She shivers involuntarily. No. Never. Painting is her portal to madness. She will never pick up a paintbrush again.

'Every woman will meet men who disdain women who have opinions, Adriana,' Christina continues as she pours out more tea.

'If you haven't yet, then consider yourself extremely fortunate. They are most exhausting.'

'They sound perfect for me, *Nonna*. I like a challenge.'

Christina lays her napkin on the table. 'Enough of this silly discussion. Etta, I wish to broach the subject of Adriana's determination to move into a flat in Bloomsbury next year with two other young girls. I do not feel it is appropriate for a girl of eighteen to be out on her own in the centre of London.'

Adriana huffs into Alice's orange fur. '*Nonna*, I still have a year to finish at Woldingham.' She shrugs. 'I might not even get into the Slade School of Fine Art.'

Christina harrumphs. 'Of course you will be accepted to the Slade, Adriana. Your grades are exemplary and your art is far beyond the derivative daubs of people your age.'

Adriana rolls her dark eyes. 'Of course I can paint, *Nonna*. Papa was a famous artist. It's obvious I got my talent from him.'

Etta sets down her teacup. 'I used to paint as well, Adriana.'

Adriana drops the cat back onto the floor. 'Yes, but Papa was a genius. Everyone says so.'

Etta bites her lip, willing herself not to let the words pushing at her lips burst out. *It was me, Adriana! I'm the genius! I painted those pictures! I'm the one who made him famous!* What good did her talent ever do her? Art had only brought her pain. She'd tried everything to dissuade her mother from encouraging Adriana in this direction, but it had been of no use.

'Adriana, most of the artists I've met live in poverty, full of anger and frustration. Isn't there anything else you would rather do? The theatre, perhaps? You do have a flair for drama.'

'I want to be an artist, Mama. I don't want to be anything else.'

'And an artist you shall be, Adriana, just as I'd always wished to be.' Christina taps at Adriana's hand with her teaspoon as her granddaughter reaches to cut herself another slice of birthday cake. 'You still have cake on your plate. It's unseemly to be a glutton.'

Adriana's eyes flash with temper. 'I see nothing wrong with having an appetite for life, *Nonna*. I intend to eat up life like it is a vast banquet. I will drink every drop and eat every crumb of life once I am out on my own. Then, if I want an extra slice of cake, I'll have it.'

'Do you hear your daughter, Etta? The way she speaks to her grandmother? Are you going to permit that?'

'Adriana, don't speak to your grandmother like that,' Etta says automatically as she sips her tea.

'I know from whom Adriana gets her insolence.' Christina folds her hands in her lap. 'As I was saying, I have great concerns about Adriana sharing a flat with several other young girls next year, and that little fit of pique of hers only serves to solidify my concern. My proposal is that you and Adriana move into my Chelsea flat. You can then keep an eye on each other.'

Adriana jumps up from the table. '*Nonna!* No!'

'Mama, I am certain Adriana would much prefer to live with her friends—'

'*Nonna*,' Adriana interrupts, 'what if my friends move into your Chelsea flat with me next year? You could charge them rent and make some money. Isn't that a good idea?'

'Etta, speak to your daughter. It's still three young girls living alone in London.'

Adriana looks over at Etta imploringly, her earlier moodiness replaced with the desire for an ally. 'Mama, I need my freedom in order to be an artist, just like you needed yours. I've heard the stories about you going to all those wild bohemian parties with Great-Uncle Roger's Bloomsbury friends. That's how you met Papa, isn't it?'

'It is not. I met your father at an art exhibition at the Royal Academy of Arts on a rainy summer afternoon. It was all perfectly above board.' Etta grins. 'But I did go to an awful lot of parties.'

Christina taps the table with her spoon. 'My point exactly. Put a young girl into an environment with artists and the result is bound to be… trouble.'

Etta sits back in her chair. 'What do you mean by that, exactly?'

'You know what I mean, Etta.'

Adriana leaps up from her chair. 'Trouble?' she shouts, her Italian accent, softened by the efforts of private elocution tutors, sharpening in her anger. 'Are you calling me trouble, *Nonna?*'

'Don't listen to your grandmother, Adriana. You were never trouble.'

'Was I a mistake, Mama? An accident?'

'Of course not. Where did you hear that?'

'You did not love Papa at all!'

'That's enough, Adriana! I loved your father more than you will ever understand. I changed my whole life for him. In the middle of a war!'

Adriana juts out her chin. 'Would you have gone to Capri with Papa if I had not been in your belly?'

'Sit down, Adriana,' Christina commands. 'I will not have this language in my house.'

'Another reason for me to move out next year, *Nonna.*' Adriana glares at her mother. 'It's true, isn't it, Mama? I was a mistake made by a foolish girl in love with a married man.'

Etta stares at Adriana's strong-featured face, so much like Carlo's. Her daughter's coal-black eyes flash like lights in a tunnel.

'You were never a mistake, Adriana. Don't ever say such a thing again. Now, sit down and finish your cake. Hettie has gone to a great deal of trouble.'

Adriana sits down gracelessly. Picking up her fork, she stabs it into the cake.

Etta rubs at the headache spreading across her forehead. It's all too much. Everything is too much. She will die if she has to spend the rest of her days fielding arguments between Adriana and her mother. Adriana's path to study art appears to be set, and her mother has her own life of WI meetings and church bazaars. There is nothing for her here.

She has to get out of this house. She has to get out of London. She can't wait for Lord Sherbrooke's will to be untangled. There's every chance that Celie hasn't been left anything at all. She's already lost everything that Carlo left her through Paolo Marinetti's machinations. There's only one answer.

She picks up the teapot and refreshes her teacup. 'I'm moving to California.'

'Wha—'

She lifts her finger to still the objections forming on her mother's and daughter's lips.

'I've made up my mind. I'm moving to California. That's all I'm going to say about it. Now, shall we have more cake? It's my birthday. It's meant to be a celebration.'

The following day

'Mama, I want to speak with you.'

Christina peers at Etta over her reading glasses. 'Is it about your mad idea to move to California?'

'Don't say that word.'

'I'm sorry, my dear.' Christina sets down her needlepoint. 'Go ahead. I do enjoy a fairy tale.'

Etta shoos Alice out of the armchair that had once been her father's favourite and sits down. 'It's a plan, Mama. I … I know people there.'

'Do you? Who do you know in California?'

'Friends from Paris.'

Christina removes her glasses and rubs the lenses with her lace handkerchief. 'Etta, how on earth do you intend to get yourself all the way out to California when you haven't a penny to your name?'

Etta takes a deep breath and juts out her chin. She won't let her mother intimidate her. Not this time. 'That's not exactly the case, though, is it, Mama?'

Christina raises an eyebrow. 'How so?'

'Celie.'

Etta feels a tweak of pleasure as she watches her mother's face blanch.

'Etta, you wouldn't. You promised.'

'That was when Lord Sherbrooke was alive. Now I understand from the newspapers that there are some issues with his will, and it made me wonder if these "issues" might have something to do with Celie. He didn't have any children with Lady Sherbrooke, so doesn't that make Celie his heir?'

Christina runs her fingers around her ear and pats her hair. 'Etta, you know nothing about this. I have been dealing with Harry's executors on Cecelia's behalf. It's far more complicated that you can imagine. Unfortunately, Lady Sherbrooke has had a few unwelcome surprises since he died and she is putting up quite a fight. If I were her, I would probably do the same. Harry was a liar and a philanderer.'

'Be that as it may, Mama, Celie ought to know that Sir Harold was her father. I'd want to know.'

Christina lays her glasses down beside her cup of tea. 'Would you really want to know that the man that you loved as a father, who loved you like a daughter, wasn't your real father? Would you want to know that you'd been abandoned by the man who'd made you?'

Etta nods. 'Yes. I would want to know because it's the truth.'

'Yes, well, Cecelia isn't you. She and Gerald had an especially close bond. She shared his passion for photography. He entrusted her with running the photography studio when he was ill. Think of your sister, Etta. It would destroy her to find out Gerald wasn't her father.'

Etta scrutinises her mother. It's true. Celie is sensitive. She's always taken any perceived criticism or reprimand to heart in a way that Etta and Jessie never do. Could she do that to her sister? Then again, the truth is being hidden from Celie, and, to her mind, that is quite wrong. Someone has to set the record straight, and if that person has to be her, then so be it. But it doesn't need to come to that ... yet.

'Perhaps you're right, Mama.'

Christina expels a sigh of relief. 'Good, I knew you would come to your senses—'

Etta holds up her hand, stopping her mother short. 'I won't tell Celie, or the newspapers, anything about you and Lord Sherbrooke so long as you fund my trip to Los Angeles.'

'I beg your pardon?'

'And provide me with money for rent and living expenses until I get myself on my feet out there.'

'Etta!'

'I'm not going to be greedy. I'll only ask you this one time. Once I'm out there, I intend to stand on my own two feet.'

'Etta, this is ridiculous. Honestly, your imaginings have become ever more outlandish since...'

'Since when, Mama? Before or after I went mad? Is that what you're referring to? I assure you, I'm quite well now. In fact, I feel quite marvellous.'

'Do you think anyone would believe you if you were to put about this rumour of Cecelia being Harry's love child?'

'I don't know. Shall we find out?'

Christina picks up her needlepoint and pulls the needle through the canvas. 'Etta, you have a chance to repair your relationship with your daughter, and you want to run off to America? Do you realise how selfish and irresponsible that sounds?'

'Adriana is seventeen. She's old enough and strong-willed enough to take care of herself. She doesn't need me.'

'And how exactly am I meant to fund such a folly?'

Etta laughs. 'Mama, you're a rich woman. You own two properties and I know you have a bank account full of savings, not to mention income from Papa's investments. For all I know, you may have a few valuable trinkets stashed away given to you by Lord Sherbrooke that you could always sell. You'll find a way.' Etta shrugs. 'Otherwise, I'll simply have to visit the post office and send Celie a telegram. Then I'll visit *The Times*. No, *The Daily Mirror*. They love these kinds of stories.'

'Etta. You wouldn't.'

Etta smiles. For so long, she has had no say in her life. Not this time. She needs to start her life over, and her ex-lover, CJ Melton, is out in California. It's time for her to take control and open a new chapter in her life.

'Mama, I would.'

Chapter Eleven

Jessie & Celie

Cairo, Egypt – August 1932

Sweet Briar Farm
   West Lake, Alberta
   Canada

July 14th, 1932

Dear Jessie,

Happy Birthday! I'm sending you out this little package now in the hope that you might receive it by your birthday next month. If it's late, I'm awfully sorry. I know how long the post can take, but at least now with air mail there's some chance you'll receive it in time. I only just received Mama's Christmas gift of a scarf and Hettie's fruitcake, which she sent via ship and train. I suspect the poor fruitcake was sat upon by a piano in the ship's cargo hold. It arrived as flat as a pancake!

How is everyone in Cairo? Thank you for sending me the photograph of your family in your beautiful garden. Shani is growing into a lovely young lady – she looks just like her father with her dark hair and eyes. Ten years old already! It's a shame she and Lulu don't live closer; I'm certain they would be great friends, although Lulu can be quite a bossy boots. But if Shani is anything like you, I imagine she is quite capable of standing up for herself.

I wonder some days why it is that time seems to move so slowly when one is young and then speed up exponentially with every subsequent birthday. Do you find that, too? It seems only yesterday that I saw you at Clover Bar in London just before Frank and I left for Canada, and that was thirteen years ago. Do you still have the photograph of you, me and Etta at the waterfall in Yorkshire that I gave you from Papa's portfolio? I keep my copy on top of my dresser. It cheers me up no end to know I am not alone in the world.

The truth of it is that it is lonely out here on the farm, and, as you know, things haven't been good between Frank and me for some years. Lulu's in school, of course, and Frank is in the fields most days and visiting his friends most evenings. Cards and drink are popular entertainments amongst many of the farmers here. Escape, I think, from the drought and the falling wheat prices. One can hardly blame them. Farms have begun to be repossessed and it is a sorry sight to see people who had been happy, productive members of the community stripped of their homes, their livelihoods and their self-worth. I had tried to keep some of Papa's inheritance as a cushion, but, in the end, I had no choice but to use it for loan repayments and our mortgage.

Frank works hard, though his insistence on pursuing turn-of-the-century British agricultural methods to farm wheat in the Canadian prairie has no doubt contributed to our persistently lower wheat yields. I've told him this time and again, as have many of the local farmers, but he won't hear a word against his methods.

Frank has always been good to Lulu and helps her with her maths homework. As far as he and I go, though, we are now little more than lodgers under the same roof. I share Lulu's room with her and have done for several years. We should never have married, Jessie. I have learned the hard way that marrying someone as a compromise is a very poor reason to marry. At the time, of course, I thought Max had been killed in the war, and I rationalised that Frank was a kind, good man who loved me and whom I would come to love one day. Only, it never happened, Jessie. I blame myself for the disaster our marriage has become, but I am a good Catholic and I will honour my vows while we are both here on this earth. I know you once suggested that I could leave Frank and take Lulu back to London with me to stay at Mama's, but I can't and won't abandon my marriage. I made the contract in a church and I will abide by it.

Oh, Jessie, I hadn't meant this to be a 'woe is me' letter! It's likely I won't even send it to you, but it's all spilling out and it feels good not to keep everything bottled up inside.

I've written before about my friend Mavis Wheatley. She and her husband Fred have been wonderful supports since the first day Frank and I arrived in West Lake back in 1919. Her son Ben is the same age as Lulu and I think he's rather sweet on her, though Lulu is in the 'boys are stupid' phase. Poor Ben follows her around like Lulu's dog Kip, hoping for a morsel of attention, but Lulu pays him no mind at all. She reminds me of you, Jessie. She's stubborn and single-minded, and doesn't suffer fools gladly (I mean this as a compliment). She's very impressed that you are studying to become a doctor. She practises her bandaging on poor Ben and Kip quite relentlessly and says she intends to be a doctor as well one day.

I've been squirrelling away some of the money I make from selling baked goods at the local store for camera film and developing solution for my photography. Frank thinks it's a waste of money, but you know how important taking photographs is to me.

Mavis and I have convinced the Women's Christian Temperance Union to open a soup kitchen here next month. Almost half of the men here are out of work now and some of the unmarried farm workers have set up tents near the train tracks. Such a sad situation.

So, that's my life. It's a shadow of all the things I used to do in London! I felt so useful and fulfilled back then, Jessie. I followed my own *heart and I felt that my life had purpose. And love. Yes, I still think of Max. I believe I always shall.*

Do you remember that Mama always called me the dutiful daughter, like it was a badge of honour? Mostly when she was reprimanding Etta for her selfishness, I seem to recall! But I've found that being dutiful is tiring and sometimes quite dispiriting. I suppose it's the reason I cling on to the photography. It's the last piece of me that hasn't been swallowed up by duty.

If you do receive this letter rather than a shorter, cheerier one, please don't waste any time worrying about me. I will manage. I always have. I always will. And please, not a word of this to Mama or Etta.

All my love, always,

Celie

PS. You were the wilful daughter, in case you were wondering.

Jessie folds the letter and slips it into the envelope. Celie is probably mortified that she'd actually posted it, she thinks. Her sister was normally one to take what came her way and forge stoically onwards without complaint.

She opens the small package wrapped in brown paper and string. A white linen handkerchief embroidered with *JMFK* lies in once-neat folds that have been somewhat compromised by the long journey to Egypt. A photograph of Celie, Lulu and Kip in a vegetable garden is tucked amongst the folds. She smiles as she stuffs the handkerchief into her skirt pocket.

She picks up her pen and bends over a fresh sheet of writing paper.

Altumanina
> *Gezira Island*
> *Cairo, Egypt*

August 13th, 1932

Dear Celie,

What a lovely handkerchief! Thank you so much. It is already in my pocket and I can guarantee it will be put to good use in this desert heat. And thank you so much for the lovely photograph of you and Lulu and Kip. I shall frame it and put in on my desk next to the one of us three sisters in Yorkshire.

All is fine here. The heat is atrocious and most of our neighbours on Gezira Island have decamped to Alexandria or further afield to Europe for the duration. The Nile has begun its annual flood and it has awakened the mosquitoes which are an awful nuisance. We are heading up to Alexandria ourselves on Monday for a fortnight, although pulling Aziz away from the hospital is like prying the lid off a Lyle's treacle tin! Then I shall be back to my final year of studies at the medical school before I start two years of residency at the Anglo-American Hospital near our house.

Aziz is well, though overworked as always, and Shani had her tenth birthday in June, as you know, and is, for the most part, the sweetest, kindest little girl. I say 'for the most part' because she can stamp her foot when she doesn't get her way. I'm afraid she has been rather spoiled by the doting attentions of her father, her Auntie Zara and our housekeeper, Marta. I try my best to even things out by having Shani help Zara in the clinic from time to time. It's good for her to see that many people don't enjoy the privileges she does.

Enough about me. I'm glad you sent me that letter, Celie. I knew from some of your other letters that things have been difficult with Frank for some time. Being dutiful doesn't mean being a martyr, and I think you lean too far in the latter direction. You are the exact opposite of Etta. She always puts her own desires before anyone else's and you always put everyone else's desires before your own.

Remember the person you were when you first arrived in Alberta, full of hope for a bright, new future. Of course, life on a farm in rural Alberta isn't going to be the same as life in London, but you aren't quite as lost as you seem to think. You taught German there for years and wrote for the local newspaper. You even had some of your articles picked up by national newspapers, don't forget that! You've brought in activists, politicians, writers and artists to speak in West Lake as part of the women's union you're involved with. You are making a difference, Celie. You just don't see it.

Why don't you approach the editor of the local newspaper with some kind of idea for a regular column? What's important to the local women in and around West Lake? I imagine maximising a shrinking household income in this economic depression is a top priority. Why not ask Mavis to help you canvas the local women to find out what they'd like to read about, and then propose that to your editor, not forgetting to indicate that it will certainly increase the paper's circulation, and, thereby, its revenue? Suggest the advertisers he might approach if he has a large female readership. I've read that make-up is flying off the shelves because of the Hollywood movies. I'm certain Max Factor and Helena Rubinstein would love to reach a new market. Why doesn't your general store become a stockist?

I know that times are tough, but that means you simply have to be as resilient as possible. Look at what's missing in West Lake, and what skills you have to fix that. Speak to your editor. The worst is that he says no, and then you step back, reassess, and move on to another idea.

You can always write me and there's no need to sugarcoat anything. Heaven knows I've never been known for sugarcoating or pussyfooting around. Mama always said I was a bull in a china shop type.

Chin up, Celie. I have every confidence in you. And, of course, I won't say a word about anything to anyone, not even Aziz.

Love always,

Jessie

PS. I'm wiring you £15. No, I won't hear a word about it. Love, J.

Chapter Twelve

Etta

Clover Bar, Hither Green, London – October 1932

Clover Bar,
  Hither Green Lane,
  Hither Green,
  London SE13

October 2nd, 1932

Dearest CJ,

  CJ, darling, why aren't you responding to my letters? I've written you at least a dozen. None of them have been returned, so I know you must be receiving them. You gave me your PO Box address in Los Angeles before everything went so wrong in Paris, don't you remember? Every morning I rush to the door as soon as I hear the post drop through the letterbox, and nothing! Darling, don't you love me anymore? You are in my thoughts constantly. Your lovely face and beautiful blue eyes hover there in the dark cave of my mind like the face of a Greek god – Apollo, I think – yes, definitely Apollo – as I negotiate my way through the interminably tedious days of needlepoint, piano, and tea with Mama, her awful friend Ellen Jackson, and any ageing bachelor or dreary widower Mama deems suitable to become my next husband.

I hope I've made you laugh! It is an awfully ridiculous situation to find myself in after the fun we had in Paris with Zelda, Scott and the Hemingways, don't you think? Hither Green is a cold, barren moon compared to Paris's burning Venus. I can't bear it much longer, darling. I shall well and truly go mad again if I have to be civil to Mama's po-faced friend much longer. I can tell by the way Mrs Jackson wipes her hands on her napkin after I hand her the milk jug for her tea that she thinks I'm a fallen woman. Perhaps she thinks I'm contagious!

Is your silence because of that awful business in Paris with Carlo five years ago? I had no idea he would come to Paris to find me after he was released from that dreadful prison in Naples so suddenly. Having him turn up at the Luxembourg Gardens like that and hit you was such a shock. I had to go back to Capri with him, you do see that, don't you? I'd planned to come back to Paris as soon as possible, tell him I'd fallen in love with you, but there was so much unfinished business between Carlo and me – well, you know how complicated life can be!

Oh, CJ, I've told you over and over in every letter how sorry I am about all that mess. I know I should have rung you or sent you a note before going back to Capri with Carlo, but it was all so confusing, and he was my husband, after all, though of course I loved you. I've always loved you, darling, but Adriana was only a child, and I am her mother, after all, and she was going through such a wild phase …

Why is life so complicated?

I told you that Carlo died in an accident on Capri three years ago. You must have read about it – Mama said it was in all the papers. What I haven't said in my letters is that I rather fell to pieces, I'm afraid, and ended up in hospital just like poor, dear Zelda. But I'm much better now and am ready to make another go at the life I'm meant to live.

Adriana is seventeen now and in her final year, boarding at school here in England. I've barely seen her since I've been home. She spent most of the summer on Capri with Cousin Stefania and was back here for only a few days around my birthday. Then she was off to York to visit some friends and then back at Woldingham last month. She is a beautiful girl with a character like a cross cat, all soft and sweet until she growls and gets her claws out, which I'm afraid she does with me quite often. She refuses to be told a thing, and has our housekeeper Hettie wrapped around her finger, though she and Mama fight like cats and dogs. They are both ever so strong-willed!

Adriana makes no secret of loathing me. She's accused me of abandoning her, as if being sent to a psychiatric hospital was my choice! She's told me that I'm weak, conceited and selfish. Honestly, how does one respond to such things? I'll tell you, CJ: by living my life the way that I intend! I'm so tired of everyone judging me. It's all so very tedious. I can't bring myself to paint. There are far too many bad memories wrapped up in painting, and I'd only ever be seen as Carlo's scandalous widow attempting to profit off his name. The art critics would find every reason to disparage my work. There's nothing those old men like better than to trivialise a woman with talent. It upsets the status quo, you see.

So, darling, here's the thing. I'm coming to California to be a film actress. Don't laugh! I can't bear the idea of painting anymore, and I have to get away from London. I've always been told I have a dramatic flair, and how difficult can saying a few lines in front of a camera be? I went to the pictures with Hettie the other day and, wouldn't you know, there was a newsreel about everything that goes on behind the scenes of making a motion picture. There was the make-up and the costumes and the sets being built and the director shouting out 'Action!' It was all so enthralling. Then, can you believe it? I saw you! Tapping away at a typewriter in a writer's hut with a bunch of other chaps, smoking away on one of your Lucky Strikes. Oh, it was so wonderful to see your lovely face! Hettie didn't believe me for a moment when I said I knew you. I was so very excited! She tapped my hand like I was a child and said, 'There, there.' I think she thought I was having one of my episodes!

No one believes me anymore, CJ. They think I can't tell what's real and what's not, but I'm as right as rain and I can't bear being treated like a fragile flower. I overheard her speaking to Mama about it, and Mama said if my 'delusions' got worse she may have to put me back in the hospital. I simply can't go back there, CJ. I simply can't.

Wouldn't it be lovely for us to start over again? We have so much lost time to catch up on, darling. I have the money, that's not a problem, but I had so wished to hear back from you (positively, of course!) before leaving for Los Angeles. We were always meant to be together, ever since that first day we met in the Paris bookshop and you teased me about being in the naughty book section. Do you remember? I remember it like it was yesterday. Knowing that I would see you at the end of my journey would make me far less anxious about this adventure.

I simply can't bear to stay here any longer, so I've booked my passage to New York for the 31st, and am taking the 20th Century to Chicago where I'll change to the Golden State Limited train to Los Angeles. I'll telegram you with my arrival date and time from Chicago. You will meet me at the station when I arrive, won't you, darling? I shall be awfully sad and quite discombobulated if I arrive in Los Angeles and your own sweet face is not there to greet me.

What an adventure this shall be, CJ! You and me together in Hollywood! Such fun we shall have!

All my love,

Etta

PS: Zelda F. has written a novel! It's called 'Save Me the Waltz' and it's published this month. I shall buy it and read on my journey. Another woman jiggling the status quo!

PPS: You wouldn't have gotten married or anything silly like that, would you? If you have, please meet me anyway and we'll simply have to discuss it. I'm certain we can find a way. Kisses always. E.

***

Los Angeles, California - November 1932

Etta steps out from the shade of the red-brick Moorish archway of the La Grande Train Station in Los Angeles and hovers anxiously in the bright November sunlight. She tips the porter who off-loads her two new Louis Vuitton suitcases from his trolley, and fans her face with Zelda's book in a meagre effort to fend off the searing heat as she searches the faces of the people milling about the station forecourt.

Her heart sinks as the minutes pass and the crowd disperses. *Where is CJ?* Panic needles her like a tormentor. What if he doesn't come? What if she really is all alone out here? How will she cope? What is she going to do?

She is about to retreat back into the cool shade of the station building when she feels a hand on her shoulder.

'Etta.'

She turns around to see him standing there, his deep-set eyes the familiar blue, the straight Greek nose, the brim of his fedora obscuring his high forehead and dark blond hair.

'CJ!' She throws her arms around him. 'CJ! You came, darling!'

CJ disengages himself from Etta's embrace and extracts a pack of Camel cigarettes and a book of matches from his jacket pocket.

'I couldn't exactly leave you to the mercy of our local pickpockets and panhandlers, could I?'

'No, well, of course not.' She frowns. 'CJ, darling? Is something wrong?'

He lights a cigarette and sucks in a long drag. Shrugging, he blows out a stream of smoke.

'What could possibly be wrong, hon? You ditch me in Paris, go back to your husband and have a great old time with him in Italy until he falls off a cliff. Then you go mad for a few years, get better, then show up on my doorstep, expecting that we'll pick up where we left off.' He points at her with his cigarette. 'You tell me if something's wrong with that picture.'

Etta staggers back like she's been slapped. 'CJ. Darling. It's all been so very difficult and complicated. I've told you all about it in my letters. You're here. You must have received my letters.'

He nods. 'I got them.'

She reaches a hand up to his face. 'Darling, I love you. I've always loved you. That's all you need to know. I'm free now. We can be together, like we used to talk about back in Paris. Do you remember? We talked about how we'd run off to America and start over.' She drops her hand from his impassive face and folds her fingers around the lapel of his brown suit. 'I'm here now, darling. We can start over.'

CJ regards Etta silently, his jaw tight. He shakes his head and throws the cigarette onto the pavement. 'Damn it, Etta!'

He pulls her into his embrace and kisses her mouth, her face, her hair. 'Why did you come back?' He kisses her again and she responds with a passion that she'd forgotten she possesses. 'Why did you come back?'

'Darling, darling, CJ,' Etta murmurs as she pulls his face to hers. 'I love you, my darling. We belong together. For ever and ever and ever.'

Chapter Thirteen

Jessie

Cairo, Egypt – December 1932

J essie and Fatima exit the door of the lecture hall into a hallway crammed with jostling medical students shouting in excited Arabic.

'Good heavens! What's going on? There's so much noise, I can't make out what they're saying.'

Fatima frowns under her *hijab* as she strains to make sense of the clamour. 'There has been a bombing at the British Residency.'

Jessie's heart jolts. 'The Residency? When? What's happened? My husband's at a meeting there today.'

The young woman squeezes Jessie's hand as she strains to listen. 'An hour ago.' She shakes her head. 'I cannot tell more than that except that many are happy for it. Many do not like the British here.'

'Has anyone … has anyone been hurt?'

'I cannot tell. It is not clear.'

'It's not clear?' Jessie swallows as she attempts to catch her breath. 'What are they saying? Please, tell me. My Arabic still isn't brilliant.'

'They are saying … they are saying … I don't know. Perhaps.' She squeezes Jessie's hand more tightly. 'Jessica, it does not mean—'

'I have to get there.' Jessie feels her legs begin to shake. 'I have to get to Aziz.'

An elbow jabs into her ribs. She glances over to see a tall student in a red *tarbouche* glaring at her with eyes glassy with fervour. He mutters something at her in Arabic as he shoves past.

'Did you hear what he called me? That was something I did understand.'

Fatima pulls Jessie into the crowd. 'I am sorry for that, Jessica, but it will not be the last time you will hear that. The mood is not good in Egypt.'

Jessie tosses some coins at the taxi driver and leaps out onto the pavement opposite the elegant white stone edifice of the British Residency on the banks of the Nile, the home and office of the British High Commissioner and Foreign Office personnel. The gates have been shut and locked against the clamouring crowd, and the police struggle to hold back the mob with their wooden batons. Jessie pushes through to a policeman in a navy uniform and *tarbouche* who eyes her with a mix of panic and suspicion.

'Excuse me,' she says as she is jostled against the barrier of batons, 'My husband was at a meeting in the Residency this afternoon. I need to get in to see if he's all right.'

The policeman shakes his head. 'No one is to enter.'

'I understand, but my husband is with the Wafd Party and they were meeting with the High Commissioner today. Please, I need to see him.'

'No. It is impossible.'

Jessie feels desperation claw its way up her body. 'He's a doctor. His name is Dr Aziz Khalid.' She strains to look past the policeman's shoulders and glimpses broken window panes and a blown-out hole in the lawn in front of the building. 'Do you … Have you…' She clears her throat. 'Has anyone been injured?'

'Madame, please—'

'Jessica!'

Jessie jolts her head toward the voice. She sees Aziz approach the gate from the Residency building with several other men and a guard of British Army soldiers.

'Aziz!' She waves frantically over the policeman's shoulder. 'Aziz!'

A British soldier unlocks the gate and the men file out onto the pavement behind the protective cordon of police. Aziz pushes past the policemen.

'Jessica, what are you doing here?'

'Aziz, I was so worried. I heard about the bomb and I came straightaway.'

He glances past her at the heaving mob. 'Darling, you should not have come. It is very dangerous. Tempers are high.'

'Nothing would have kept me away.'

He takes hold of her elbow. 'Come, let us get out of this place. There are many angry people here today, and more will come, I am certain. There is much sympathy for the man who did this.'

They dodge through the crowd and the traffic and hurry down the river path. When they are a safe distance away, they sit on a bench under the feathering branches of a jacaranda tree beside the river. Aziz reaches into his jacket pocket and removes a packet of cigarettes and a book of matches. He lights the cigarette and inhales deeply. He blows out the smoke with an exhausted sigh.

'We were sitting in the boardroom discussing the Wafd Party's concerns about the high level of corruption and favouritism in Prime Minister Sidqi's People's Party government when we heard a bomb explode just outside in the garden. It shattered a few window panes, but nothing more than that. No one was hurt, *alhamdulillah.*'

'That's a relief. I was so worried. I thought—'

'You needn't worry, Jessica.' He brushes a strand of her hair out of her eyes. 'I am invincible, don't you know this?'

'Don't joke, Aziz.'

He nods. 'I am sorry. It is a serious situation.' He takes another long drag on the cigarette and blows out the smoke.

'The economic situation in Egypt is terrible, with cotton prices half of what they were just a few years ago. People are suffering and they see this grand building and the British enjoying their lives at the Shepheard's Hotel bar and the Gezira Sporting Club, and they are angry. So, someone throws a bomb at the British Residency. I understand it, but it is not just the British at fault. The king turns a blind eye as long as he is kept in the comfort to which he is accustomed, which the British are very happy to accommodate as it serves their purposes, and Sidqi's government is nothing more than a pseudo-dictatorship benefiting the corrupt contractors and British investors in the Prime Minister's vanity projects. Projects which he tells the Egyptian people will benefit them, but will only serve to line his own pockets and those of his cronies.'

Jessie shakes her head as she glances back to the crowd in front of the Residency in the distance. 'It seems nothing ever really gets better, does it, Aziz? People will always find something to fight about. I thought we'd all learned our lesson after the Great War, but it seems not. I worry about you, and Zara, and Shani, too. What kind of world will our daughter be facing when she's older?'

Aziz tosses the cigarette butt onto the pavement and stubs it out with his shoe. 'Zara and I can take care of ourselves, darling. As for Shani, all we can do is equip her the best we can for whatever the future holds.' Rising from the bench, he holds out his hand to Jessie. 'Come, *habibti*. I do not wish to stay here any longer. Let us go home and hug our daughter.'

Part II

1933

Chapter Fourteen

Christina

Bishop House, Portman Square, Marylebone, London – January 1933

Christina rings the doorbell and steps back onto the tiled stoop while she waits for the black door, its gloss paint polished to a high shine, to open. She taps her booted foot in irritation and glances at the Cartier wristwatch that had been one of the last of Harry's gifts to her before their relationship had crashed upon the rocks of distrust and disappointment and sunk like a ship wrecked in a storm. She shouldn't have to wait to enter her family home – the home that was now half-owned by her daughter, Cecelia.

The door opens and a young maid in a neat black and white uniform eyes her quizzically. 'Yes? May I help you?'

'I'm here to see Miss Adam.'

'May I ask who's calling? Have you a card?'

Christina huffs impatiently. 'Tell her it's Mrs Fry. She knows who I am.'

'Of course.' The maid opens the door and gestures for Christina to enter. 'Please wait here and I will let her know of your arrival.'

Christina watches the maid disappear through the French doors into the drawing room. She pulls off her black leather gloves and slips them into her crocodile handbag as she surveys the familiar entrance hall with its soaring height and classical pilasters, the black and white marble tiled floor on which she would play hopscotch, the grand staircase she used to love to watch her beautiful Italian mother, Isabella, sweep down to join her glamorous guests at one of her parents' many house parties, and the Venetian chandelier that her grandfather had instructed the best glassblowers on the island of Murano in Italy to make for the house back in 1840. How she missed this place. She'd been so happy here until her mother and her newborn brother died of the Russian flu back in 1891. After that, nothing was ever the same again.

She hears the click of heels on the marble and turns to see Dorothy Adam, slender and elegant in a tailored forest-green day dress that Christina recognises as the work of her favourite London couturier, Madame Isobel. Quite the change from the dowdy girl in the cheap dress she'd first met in Dorothy's rundown Chelsea flat almost eight years ago.

'Christina Fry. To what do I owe the pleasure?'

Christina eyes the younger woman, not even forty yet, she guesses, and looking even younger than that with her pale complexion and stylishly short waved auburn hair. A younger version of herself. Harry had certainly had a type.

'You can't be surprised to see me, Dorothy.' She takes a letter out of her handbag and waves it at the stylish young woman. 'What's the meaning of this letter from your solicitors barring my right of access to this house and to cease and desist my alleged harassment of you? You know as well as I do that my daughter has nominated me as her representative in matters relating to

Harry's bequest of half of this house to her. I have every right to write you letters demanding access. By rights, I can claim half of the rooms for her.'

'Your daughter is in Canada. I can't see how half of the rooms in this house would do her any good. Besides, I require the rooms for my students.'

'Your students? What are you talking about?'

'I am quite in demand as an elocutionist for all the young women dreaming of stage and cinema stardom,' Dorothy says as she walks across the hallway to a Georgian demilune table. She opens a silver box and removes a slim cigarette. 'Alexander Korda sends me all his newly-signed young hopefuls to transform from Cockney sparrows into West End nightingales. They stay here until I deem them ready. It's quite a lucrative business.'

'You're running a business out of my lovely home?'

Dorothy shrugs as she lights the cigarette with a crystal lighter. 'It's not your home any longer, Christina. As you know, Harry rented Bishop House to me for a penny after he bought the house from your aunt just before she died. I had a roof over Christopher's and my head, but I needed money for us to live on and I'd had enough of the subsistence wages of a typist. So, I sold that awful flat he bought me in Chelsea and started up this business in order to rub shoulders with the London theatre and cinema crowd. I decided that if I couldn't be an actress myself, I would make another way into that world.' She sucks at the cigarette and blows out a puff of smoke. 'I had Noël Coward and Gertrude Lawrence here at my New Year's Party. He played the piano and she sang. It was most delightful.'

Christina watches Dorothy as she smokes the cigarette, the very model of a self-assured socialite. Dorothy had seemed so timid and self-effacing when they'd first met. She'd been so easily manipulated into joining her battle to have Harry recognise Cecelia, and Dorothy's son Christopher, of course, as Harry's... Well, if not his heirs, at least his beneficiaries. But Dorothy was cleverer than she'd given her credit for. She should have paid attention when Dorothy had told her she'd once been an actress.

She'd made a fatal mistake – she'd underestimated Harry's ex-lover, and now Dorothy and Christopher were the ones living in the house, not she nor Cecelia. And it was obvious Dorothy wasn't going to leave Bishop House without a fight.

'This is a private residence, Dorothy. I am quite certain the Portman Estate would take a dim view of you running a business out of this house.'

Dorothy leans against the table and blows out a puff of smoke. 'Ah, but that is only if someone tells them, isn't it?'

Christina winces as Dorothy taps out grey cigarette ash into an antique porcelain dish. 'What makes you think I wouldn't?'

'Because it might cause me to become quite vindictive, Christina. Bishop House is my son's home, the only real one he's ever known. I'm administering the trust until he comes of age in two years, when he will take control of his share of the house. Should you do anything to disrupt our lives in the meantime, it will be my intention to ensure that he inherit the whole house, rather than simply half. We've lived here for almost six years. Don't they say possession is nine-tenths of the law?'

'That's just a saying. It means nothing. Half of this house is Cecelia's.'

Dorothy scrutinises Christina with her pale green eyes as she exhales a stream of white smoke. 'I'm very happy to test it out if you force my hand, Christina.' She stubs out the cigarette in the porcelain dish. 'Now, if you excuse me, I have a meeting at London Studios with Mr Korda's latest protégé, a Merle Oberon. Not her real name, of course. I'm meant to make her sound like a proper star and I intend to do just that.'

Chapter Fifteen

Etta

Paramount Pictures, Hollywood, California – February 1933

Harvey Tubman, the second assistant director of the Marx Brothers' latest picture, *Grasshoppers*, sits back in his desk chair and stretches his arms. He takes a mug of coffee from a harried intern who looks, to Etta Marinetti, no more than fifteen, then fixes a dead-eyed stare on her through his horn-rimmed glasses.

'Okay, hon. Ya can dance a little and ya got a good shape.' He rakes his eyes over her face. 'How old did ya say ya were?'

Etta hesitates a fraction of a second. 'Twenty-six. Just turned.'

He shrugs as he lights up a cigarette. 'Gettin' on a bit for this game, aren't ya? That an English accent?'

She smiles, offering him a view of the dimpled cheek that has served her so well in the past. 'Yes, from London.'

He blows out a puff of smoke and clicks his tongue against his cheek. 'Ya gotta learn to speak American if ya want to act in the pictures now everything's turning into talkies. This was so much frickin' easier when no one talked on screen. As long as ya looked good, ya could sound like a foghorn and no one gave a f—' He clears his throat. 'Can ya carry a tune?'

'Sing?'

'Ya. *La la la la*. This is the entertainment business.'

Etta nods, setting the marcelled curls of her golden bob jiggling around her ears. 'Yes, of course.' She straightens her shoulders and juts out her chin. 'I was in the chorus for *Funny Face* at the Winter Garden Theatre in London,' she lies. 'Mr Fred Astaire himself chose me for the chorus line. He said I was a star in the making.'

Harvey Tubman grunts. 'If I had a dime for every time I've heard that one, I'd be richer than Rockefeller.' He takes a gulp of coffee and waves at Etta with his cigarette. 'So, show me what ya got.'

Etta glances around the office where a bespectacled middle-aged woman in a mustard mohair twin set and pearls is busy scribbling notes on a clipboard. The boy intern stands beside her, his skinny body vibrating in anticipation of a shouted order.

'Uh, now? Without music?'

'Do I look like Duke Ellington?' Harvey Tubman looks over at the scribbling woman. 'Do I look like Duke Ellington, Marge?'

The woman looks up from the clipboard and smiles joylessly. 'You don't look like Duke Ellington, Mr Tubman.'

He waves his hand at Etta, sloshing drips of coffee onto the pile of scripts and paper on his desk. 'Just sing, f'Crissake.'

'Oh. Yes. Of course.' Etta clears her throat and, after taking a breath, launches into 'I Wanna be Loved by You'. She is about to start the second verse when Harvey Tubman clicks his fingers and holds up his hand.

'Fine. Fine. You're no Fanny Brice but ya can carry a tune.' He waves his cigarette at the boy. 'Hey kid, get me another coffee and make sure this one's hot.' He scowls at the mass of papers on his desk, and begins rifling through the piles, frowning and muttering as he searches fruitlessly for some misplaced document.

Etta shifts in the hard chair. 'Is there anything else—'

He looks up and blinks at her owlishly through his glasses. 'What are ya sittin' there for? Ya got in. We start shootin' the picture in three weeks. Marge, get her a contract and send her over to wardrobe, will ya?' He sits back in his chair and scrutinises Etta. 'What did ya say your name was?'

'Etta Marinetti.'

He nods as he sucks on his cigarette. 'Gawd, no. Too many syllables. What about … Martin … nah, too ordinary … Melvin … nah, sounds like a librarian…'

'M-m-m-Marine?'

Harvey Tubman jerks his head around to see the young intern quivering in his knickerbockers as he attempts not to spill the contents of the newly filled coffee mug over Harvey Tubman's desk.

He grabs the mug. 'What did ya say, kid?'

'M-m-m-Marine. L-l-l-like the sea.'

Harvey Tubman takes a gulp of coffee as he eyes the boy. 'Catchy. I like it. Ya like it, Marge?'

Marge nods as she hands a document to Etta. 'I like it, Mr Tubman.'

'Etta Marine. That's it. That's your new name. I tell ya, Etta Marine, ya wouldn't believe some of the names I gotta deal with. Ya know John Wayne's real name is Marion Morrison, can ya believe it? What were his parents thinkin'?' He clucks his tongue. 'Marion, I tell ya.'

Etta signs the contract and extends her gloved hand to Harvey Tubman. 'Thank you very much for believing in me, Mr Tubman. I assure you, you won't be disappointed.'

His beefy hand engulfs Etta's. 'Hon, you're just a contract extra. It's not like you're the star.'

Etta favours him with her dimple. 'Not yet, Mr Tubman. But I will be.'

Harvey Tubman's characteristically saturnine expression cracks into a facsimile of a smile.

'Okay, maybe I'll get ya a line or two. You'll get a few more dollars and a credit. I'll get wardrobe to throw some silver lamé on you for the party scene and you'll be fine. Oh, and hold off the potatoes. Camera puts on twenty pounds and, trust me, Etta Marine, ya can't afford it.'

———————

Etta steps out of the Paramount Pictures office building and leans against the wall as her heart pounds against her ribs. She takes a deep breath and lights a cigarette. She inhales, savouring the acrid taste of smoke and tobacco, and watches the construction crew hammer and saw the façade of an English manor house into life in the vast yard as a parade of chorus girls and cowboys filters past.

Finally. She's lost count of the auditions she's been on since she'd arrived in Hollywood in November. Her mother's money is running out, and she needs this job, or she'll have to ask for more, which is a terrible nuisance. She hates to have to blackmail her mother, but, really, what choice does she have? Her mother has money, and she has her mother's secret. It is an even trade. Damn Paolo Marinetti for contesting Carlo's will in the Italian courts! He's made things ever so disagreeable!

She'd never thought it would be so difficult to get noticed in Hollywood. She'd always been so assured of her ability to capture the attention of the less-favoured. But here she is just another girl looking for a break. If anyone finds out she's almost forty, she'll be dead in this town. And then what? Back to stultifying teas at her mother's or painting lemons on Capri? Over her dead body.

She stubs out the cigarette under her shoe and waits as a cluster of mounted cowboys passes by. At least things have worked out with CJ. He'd had her worried when she'd first arrived, being so awfully cold and distant. She smiles as she remembers the night she'd finally won him back. It had taken all her wiles, helped by a new silk peignoir from Bullocks Wilshire, and several dry martinis. He'd succumbed, of course. She'd never really doubted that he would. Of course, it had been perfectly natural for him to have been upset about her going back to Carlo all those years ago. But really, how could she not? Carlo was her husband. But, now, Carlo is dead and she has a life to live, and she's decided she's going to live it here in Hollywood with CJ.

She opens her handbag and slips out a silver flask. Unscrewing the cap, she takes a deep swallow, shivering as the gin burns its way down her throat.

'Ah, a kindred spirit. Always thought the olive was a waste of time myself.'

Etta coughs and turns around to see the familiar thick black moustache and eyebrows of Groucho Marx. He pulls a cigar out of his breast pocket. 'Mind if I don't smoke?'

'Yes, no. Uh—'

He stuffs the cigar back into his pocket. 'Another beautiful girl struck dumb. Is it the moustache or the eyebrows? Or maybe the glasses? Girls don't make passes at boys who wear glasses.'

Etta screws the top back onto the flask and drops it back into her handbag. 'I'm terribly sorry, Mr Marx. I know I shouldn't have—'

'If I had a dime for every time I've heard that, I'd be as rich as Rockefeller.'

Etta laughs. 'It's the second time I've heard that today.'

'What? Is somebody stealing my jokes? How dare they!'

Etta glances at her handbag. 'You won't tell anyone, will you, Mr Marx? I need this job on your picture. The truth is, I'm awfully nervous. They told me I had to learn to speak like an American now that they're making talkies or I'd never make it in the pictures.'

'And they tell me I'm supposed to make people laugh. Harpo says if I keep at it, I might manage it one day.'

Etta giggles. 'Oh, you always make me laugh, Mr Marx.'

He wiggles his wire-rimmed glasses with his finger. 'Then my work here is done.' He heads down the steps. At the bottom, he turns around and nods at Etta's handbag. 'If you don't mind me saying, drinking gin like that is a waste of a good martini.'

Chapter Sixteen

Celie

West Lake, Alberta, Canada – March 1933

Ol' Man Forbes slides the Eaton's package across the battered wooden counter to Celie.

'This came for you yesteday, Mizz Jeffries,' he says in his gravelly Georgia drawl. 'From Toronto. Must be somethin' pretty special for it to come all that way.'

Celie shifts her eyes toward her daughter, Lulu, who is peering longingly at the Easter jellybean display in the candy counter. 'It's nothing special, Mr Forbes.'

He winks at Celie. 'Gotcha. Nothin' to do with some little girl's birthday next week. No, I expect it's nothin' to do with that at all.'

Lulu darts a look at the shopkeeper. 'How'd you know it's my birthday next week, Mr Forbes?'

'A little birdie told me.'

Lulu wrinkles her freckled nose. 'That's ridiculous. I bet it was Benji Wheatley.'

'Lulu Jeffries!' Celie chides. 'Manners, please.'

Lulu rolls her large blue eyes and sighs with the exasperated weariness of a worldly almost-thirteen-year-old. 'I'm sorry, Mr Forbes.'

'No harm done, darlin'.'

Lulu shrugs. 'I was simply stating a fact. Everybody knows birds don't talk. Except for parrots, of course. They talk but it's not like they know what they're saying, even if Benji says they know. But that's just ridiculous. Parrots just repeat sounds. Benji Wheatley really is such a ridiculous boy.'

'Is "ridiculous" your word of the week, Lulu?'

'Yes, Mommy. Miss Evans had us write out ten sentences with it yesterday at school. I like it better than last week's "questionable", or even "peculiar" the week before, which had been my favourite before "ridiculous".'

'I may have to have a word with Miss Evans about her word of the week choices.'

Lulu turns her attention back to the contemplation of the tiny egg-shaped jellybeans which Ol' Man Forbes has painstakingly arranged by colour – mauve, blue, green, yellow, orange, pink and white – in glass jars behind the glass. A sign urging customers to 'Buy an Easter treat for your sweet' is plastered across the glass frontage.

'Benji gave Lizzie Philby a Mickey Mouse pencil case on Monday.'

'Well, isn't that nice of him.'

'Mommy, it isn't nice at all! He was supposed to give it to *me* for *my* birthday. I told him I saw it in Mr Forbes's store and I said how much I liked it.' She crosses her arms and huffs. 'I don't want him to come to my birthday party.'

Celie smiles apologetically at the shopkeeper as she signs the credit note for the postage. 'Ben Wheatley is a very nice, polite and thoughtful boy, Lulu. You're lucky to have him as a friend. He is under no obligation to give you anything just because you expect it. You should be nicer to him.'

Lulu lifts and drops her shoulders as she sighs dramatically, and Celie presses her lips together to suppress at smile at Lulu's obvious jealousy of Ben Wheatley's attention to Lizzie Philby.

Ol' Man Forbes clears his throat as he impales the credit note on an overflowing spike. He glances over at the small, sturdy figure of the bob-haired girl fixated on the temptations of the candy counter.

'I suppose it's ridiculous to suggest a bag of jellybeans for the birthday girl.'

'Oh, I don't know, Mr Forbes,' Celie says. 'Don't you think jellybeans are far too ridiculous for a young lady who's about to turn thirteen? Perhaps an extra helping of broccoli at supper would be much more sensible. I hear broccoli is very good for the bones of growing children.'

Ol' Man Forbes winks at Celie. 'I love me some broccoli the way Mizz Forbes makes it,' he says, smacking his lips. 'It's good with mashed turnip and butter meltin' all over it. Yes, sirree, I've got a hankerin' for some broccoli now.'

'But I like jellybeans,' Lulu protests. 'I'm not even thirteen until next week.'

Celie reaches into her handbag and retrieves the small red leather coin purse. She snaps it open and pokes at the coins. Eight cents. Two cents short for a bag of jelly beans. Jessie's money had been eaten up by household bills, credit repayments, two precious rolls of film and Lulu's birthday present.

'No, I'm sorry, Lulu. Not today.'

'Mo-therrr,' Lulu groans. She stomps over to an old wooden chair by the display window and flops into it. 'No, no, no, Lulu. That's all I ever hear.'

Celie snaps shut the change purse and drops it into her handbag, conscious of the shopkeeper's studied busyness as he rearranges tins of Deep Sea Fancy Pink Salmon on the back shelf. It was becoming more and more of a challenge eking out the diminishing household money Frank begrudgingly handed over to her on the thirtieth of every month. The pennies she made from selling her baked goods to Ol' Man Forbes didn't go very far.

Maybe she should do as Jessie had suggested and approach Rex Majors at the *West Lake News* about a column directed at women readers. She'd used the last of Jessie's money to pay for a chemistry set from Eaton's Winnipeg store for Lulu's birthday, as well as for the ingredients for a chocolate cake, thirteen tiny candles, and some navy wool for a new dress for Lulu.

She knows it will cause yet another fight with Frank. She hadn't told him about Jessie's money, of course, or he would have demanded that she give it to him. He'll protest about the extravagance of the chemistry set. He'll want to know where she got the money, and accuse her of hiding some of her father's inheritance from him. Then he'll accuse her of undermining him, of making him feel … ridiculous. Her shoulders slump in exhaustion at the thought of the impending argument. Nothing ever seems to get easier.

After she'd received Jessie's letter in September, she'd felt re-energised. Jessie was absolutely right – she *is* capable and she *is* resilient. She'd planned to speak to Mavis about canvassing the local women about what they'd like to read in the paper and then approach Rex Majors with some columns for him to trial. But then the school governors had asked her to replace Mabel Prince on the school board when the Princes' farm had been repossessed and they'd gone off to Victoria to live with Mabel's sister's family, and then Frank's health had taken a turn in December with a bad flu, and she'd spent most of that month making mustard plasters and boiling up pans of water and VapoRub to help Frank breathe. Then Miss Evans had asked her to help organise the Saint Patrick's Day concert at Lulu's school, and now there's Lulu's birthday party to organise. The months just slip away, and when she looks in a mirror, she no longer sees the enthusiastic young idealist she once was. All she sees now is an exhausted middle-aged woman.

'Mizz Jeffries, would you mind watching the store while I hop next door? Forgot my lunch again, and all that talk about food's got my stomach grumblin'. Mizz Forbes'll have some cold fried chicken and cornbread waitin' for me in the fridge.'

'Of course, Mr Forbes. Take your time. Fred Wheatley's giving us a lift home. He told us to drop by the garage when we're done.'

The shopkeeper disappears behind the beaded curtain to the storeroom, and the backdoor slams. Celie steps behind the till and sets her handbag and the Eaton's package on the counter. She looks over at her sulking daughter.

'Lulu, why don't you read the Mickey Mouse comic book over there on the magazine table? Be careful with it. You'll have to put it back before we go so that somebody can buy it.'

'All right,' Lulu says grudgingly.

Celie unwraps her scarf and unbuttons her coat and hangs them on a hook by the display shelf. She sits down on a stool behind the ornate brass cash register. She notes the amount still flagged up on the register: $17.42. Who in this town had paid that amount in cash? She can't remember the last time she'd spent that much on anything other than bills.

The income from last year's wheat harvest had barely been enough to cover paying the minimums on those bills. Wheat prices were now down to thirty-eight cents a bushel from over a dollar in two years. How were they expected to keep a household afloat, with loan payments on the house and farm equipment coming due every month? And that wasn't even counting the utilities and food bills, animal feed, Lulu's school books, Frank's tobacco, groceries, and the credit they are still paying off on the piano, the sewing machine and the refrigerator.

Sometimes she feels like she is a rudderless boat adrift in a sea of sun-beaten Alberta wheat. She is so far away from her mother and her sisters, out here on the Canadian prairie. So far away from everything and everyone who had once been so important to her; who are still important to her.

So far away from Max Fischer.

No. I mustn't think about Max.

She glances over at Lulu, who is picking at hangnails around her bitten fingernails as she reads the comic. *Do you have children, Max?*

The back door slams and Ol' Man Forbes emerges through the beaded curtain, wiping his mouth with his white handkerchief.

'Thank you, Mizz Jeffries. Gobbled up my lunch as fast as I could. Didn't want to take advantage.'

'Not a problem at all, Mr Forbes.' Celie slides off the stool and grabs her coat and scarf from the hook. She loops the scarf around her neck and buttons her coat. 'Anyway, it was quiet as a church on a Monday.'

She picks up the package and her handbag and gestures to Lulu to replace the comic book. 'Let's get going, Lulu. We've taken up enough of Mr Forbes's time.'

He wags a sausage-like finger at Celie. 'Hold on a minute, Mizz Jeffries.' He slides open the back panel of the candy counter. 'The jellybeans is on me. Consider it an early birthday present for Lulu.'

Lulu jumps out of the chair. 'Oh, yes, please, Mr Forbes!'

'Really, Mr Forbes, you needn't do that.'

He holds up a metal scoop and a small brown paper bag. 'What a body needs to do and what a body wants to do are rarely the same thing.'

Lulu sets the comic book reverentially back on the table and hurries over to the candy counter. '*Pleeeze*, Mommy. I've been ever so good, even though it's been *sooo* boring.'

Celie sighs in good-natured defeat. 'All right, Lulu. But just because it's your birthday soon.'

'All right, then, Mizz Lulu,' the shopkeeper says to the excited girl. 'Now, what colours do y'all want? I'm partial to the orange ones, though Mizz Forbes favours the pink ones herself.'

Celie and Lulu step out of the store onto the new concrete sidewalk. Celie tucks the Eaton's package under her arm and loops her handbag over her wrist.

They are half-way across the road to Wheatley's Garage when a battered black flatbed truck pocked with rust veers around the corner from Church Road into the high street. They leap onto the concrete sidewalk in front of the garage and watch the truck splash through the slush like a speeding boat. As the truck flies by, Celie glimpses the stony face of Emma Philby at the passenger window, young Lizzie Philby in tears beside her. A filthy canvas tarpaulin flaps over the flatbed, exposing the Philbys' upright piano, the ivory keys jiggling like loose teeth.

'Mommy, it's Lizzie! Where are they going?'

Fred Wheatley joins them on the sidewalk, tugging his flat cap onto his cropped ginger hair and turning up the collar of his jacket against a blast of frigid air. He slaps his large hands together and huffs into his cupped palms. 'That wasn't the Philbys, was it?'

Celie nods. 'Yes, it was.'

Fred clicks his tongue as he shakes his head. 'Looks like no one's safe from the bank these days. Cryin' shame.'

'Mommy, where are they going? I'm supposed to go to Lizzie's birthday party in April. I braided her a bracelet from Betsy's tail hair and everything.'

Celie wraps her arm around Lulu's shoulders. 'I don't know, darling.'

She watches the truck bump along the road until it diminishes to the size of an ant on the flat horizon beyond the last grain elevator. She feels her stomach drop and she takes a deep breath to calm the nausea that washes over her. Emma Philby, the president of the Women's Christian Temperance Union, and head of the school governors; who ran the local hospital's fund for an X-Ray machine, and organised any number of bake sales and tombolas for various causes; who treated everyone, Celie in particular, like they were her minions, and held herself and her abilities in the highest of regard. How could this Emma Philby have lost everything?

The woman was arrogant and superior, to be sure, but she was as solid and reliable as an ornery mule. Emma Philby was untouchable. As long as Emma Philby stood, officiously directing the town's clubs and events, everyone was safe.

For the first time since the stock markets crashed in 1929, Celie is truly afraid.

Chapter Seventeen

Etta

Grauman's Chinese Theatre, Hollywood, California – March 23rd, 1933

The taxi draws up against the kerb behind a Rolls Royce limousine, which is disgorging a beautiful blonde woman wearing a skintight eau de nil satin gown that teases the exposure of more than her décolletage as she slides out of the car into the arms of a tall, broad-shouldered male companion in white tie and tails.

'Oh, my word, CJ. Isn't that Jean Harlow and Clark Gable? Don't they look glamorous!' Etta squeezes CJ's arm. 'Pinch me, darling. If my sisters could see me now! Oh, look! They've got King Kong's head on display over there by the entrance! They're taking pictures. Oh, I want us to have our picture taken over there! You and me here at the premiere of *King Kong*! I'll send copies to everyone back home and Celie and Jessie, too. Wouldn't that be the bee's knees?'

CJ hands the taxi driver some change. 'Sure thing, honey.' He peers out the window at the crowd craning their necks to spot the famous faces parading on the red carpet into Grauman's Chinese Theatre, and runs his fingers inside the starched collar of his dress shirt to loosen its hold on his neck. 'Remember, we're just staying for the movie, Etta. No parties tonight. I've got a deadline on the Cagney script due tomorrow and I need to be *compos mentis*. We need the studio to greenlight one of my screenplays or we'll be joining the line at the soup kitchen downtown.'

'Yes, yes. I promise, darling. Now be a doll and open my door.'

As they walk up the red carpet past the screaming throng, she smiles and waves, and is gratified when the screams intensify. She may not be famous yet, but making people believe it is the first step. It's all an act, and she's in the right town to reinvent herself.

So what if she'd had to spend a chunk of her mother's money on the *King Kong* tickets that Harvey Tubman's PA, Marge, had touted to her for the extortionate sum of fifteen dollars? Then, of course, she'd had to buy a new gown and shoes and have her hair freshly marcelled, and rent CJ's tuxedo … but, really, it was all necessary. She has no intention of wasting years in chorus lines and walk-on roles.

She'd been famous before – maybe infamous is a better word, though, what with all the commotion over Carlo's imprisonment for his first wife's murder and the circumstances of his death at the Grotta di Matromania on Capri – but this time she intends to be famous in her own right. The way she should have been famous as the real painter of Carlo's lauded paintings.

She reaches out and squeezes CJ's hand as they head under the towering pagoda portico and through the doors into the Chinoiserie extravaganza of the theatre's lobby.

'This is the best day of my life, CJ.'

He smiles at her childlike excitement. 'I'm sure it won't be the la—'

'Oh, look! It's the Marx Brothers!' Etta releases her grip on CJ's hand. 'I must go say hello to Groucho. He needs to know I'm still up for doing his movie even though it's been postponed till the summer. You don't mind, do you, darling?'

'CJ!' Etta calls out as she spots him standing beside one of the towering orange pillars either side of the entrance, smoking as he watches the glamorous throng pile into their waiting cars.

'There you are! I've been looking all over for you.'

'Really? The last I saw of you, you were wrapped up in conversation with Clark Gable and Cary Grant.'

'Oh, don't be like that. It was business, darling. I've got to see and be seen.' She takes his cigarette from his lips, sucks at it and returns it to him. She blows out a puff of smoke and loops her arm through his.

'Groucho's invited us to his place for drinks. There's a whole bunch going. He's promised that Harpo may even talk. Wouldn't that be something?'

CJ stubs out the cigarette. 'Etta, I've got to get home. You said we'd just come to the movie and leave. You've already been chatting everybody up for over an hour. It's time to go.'

'Oh, please, CJ. Just for an hour. Okay, half an hour. Just to put in an appearance. It's important to me.'

'Honey, I can't. I'm sorry.'

Etta's face hardens. 'CJ, I've made it to Hollywood. I'm making friends with important people. People who can help my career. I'm not going to waste this opportunity.'

CJ nods. 'I get it. It's always all about what Etta wants, isn't it? I'm starting to understand Carlo a lot more.' He turns away abruptly and heads down the red carpet.

'CJ? What did you mean by that? CJ, you're not leaving me here alone, are you? CJ!'

He turns around. 'I'll hold a cab for five minutes, then I'm leaving.'

'CJ!' Etta stamps her foot as CJ disappears into the crowd.

'I smell a whiff of a lover's tiff.'

'Mr Marx!'

Groucho Marx offers her a martini. 'This is a much better way to drink gin. It's even got the olive.'

Etta accepts and takes a generous gulp. 'Thank you. It's just a silly little thing.'

'That's what my wife said on our wedding night.'

Etta laughs. 'It looks like I've been stranded.'

'Not on my watch.' He points at her feet. 'Move! Move! I said not on my watch!' He spies his watch on his wrist. 'Would ya look at that. It was there all the time.' He offers her his arm. 'C'mon, Miss Marine. I promised you a talking Harpo, didn't I? That's something you definitely don't want to hear.'

Etta takes one last look toward the road. 'Mr Marx, I wouldn't miss it for the world.'

Etta slips off her shoes and tiptoes into the shadowy bedroom where CJ lies asleep in a T-shirt and trousers, a cigarette butt extinguished between his fingers. She sets her shoes down beside the wooden wardrobe and, hitching up her silver satin dress, climbs onto the bed. CJ stirs and stretches. He reaches across and pulls her closer as he yawns.

'So, you decided to come home. I thought I'd lost you to a screen god.'

Etta runs a finger along his lips. 'Of course, darling. Gable has nothing on you.'

CJ grunts. 'Flattery will get you nowhere.'

She presses kisses onto his neck. 'No? Did I ever tell you that you have a place here, this little dent just above your collarbone,' she says as she runs her lips along the indentation, 'that makes me quiver whenever I think about it?'

'Ummm, is that so?'

She shifts her body until she sits astride him. She leans over and kisses him full on his mouth. 'I like it when you're sleepy like this.'

He yawns again and throws his arms back onto the pillow behind his head. 'So you're being CJ tonight? Staying out late, sliding into bed, waking me up to have your wicked way with me?'

'You've been a good teacher.'

CJ laughs as he runs a hand along the naked skin of Etta's arm. 'Is that so?'

Etta sits up and slides the dress over her head, her naked body catching the moonlight filtering in through the thin curtains. 'Maybe there are one or two things I can teach you.'

CJ brushes her right nipple with his thumb until it hardens into a peak. 'Is that right?'

Etta leans over and whispers into CJ's ear. 'Why don't we find out?'

Chapter Eighteen

Jessie

Altumanina, Cairo, Egypt – June 1933

J essie is about to turn the front door handle of the house when the door flings open and she is suddenly face to face with a striking Black woman of about forty in a man's white shirt and khaki trousers.

'Ruth?'

Ruth Bellico throws open her arms and pulls Jessie into an enthusiastic embrace.

'Jessie Khalid!' she exclaims as she kisses Jessie on the cheek. 'Where've you been? Shani and I have been playing sentinel at the door waiting for you. She's on temporary relief helping someone called Marta in the kitchen.'

'Ruth? What on earth are you doing here? I thought you were off in Germany covering all that political to-do there for the American papers.'

'Actually, I'm just back from Chicago where I was covering the opening of the World Fair.' She throws up her hands as if she is

110

reading a large sign. '"A Century of Progress" – that's the fair's slogan, although I don't know how you can call it progress when almost thirteen million Americans are unemployed, families are setting up home in packing crates and abandoned cars, and gangsters are running riot across the country. We've got a new president and who do you think is on the front pages of all the papers? Some runaway killers named Bonnie and Clyde! And the people lap it up. They can't print enough newspapers!'

Jessie shuts the door and sets down her schoolbag on the central table's black marble top. 'Scandal sells. It's the same in London. It's always been that way, and probably always will be. Come out to the terrace and tell me all about what you've been up to. Have you had any tea while you've been waiting? Shall I ring Marta for some?'

'Don't bother. I had the pleasure of your mother-in-law's company for tea when I got here.'

Jessie raises her eyebrows. 'How did that go?'

Ruth follows Jessie through the vast entrance hall and into the grand drawing room with its tasteful and expensive French antiques.

'She suggested that I visit a manicurist and a "good French couturier" she knows, and thought I could benefit from a visit to her *coiffeuse* as well. She's given me all their addresses and told me I was very fortunate to have an introduction from her, as it would guarantee the best service. Then she excused herself and said she needed to lie down as she had a headache brought on by her "unexpected hostessing duties".'

'Oh, dear. I'm sorry, Ruth. Layla is … well, she's unique.'

'Yeah, I got that.'

Jessie opens the French doors to the terrace and makes her way over to her favourite wicker chair. She flops onto the plump chintz cushions and kicks off her shoes.

'How long has it been, Ruth? Two years?'

Ruth settles onto the wicker settee. 'Three. I stopped by en route to Libya to report on the Italian invasion and we all went out to dinner at Shepheard's Hotel, do you remember?'

'Ah yes, I remember. The *maître d'* was quite taken with Shani and gave her a second helping of ice-cream, much to Layla's disapproval, which made it all the more delightful in my view.'

'It was a great night. Then the things I saw in Libya just a week later...' Ruth runs her hand through her waved bob. 'Honestly, Jessie, sometimes I wonder why I bother reporting on war and politics when scandal is all anyone seems to want to read about in the papers. Maybe I should sign up for one of the scandal sheets in Hollywood and have done with it.'

'If you do, you're more than likely to bump into Etta. She's out there living in sin with CJ Melton trying to become the next Jean Harlow.'

'Is she now?' Ruth chuckles as she takes a packet of cigarettes and a metal flint match lighter out of her trouser pocket. 'She's a little old for that, but good luck to her.' She sticks a cigarette between her lips and strikes the flint match along the grooved side of the lighter until the end flares, then she lights the cigarette and inhales. She smiles at Jessie and throws her the lighter as she exhales a stream of smoke.

'Souvenir from the World Fair. It's got the logo stamped on it and all. Give it to Aziz. I know you don't smoke.'

Jessie pockets the lighter. 'Thanks. He'll like that. He's always bringing odd little gadgets back from the souk. You can find all sorts here in Cairo.'

Ruth tilts back her head and examines Jessie as she exhales a puff of smoke. 'Truer words were never said.'

Jessie frowns. 'What do you mean?'

Ruth leans across the arm of the settee and taps the cigarette ash into a brass ashtray. She settles back against the cushions and scrutinises Jessie with her dark eyes.

'Jessie, you know I like you, don't you?'

'Yes, of course. I like you, too, Ruth. You're one of my best

friends, even though we haven't seen each other for three years.'
Jessie laughs. 'Maybe that's why we're friends.'

A smile flits across Ruth's lips. 'Friends. Sure, of course.' She
shakes her head as she takes another drag on the cigarette. 'I was
just thinking … Never mind.' She glances at her wristwatch.
'Good grief. Is that the time?' She stubs out the cigarette in the
ashtray. 'I've got to love you and leave you, hon. I've got a dinner
meeting with a German film director who's in town making a
picture. They're filming a big musical number at the Sphinx the
day after tomorrow and I'm hoping to get onto the set and take
some pictures for *Photoplay*.'

'Oh no! You can't go yet. You've just got here. Stay for dinner.
Marta always cooks far too much. If you go now, you'll miss Aziz.
He's out at a meeting tonight but he'll be home in an hour or so.
He'd love to see you.'

Ruth rises from the settee and, bending over Jessie's chair,
gives Jessie a quick peck on her cheek. 'Another time, honey.
Maybe next time you can come to me.'

Jessie laughs. 'Come to you? The woman with no fixed
address? How do you figure I'll manage that?'

'You've got a point.' Ruth touches her forehead in a salute.
'Don't get up, Jessie. Rest your feet. I know the way out.'

'Are you sure? Do you need a lift? Mustapha can drop you
anywhere you like.'

'Don't worry, I've got it covered. I'm an intrepid reporter,
remember? See you when I see you. I'll try to give you a call
before I leave. Maybe we can meet for a drink at Shepheard's.'

'Sure, Ruth. That would be lovely.'

At the doors to the sitting room, Ruth turns back to face Jessie.
'And, hon, ask your mother-in-law for her manicurist's details. I
think your poor feet could use a pedicure.'

Chapter Nineteen

Celie

Sweet Briar Farm, West Lake, Alberta, Canada - July 1933

Mavis Wheatley flips over the page of her notebook and runs her finger down the list of names and comments she's scribbled across the page.

'Oh, yes, Rosita Majors suggested a column on "Fifteen Ways to Clean Your Home with Baking Soda", and Muriel Evans said she's discovered that cola is a miraculous cleaning product. She's happy to talk to you about that. Molly and her friends all want to include a petition for Mr Forbes to stock Tangee lipstick. Now that she's eighteen, all she thinks about are boys, movies and make-up.'

Celie nods as she jots down her notes. 'Right. So, it's the practical things everyone's interested in.' She taps the eraser of her pencil against her cheek as she frowns. 'Doesn't anyone want to know what the government plans to do to help us out of this Depression? Prime Minister Bennett seemed to think that raising import tariffs was the answer, but now no one wants to sell to us.

And he's holding back the sale of our wheat abroad waiting for export taxes to go down and wheat prices to improve, but all that's happening is that we've got grain elevators stuffed with wheat and no one to sell it to. It's an economic disaster, Mavis.'

Mavis grins at Celie as she brushes an errant clump of her unruly dark blonde bob behind her ear.

'Slowly, slowly, Celie. Don't scare Rex off at the start. Soften him up with "Twenty Ways Vinegar will Change Your Life" before you slip in politics. Men can get awfully nervous when women think about the big issues. They hate being challenged by us, don't they? They much prefer thinking that our brains are inferior.'

Celie picks up a digestive biscuit and dips it into her tea. 'I think they're afraid that we'll figure out what a mess of things they've made, Mavis. I hope Lulu has a better time of things when she's older.'

Mavis helps herself to a third biscuit. 'Absolutely. And Molly, too. But right now, women in West Lake need to know how to run a household and raise children on no money. That's their priority.'

Celie nods. 'First things first.'

'First things first. Then, in a few months, go for the jugular.'

Celie rises and heads to the sink to refresh the kettle. As she's filling it, she looks out the window and watches Lulu squeal with delight as Ben Wheatley pushes her in circles on the tyre swing Hans had hung from the maple tree years earlier.

She smiles. It's good to hear their laughter. It had been a hard four years of stifling heat and drought, with Frank's mood sinking with their bank balance.

Where had it had all gone wrong? Was it Frank's profligate spending on their Montréal honeymoon when she'd urged caution? His stubborn reliance on outdated British farming methods for growing barley out on the baking, windswept Canadian prairies? Was it her acceptance of the Saturday job teaching German immigrants English? Or was it the realisation that his dream of a new life of prosperity and happiness with his wife and daughter on a farm in Canada after surviving the horrors of the Great War was as fragile as a balloon with a slow leak? And that that slow leak was her love for another man. Max Fischer. A German.

'Mommy! Come quick! There's a big black rain cloud coming!'

Celie glances up at the sky where Lulu is pointing to the cloud floating in from the south. She sighs with relief. Finally, rain. She sets the kettle down on the stove and points out the window. 'Looks like we've got some rain coming, Mavis. Come help me bring in the laundry, would you?'

'Sure thing.'

Celie grabs the laundry basket out of a store cupboard and waves to the children as she and Mavis hurry down the porch steps.

'Lulu! Ben! Come help us get the sheets in before it rains!'

The children run over to the clothesline and slide into easy teamwork – Ben unclipping the wooden pegs and Lulu bundling the sheets into the laundry basket – as Kip spins around the garden barking.

'Daddy will be so happy, won't he?' Lulu says as she stuffs a pillow case into the basket. 'He's been ever so cross. He shook his fist at the sun yesterday and yelled, "Hell and set fire to it!"'

'Louisa Jeffries! That is no language for a young lady. What must Ben think?'

Ben tugs at a sheet. 'I've heard worse when Ol' Man Forbes and Pastor Dinklage come round to play Pinochle, Mrs Jeffries.'

A large drop hits Celie on her head, and she brushes at it automatically. Then another hits her shoulder.

Lulu screams.

'Lulu, what is it?'

She gasps at the sight of her daughter flapping at the grasshoppers dropping into her hair. The swarming insects fall out of the sky, landing on every surface.

'Oh, my word!' Mavis says as she flaps at the descending cloud of insects. She grabs two sheets from the basket and tosses one to her son.

'Ben! Lulu! Put this over your heads and run into the barn! Hurry!'

Celie joins Mavis under a sheet and the four of them run blindly through the buzzing swarm into the shelter of the barn, Kip barking at their heels.

'Shut the door, Ben!' Mavis yells. 'Hurry!'

'Mommy!' Lulu screams. 'They're all over me!'

'Flap the sheet, Lulu. They won't hurt you. It's the wheat they're after.'

Ben whips the sheet away from Lulu and stamps on the insects. 'There, Lulu. They're gone.'

Celie opens her arms to her daughter. 'Come here, sweetheart. They're just insects. They're nothing to be afraid of.'

Lulu runs to Ben and throws her arms around him. The boy pats her on the back. 'Don't worry, Lulu. I'm here. I'm your best friend for ever.'

Celie stares at Ben and Lulu, and she knows, as sure as she knows that their crop is being decimated by the plague of grasshoppers, that Lulu is no longer a child and that nothing will ever be the same.

Chapter Twenty

Christina

London/Capri - September 1933

Clover Bar, Hither Green, London

Hettie tromps into the dining room and thrusts a yellow telegram envelope at Christina, who is dolloping marmalade on a slice of buttered toast.

'Just came for you.'

'Can't you see my hands are full, Hettie?' Christina says as she nods at the table. 'Just put it down. I'll read it in a minute.'

'I can read it to you, being as your 'ands are full.'

Christina raises an eyebrow. 'Hettie, I know you make it your business to know everything that goes on in this house, but I most certainly do not require you to read my telegrams.'

Hettie shrugs her broad shoulders as she sets the envelope beside Christina's teacup. 'Suit yourself. You'll tell me about it in a minute anyway. 'Fought I'd save myself trekking back from the kitchen.'

'I shall do no such thing.'

Hettie grunts as she collects the empty toast-rack and heads out the door into the hallway. Christina wipes her fingers with her napkin. She should probably have let Hettie go years ago. It's too late now, of course – Hettie knows far too much about Harry. Ah well. She and Hettie are like a pair of old shoes that would be useless without each other. If truth be told, she rather enjoys their sparring. It keeps her wits sharp, which, heaven knows, she needs, given Etta's intrigues, Adriana's temper and Dorothy Adam's irritating intransigence.

She slits open the envelope with the end of her spoon and sets her reading glasses on her nose.

11.00 CAPRI ITALY 20 SEPT 33
DEAR MRS FRY – STEFANIA VERY ILL – HEART ATTACK –
DOCTOR
SAYS NOT LONG – MY GRANDMOTHER VERY UPSET –
PLEASE COME – MARIO SABBATINI

———————————

Three days later, Centrali train station, Naples, Italy

'Signora Fry! Adriana!'

Adriana spots the tall, slender young man waving his hat at the end of the train platform and grabs Christina's arm.

'It's Mario! Over there, *Nonna!* I knew he'd come.' She drops her suitcase onto the paved platform and elbows her way through the stream of departing passengers as she dashes to greet him.

'Adriana! Adriana, come back here at once!'

Christina expels a huff of exasperation. *Mario, Mario, Mario.* It had been all she'd heard from Adriana on the interminable train journey from London to Naples. She'd warned her granddaughter that a young man of thirty was hardly going to be interested in a girl of eighteen who was just starting her art studies in another country, but it had been like throwing pebbles at a brick wall. Her words had bounced off Adriana, leaving no indication of any impact whatsoever.

She tuts as she sees Adriana throw herself into the young Italian's embrace. The results of her hard work teaching her granddaughter propriety over the past four years will no doubt succumb to the laxity of the existence Adriana had always enjoyed on Capri. She will have to remind Adriana of the seriousness of their visit and hope that it will inspire a sense of decorum in her lovesick granddaughter, though she knows only too well the spell this island can have on a romantic young girl.

She watches Adriana grab Mario's hand and drag him through the passengers to where she has been abandoned with their luggage.

'*Nonna*, Mario is coming to Capri with us! Isn't that wonderful?'

Christina smiles tightly at the handsome, dark-haired Italian as she hands him her vanity case. 'Thank you for meeting us, Mario. I hope we didn't take you away from your teaching responsibilities at the Accademia di Belle Arti.'

Mario waves away her concerns. 'That is nothing. Of course, I would come to meet you, Signora Fry. You are like my own family and Adriana is like my own little sister.'

Adriana's thick dark eyebrows draw together. 'I am not a child, Mario. I am an independent woman of eighteen. I am studying at the Slade College of Fine Art and I am living in my own flat in London.'

Christina raises her hand to attract a porter. 'Adriana, you are living rent-free in my Chelsea flat with two other girls and Hettie visits twice a week to wash your clothes, clean the flat and cook you two good meals. I give you an allowance for your other food and necessities. You are hardly independent.'

Adriana rolls her dark eyes. '*Nonna*, I am a student. How can I be expected to pay for all of that myself? Isn't that true, Mario?'

'Well, I don't really—'

'Some students have part-time jobs to help them pay their way, Adriana,' Christina says as watches the porter approach with a trolley. 'Your mother, for all her many faults, worked at the Omega Workshops when she was at the Slade.'

'And how did that turn out, *Nonna*? Mama only got herself into trouble working while she was studying, didn't she? I'm saving you that anxiety.'

Christina sighs wearily. 'Fine. I shall expect you to come top of your class. You will have some catching up to do when we get back to London, what with missing a fortnight of your first term. You really should have stayed in London and got on with your studies. Heaven knows I am paying enough. Your mother's the one who should be here. I am most disappointed that she's made no effort to come. Etta owes our cousin Stefania a great deal.'

Adriana grunts as she hands Mario her suitcase to stack on the porter's trolley. 'Mama's too busy trying to be a Hollywood star. It's embarrassing. I'm glad she changed her name. I don't want anyone knowing that Etta Marine is my mother.'

A whistle blows and a group of men in black shirts and beige knickerbockers barrel down the platform, shoving Christina and Adriana unceremoniously out of their way.

'*Lui è lì!*' one of them shouts as he points at a man coming off the train.

Christina clutches Mario's hand to steady herself. 'What on earth?'

Mario's expression stiffens. 'It is the Blackshirts. Mussolini's *Camicie Nere*. They are nothing but thugs.'

The whistle blows again, piercing the men's shouts with its

shrillness. The Blackshirts push their victim, a middle-aged man in a grey coat and black fedora, against a train carriage. Then they clamp his arms behind him and frogmarch him down the platform.

The man turns and catches Christina's eye as he stumbles past her, but it is not fear she sees in his dark eyes. It is defiance.

Villa Serenissima, Capri

The arched wooden door of the villa swings open and Liliana Sabbatini, Stefania Albertini's lifelong friend and housekeeper and Mario's grandmother, throws open her sturdy arms to pull Christina into her embrace.

'Thank the Blessed Lord you have arrived!' Liliana exclaims in Italian as she kisses Christina's cheeks. She releases Christina and hugs Adriana. 'My angel, my beautiful child. You travelled well? You are not too tired from the journey? Mario did not keep you waiting at the train station?'

'We're both fine, Liliana,' Christina answers in Italian as she takes in Liliana's appearance – the familiar face lined and heavy, the raven hair now pure white, the body roundly sturdy in a black dress and ubiquitous apron. She is relieved to see that, despite the housekeeper's advanced age of eighty-one, Liliana appears to be as strong and capable as ever.

'Mario is arranging a cart to bring our luggage from the funicular. He has been more than helpful. He is a credit to you, Liliana.'

'He is a good boy,' Liliana says as she ushers them into the hallway, where the glazed Vietri sul Mare floral floor tiles gleam brightly in the sun streaming in from the window overlooking the garden. She shuts the door behind them and gestures to the large white-painted sitting room to the left. 'Sit, sit. Stefania is resting, so I will bring us *tisana* and *biscotti* and tell you what has happened.'

Adriana loops her arm through the housekeeper's. 'Let me help you, Lili,' she says as they head into the elegant room filled with handsome Italian antiques and furniture upholstered in plush green damask. 'It will be so nice to talk to somebody other than *Nonna*. You can tell me all about Mario.'

'Please don't fan the flames, Liliana,' Christina says as she unpins her hat and sets it on the hallway table. 'You know how obsessed Adriana is with your grandson.'

Liliana laughs and pats Adriana's hand. 'This is because she has good taste. There is no man better than a Sabbatini, may the Lord bless my dear departed Angelo.'

Christina watches them disappear through the doorway to the kitchen, then she turns toward the open glazed doors to the balcony and heads outside into the fresh autumn air. She walks over to the black iron railing and looks past the garden's cypress trees to the view of the turquoise Tyrrhenian Sea and the distant coast of the Italian mainland. Leaning against a stone pillar, she picks a perfumed blood-red bloom from the climbing rose. She lifts it to her nose and drinks in its scent as the soft sea breeze eases the weariness from her body.

It was on a September day just like this, on this same terrace forty-two years before, that Cousin Stefania had guessed her pregnancy. The sky had been the same sharp blue, the sea the same sparkling turquoise, and the heady-scented roses the same rich red. She had been so in love with Harry then, so sure that he would marry her when she told him that she was expecting his child, then so absolutely devastated when he'd abandoned her to her fate.

If it hadn't been for Stefania and Liliana, and Liliana's husband, Angelo, who had rescued her from an act of folly at the cliff in front of the Grotta di Matermania, she never would have survived that next difficult year. There would have been no

Cecelia, no Jessica, no Etta, no Adriana, no Louisa and no Shani. She owed her mother's cousin, Stefania Innocenti Albertini, her life and the lives of all her beloved family.

She runs her fingers over the rose's velvet petals. And now, Stefania is dying. It does not seem possible that the woman who had been there for her, and for Etta, in their most vulnerable states, who had been the shoulder to cry on, to confide in, who had carried the secret of Cecelia's father's identity all these years, is reaching the end of her earthly days.

Christina's throat tightens and she swallows a sob. She grits her teeth and sucks in several deep breaths as she wills her body to regain its composure. She must be strong. She *will* be strong. Not because of a sense of duty, but because of love.

'Tina, *cara mia*, come let me kiss you.'

Stefania gestures for her to approach, and Christina is taken aback by the thinness of her elderly cousin's wrists and the blue veins rising like vines on the back of her hands. The once plump cheeks have sunken and blue crescents have carved themselves under Stefania's brown eyes, though it is obvious that Liliana has made an effort to keep Stefania's grey-streaked black hair coiffed into neat marcelled waves.

She bends to kiss her cousin. 'Stefania. You're looking so well. You had me and Adriana worried.'

The older woman laughs, the sound surprisingly robust coming from such a frail body. 'You have always had tact, Tina. It is an English trait, I think. It is a skill we Italians have yet to learn.'

She looks past Christina to Adriana, who hovers awkwardly by the door. 'Adriana, since when have you become shy? Come kiss your ancient cousin.'

Adriana rushes over to the large mahogany bed and bursts into tears as she throws her arms around Stefania.

Christina clears her throat. 'Adriana, please. Decorum.'

Stefania brushes her hand over Adriana's dishevelled golden curls. 'Leave her be, Tina. It is not a bad thing to feel.'

She kisses Adriana's forehead and wipes the girl's tears with the corner of the sheet. 'My, you have become a beautiful young woman, *cara mia*. I can see your mother and your father in your face. It is a good mix.'

Adriana sniffs and rubs at the tears on her cheeks. 'The girls at my boarding school used to tease me for my black eyebrows and eyes and my blonde hair, and for my Italian accent. They always called me "that ugly foreign girl" and told me I would never belong in England.'

'Why didn't you tell me this, Adriana?' Christina says, shocked. 'I would have had the headmistress right on to those girls and their parents.'

Stefania shakes her head. 'It is why she never told you. Isn't it, Adriana?'

Adriana nods. Her lower lip quivers and a sob wrenches out of her body. 'Oh, Cousin Steffi, I'm so sorry I was so wild and horrible when I lived here with you.'

Stefania cups Adriana's tearful face with her hand. 'You must never worry about that, *il mio angelo*. Liliana and I always loved having you here despite all the cakes and biscuits she had to make for the mayor after your altercations with his daughter. You are the sun in our lives, Adriana. Never forget that.' She kisses Adriana's flushed cheek. 'Now, why don't you find Mario and go to the lemon seller and buy several fat lemons so Lili can make her delicious *Torte Caprese Bianca*? She will give you some money. I have a few things I need to talk to your grandmother about.'

Adriana kisses the old woman's cheek. 'I love you, Cousin Steffi.'

'I love you, too, *mio piccolo angelo*.'

After Adriana has left, Christina settles into the bedside chair.

'Can I get you anything, Stefania? Water? *Tisana*? I know how much you like your peppermint *tisana*.'

'Not right now, Tina. I wish to speak frankly with you.'

Christina folds her hands in her lap. 'Of course.'

Stefania smooths the embroidered bedcover covering her lap. 'Liliana has convinced herself that I shall recover from this. She tells me that she visits Father Izzo at Santo Stefano every morning to pray for my recovery.' She smiles sadly. 'It will be of no use. I know my time is near.'

Christina leans forward and rests her hand on Stefania's thin arm. 'No one but God can possibly know this.'

'You can know. I do. I feel it.'

Christina drops her hand and sits back in her chair. 'Are you afraid?'

Stefania looks down at the bedcover and picks at a loose blue embroidery thread.

'The thought of not being here, being me, Stefania Albertini, is frightening, I will not deny that. But I am eighty-four years old and I am a good Catholic woman. I have lived a long and happy life. I believe I will meet my Federico in Heaven and your mother, Isabella, too, whom the Lord took from us far too young. I choose to believe that they will be waiting for me.' She shrugs as she looks at Christina. 'It is a comfort, at least, to believe this. I cannot allow myself to think otherwise.'

Christina runs her fingers around her ear and nods. 'I understand.'

'This is not what I wished to speak to you about, Tina.' Stefania nods at the chest of drawers. 'Cecelia's Italian birth certificate is in the folder over there. It is best that you take it back with you to London. I am leaving Villa Serenissima to Adriana in my will and I am concerned that Carlo's son, Paolo, may try to find a way to claim the villa as his when she is in England. I would not wish the birth certificate to fall into his hands.'

'How would that happen, Stefania? Liliana is here and Mario visits often. They will keep an eye on the villa.'

Stefania sighs wearily. 'You have not experienced the barrage of letters and telephone calls I have had from Paolo's solicitors since Carlo's death, wanting to know about Etta's frame of mind, whether she and Carlo were together as man and wife, proof of their marriage, proof of Adriana's parentage. It has been one thing after another. Paolo is like a dog digging out a rabbit's lair. He will never cease until he gets what he wants. He wants this villa. I know this for a fact.'

'Why would he want the villa? Paolo has already successfully contested Carlo's will and taken everything Carlo wished Etta and Adriana to have. Etta has told me he is wealthy beyond measure, heading up a large automotive company in Milan.'

Stefania pierces Christina with her dark gaze. 'Paolo wishes to destroy them, Tina. He will not be satisfied until he has left them nothing. It is his revenge on Carlo for abandoning him to his grandparents when he was a boy, and on Etta for stealing Carlo away from Paolo's unfortunate mother.'

'That's ridiculous. Etta didn't know Carlo was married when she left for Italy with him.'

Stefania shrugs her frail shoulders. 'It is a fiction Paolo has created in his head, but it is one he believes.'

Christina frowns. 'And Adriana? Why is he so vindictive toward her? She is an innocent in all this.'

'Don't you see, Tina? Adriana was the beloved child. In Paolo's mind, she stole Carlo's love away from him. He will never forgive her for that.'

Christina rubs her forehead. 'I see.' She frowns. 'What has Cecelia's birth certificate to do with any of this? Adriana is regularly at Clover Bar. I would dread for her to find it. Surely it's safer here in Italy with Liliana.'

'Tina, if that birth certificate ever falls into Paolo's hands, you can be certain he will use it to blackmail you into forcing Adriana to give the villa to him. I do not trust him one centimetre and neither should you.'

Stefania reaches across the bed and grabs hold of Christina's hand. '*Cara*, I am making you the executor to my will. I trust no one like I trust you, and you have a clear head. I will leave some of my late husband's investments to Liliana and some to Etta in the vain hope that it will help her find some security in her life, and I am leaving the villa to Adriana. Please do all you can to fight Paolo if he tries to interfere with my wishes. I will not have that man in this house.'

Christina nods. Paolo had been an innocent victim of his parents' estrangement, that was clear, and despite the privileged life he had lived with his mother's parents, this feeling of abandonment had obviously festered until it had eaten away any vestiges of empathy in Paolo's soul. If he were a kinder man, she would feel sorry for him, but he has proved himself to be selfish and vindictive.

Christina squeezes her cousin's thin, cold hand. 'Of course, Stefania. So long as I live, Paolo Marinetti will never get his hands on your money or this house. You have my word.'

'Mario? Mario, wait a minute! You're walking too fast.'

Mario turns around on the cliff path, laughing. 'You are too slow, Adriana. You used to be as surefooted as the mountain goats. I think you're becoming an English girl, taking buses and taxis everywhere.'

'I am not! Don't you dare say that! I'm as Italian as you are!'

He holds out his hand. 'You are certainly Italian in your character, *stellina mia*.'

She takes hold of his hand and they continue along the path to the Arco Naturale. '*Stellina*? I am your little star?'

'It is just an expression.'

Adriana pulls her hand away. 'I'm not a child, Mario. I'm a woman. Can't you see?'

Mario looks at Adriana, taking in the thin flowered dress blowing against her full-figured body, the dark, flashing eyes with their eyebrows like spears, and the golden curls, cut short in the fashion, flying about her face in the breeze. It is like he is seeing her for the first time. He *is* seeing her for the first time. He sucks in his breath.

'Adriana.'

She steps forward and, pushing aside his unbuttoned waistcoat, rests her hand on the white linen shirt over his heart. 'Mario. My Mario.'

They stand like this for some time, aware only of their breaths, the warmth emanating from their bodies, the beating of their hearts. Expelling an anguished breath, Mario pushes Adriana's hand away and turns his back on her. He faces the sea, though his mind is such a jumble of confusion he sees neither the fishing boats bobbing on the waves, the sun-kissed Italian coast in the distance, nor the screeching gulls circling the cliffs.

'Adriana, I am twelve years older than you.'

'This is nothing, Mario. My father was eleven years older than my mother.'

He looks at her over his shoulder. 'I have known you since you were a child. You have been like my little sister.'

Adriana approaches him and wraps her arms around his waist. She rests her chin on his shoulder. 'But I am not your sister. I am Adriana Christina Marinetti and you are Mario Sabbatini. I love you, Mario. I have always loved you.' She whispers into his ear. 'Say it to me again. *Stellina mia.* Say it.'

Mario turns around and pulls her into his embrace. '*Stellina mia,*' he says, burying his head against her shoulder. '*Stellina mia, stellina mia, Adriana, il mio bell'angelo.*'

And then he is kissing her neck, and her face, until, finally, their lips meet as they were always meant to.

Christina staggers away from the bed where Liliana sits beside Stefania's body, caressing the dead woman's hair as she whispers the Hail Mary over and over.

It had happened so suddenly. She had gone to fetch the peppermint *tisana* and some biscuits to share with Stefania. She hadn't been gone more than a quarter of an hour.

She clutches at a bedpost, her breath shallow and uneven. A dull throb pulses against her breastbone and a heaviness presses against her chest like an iron weight. She shuts her eyes and gasps for breath.

'Christina?' She feels Liliana's hand on her arm. 'Christina? Are you all right?'

She clutches Liliana's hand and allows herself to be guided to the bedside chair.

'It's nothing,' she says in Italian. 'I am fine. It is simply the shock.'

Liliana brushes her hand through Christina's hair like a nanny comforting a child. 'You are not fine, my angel. You must rest.'

Christina takes a breath and straightens her shoulders. 'Really, Liliana, I'm fine considering what has just happened. I was simply overcome by emotion.'

Liliana nods. 'All the more reason for you to rest.' She looks over at Stefania. 'I will make her comfortable for her journey to Heaven.'

Christina glances over at Stefania, as still and pale as a wax mannequin under the bedcovers. Her cousin is gone, her essence departed, leaving nothing behind but the frail vessel which had held her spirit for eighty-four years. Stefania had been right. It had been her time.

'Have Mario call the undertaker. I will speak to Father Izzo about the funeral arrangements and Stefania's solicitor about the will.'

'Mario has gone out.'

'Gone out? Now? Where has he gone?'

'Don't you remember? Stefania sent Mario and Adriana out to buy lemons for *torte*.'

Christina sighs and runs her fingers over her ear. 'That's most inconvenient. What need do we have for lemon cake today? I shall call the undertaker myself.'

One week later

Adriana loops her arm through Christina's as they stand beside Stefania's grave. The other mourners – the men in black suits dusted off from years at the back of wardrobes, and the women in unadorned black dresses and veils – file out along the paths between the magnificent family·mausoleums and weeping stone angels of the island's Catholic cemetery.

'I will miss her.'

'I will miss her, too, Adriana. More than I think she would ever have understood.'

Christina watches Mario shake the old priest's hand and pass him an envelope, which she knows holds several thousand *lire*. Everything is about money, both in this life and in the afterlife.

'Come, Adriana. Liliana is waiting for us at the entrance. We must return to the villa. Most of the town will be there shortly to celebrate Stefania's life. It seems she touched many people here with her charitable work.'

Adriana nods. 'In a minute, *Nonna*. I want to wait for Mario.'

'Mario will come in his own time. You follow him around like a puppy, Adriana. It is not becoming. I can't imagine that he—'

'You can't image that he what?' Adriana pulls away from her grandmother. 'That Mario would be interested in me, because I am such a child?' She laughs, her coal-black eyes flashing. 'You know nothing, *Nonna*. Mario loves me and I love him.'

'What are you talking about?'

'We love each other, *Nonna*.' Adriana juts out her chin. 'We intend to be married.'

'Don't be ridiculous, Adriana. You're only eighteen and you have a place at the Slade waiting for you back in London.'

'*Nonna*, I am not going back with you.'

'Adriana! You most certainly shall be coming back with me.'

Mario approaches them and gestures in the direction of the entrance gate. 'Shall we go?' He looks from one woman to the other. 'Is something wrong?'

Christina eyes the young Italian coldly. 'Adriana has just informed me that you both intend to marry. Just when exactly is this folly meant to occur?'

Mario looks at Adriana. 'What's going on?'

'Mario, it's true, isn't it? We love each other. People who love each other marry.' She takes hold of his hand. 'I didn't tell *Nonna* anything that isn't true.'

Mario pulls his hand away. 'Adriana, we are not getting married.'

He looks at Christina and shakes his head. 'I am sorry, Signora Fry. It is true that something has happened between Adriana and me since you arrived on Capri—'

'What do you mean by that?'

Mario presses his hands to his forehead. 'No, no. I respect Adriana. I would not touch her until we marry.'

'See, *Nonna*? We *are* getting married.'

Mario shakes his hands in the air. '*Santa Maria*, Adriana! We are not getting married. You have been here only one week. *Madonna!* I am so, so sorry for the confusion, Signora Fry.'

'Signora Fry?' Adriana shouts, poking Mario in the chest. 'You apologise to my grandmother and not to me? Fine, you can marry my grandmother, *idiota!* I would never marry you, anyway. You're an old man for me!' She spins around and stomps down the path back to the town.

Mario rubs his forehead as he watches her go. '*Merda*.'

'It most certainly is that, Mario.'

Mario's eyes widen. 'I am sorry, Signora Fry. I forgot you speak Italian.'

'Adriana is young, Mario, and she's always had a temper. She needs to grow up before she marries anyone.'

Mario nods. 'I think this is true.'

Christina hooks her hand through the crook of Mario's arm. 'Let her do her studies in London, experience some adult responsibilities,' she says as they head down the path. 'Give her time. If you are meant to be together, it will happen. I have learned it is best not to rush these things.'

'She hates me, I think.'

'Maybe that's a good thing for now. Mario, you need to live your life too. You may find someone else. Someone … more appropriate. I am certain there are many lovely young women in Napoli.'

'There are. Many. The problem is, I do not love any of them. I love … I love Adriana.'

'My poor Mario. Love is a blessing and a curse.'

Chapter Twenty-One

Jessie

Cairo, Egypt – November 1933

Fatima pushes open the front door of the new medical building as she and Jessie step out into the large central courtyard with its double-tiered fountain and newly planted trees.

'How did your portfolio assessment go today, Jessica? I am always so nervous with the eyes of the assessors on me. I dropped my pencil twice when I presented my appendicitis case. I do not think Professor Mahmoud was very impressed.'

'Why were you holding a pencil?'

'To keep my hands from shaking! It was a bad idea, I think.'

'You're a fine student, Fatima,' Jessie says, clutching her schoolbag against her chest to avoid being jostled by the departing medical students. 'You really needn't be nervous. You'll make a wonderful doctor. You were far better than I was during our paediatric rotation.'

Fatima laughs. 'This is true. You must learn patience, Jessica.

Telling a four-year-old to sit still or you will jab the needle right through their arm is not best practice.'

'I know. I'm much better when the patient is unconscious. They don't fidget or talk back. Give me a surgical rotation any day.'

The young Egyptian woman waves at a young man in a khaki uniform and a black *tarbouche* standing in the shade of a neatly clipped tree at the medical school's entrance.

'Who's that? He looks very dashing.'

'He is my brother, Rami.' She kisses Jessie hastily on her cheeks. 'I must go. He is waiting to take me home. He becomes very impatient if I am late.'

'All right. I'll see you in the hospital canteen for lunch tomorrow. I'm starting my parasitology rotation. I expect to be spending quite a bit of time hovering over a microscope.'

Fatima laughs. 'For which I am certain Cairo's children will be thankful.'

When her friend has gone, Jessie looks up at the November sky and watches a lone puff of cloud scuttle across the sharp North African blue. It has been a good day. Her presentation on her essential thrombocythemia case had gone well and she had earned a nod of approval from Doctor Mahmoud. Joy buzzes through her body, setting her nerves tingling. How has she any right to be this happy? How has she been so lucky in this life?

She hurries down the path to the road and steps out onto the pavement. She sees Mustapha waiting for her beside the new Aston Martin. He takes her schoolbag and gestures down the street where a group of young men in the same uniform as her friend's brother are marching toward them to the beat of a drum. Two of the men at the front hold up a large banner in Arabic.

'We must wait until they pass.'

Jessie shields her eyes with her hand and squints at the banner. 'Young Egypt … Young Egypt…'

'Young Egypt Party.'

She stands beside Mustapha and watches the marchers approach. The rhythmic thump of the drum and the pounding of the men's booted feet on the tarmac draw a crowd from the medical school. The marchers' fixed stares and their goose-stepping stride unnerve her. She has seen something similar somewhere before, but she can't remember where.

'Who's the Young Egypt Party?'

Mustapha shrugs.

'It is a new party,' a voice pipes up from behind her.

She turns around and recognises one of the male students from her medical class.

'We call them the Green Shirts,' he says. 'My brother is a member.'

'What kind of new party?'

'It is a party of Egyptian youth who wish to see the union of Egypt and the Sudan, and break the chains which bind us to Britain. Why do we need Britain when there are many Arab and Muslim countries who can become our allies?'

'But the Wafd Party—'

'The Wafd Party is nothing but a lackey to the British. It is a party of old men and old ideas. The founder of the Young Egypt Party, Ahmed Hussein, is a man of the future. Like Hitler and Mussolini, he believes that an organisation of order and obedience with one specific goal is the answer in this time of chaos we live in. As soon as I graduate next year, I will join as well.'

Jessie turns back to watch the men file past. That was it. She'd seen a newsreel at the cinema of Hitler's Brown Shirts, goose-stepping down a street in Munich. Something about it had sent a chill down her spine. It had seemed … ominous. Now, watching the tense, glassy-eyed faces of the marchers, the feeling comes over her again, only worse, because this time she is living it.

She catches the eye of one of the final marchers and gasps. He stares at her for a brief moment, his fine-boned face expressionless, then he turns his gaze forward and marches past.

Isham. Zara's husband.

Mustapha opens the car door. 'We can go.'

She nods and climbs into the car. But as it pulls out into the road and speeds toward Gezira Island, she can think only of one thing.

What has Zara got herself into?

Part III

1934

Chapter Twenty-Two

Celie & Etta

Sweet Briar Farm, West Lake, Alberta, Canada – February 1934

5 Santa Rosa Apartments
   Hollywood
   California

January 9, 1934

Dearest Celie,

It's me, your prodigal sister! I'm so sorry it's taken me so long to write you back. Your Christmas letter was such a sweet read. Lulu sounds like a girl who knows her own mind! Fancy telling the Girl Guide leader that she has no need to learn to bake for her Baking Badge because 'Mama does it perfectly well and, besides, I want to be a doctor when I grow up just like my Auntie Jessie and doctors don't need to bake.' I laughed my socks off! She has that stubborn Fry blood running through those clever veins of hers.

Reading about Lulu made me think about Adriana. I do so miss her. It's been over a year since I've seen her. She was rather cross with me when I left London, but she'll understand one day when she has things she wants to do. She's doing ever so well at the Slade School of Fine Art. Mama writes me regular updates as Adriana is such a poor correspondent. Not even a birthday or Christmas card from her! Oh well, the callowness of youth. She will be nineteen this May, can you believe it? I was twenty when she was born. How is it possible that time has passed so quickly?

I'm terribly busy here in Hollywood. I have an audition tomorrow for a part as an Egyptian servant in Cleopatra' starring Claudette Colbert. It's a big picture, with scads of people. It's being directed by Cecil B. DeMille. Can you believe that, Celie? I might be in a picture directed by the great Mr DeMille! It's so awfully exciting being out here!

I know I should have gone out to Capri to be with Mama and Adriana for Cousin Stefania's funeral in September. Adriana sent me a horrible telegram accusing me of being an awful person for not going to the funeral after all Cousin Stefania had done for me. I was in the middle of filming a very important scene in a Bing Crosby picture called 'Going Hollywood'! I mean, a Bing Crosby picture, Celie! I couldn't possibly have left and let some other pushy hopeful steal my place, could I? Besides, Cousin Stefania was already dead. She wouldn't have been upset if I wasn't there.

I feel that my acting career is finally moving in the right direction after that to-do on the Marx Brothers' 'Duck Soup'. It's a shame the wardrobe mistress found that flask of gin in my make-up case. Did you know they were going to call the picture 'Grasshoppers'? Groucho said it was because the producer said animal pictures are big. I don't think 'Duck Soup' is much better, but what do I know?

Anyway, some jealous chorus girl must have planted the flask there. I know I would have been marvellous if they hadn't fired me. Groucho told me so. You must visit your local picture house to see '42ⁿᵈ Street'. I'm one of the dancing secretaries in the big number at the end. Oh my, did my feet hurt after that! I made CJ buy our downstairs neighbour a fruit bowl to apologise for all the stamping around I did in our apartment practising the steps. CJ said I don't look a day over twenty-five in the picture. The darling man! I've fudged my birth certificate, of course. If anyone finds out I'm thirty-nine I'll be run out of town! Women aren't permitted in Hollywood once they hit thirty, did you know that? Ha! Ha! I'm only kidding!

Celie chuckles. The local picture house? How big did Etta think West Lake was? She takes a sip of tea and turns over the page.

Celie, I need to ask an awfully big favour of you. Do you think you might be able to wire me a few dollars? You know I had to spend all of Papa's inheritance on Carlo's legal bills. I barely used a penny on myself, except for a few meagre dresses from Chanel for my meetings in Paris. One had to look the part to sell Carlo's paintings. Mama lent me some money to come out here, and I felt awful about it, but I'd had no choice. She was so obtuse, saying I was irresponsible and selfish, but I have only one life to life, Celie, and I intend to live it my way. She eventually saw my point of view. Truthfully, I think she was relieved to be rid of me, after the to-do at the WI Summer Tombola. I mean, really, when they invite people up onto the stage to sing a song of their choice, they shouldn't get all huffy when someone sings 'Find Me a Primitive Man'!

I really would rather not bother Mama for money again. It would be absolutely too headache-making. I'm sure you understand.

You've probably heard from Mama that Carlo's dreadful son, Paolo, contested Carlo's will and took all of Adriana's and my money. Darling Cousin Stefania left Adriana Villa Serenissima and me a few lire from some old investments of hers in her will, but that's tied up in Italian red tape, so I don't expect to see that for years, if ever.

The thing is it's awfully tough here right now. A shanty town is growing up around Los Angeles – little huts made of cardboard and pieces of wood. All these poor unemployed people from all over the States seem to think things are better out here in the west. If anything, it's worse because everyone is coming here! I can barely step outside the apartment without some pathetic wretch asking for a dime for food.

My acting work keeps food on the table and CJ has contract work at MGM writing screenplays, so he pays the rent and utilities. I'm so pleased he chucked in his newspaper job to become a screenwriter. It's ever so much more exciting than being a boring old reporter, don't you think?

We're not out on the street, of course, but there simply isn't any money for anything else. I've been sneaking things out of the wardrobe departments when I can so I can keep myself looking the way an aspiring actress should. Appearances are everything here. I'd so much appreciate some money to buy some proper clothes for myself. The shoes I'm wearing are three years old! I'm absolutely embarrassed about them. And I would die for a proper permanent wave and a colour. Platinum blonde is all the rage here thanks to Jean Harlow and Mae West. I think it would suit me terribly well.

Anyway, I know how prudent you've always been with money. Jessie is, too, of course, but I asked her and she turned me down flat. Can you believe that? And she's my twin! She had the audacity to say that my need didn't appear to be that urgent, and that she is using her inheritance to pay for her medical studies and fund her health clinic. Aziz is rich enough to do that! That's Jessie and her silly pride, isn't it? She can be so very mean.

I promise, promise, promise I will pay it back with 5 per cent interest, so it's a win-win situation for both of us. Perhaps I might even take the train up to Alberta and pay you back personally. Wouldn't that be fun? You can show me all the high points of West Lake!

I must go. CJ's just come back from work and has brought some Chinese food from Man Fook Low in Chinatown. We've seen Mae West there more times than I can say. Los Angeles is such an exciting place to live, Celie. I never know whom I'm going to see when I step outside my door.

Please, please, Celie. Do be a doll and say yes. I've written down my bank details below.

Lots of love always,
Etta X

Celie sets the letter down on the kitchen table. *Oh, Etta. What have you got yourself into this time?* She looks over at the basket of eggs on the kitchen counter, and the half loaf of bread she has been trying to eke out over the past few days. She can already hear Frank. *'Eggs again for supper? Are you trying to turn me into a chicken, Celie?'* But what can she do? Frank can no longer afford the fuel for the tractor, which sits in the backyard like a hulking metal vulture, while he treks in the fields behind Betsy harvesting the wheat that he sells for almost nothing. She can't remember the last time they'd had a roast, or a cake, let alone coffee. And Etta is worried about her unfashionable shoes!

She drops her head into her hands and massages her forehead. Etta has to grow up. Her sister has made her choices, all of them selfish and irresponsible as far as she can see. Etta has never thought of anyone except herself, not even of her own daughter, Adriana. At least Adriana has found her feet in London and is excelling at art college. Perhaps it's a blessing that she has escaped Etta's influence.

Celie folds the letter and slips it back into the envelope. She will send Etta a telegram tomorrow. Etta will have to find somebody else to pay for her shoes.

Chapter Twenty-Three

Jessie

Khan el-Khalili Souk, Cairo, Egypt – February 1934

Jessie licks at the sticky Lebanese pistachio ice-cream called *booza*, which she has twisted around a small flat wooden spoon, and dabs at her lips with her fingertip as the cold sweet melts on her tongue.

'Is there anything else you need to buy while we're in the souk today, Zara? I really should get back soon to study up on ophthalmology for my next rotation.'

Zara tosses her empty ice-cream cup and spoon into a brazier and shakes her head.

'I would like to look at the shoe stall. I am hoping they have brought in some new shoes from Spain.' She casts a withering glance down at Jessie's scuffed brown shoes. 'You should buy some yourself. Your shoes do not become you.'

Jessie laughs as she hands her half-empty cup of *booza* to a child who has been following them, pleading for a taste.

'You sound like your mother. She disapproves of everything I wear, but I really can't be bothered about fashion. I'm quite happy to leave that to Etta.'

Zara stops at a stall displaying colourful *hijabs* on faceless cork mannequin heads the vendor has strung up over the sales table. She picks up a sky-blue *hijab* from the table.

'What do you think of this one?'

Jessie presses her hand to her lips to stifle a yawn. 'It's very nice. It would suit you.'

Zara glances at Jessie. 'Not for me, Jessica. For Shani.'

'Shani? What are you talking about?'

Zara folds the blue fabric and returns it to the sales table. 'Shani will be twelve years old in June. She will need to start wearing a *hijab*.'

'June is months away. We don't need to talk about this now.'

Zara rests her hand on Jessie's arm. 'Jessica, you have buried this conversation for many years and Aziz has supported you. But our mother has been speaking to him about Shani's religious training and he believes, as I do, that Shani must begin her regular prayers and learn about Islam once she turns twelve.'

Jessie bites her lip as irritation pricks at her like a mosquito. 'Well, he has not told me as such, and until I speak with him, I don't wish to talk about this any further.'

'Jessica—'

'Zara. I said enough.'

'But Jessica—'

'Zara, Shani is Catholic. My mother and Marta had her baptised in the Roman Catholic Church just after Shani was born.'

Zara gasps. 'I did not know.'

'Neither did I at the time. I was in the hospital recovering from the birth. I didn't find out until several years later. I was furious with my mother, but it's done.'

Zara draws her dark eyebrows together beneath her *hijab*. 'Does Aziz know?'

'Yes, of course.'

'What did he say?'

'Zara, this really isn't any of your business.'

'You are wrong, Jessica. You are not Muslim and I am. As Shani's aunt, it will be my responsibility to teach her about being a good Muslim woman.'

Jessica rubs at her throbbing forehead. She'd known for the past few months the subject of Shani's religion would have to be addressed soon, but she'd pushed the issue to the back of her mind in a vague hope that the problem would disappear. She had enough to deal with, what with the overcrowding in the clinic, her medical studies and her concerns about Aziz's safety in going to church, let alone teach Shani how to be a good Catholic, but she couldn't accept Shani wearing a *hijab* and becoming Muslim either. She didn't have the time or energy to deal with this. As far as she was concerned, Shani was Catholic and she was happy to ask Marta to take her to the Orthodox Church every Sunday and be done with it. But then there was Aziz, and Zara, and Layla to think about ... and how much they wanted Shani to become Muslim. It's just all too much to think about.

'Please, Zara. Let's go look at these shoes and go home. I'm feeling very tired.' She glances over her shoulder. 'And Mustapha must be awfully bored waiting for us.'

Zara sighs, her shoulders heaving under her black *jellabiya*. 'As you wish.'

They walk on through the narrow alleys of the market in silence, Jessie following her sister-in-law's slender black-clad figure.

'Zara?'

'Yes.'

'I saw Isham.'

Zara turns around. 'You did? When?'

'A few months ago. He was in a march outside of the medical school for the Young Egypt Party.'

Zara juts out her chin. 'Yes. He is a member.'

Jessie runs her tongue over her lips. 'They looked … they looked very military. Someone said they're called the Green Shirts.'

'It is necessary to have structure if we are to achieve the aim of a unified Egypt and Sudan under Egyptian rule.'

'That's what the Wafd Party is trying to do through the proper channels.'

Zara grunts. 'They are too slow. They try to make everyone happy – the British, the king, the Nationalists – it will never happen with them.'

'It's just that … I have a bad feeling about it. Please, be careful.'

Zara's guarded expression softens. She reaches out and takes hold of Jessie's hands.

'Jessica, please do not worry about me. I am a capable woman, and Isham is my husband. I have my life to lead, as you have yours.'

'That's another thing. When are you going to tell your mother and Aziz about your marriage? I hate being the keeper of secrets, especially from my husband.'

'I know. It means a great deal to me that you have not told anyone. I will tell them when the time is right. I promise.' She slides her arms around Jessie and pulls her into an embrace. 'You are my English sister, Jessica. You have been there for me many times. I will always be here to help you as well.'

Jessie relaxes into Zara's embrace. 'I'm glad you're Aziz's sister. I don't know how I would have managed your mother on my own.'

Zara pulls away suddenly and points at the shop sign behind Jessie. 'Jessica, look! It's the fortune-teller. Do you remember when we went there when you were carrying Shani in your belly?'

Jessie looks up at the wooden sign, the paint now worn and faded after so many years.

'I remember. She said that I was on a path that would divide, with one direction leading to happiness and the other to sadness. It's a lot of rubbish, if you ask me.'

'She knew you had a twin sister and that you had Shani in your belly. And she knew about Aziz as well.'

'Zara—'

Zara grabs Jessie's hand. 'Come, let us visit her. Perhaps she can tell me if Isham and I will be blessed with a child, even though I am past forty.'

'You go, Zara. I'll go buy some notebooks at the stationery stall and I'll meet you back here in an hour.'

The beaded curtain in front of the shop entrance clatters as a woman in a gold silk turban and a black *jellabiya* embroidered with gold at the cuffs and collar exits. The musty floral scent of frankincense and patchouli wafts around her like a perfumed cloud.

'Mama?'

Layla Khalid's heavily kohled amber eyes widen when she recognises Zara and Jessie.

'Zara! What are you doing here?'

'I didn't know you visited the reader.'

'It is not your business to know everything I do, Zara.' Layla eyes Jessie's plain navy dress and her scuffed shoes. 'Jessica, you really should make more effort when you leave the house. People will think Aziz is poor.'

Zara steps past her mother and pulls back the beaded curtain. She waves at Jessie. 'I will leave you with Mama while I find out my future.' The curtain rattles behind her as she disappears into the shop.

Jessie regards her mother-in-law. 'Well, here we are. Do you want to look at shoes?'

'I have no interest in any shoes that are sold in this place. I buy only Italian shoes from Cicurel.'

'Fine. I'm off to buy notebooks.' Jessie nods at Mustapha who is standing patiently in the shadow of an olive seller's stall. 'Why don't you ask Mustapha to drive you home? Zara and I can take a taxi later.'

'Jessica,' Layla says, her eyes narrowing. 'The reader told me something about you that you may wish to know.'

'Really? You don't strike me as the superstitious type.'

Layla raises a finely arched eyebrow. 'You are not curious? Do you not wish to know your future?'

'I am quite happy to live my life one day at a time. You might wish to do the same, rather than listening to fantasies put about by fortune-tellers.'

Layla shakes her head, setting her gold earrings swinging. 'I am sorry for you, Jessica. You live in a very narrow world. It is well that Shani has a grandmother who will ensure that her education is not limited to only that which can be seen and heard.'

'Please keep Shani out of all of this. I won't have you filling her head with nonsense.'

'If you spent your time at Altumanina rather than at the medical school, you would have more influence on your daughter.' Layla shrugs. 'As it is, Fate has seen fit that I am there to step into the void left by her mother.'

'Layla, leave my daughter alone.'

'I will not leave my granddaughter to be an infidel like her mother.'

The beaded curtain rattles as Zara rushes out, tears streaming down her face.

Jessie gasps. 'Zara? What's wrong?'

'It is nothing. It is nothing,' she says between sobs. She wipes at her face with her *hijab*. 'Please, I want to go home.'

'Zara, don't pay any mind to what that woman said. She can't possibly know anything about you.'

Zara wipes at her streaming eyes. 'You are wrong, Jessica. She knows everything.'

Chapter Twenty-Four

Christina & Etta

Clover Bar, Hither Green, London – March 1934

Santa Rosa Apartments
Hollywood
California

March 8th, 1934

Dear Mama,

How are you and Adriana? I trust you are well and that Hettie isn't slowly poisoning your tea with arsenic. I hope you haven't told her you'd leave her something in your will. It would be all the motivation she would need!

Do ask Adriana to write to me, please. The only response I get to my letters is a well of silence. It is like dropping pennies into a bottomless pit. I'd like to know what she'd like for her birthday. I'm sure she would love something from Hollywood. If I were her, I know I would!

Which brings me to the meat of the matter. Mama, I know I said that I wouldn't ask for any more money once I got out here, but things have been so much tougher than I ever imagined. I thought that I'd have been at least a second lead in the pictures by now, but it's so terribly competitive out here, and there are so many beautiful young girls. It's quite dispiriting. But, then, I remind myself that they're not me, and it is only a matter of time before my unique talent is recognised. That's what CJ says, too. He's such a sweet man. I'm sure you would adore him if you were ever to meet, though that is hardly likely, is it?

He tries so very hard to keep the wolf from the door, but he's paid a pittance hammering away at scripts at the studio. He only gets a bonus if one of his scripts gets made, can you believe it? He is such a talented writer – so much better than Scott Fitzgerald or Ernest Hemingway, which I tell him night and day. He threatens to go back to being a newspaperman, but that is so dull compared to working in the pictures, don't you think? I tell him that he'll be collecting an Oscar for best screenplay before you know it. Then, we'll be made!

So, money. Such a dreary subject, don't you think? I've asked both Jessie and Celie for a loan, and both have been most unhelpful, which is a great disappointment to me. I mean, we're sisters, and sisters are meant to help each other, aren't they, Mama? They haven't been any help at all. Celie even told me that I was lucky to have shoes!

I'm sending you my bank account details, if you would send me two hundred dollars that would be wonderful. I don't know what that is in pounds, but I'm sure your bank manager will tell you. I know it's rather a lot, but it would give me and CJ a cushion, and I wouldn't have to bother you again, because by the time it runs out, I'll be headlining with Clark Gable, mark my words!

I promise our little Celie secret is safe with me if you wire me the money as soon as you can. If you feel you can't, well, the post office is just a short walk away and it wouldn't take me more than half an hour to send Celie a telegram about you and Lord Sherbrooke. I feel just awful having to say that, but I feel it's best to be clear. Needs must! Misunderstandings are a terrible bore.

All my love to you and Adriana, always.
Yours ever,
Etta X

Christina removes her reading glasses and lets them fall against her chest on their silver chain. She sets the letter on the table and rubs her forehead. *Oh, Etta, you silly girl. You are so singularly self-absorbed that you believe the world should revolve around you and your petty needs. Is it any wonder that your own daughter refuses to speak to you? What have you ever done for her? You should never have been a mother. You have no idea of the responsibilities and the sacrifices that are required.*

Alice the cat jumps up onto the table and flops on top of the discarded letter, rolling onto his back for attention. Christina rubs his belly absentmindedly. Perhaps she'd been too lenient toward Etta when she'd been growing up. Cecelia had been so easy. Always diligent with her schoolwork, earnest, hard-working, reliable. Of course, there'd been the little blip with her romance with Max Fischer, but that had all worked out in the end.

There'd certainly been run-ins with Jessica before she'd left to nurse in the war. Jessica was far too stubborn and wilful for her own good. But Jessica was strong, smart and determined, which were admirable qualities, even if her single-mindedness sometimes lacked grace. And she seemed to have done quite well for herself in Egypt, which is all a mother can hope for.

Cecelia had never caused her a moment's concern, and Jessica had been so unwavering in her pursuit to become a nurse that Christina had rather taken her eye off the ball with Etta. If truth be told, she'd rather enjoyed her youngest daughter's airy spirit and artistic bent.

Etta had reminded her of herself before Harry had changed her life for ever. She'd been only too happy to encourage Etta's artistic leanings. She'd seen herself in Etta, but then Carlo had entered Etta's life, and … well, that turned into a disaster. Perhaps part of that disaster is her own fault for indulging Etta's whims, because she'd seen, through Etta's life as an artist, a chance to live the life she'd wanted for herself all those years ago.

Still, this current situation with Etta is untenable. She has indulged Etta's capriciousness and her threats to reveal the identity of Cecelia's father long enough.

She sets the cat onto the floor and reaches for her fountain pen and a piece of writing paper.

Clover Bar,
   Hither Green Lane,
   Hither Green,
   London SE13

March 20th, 1934

Dear Etta,

   I am sorry to hear of your money troubles. I had thought we'd reached an agreement when you left for America, which you assured me at the time would not be revisited. Of course, perhaps you don't recall the details of our discussion, being as you were so recently released from a lengthy stay at the Maudsley Hospital.

   I can certainly understand if you are unable to recall events accurately, being as you are susceptible to some misinterpretations of reality. It is a shame that you felt compelled to leave your home here in London, where you were making such good progress, for what can only be described as an impulsive folly to become an actress in Hollywood.

   How have you been feeling, my dear? There were days when you were at Clover Bar where you seemed quite certain that you were back in Capri with Carlo, and Adriana an infant in your arms. It was quite disconcerting for Adriana, and no doubt contributed to your estrangement, but I had entertained the expectation that you would recover your relationship with your daughter as you recovered the health of your fragile mind. But, then, far too soon in my opinion, you insisted on leaving on this foolish escapade. I am truly ashamed at my part in funding this folly, and cannot, in good conscience, continue supporting this situation. Quite frankly, Etta, if I send you money this time, it will only encourage you to continue to lean on me again and again in the future. You are an adult woman, living in sin, no less, and you simply must stop expecting other people to rescue you from the situations in which you find yourself.

As to your threat of revealing to Cecelia that Lord Sherbrooke is her father, well, this is truly absurd. Who in their right mind would believe you, after the fantasies you wove during your two illnesses? They would simply think that you were succumbing to yet another delusional episode. I am certain I can persuade the Maudsley Hospital to take you back should this be necessary or find a similarly suitable hospital in California.

With loving concern,

Mama

Chapter Twenty-Five

Jessie

Altumanina, Cairo, Egypt - June 1934

Jessie tears open the telegram envelope and reads through the brief message.

10.00 LOS ANGELES USA 27 JUNE 34
DEAR DR JESSIE – YOU DID IT! – CONGRATULATIONS! –
HAPPY
BDAY TO SHANI TOO – RUTH X

Aziz looks up from the grapefruit he is eating for breakfast. 'You are smiling. It must be good news.'

'It's from Ruth. Congratulating me on my graduation and wishing Shani a happy birthday. I'm amazed she remembered considering how busy she is.'

'She is a good friend.'

Jessie smiles. 'Yes, she is. Speaking of friends, did I tell you I had a letter from Lady Evelyn Beauchamp yesterday? Lord

Carnarvon's daughter? You remember? We met her down at the Tutankhamun dig with her father and Howard Carter. She introduced us to Ruth in the camp there.'

'Of course I remember her. A very charming young woman. It's a terrible shame about her father. Dying from an infected mosquito bite just a few months after the discovery of the tomb is a terrible fate.'

Layla Khalid, dressed in her customary black silk *jellabiya*, enters the dining room as erect and imperious as a black swan gliding through water.

'A fate he deserved. He had no business disturbing the tomb of a pharaoh.' She slides into a chair beside Zara, which Mustapha pulls out from beneath the table, and lays a linen napkin across her lap. 'His daughter will be fortunate if she escapes the pharaoh's curse. I understand she entered the tomb as well.'

Zara rolls her eyes as she drizzles honey onto a piece flat *baladi* bread. 'Mama, please be nice. It's a special day.'

Shani looks up from her favourite breakfast of *baladi* bread and *foul* – a mash of fava beans, cumin, lemon, olive oil, salt and pepper. 'Is King Tutankhamun's tomb cursed? You and Baba were there, too.'

Jessie frowns at Layla. 'No, darling. That's just silly superstition. Lord Carnarvon got a blood infection and he died. It was very sad and unfortunate, but it was not a curse. Don't let your grandmother fill your head with these ridiculous notions.'

Layla glares at Jessie. 'It is not a ridiculous notion. The Curse of the Pharaohs is common knowledge. It is why Egyptians had the good sense to leave the tombs alone. The European tomb thieves deserve whatever the curse visits upon them.'

'Enough, Mama,' Aziz says as he accepts a refill of coffee from Mustapha. 'We have more important things to discuss today.'

He looks across the table at Jessie and his dark eyes alight as he smiles. 'We have my wife's graduation from medical school and our daughter's twelfth birthday to celebrate.'

Layla waves away Marta's offer of a plate of *foul* but accepts a grapefruit. She beckons to Mustapha, who brings her a package wrapped in white tissue paper and pink ribbon.

Layla takes the package and hands it across the table to Shani. 'It is indeed an important day. Happy Birthday, Shani. Unwrap it now. There is no need to wait.'

Shani's eyes light up. 'Thank you, Nana Layla.' She carefully unties the pink satin bow and pulls apart the tissue paper. Her eyes widen as she lifts out a long lavender silk chiffon scarf. 'Oh, Nana Layla. It's beautiful.'

'It is a *hijab*, Shani. A very expensive one.' Layla casts a defiant glance in Jessie's direction. 'You are twelve now, and you must wear one as a good Muslim girl. Zara will tie it on you.'

Jessie glances at Aziz who shakes his head surreptitiously. She grits her teeth. 'It's a very nice gift, Layla. Shani, why don't we put it away and you can wear it for special occasions? Like Eid al-Fitr and Eid al-Adha?'

'Mama, can't I put it on now? It's my birthday, after all. Isn't that a special occasion?'

Jessie presses her lips together as she absorbs the tense expressions of her Egyptian family. 'I … I suppose. As you say, it is your birthday.'

Shani leaps out of her seat and hugs her mother. 'Thank you, Mama. I will be a Christian *and* I will be a Muslim. I am both, after all, aren't I?'

Layla frowns. 'Shani, you cannot be both.'

Aziz throws his mother a warning look. 'Mama, not now.'

'But, Aziz—'

Zara rises from her chair and beckons to her niece. 'Come, Shani. Bring me your *hijab* and I will put it on you. You will be the prettiest girl in Cairo today.'

Jessie sits back in her chair and squeezes her hands together as she watches Zara tie the scarf around Shani's dark hair. She glances over at Aziz. He is smiling. They are all smiling, Shani the broadest of all.

Her mind spins in a confusion of emotions – fear, worry, trepidation, incredulity, shame. Why can't she accept her daughter's embrace of Islam? Christianity and Islam share the same God, the Old Testament, even the same angels. Perhaps she needs to learn from her daughter's even-tempered acceptance of the two faiths. Shani is right, after all; she is both Christian and Muslim, and she, as her mother, will need to embrace that fact despite her own misgivings.

'Mama, what do you think?'

Jessie looks at her daughter who beams at her from the folds of the lavender *hijab*.

'You look very nice, Shani.' She clutches the arms of the chair and rises. 'Now, Baba has promised to take us for a camel ride at the Sphinx and the Pyramids today. Let's get ready before it gets too hot. Then we can come back and have a celebration picnic out in the garden.'

———

Later that night, Aziz joins Jessie on their bedroom balcony. 'I was very proud of you today, *habibti*. I know it was difficult for you to see Shani in a *hijab*.'

'It was.' Jessie sighs. 'I feel so guilty. It shouldn't upset me so much, but it does.'

He takes her into his embrace and kisses her forehead. 'You needn't worry. Zara will be a good guide for her.'

'Perhaps. At least it won't be Layla.'

Aziz frowns. 'What do you mean, "perhaps"?'

She chews her lip, the revelation of Zara's marriage to Isham threatening to tumble out of her mouth. 'Nothing. You're right. Of course you're right. I just want Shani to have the freedoms I've had. I worry that she won't.'

'Don't worry. Shani is a strong girl just as her mother is a strong woman. She will do what she wishes in life, I have no doubt.'

'I hope so.'

'Darling, I wish for Shani to be happy in her life. I will ensure she has the freedom to choose her path, just as I supported Zara in her refusal to marry any of my mother's proposed suitors.'

'You're not so keen on Zara's politics, though.'

'It's true, I'm not. But she has her own mind and I respect that.' He kisses Jessie lightly on her lips. 'Enough of Zara and Shani. Today is about you as well, Dr Jessica Khalid.'

Aziz reaches into the breast pocket of his jacket and removes a small red satin box. He opens the lid. 'Congratulations, my beautiful wife. I am so very proud of you.'

Jessie gasps at the gold ring surrounded by small, perfect diamonds. 'Aziz! Good heavens.'

He takes hold of her left hand and slides the ring down her ring finger until it nestles above her wedding band. 'It is an eternity ring. To remind you that you have my love for all eternity.'

Jessie looks up at her husband, still so handsome despite the years of arduous hours at the hospital and government work.

'I love you, Aziz. For all eternity.'

Chapter Twenty-Six

Christina

Clover Bar, Hither Green, London - July 1934

Christina looks up from the needlepoint rose she is working on and glances at Hettie, who is making a weak show of dusting the family photographs on the piano as she surreptitiously parts the lace curtains to peer out the window.

'Whatever are you doing, Hettie? The sight of your face at our window will frighten off Mr Brandt before he reaches our doorstep.'

Hettie steps back from the window with a huff. 'Excuse me for still 'aving red blood coursing through these Cockney veins. Can't remember the last time we 'ad a young man 'ere for tea. You can't begrudge me a look.'

'I suspect Mr Brandt is visiting us out of a sense of duty to Cecelia. I don't imagine he is coming here in a romantic frame of mind.'

Hettie shrugs. 'No 'arm in looking. I ain't dead yet.'

The rattle and squeak of the front gate filter in through the window and Hettie thrusts the feather duster at Christina, who stares at it like it's an alien creature.

'Hettie! What am I meant to do with this?'

But Hettie is already out in the hallway greeting the newly arrived guest while the doorbell chimes are still resonating through the house. Christina stuffs the duster under her chair cushion and resumes pulling a red embroidery thread through the canvas with her needle.

'Mr Brandt's 'ere,' Hettie announces in the sitting room doorway.

'Thank you, Hettie. Please take his hat as you should have done when he first arrived.'

Hettie rolls her eyes and takes Hans's grey felt fedora, which he extends to her with a smile and a wink. A girlish giggle escapes from her as she gestures with the hat for him to enter the sitting room.

''Er ladyship's expecting you. I'll get the tea.'

Christina observes the tall young man with the neat, brilliantined blond hair and good English grey wool suit. Impeccable down to the polished black shoes, blue striped tie and neat white handkerchief in his breast pocket. A box of expensive Bendicks of Mayfair mint chocolates in his hand. A man with an attention to detail. Such a pity he's a German. She will never be able to forgive them for Gerald's death by a German bomb.

She sets down her needlepoint and rises to greet her visitor with a handshake.

'Mr Brandt. I'm so delighted you could come to tea today. Cecelia has written me all about your terribly important position at Vickers Aviation. It's good of you to find the time to visit.'

'It is my very great pleasure, Mrs Fry, although I'm known as Henry Brand here in Britain. It makes things … easier. But please call me Hans. It is my name, after all.' He offers her the box of chocolates. 'Mrs Jeffries said you were fond of chocolate and that I should bring you some in order to ingratiate myself to you. I have it on good authority that Bendicks makes the best mint chocolates in Britain.'

Christina accepts the gift and places it on a side table.

'Consider yourself ingratiated. We shall have some after tea. Now, do have a seat and tell me about how you came to know my daughter in Canada.'

'… And she is a stickler for precise grammar and pronunciation.' Hans laughs. 'She despaired of the hard "r's" of Canadian English, but I am afraid that was a battle she couldn't win. Lulu is Canadian through and through.'

Christina smiles as she sets down her teacup. 'Cecelia has always been my diligent daughter. She was never a worry to me, unlike her sister Etta who's now off attempting to be an actress in Hollywood. It is quite beyond comprehension. I feared Etta's daughter, Adriana, would be similarly flighty, but she is studying art here in London at the Slade and quite excelling at it. She appears to have inherited her father's talent. I was hoping she would join us today, but apparently there's some modern art exhibition that her class is attending. She said she'd try to come, but it seems she's been delayed. Another time, perhaps.'

Hans accepts Christina's offer of another of Hettie's currant scones and sets it on his plate. 'That would be my pleasure. Family is important. My stepfather passed away a few years ago, but now that I am in England, I've been able to visit my mother and stepbrother in Heidelberg a few times.'

'Heidelberg? Cecelia knew someone from Heidelberg once.'

Hans looks up from the piece of scone he is buttering. 'Did she? She never mentioned this to me.'

'It was a young man she knew before she married her husband. A Maximilian Fischer. He was Cecelia's German teacher at the university here, but it was quite a long time ago. Before the war.'

Hans dollops a spoonful of strawberry jam onto the scone. 'How very interesting.' He smiles. 'It is a small world, isn't it, Mrs Fry?'

Christina is seeing off Hans Brandt in the hallway when the front door flies open and Adriana whips into the house like a gust of wind.

'Oh, *Nonna!* I am awfully sorry. I tried to arrive earlier, but the bus to Charing Cross took for ever and then I missed the train.'

She thrusts out her hand to Hans. 'You must be Auntie Celie's German student.' She slams the door shut and smiles at Hans as she unpins her hat. A shock of cropped blond curls escapes from the confines of the felt cloche hat. 'I've been dreaming about Hettie's scones. I hope you haven't eaten them all.'

Hans stares at Adriana before finding his voice. 'No, uh, no, they were quite irresistible, but I restrained myself from having a third.'

She flashes him a broad smile. 'Wonderful.' She edges past him and heads down the hall toward the kitchen. 'Hettie! Hettie! I am home. Where is my scone!'

Christina suppresses a smile as she watches her visitor's gaze follow Adriana. She hands him his hat. 'That was Adriana.'

'Right. Yes. Of course.'

Clearing his throat, he puts on his hat and offers his hand to Christina. 'Thank you very much for inviting me to tea, Mrs Fry. It's been a great pleasure to meet you and to see where my favourite teacher came from.'

'The pleasure is all mine, Mr Brandt. You must come again. I shall ensure Adriana is here next time.'

Hans shuts the door of his boarding house and hangs his hat on the hat rack. He is sorting through the stack of post when his landlady appears from the sitting room in a floral housedress, carrying a feather duster. She eyes him with the passive aggression she reserves for her foreign lodgers.

'There was a telephone call for you while you was out.' The woman digs into the pocket of her floral apron and retrieves a slip of yellow paper. 'Foreign bloke. 'Ere's the number. Tea's at six. Shepherd's pie tonight wiff treacle pud for pudding.'

'Thank you, Mrs Wright. That sounds delicious.'

He watches the woman's squat frame waddle down the hallway, then picks up the receiver on the hallway phone and dials the number.

'It's Henry Brand.'

He nods as he listens to the voice on the other end.

'Of course. I understand. I will arrange it. No, it won't be a problem. Yes. Yes. I will be discreet. No one will suspect a thing.'

Chapter Twenty-Seven

Celie

Sweet Briar Farm, West Lake, Alberta, Canada – September 1934

'*S* *chatzi, take the picture! The swan is coming for me!'*

She laughs as Max tosses the oats into the river and jumps back from the hissing swan, his arms flailing at the bird's flapping wings. 'Hold still, silly!'

'Nein, Liebling. I concede defeat to Mr Swan.' He treks up the muddy bank and holds out his hand. 'Help me up.'

'Don't be silly. You can manage perfectly well. I'll get mud all over my shoes.'

'Ah, is this how it is? You think only of your shoes when the man who adores you above all others is sliding to his death by swan attack.'

She rolls her eyes and, releasing the camera to hang from its strap around her neck, holds out her hand. 'When you put it like that, I suppose I must. What would poor, weak men do without women?'

Max grabs hold of her hand and, pulling her into his embrace, kisses her passionately. She feels herself soften against the heat of his body, like sugar melting into caramel.

'You fooled me,' she says between their kisses.
'I wanted to touch you.'
'What if someone sees us?'
'There is no one here but the swan.'
'Then kiss me harder.'

———

The next morning, Celie waves off Lulu on her bike and watches her speed down the dirt road to where Ben Wheatley is waiting for her on his bike at the junction. They'd both grown over the summer; at fourteen, Ben is as tall and lean as a tree taking root in fertile ground, and Lulu has suddenly sprouted up and is almost as tall as Celie. Where did the years go? Wasn't it just yesterday that she'd sat on her suitcase at the West Lake station contemplating the baby in her belly and the new life ahead?

She turns to head back into the house, stopping to pinch off the wilted heads of the cosmos flowers lining the path. A Red Admiral butterfly flutters over a pink cosmos and Celie watches it as it lands on a petal and spreads out its orange-banded brown wings in the warm September sun. It will be off, too, in another week or so, flying south to winter in Texas, as the cool autumn air sweeps down from the Rockies in the west onto the flat plains of central Alberta. Then, too soon in her opinion, the first snow flurries will fall, and another long, frigid Canadian winter will be upon them.

She sighs.

She hates the winter. She has come to loathe every snowflake, every icicle hanging from their eaves, every crunch of ice underfoot. The layers and layers of clothing, the frostbitten fingers and toes, the chilblains, and the bronchitis and colds. But she won't think of that today. She dreamed of Max again last night, and she feels happy and light. She will make herself a cup of tea and sit on the bench on the front porch and enjoy the morning.

Then she will get her camera and spend the day taking photographs, though she really should finish writing the article on '20 Ways Toothpaste Can Polish Your House' for the *West Lake News*. She'll finish that tomorrow. Today will be her day.

She hears a car engine and turns to see the post office truck bounce down the road toward the house. She walks down the path and unlatches the gate in the picket fence as the truck squeals to a stop by their mailbox.

'Morning, Mr Evans. Lovely day, isn't it?'

'Mornin', Mrs Jeffries.' The postman holds out a pile of mail to her through his open window. 'A bit of a stack for you today.'

Celie takes the post. 'Thank you. Would you like a cup of tea? I'm just about to make some.'

'Thanks, but I've got to be on my way. No rest for the weary!' He tips his peaked cap and grinds the gears as he shifts into drive. 'Good day, Mrs Jeffries.'

'Good day, Mr Evans.'

Celie shuffles through the mail – bills, second notices, something from the bank, all addressed to Frank – when she spots a letter with a blue airmail etiquette addressed to her. English stamps, but she doesn't recognise the handwriting and there is no return address.

She climbs the steps up to the porch and, settling on the bench, tears open the envelope.

24 Avonmore Road,
  London W14

August 25th, 1934

Dear Mrs Jeffries,
   Hello from London. Please excuse my tardiness replying to your Easter letter. I have moved to new rooms in Kensington and there was a

delay having my post forwarded from my old address, and then I was in Germany for the past few weeks visiting family. I am catching up now, and you were the first on my list.

I have enclosed a postcard of the view of the Neckar River and the castle in Heidelberg taken from the Philosophenweg, or the Philosopher's Walk … but, of course, you know that. You speak German, after all! I spent a lovely visit there earlier this month with my family. We all went hiking down in Bavaria as we used to do when I was a boy, and it was quite beautiful up in the mountains.

Celie's heart thumps against her ribcage. *His family? Does he mean Max? Did he see Max in Heidelberg?*

Last month I did as you asked and rang your mother, who very graciously invited me to tea. She is a very charming woman and quite the excellent hostess. I was treated to scones and tarts and cucumber sandwiches and a great deal of tea. I had the pleasure of meeting your niece Adriana briefly as well, who arrived just as I was leaving. It was a very pleasant day.

My work is going very well at Vickers. I am on the design team for a new aircraft, which is quite exciting and most challenging. I am so very grateful for all your patience, teaching a rather thickheaded boy the mysteries of English grammar and pronunciation. I would most likely still be working on my Uncle Klaus's farm in Alberta without your patience and guidance. It is a great thing to have someone believe in and encourage one's abilities, and I am certain that I am not the only student who has benefitted from your enlightened instruction.

How are Mr Jeffries and Lulu? And Kip, of course. He mustn't be forgotten. I miss everyone, and your apple pie, which gives my Aunt Ursula's Quetschekuche stiff competition.

My stepbrother, Max, is a lawyer in Heidelberg and I see him whenever I visit Germany. With everything that is happening in Germany, he is extraordinarily busy. He has complimented me on my

English, and I told him about the excellent teacher I had in Canada. He said he'd known someone who'd emigrated to Alberta after the war. Isn't the world full of strange coincidences?

I will sign off now and wish you all the best as I think about your apple pie!

Cordially,

Hans

PS: I once had a university professor who claimed that there are no such things as coincidences. That is an interesting perspective, isn't it?

Celie sets the letter down beside her on the bench, her head spinning with a confused mix of excitement and trepidation. She picks an apple out of her apron pocket and, biting into the hard red skin, watches a flock of crows flap into the flat white sky above the dusty fields with their sparse offering of wheat.

What if Frank discovers the secret she's been harbouring since the day she saw the photograph of Hans and Max in Ursula's Brandt's house – the photograph she'd stolen and hidden away in her father's old photographic portfolio? The secret that Max and Hans are stepbrothers; the secret she has been so careful to hide? Frank would accuse Hans of being her accomplice somehow, of passing letters between her and Max. Frank would go mad with jealousy. There's no telling what Frank would do.

She knows she should destroy the photograph. Max is a closed chapter in her life. She takes another bite of the apple and watches the crows settle down on the weary wheat. But she hasn't destroyed it because it's the only picture she has of Max since Frank burnt all her other photographs of him one night in a fit of jealous rage. She hasn't destroyed it because, buried under the weight of stoic disappointment as the wife of a war-haunted drug addict, she still harbours love for Max, despite knowing it is pointless and that she will never see him again.

Now, for the first time in a very long time, she feels a flutter of hope. Perhaps there *is* no such thing as a coincidence. Perhaps the world *is* pushing her and Max together again. Maybe their story isn't finished.

Chapter Twenty-Eight

Etta

Santa Rosa Apartments, Hollywood, California – September 1934

The postman straightens his shoulders and smiles broadly at Etta as she waves at him from the balcony of her Spanish-style apartment building. He tips his peaked cap.

'Mornin', Mrs Marinetti. Lovely day today.'

'G'morning, Mr Dunphy! Any post for us today?'

The postman holds up a stack of letters.

'Oh, lovely!' she says as she pulls her silk dressing gown around her body. 'Hold on a minute. I'll be right down.'

She rushes down the outside stairs in her bare feet, tossing a flirtatious smile at the postman as she collects the post. 'That's what I call first class service! You are a credit to your profession, Mr Dunphy.'

He clears his throat as he adjusts his wire-rimmed glasses. 'It's Michael, Mrs Marinetti. Uh, Mike.'

'What a strong name. It certainly suits you.' She hugs the

173

letters against the thin silk covering her breasts. 'Thank you very much for your personal service, Mike Dunphy. You are a doll.'

She spins around, not mindless of the way the silk clings to her body as she moves, nor of the postman's reddening face, and hurries up the stairs. She slams the apartment door behind her and shuffles through the letters. Bills, more bills, a postcard from Jessie from Alexandria that has taken two months to reach her, and a letter with a French stamp addressed to her in spidery black handwriting. Nothing from her mother after that awful letter she'd received in April.

The nerve of her mother calling her delusional! She'd had half a mind to stomp right over to the post office and wire Celie about her real father. But then, her mind had gotten into a muddle. Had she imagined it all? She'd been so certain … she'd found Celie's Italian birth certificate in Villa Serenissima with Harry Grenville's name on it, hadn't she? Or had she? And then she'd thought of Carlo in that awful prison, and Adriana crying in her cot, and then being strapped down in the hospital, biting down on a rubber block, and then … No, she can't go back there. Not ever.

'Any mail for me, hon?' CJ calls from the bathroom.

'Just bills, darling.'

After lighting a cigarette, she takes the letter out to the small café table on the balcony and settles onto a chair as she slits open the envelope with a red-painted fingernail.

Galerie DuRose,
62 rue la Boétie,
Paris

September 4th, 1934

Dear Madame Marinetti,
You are no doubt surprised to receive this letter from me after all these years. Your mother was most kind to furnish me with your address in

California. I managed to locate Mrs Fry through your late relative, Signora Albertini's, housekeeper in Italy. I had been in touch with Signora Albertini to discuss the sale of Carlo's paintings after his death. It is a shame that your stepson gave them to a second-rate dealer in Rome to sell. I would most certainly have sold them for higher sums, and would, naturally, have been happy to assure you of a commission, as I understand all the sale revenue went to Carlo's son. Such a shame! I always thought we worked very well together when you were in Paris.

François DuRose? Carlo's art dealer? What on earth could he want?

I understand that you were incapacitated for a time after your husband's unfortunate death. I trust that you are now well recovered and are enjoying your new life in California. Now, as to why I am writing.

Etta exhales a puff of smoke and turns over the letter.

The world, as I am certain you are aware, is in the grip of a terrible economic depression, and the sale of art has, as a consequence, suffered a tremendous decline. I have managed, for the past few years, to weather the storm owing to the excellent reputation of my gallery, and the superlative service I give my clients and customers, from which you, yourself, have benefitted in the past.

Unfortunately, the economic situation has resulted in an oversupply of artwork on the market as owners seek to divest their investments. Prices have plummeted as the buyers with money have melted away, their assets dried up by bank failures and foreclosures. All of this is to say that I find myself in a tenuous position financially. What has this to do with you, you may well be asking?

Etta huffs. *You've got that right.*

Madame Marinetti, it has come to my attention that the 'new period'
Marinettis that you supplied to my gallery to sell were, in fact, fakes. I, of
course, would never have agreed to sell these paintings had I known this.

Etta yanks the cigarette out of her mouth and stubs it out in a
pot of petunias. *What a liar!* Of course he'd known the paintings
were fake. Carlo had been in prison for two years when he'd
agreed to sell the paintings Carlo had left in storage in London
and Naples. He'd been as delighted as she when the paintings had
sold so well, owing to Carlo's infamy after his arrest for his wife
Marianna's murder. François DuRose had then been more than
happy to sell the 'new period' Marinettis she'd painted in Carlo's
name, and he'd encouraged a continued supply, despite knowing
that Carlo, stuck in prison with an injured right hand, could not
possibly be the artist. François DuRose had been involved in the
fraud as much as she had.

I should imagine the authorities would be most interested to learn of your
fraudulent activities. Do not think that your residency in America will
protect you if this scandal should come to light. I would expect the
authorities there would be quite interested to deport you back to France to
face the consequences.

I am certain you would agree with me that such a fate is one which
you would prefer not to face. In this regard, I aim to help you. I propose
that I vow an oath of silence on this matter in return for a sum of – I will
put it in American dollars as I remember that you had some difficulty
understanding the value of French francs – $1,000. This is a tidy figure, I
am certain you agree. Obviously, it would be my preference to receive it
in one deposit; however, I am a reasonable man and am happy to agree to
regular payments of $200 over the next six months, or even $100 a
month over a year, though, of course, interest would be attached if you
don't pay the full sum at once. Your mother has informed me of your
great success in Hollywood so I am certain you will find my modest
request more than reasonable and easily dealt with.

It goes without saying that, should you decline this offer, I will be left with no option but to contact the authorities about your fraudulent activities with regards to Carlo Marinetti's paintings.

I have included my bank details on the reverse of this page. Please telegram me upon receipt of this letter to acknowledge your agreement to my terms. Any delay in payment shall result in added interest of 25% monthly until the debt is paid in full.

I remain your indebted servant,
François DuRose

Etta stuffs the letter into her dressing gown pocket and strides into the apartment's tiny living room. *A thousand dollars! How dare he blackmail her?* She picks up her cigarette pack and a lighter and lights another cigarette.

CJ comes out of the bedroom tying his tie. 'Everything okay?'

Etta exhales a stream of smoke. 'Yes, darling. Just Jessie giving me a hard time in a letter. You know … sisters.'

'Can't say I do, baby.' He looks into the hallway mirror and adjusts his tie. 'How about I pick us up some chop suey from Man Fook Low tonight?' He yawns and rubs his eyes. 'These late nights working on rewrites for the next Garbo picture are killing me, and I won't even get a credit for them.'

'CJ! We've got the première for *The Barretts of Wimpole Street* tonight. Norma Shearer and Irving Thalberg are having a party at the Trocadero afterwards and Goucho's got us on the guest list.'

'Oh, hon, can we do a raincheck? I'm worn out, and, honestly, those parties are full of posers and leeches. I don't have the stomach for it.'

'Well, you trying to talk about the Depression and European politics isn't going to make you any friends in Hollywood, CJ.'

She walks over to him and smooths down his collar as she looks at him in the mirror. 'You need to lighten up, darling. You've gotten so serious, and by that, I mean dull.'

He cocks an eyebrow at his reflection. 'Oh, really? I'm dull now, is it? And here I was thinking you appreciated my incredible intellect.'

She gives him a quick peck on his lips. 'I don't cuddle up to your intellect in bed at night. Besides, intellect is all very well and good, darling, but it's not going to get you very far in Hollywood. You need to go out and schmooze people. Get them interested in you. That's what Groucho said and he should know. He says people try to schmooze him all the time.'

'Etta, I can't do it. I just don't have it in me.'

'CJ! You promised!'

'I don't remember promising anything.'

'Well, you didn't say you wouldn't go.'

'I'm saying it now, Etta. I'm not going.' He picks his hat and suit jacket off a hook on the wall.

Etta stamps her foot. 'CJ! What will it look like if I turn up on my own?'

'You'll have all of Hollywood's leading men rubbing their hands at their good fortune. You'll love that. Etta, you're sucking the life out of me. Everything's about what you want. Well, what about what I want?'

'If you don't come to the party tonight, I'll be very cross.'

CJ shoves on his fedora and opens the door. 'It's not like I haven't seen that before. Knock yourself out.' The door slams behind him.

Etta stares at the door as she seethes with fury. She picks up a cheap ashtray from a trip they'd made to Tijuana, and launches it across the room, wincing as it smashes against a wall. *Damn CJ! Damn François DuRose! Damn her mother! Damn her sisters! Damn them all!*

She stubs her cigarette out in a plate of congealing eggs and reaches for the bottle of gin on the sideboard. Grabbing an empty glass on her way past the kitchen counter, she walks into the bathroom. She plugs the bath, turns on the tap, and dumps a stream of bubble bath into the coursing water.

Untying her belt, she lets the dressing gown slide to the floor and, after filling the glass with gin, watches the foam grow into an organic form. She takes a large gulp and shudders as the bitter alcohol burns its way down her throat. She wonders how long it would take before the foamy mass filled the room and engulfed her.

Part IV

1935

Chapter Twenty-Nine

Celie & Frank

West Lake, Alberta, Canada – March 1935

'There they are!' Mavis calls out as the two men stamp snow off their boots on the porch. 'Get them some beer, Celie. I don't want to see any grumpy faces today. We're gonna have fun, aren't we, kids?'

'Sure thing, Ma,' Ben Wheatley says as he sends Lulu's playing piece sliding down a snake where they're playing Snakes & Ladders.

'Ben Wheatley! Why'd you do that?' Lulu protests.

'Because that's how it works, Lulu. Your go.'

'It's my birthday party, Ben. You're meant to let me win.'

'It's my birthday party, too, Lulu. And wouldn't you prefer to win fair and square?'

'I guess, but you're going to be sorry you did that.'

Celie smiles at Mavis as she sets two glasses of beer on the dining table. 'Looks like Ben has discovered that logic is Lulu's Achilles heel.'

'Ben's had a lot of experience with Molly.'

Mavis squints as Molly Wheatley turns up the volume on their phonograph machine.

'Molly! Change the phonograph record, will you? We've had enough of "Minnie the Moocher". Put on some Cole Porter. Arthur Wheatley, what are you doing with that beer? I hope that's for your father.'

'Aw, Ma. I'm eighteen.'

'Which means you're not twenty-one.'

Celie laughs as she sets down two bowls of steaming stew and fat white dumplings on the table. 'I'm glad I don't have a boy. All I need to keep Lulu away from is the sweet counter at Mr Forbes's.'

The front door swings open and Fred Wheatley and Frank enter the large living room, where a fire crackles in the stone fireplace. Celie brings them around the glasses of frothy golden beer and glances at Frank's empty hands.

'Did you leave the presents in the porch?'

He looks at her blankly. 'The presents?'

She glances at Fred who is already half-way to the kitchen. She lowers her voice. 'The gifts for Lulu and Ben. You were meant to collect them from Forbes's shop.'

'Celie—'

She sighs. 'Frank, I spent all the money I'd saved up from my articles for the *West Lake News* on those gifts from Eaton's. All you had to do was pick them up. What are we meant to do now? Lulu will be heartbroken thinking we forgot. The Wheatleys have gone out of their way to host the party this year *and* they gave Lulu the latest Nancy Drew book. What are we supposed to say when we don't have anything to give Ben?'

'What do you want me to say, Celie? "Sorry, I forgot to pick up the birthday presents because I was floundering around in Fred's garage losing him money on everything I touched?" It's not the end of the world. I'll pick them up tomorrow. One day isn't doing to make a difference.'

'Forbes's is closed for inventory tomorrow.'

'Fine. Monday then.' Frank thrusts the beer glass into Celie's hands as a cough rattles up through his diaphragm. He pulls the rag out of his back pocket and presses it against his mouth until the coughing fit subsides.

'Frank?'

He looks at Celie and sees her staring at the blood-spattered rag.

'Celie, I—'

'Supper, everyone!' Mavis calls from the dining table. 'Don't let it get cold! We've got two birthday cakes to eat and Charades to play later. Arthur, I said no beer.'

At home later that night, after Lulu has gone to bed, Celie follows Frank into his bedroom and shuts the door.

'How long have you been coughing blood, Frank?'

'Celie, I don't want to talk about it. I'm fine.'

'There was blood on that handkerchief, and your breathing's been getting a lot worse. Your clothes are hanging off you. I wake up almost every night to your coughing and I'm in Lulu's room.'

'Sorry to inconvenience you.'

Celie sighs. 'I don't mean it like that. You're not well, Frank. You need to see the doctor.'

'We don't have any goddam money for me to go to a doctor!' He sits on the bed and, yanking at a boot, throws it across the floor.

'Frank, please. We'll find a way. I'll ask Jessie—'

'You will not beg money off your sister!' He tosses his other boot onto the floor. 'I am not a charity case. I said I'm fine. Just go. Leave me alone.'

'Frank, morphine isn't the answer. You need help. I'm worried about you.'

Frank turns on the bed to look at Celie. 'Are you? Really? Wouldn't it solve all your problems if I dropped dead?'

'Frank!'

'It's true, isn't it? You'd be free. Free to go back to England. Free to go back to Max Fischer—' His voice breaks and dry sobs wrack his body as all the years of frustration and disappointment overcome him.

'No, Frank, no.' Celie joins him on the bed and holds him as he weeps the tears of a man facing the failures of his life.

He clutches Celie's hand and looks at her through eyes glassy with tears. 'I'm sorry, Celie. I'm so, so sorry. I'll stop. I promise. I will.'

Chapter Thirty

Christina

St Saviour's Catholic Church, Lewisham, London – April 1935

Christina fingers the black onyx rosary beads as she kneels in the pew in the empty nave of St Saviour's Church. The peace she usually finds here, particularly on the afternoons she slips away to be alone with her thoughts, is eluding her today. She shuts her eyes and breathes in the chilly air, which still holds the faint scent of frankincense from the Wednesday morning service.

Why are her daughters causing her so many problems? Not Jessica, of course. Jessica has always been self-sufficient to a fault. Etta, on the other hand … Etta's silence is worrying. She hasn't heard a word from Etta since she refused to send her any more money to fund her rash adventure in Hollywood. She'd felt awful about threatening Etta with the psychiatric hospital, but her daughter had brought it on herself with her threats to reveal the secret of Cecelia's father. It simply won't do, and the only way she can think of controlling Etta is by using that threat, as much as it pains her to do so.

She rubs a rosary bead between her fingers and begins to recite a Hail Mary in her head, but finds her mind drifting. The battle with Paolo Marinetti over possession of Villa Serenissima, which he claims, with no foundation whatsoever, is part of his father Carlo's estate, is ongoing, although Liliana and Mario Sabbatini are doing everything in their power to keep him from accessing the property. She has lost count of the legal letters Liliana has forwarded her from Paolo's lawyers. A spurious claim, but one which has forced her to engage the services of expensive lawyers in Naples.

That isn't her only worry about Capri. What if Paolo does manage to gain access to Villa Serenissima? She should never have left Cecelia's birth certificate there. Despite Stefania's entreaties, it had seemed the safer option rather than take it back to Clover Bar, with Adriana in the house and Hettie's penchant for snooping. She'll have to figure out what to do about it. She can't afford for it to fall into the wrong hands, either in Italy or England.

And now, this latest development. A letter from Dorothy Adam's solicitors this morning with the news that Christopher Adam has come of age and is now the owner of half of Bishop House. And that he has nominated his mother, Dorothy Adam, to press suit against Cecelia to claim the house in its entirety owing to Cecelia's continued absence from the UK, and negligence in contributing to the costs of its maintenance over the past three years, despite regular requests.

The nerve! She rises from the leather-clad kneeler and sits on the hard bench. Why should she agree to the extortionate maintenance costs that had been presented by Dorothy Adam's solicitors? The house is in perfectly good order – she checks on it regularly – and it certainly doesn't require a new roof!

This legal suit is simply another ruse for Dorothy to line her pockets and obtain possession of the entire house. Christina wouldn't be in the least surprised if Christopher Adam knows nothing about it. No, this has Dorothy's stamp all over it.

She picks up her purse from the pew and drops her rosary inside. She will have to deal with this as soon as possible. *Dorothy will not win. Not so long as I've got breath in my body, so help me God.*

Chapter Thirty-One

Jessie

Cairo, Egypt - April 1935

Jessie pulls on her white hospital gown as she rushes down the corridor toward the orthopaedic ward, almost upending an orderly carrying a bedpan in the process.

'Sorry, Ibrahim! So sorry!' she says as she collects the notebook she has dropped on the terrazzo floor. 'Have you seen Dr Salah and the other interns?'

'Ward 6. You are late, Dr Khalid. He will not be pleased.'

'I know. It couldn't be helped. The students were protesting on the Corniche again and it slowed all the traffic down.'

The orderly shrugs. 'This is life.'

Outside the open doors to the ward, Jessie pauses to catch her breath. She pats her hair into place and enters the eight-bed ward as unobtrusively as she can manage.

'Dr Khalid! So good of you to make the time to join us.'

She winces apologetically. 'I'm sorry, Dr Salah. It won't happen again.'

The doctor smirks as he addresses the interns gathered around the bed of a patient whose plastered leg is suspended from a complicated pulley system attached to the ceiling. 'It seems we must adjust our schedules to women, now, gentlemen. It was so much easier when they understood their place resided in the home. It seems that the British have a great deal more than the Sudan to answer for.'

Jessie feels the blood rise in her cheeks. *What an arse! How dare he say things like that! This is the twentieth century, not the Dark Ages.* She catches the eye of one of the male interns who leers at her before turning his attention back to Dr Salah's case assessment.

She spies Fatima fruitlessly attempting to peer between the shoulders of two of the interns on the far side of the patient's bed.

Why does it have to be so difficult? Why are the men so angry at women's progress? We all have brains and ability. Why do they close ranks against us when we want nothing more than the chance to live the lives we wish and which we have trained for? Are they so insecure?

'… yes, Dr Hamdy, you are correct. Traction is used to control pain from muscle spasm. Anyone else? What are the other reasons we use traction to heal a broken limb?'

Jessie raises her hand. Dr Salah glances at her then nods to another intern. 'Dr Nabil?'

'It maintains anatomical reduction.'

'Indeed. Can anyone else tell me what anatomical reduction is?'

Jessie clears her voice. 'Dr Salah, if I may?'

Silence falls over the ward as even the patients and nurses turn to stare at the impudent woman.

The chief surgeon stares at Jessie coldly. 'Can anyone else tell me what anatomical reduction is?'

Anger flashes through Jessie, prodding her to push through the wall of interns to the patient's bed. 'Anatomical reduction involves the aligning of the fragments of the broken bone to reconstruct the fractured bone as precisely as possible. The goal is to allow the bone to recover its original form as closely as possible as it heals.'

The doctor glares at Jessie and turns back to the other interns. 'Once again, can anyone tell me the benefits of anatomical reduction?'

'Not only that, he totally ignored me and asked the question again!' Jessie stomps across the bedroom floor as she throws her belt on a chair and begins unbuttoning her blouse. 'What am I meant to do, Aziz? Just ignore it? I have half a mind to make a formal complaint to the head of the hospital.'

Aziz stubs out his cigarette in an ashtray and walks over to Jessie. He opens his arms. 'Come. Let me hug you.'

Jessie sighs and leans against his body as his arms envelope her. 'I knew medicine would be challenging, but it's nothing compared to the daily fight for respect that I, and Fatima, and all the other women doctors have to deal with.'

'I am sorry for that.' He looks down at his wife. 'You are pioneers here, Jessica. You are carving a path for the other women who will follow you. It is a battle worth fighting.'

She gives him a quick kiss and turns to sit down at her dressing table. 'You're right. Of course you're right. It's just been a difficult day. Mustapha and I were caught in another student demonstration this morning, which made me late, and then there was the business with Dr Salah, not to mention your mother.'

Aziz sits on the bed and unties his tie. 'What did my mother have to say now?'

'She's upset that Shani is spending so much time with Marta in the kitchen. She says it's a waste of Shani's time as she is a Khalid and will have servants to cater for her when she's older. This led, of course, to her telling me, once again, that I was an irresponsible mother for abandoning my child to the care of a servant.'

Aziz smiles as he undoes his cufflinks. 'Oh dear. What did you say to that?'

'I reminded her that both you and Zara had been brought up by nannies, and asked her if she, by her own argument, had also been an irresponsible mother.'

Aziz laughs. 'I should have liked to hear Mama's response to that.'

Jessie pulls her brush through her brown bob. 'You didn't miss anything. She huffed off, complaining of a headache. She has an awful lot of headaches.'

She sets down the brush and turns around on the stool to face her husband. 'Aziz, do you think I'm an irresponsible mother?'

'Of course not! Why would you think such a thing?'

'It's just that I spend so much time at the hospital and in the clinic. Sometimes I feel like I've barely been around for Shani. She's growing up so fast. Sometimes I look at her and wonder where the time's gone. I've missed so much. I wasn't there for Shani's first step, and I wasn't there when she lost her first tooth.'

Aziz smiles. 'I think Shani will survive.'

'I feel so guilty. I blame Etta for being selfish, but I think I'm just as bad.'

'You are not like your sister, *habibti*. You wish to make things better for others. Etta wishes only to make things better for herself.'

'Maybe.' She smiles. 'You always knew how to make me feel better.'

'I am your husband, Jessica. It is my job and my pleasure.'

Jessie picks up her brush again and begins to pull it through her hair. 'I was worried about you tonight, Aziz. With all these demonstrations and the Green Shirts causing trouble, it's not safe out there at night. Why do your political meetings have to run on so late?'

Aziz rises from the bed and tosses his tie and cufflinks on top of his dresser. 'It is precisely because of the Green Shirts and the student demonstrations that the meetings are running so late,' he says as he lights another cigarette.

'What about Zara? She's in the Young Egypt Party.'

Aziz blows out a stream of smoke. 'It is a concern. I feel, sometimes, that she is wilfully ignorant of the situation she has put herself in. It is why I have Mustapha follow her.'

'You have Mustapha follow her?'

'Yes, of course. I assure you, it is not for any other reason than for her own safety. I will not have any harm come to her.'

Jessie nods. 'I understand. If I were you, I would probably do the same.'

Jessie stares at her reflection as she brushes her short brown bob. *Has Mustapha seen Zara with Isham? What does Mustapha know and why hasn't he told Aziz?*

Chapter Thirty-Two

Celie

Edmonton, Alberta, Canada - May 4th, 1935

'Good heavens, Mavis!' Celie exclaims as they fight their way through the crowds lining 102nd Avenue in Alberta's capital city. 'It looks like all of Edmonton has turned out for the May Day parade. And here I told Frank you were treating me to a quiet day of lunch and the pictures as a birthday treat.'

'I'm glad Frank's feeling so much better. That was an awful flu he had.'

'Yes, yes, it was.' Celie smiles self-consciously. It's best that Mavis and Fred think that Frank's only had the flu. Only she, Frank and Dr Addison know the truth: that Frank's lungs are rotting from the mustard gas he'd been exposed to in the war.

'Frank's much better now. He actually insisted I come after being his nurse for the past month.'

Mavis squeezes Celie's arm. 'I'm glad, but I'd totally forgotten it was the May Day parade today. It looks like everyone's come out to protest the government.'

'I don't blame them in the least,' Celie says as she shuffles by several women with baby carriages waving and clapping as a wagon passes by with three stuffed figures dressed as 'Capitalism', 'Fascism' and 'War' sitting astride sawdust bags labelled 'Money'.

'But Prime Minister Bennett's "New Deal" is promising all sorts of things, Celie. Unemployment insurance, an old age pension, minimum wage—'

'It all sounds lovely, Mavis, but it's too little, too late.' She thrusts her hand at a line of cars being drawn by horses in the parade, led by men brandishing a banner with 'Bennett's Buggies' painted in red letters.

'People can't afford petrol anymore, so they've got horses pulling their cars, and our Prime Minister has the nerve to say the provinces are rich enough to manage their own problems! His government won't last out the year, mark my words. Good riddance to bad rubbish.'

Mavis grabs Celie's hand and pulls her past the tall white-painted frontage of the J.A. Werner Hardware store where a cluster of men are unfurling a banner which proclaims, 'People's Unity: The Gravedigger of Capitalism'.

'Wait! Wait, Mavis.' Celie stops beside a boy selling black armbands under a sign exclaiming, 'Mourn the Death of Capitalism!'.

Mavis releases her hold on Celie's hand. 'What is it?'

Celie pulls her camera out of her canvas shopping bag and loops the leather strap around her neck. 'I've got to take some pictures. This kind of opportunity doesn't come every day.'

Mavis frowns as a contingent pass by waving placards urging viewers to 'Join the Communist League'. 'I don't think Rex Majors is going to be too keen to publish this kind of stuff. He's a Conservative to his core.'

Celie focuses the lens and snaps an image as the parade marches by. 'Writing a column about "Cakes, Carrots and Crafts" during the world's worst financial depression is like buttering burnt toast. This is the burnt toast, Mavis.'

Mavis shakes her head. 'I have a feeling Rex has met his match. I've never met anyone with such a social conscience. Where did you get that from?'

Celie shrugs. 'I've always been this way. I just believe in fairness. The way I see it, we're all set down on this earth together for a short period of time. Doesn't everybody deserve a fair shake? Who benefits if only the wealthy have the wherewithal to live comfortable lives? Who benefits when the leaders of countries with imaginary borders wage war over the same disputed ground, killing thousands of people in the meantime? Who benefits when half the population – the female half – have no voice in the running of their country or their own lives? In the end, no one benefits. I believe if one person suffers, we all suffer. Maybe not immediately, but eventually. Why is it so difficult for everyone to understand that we are all in this together? It does no one any good to sweep things like this parade of people voicing their resentment at the status quo under the rug. The current situation is not fair, and that really upsets me.'

'My word, Celie. Where did all of that come from?'

Celie smiles at Mavis over the top of the camera. 'This is history in the making, Mavis, and we're here right in the middle of it. I'm a photographer. I *have* to record this. It's in my genes.'

'You should be a politician, Celie. You'd get this country sorted out in no time.' Mavis extends her hand. 'Give me your shopping bag. I need some new garden gloves. I'll go into the hardware store while you take your pictures. Then we can head over to Johnson's Café for lunch. I'm fit to eat a tiger.'

Celie pops the film out of the camera and stuffs the roll into her coat pocket. She is winding a new roll of film into the camera when a voice addresses her from behind.

'You have a good eye.'

She turns around. A tall square-shouldered man in a brown wool suit tips the brim of his slouchy fedora.

'I beg your pardon?'

The man holds up his Rolleiflex camera. 'I've seen you taking pictures. Looks like I've got competition. Who are you working for?'

Celie smiles politely and turns back to watch the parade. 'No one. I'm just taking pictures for myself.'

The man joins her at the front of the crowd. He peers into the viewing lens on top of his camera and snaps a picture of six pallbearers carrying a wooden coffin labelled 'Capitalism'. 'You should be working for somebody. You know how to find the story. You're not just taking holiday snaps.'

'Is that what you think women armed with a camera do? Take holiday snaps?'

He turns his head as he looks at her. 'Touché. I suppose I do.'

She focuses the lens and snaps a picture of women pushing baby strollers between marchers carrying banners demanding 'Equal Pay for Women Workers'. 'I've been taking pictures most of my life. My father was a photographer, as was my grandfather.'

'In England? I can tell by your accent you're not from this side of the Atlantic.'

She nods as she resets the viewfinder. 'London. I worked in my father's photography studio. I took pictures and wrote for the *Daily Mirror* during the war.'

He whistles through his teeth. 'That's impressive.'

Celie glances at the man, whose head is bent over the viewing lens as he focuses on the Boy Scouts trooping by. His short hair is as dark as the fur of the black bear she'd once seen trundle by the house in the spring thaw, and his square-jawed face is tan and weather-beaten, like a wind-battered cliff. He could be forty-five or fifty-five.

He looks over at her, and his eyes, as translucent as green glass, wrinkle at the corners as he smiles. 'You're looking at me like I'm an amoeba under a microscope.'

Celie feels her cheeks flush. She turns back to watch the parade. 'Certainly not.'

She glances unseeingly at her wristwatch. 'Oh, dear, is that the time? I'm terribly late to meet a friend.' She offers her hand awkwardly to the man. 'Good luck with your pictures.'

He grins as he shakes her hand. *'Life.'*

'I beg your pardon?'

'Life Magazine. That's where you'll find my photographs.'

'Oh. Well, I shall look out for them.' She turns and pushes through the crowd toward the café.

'Robson McCrea,' he shouts after her.

She looks over her shoulder and sees him smiling at her.

'It was very nice to meet you, Mr McCrea. I'm Celie Jeffries.'

'There you are!' Mavis says as she steps out from under the huge clock over the front doors of Johnson's Café. 'I thought you'd gotten swallowed up by the marchers.'

'Sorry I'm late. I've just had the most unusual encounter.'

'That doesn't surprise me,' Mavis says as she opens the door to the café. 'It's not every day you see gravediggers in a parade. Did you get some good pictures?'

'Yes. I've used up two whole rolls of film. I think I might use Mama's birthday money to buy another couple of rolls while we're in town.' Celie frowns as she follows Mavis to a table by a window. 'Although I really should use it to pay down our Eaton's account.'

'Don't be silly. Birthday money is birthday money. Spend it on yourself.'

Mavis waves at a pair of women at a table in the far corner. 'Oh, look! It's Rosita Majors. I think that's her sister, Edna, with her. That's right, I remember she lives in Edmonton. She's waving at us to come over.'

'Oh, um, right. I wasn't really expecting—'

Mavis pokes at Celie's arm. 'Come on. They're not going to bite. You're spending too much time at home. You're turning into a right old hermit. You need to loosen up and socialise a bit.'

'I suppose. Let's go socialise.'

'Wonderful. Oh, what was that you said about an unusual encounter?' Mavis asks as they head across the café.

'It was nothing. Does Rosita have a new hat? Do you suppose she got it at Hudson's Bay?'

'It does look new, doesn't it? You can't buy anything like that in West Lake.' Mavis stops abruptly and grabs Celie's arm. 'I know! Let's go hat shopping at Hudson's Bay this afternoon. It's been ages since we've had new hats. Won't that be fun?'

Celie watches the flat brown plains, still wet from the recent blizzard, spread out to the horizon as the train steams north toward West Lake. The dump of snow on the last day of April had been a blessing after the dry spring, and though she was the last to celebrate frozen fingers and chilblains, she'd been as happy as everyone else to see the snowfall. Maybe it's a sign that the drought is finally over. They were desperate for a good wheat year after five terrible harvests.

She glances over at Mavis, who is snoozing, open-mouthed, beside her, the new Hudson's Bay hatbox tucked in her arms like a baby. She hadn't bought a new hat for herself in the end, nor any film. It hadn't felt right to spend money on frivolities when she was making dresses for herself and Lulu out of flour sacks. She'd become a dab hand at using homemade dyes, rickrack, ribbon and buttons to disguise the plain white cotton. She'll use the last of her developing solution to process the photographs she'd taken in the hope that she can sell the story to Rex Majors at the paper. She'll buy new film with any money she earns from that.

She runs her finger idly over the window glass. Robson McCrea. Why is she thinking of him now? He is just a stranger who popped into her life for a handful of minutes. He's probably already forgotten their meeting. *Life Magazine*, he'd said. Ol' Man Forbes gets *Life* into his store, and though she's often thumbed through the pages of photography, she's never splurged on buying a copy. She can just imagine what Frank would say if she wasted ten cents on a magazine!

She'll look out for Robson McCrea's name now when she thumbs through the magazine. She's just curious. About his photos, of course. Not him. That would be ridiculous. He's just a stranger, after all.

So why did she tell him her name?

Chapter Thirty-Three

Christina

Bishop House, Portman Square, Marylebone, London - May 1935

Christina smiles a tight smile at the maid who greets her at the door of the Portman Square house.

'I'm here to see Mrs Adam. Tell her Mrs Fry wishes to have a word.'

'That's not necessary, Mary,' Dorothy Adam calls from the hallway. 'I'll speak to Mrs Fry. Go back to polishing the silverware.'

Christina nods to Dorothy Adam, who, in her smart navy jersey Chanel dress and with her auburn hair subjected to an expensive perm, appears to have adapted to the role of chatelaine of a grand London house as if it were one she was born to.

'Hello, Dorothy. You're looking terribly well.'

Dorothy casts her pale green gaze over Christina. 'What do you want, Christina?'

'I should very much like to have a word.'

'I can't see that we have anything to talk about. My solicitors were quite clear in their letter to you.' She makes a movement to shut the door.

Christina steps forward and holds the door open.

'Wait. I've had time to think about this situation. It's absurd for us to be at loggerheads about the house, with both of our children involved. I'd very much like to clear the air. For their sakes, if not for ours.'

Dorothy smiles coldly. 'You don't need to act the contrite opponent, Christina. You're here because Christopher has just turned twenty-one and you're worried you will lose this house once and for all.'

Christina juts out her chin. 'Dorothy, half of this house is Cecelia's. Christopher's coming of age doesn't change that.'

'Is that so? What do you intend to do about it? Your daughter hasn't rushed back from Canada to stake her claim, nor has she contributed to any of the extraordinarily high maintenance fees incurred by Bishop House, no doubt the result of years of neglect on the part of your family. However it's happened, the house has finally found itself in good hands.'

Christina's jaw tightens. 'My family always took impeccable care of this house. I can only imagine that its current tenants have neglected their duty of care.'

Dorothy moves to shut the door, but Christina holds firm. 'I have had quite enough of this conversation, Christina. You shall hear from my solicitors.'

'I am Cecelia's representative, Dorothy. I have been very vocal about "staking her claim". I assure you that she has every intention of moving to Bishop House when she returns to London.'

'When will that be? Harry died three years ago. Cecelia has had plenty of time to visit London to view her inheritance.' Dorothy's green eyes narrow. 'Does she even know? Have you even told her?'

'What are you insinuating?'

'Mummy!'

A dark-haired young man in the white trousers and jumper of a cricketer bounds up the steps.

'Hello, there!' he says, offering his hand to Christina. 'I remember you. You used to visit us at our old flat, didn't you? Jolly nice to see you again.'

'Mrs Fry was just leaving, Christopher.'

'Oh no, Mummy, we can't have that.' Christopher smiles at Christina, his blue eyes as guileless as a child's. 'Do come in for tea, Mrs Fry. Cook makes the best shortbread biscuits. She promised me some after my match, as long as we won.'

Christina bestows a generous smile on Christopher Adam and offers him her arm. 'That would be lovely. And did you win?'

'Of course!' Christopher says as he accompanies her into the house. 'I always win!'

'… And I'll be starting law school at Cambridge in the autumn. I won't even need to change my dorm room!'

Christina declines the offer of a second shortbread biscuit from Christopher. 'The apple doesn't fall far from the tree.'

'I beg your pardon?' Christopher laughs. 'Oh, no, my father wasn't a lawyer. He was an accountant, wasn't he, Mummy? He was killed in the war when I was a baby. I never knew him. Mummy brought me up.'

Christina raises an eyebrow at Dorothy. 'I see. I'm terribly sorry about that. It's a shame to grow up without a father.'

'Oh, it's been all right. You don't miss what you don't know, isn't that right? Anyway, my great-uncle left Mummy this house in his will a few years ago.'

Christina glances at Dorothy, who raises her chin in silent defiance. 'Is that so?'

'Incredible, isn't it?' Christopher says as he wipes shortbread crumbs off his lips with a napkin. 'I didn't even know I had a great-uncle! This is so much better than that flat we had in Chelsea, isn't it, Mummy?'

'Indeed it is, Christopher.'

Christina smiles at the young student, who is onto his third shortbread biscuit. 'What sort of law are you interested in, Christopher?'

'Oh, criminal, of course. I quite fancy swanning about a courtroom in my wig and gown.' He laughs. 'My friends call me "The Thespian" because I've been active in the Cambridge Footlights ever since I went up there. Mummy was an actress before she was married, did she tell you that?'

'Yes, she has mentioned that.' She smiles at Dorothy. 'Where did you say you performed, Dorothy? The Windmill, was it?' she asks, naming one of London's infamous burlesque theatres.

'I was a classical actress,' Dorothy responds tightly. 'My Ophelia was the talk of London back in the day.'

'Not Lady Macbeth?'

The front door slams and an attractive brunette woman in her twenties appears in the sitting room doorway. 'Oh, I'm awfully sorry, Mrs Adam. I didn't know you had company.'

'Not a problem, Vivien. Mrs Fry is just leaving. I'll meet you in the conservatory in a few minutes.'

Dorothy turns to Christina. 'I'm afraid I must cut our delightful visit short.'

Christina collects her handbag and rises. 'It's been a great pleasure, Dorothy. I trust it won't be too long before we meet again.' She glances at Christopher. 'We have so very much in common.'

Christopher jumps to his feet and extends his hand to Christina. 'Awfully nice to meet you, Mrs Fry. Do come by again soon. I'll ask Cook to make her ginger biscuits. They're even better than her shortbread.'

Chapter Thirty-Four

Etta

Santa Rosa Apartments, Hollywood, California – June 1935

ALS, 4pp. Princeton University
   Sheppard and Enoch Pratt Hospital
   Towson, Maryland

June 9th, 1935

Dearest Etta,

   Thank you, darling, for your lovely letter telling me all about your adventures in Hollywood. I remember what a gay time Scott and I had there in our little bungalow at the Ambassador Hotel back in 1927 when he was working on that awful movie 'Lipstick'. So many parties and frolics and such naughtiness! Oh dear, I just remembered I got awfully cross with Scott for flirting with a little floozy and set my clothes alight in the bathtub and burnt the whole place down! What a time it was!

   I do so wish I could join you and your darling CJ out there, but my dear head is quite getting the best of me. Scott has found me this lovely sanatorium and they're taking wonderful care of me. They have me painting and going for walks in the grounds. The roses are blooming and I adore sticking my nose into them and sniffing up the delicious perfume. It is joyous joyfulness.

It has been over a year now, but I am still dreadfully disappointed in the response to my art exhibition in New York last April. The New Yorker said my paintings were filled with 'whatever emotional overtones or associations may remain from the so-called Jazz Age'. I memorised it. Oh, it does vex me. Why can't they see me as an artist rather than some dusty souvenir from the 'so-called Jazz Age'? I am so much more than one of Scott's flapper girls.

My poor little book, 'Save Me the Waltz', has been another disappointment. It's been over a year since it was published, but it's only sold a little over a thousand copies. My editor at Scribner's, Mr Perkins, said Hemingway told him that he'd shoot him if Scribner's ever published a book by any of his wives!

Why is it so very difficult for me to be taken seriously as an artist? I now know how frustrated and disappointed poor Scott was after 'The Great Gatsby' sold so poorly. I really should have been more sympathetic at the time. Telling him to just go write another one and put in some cats possibly wasn't the height of sensitivity. As you know, Scott finally did publish 'Tender is the Night' last year, but that one's sold worse than 'Gatsby'! He's back to writing short stories for the Saturday Evening Post to cover my medical bills and Scottie's schooling, and drinking himself into hospital stays. Hemingway tells him he's 'whoring' his talent writing for popular magazines. I told Scott that if anyone knows anything about whoring, it's Hemingway.

It is an odd world, isn't it, when a talentless boor like Hemingway has books flying off the shelves, and me and my poor Scott can barely sell enough to buy groceries. The man writes like an ape – all one-syllable words. There is no accounting for taste. It seems talent isn't a requirement for success.

I must sign off to get this into the post today. We are having chocolate

cake for dessert tonight and I am so very happy. Saturday is my favourite
day of the week. Do write me about your adventures, and have all the fun
that I'm missing.

    Love and kisses,

    Zelda

Etta folds the letter and leans on the balcony railing. So much for
getting Zelda out to Hollywood. She feels awful about Zelda's
mental condition, of course; she'd been there herself. But she is
obviously made of sterner stuff than her old friend, who seemed
to go from one sanatorium to another.

Zelda is right about one thing: talent isn't a requirement for
success. She has talent. The paintings that she'd painted under
Carlo's name had sold better and made more money than any of
Carlo's own paintings ever did. And yet, when she'd finally
persuaded Monsieur DuRose in the Paris art gallery to exhibit her
own paintings, she'd only sold two, and one of those was to CJ.
That failure stole her love of art from her. Zelda is right about
another thing: there is no accounting for taste.

Maybe she does or maybe she doesn't have acting talent. After
being in Hollywood for over two years, she's come to understand
that talent is the least of the requirements for fame. What is more
important is that elusive thing called star quality. That charisma
that lights up the screen and makes the audience's hearts thump
with admiration or delight or desire. Now, more than ever, when
the world has fallen to pieces in the worst drought and financial
depression ever known, people need gods and goddesses to bring
some magic into their dull, dreary lives. In the 1930s, Hollywood
is Mount Olympus and she is half-way up the mountain.

She knows she has that star quality. She's always been one to
be noticed. She's been used to admiring glances from both men
and women all her adult life. You either have 'it', like Clara Bow
and Greta Garbo, or you don't, like all the other starlets who have

shone and burned out like dying embers. She has 'it'. She knows it in her bones.

She looks at her reflection in the vanity mirror and runs her fingertip along the faint lines fanning out from her eyes as panic jabs at her solar plexus like a bony finger. She is forty-one in August. She needs someone in power to notice her before it's too late.

The front door slams and CJ enters the apartment, throwing his fedora onto the small metal table topped with garish yellow Formica. 'Hey, doll,' he says as he joins her on the balcony. He gives her a peck on her cheek and nods at the letter in Etta's hand. 'Another letter from your mother telling you to go home?'

Etta raises an eyebrow and smiles, aware of the attractive dimple it forms in her cheek. 'What was that?'

'What was what, hon?'

'You kissed me like I'm your grandmother.'

CJ laughs and, pulling her into an embrace, kisses her until a suggestive whistle from a passing cyclist breaks them apart. He grins. 'Better?'

Etta laughs. 'Much better, darling.'

She follows him into the tiny living room with the saggy sofa she'd covered with a paisley throw she'd filched from the MGM wardrobe department, and wanders over to the kitchenette. She drops the letter on top of the other bills and letters stacked in a fruit bowl and puts the kettle onto the hotplate to boil.

'Tea, darling? I splurged on Earl Grey.'

'Sure, baby.' CJ takes off his suit jacket and throws it over one of the two metal chairs at the table. He picks the letter out of the fruit bowl. 'Ah, Zelda. In another hospital?'

Etta measures out several spoonfuls of loose tea into the teapot. 'Yes, read it if you like. Poor Zelda. There but for the grace of God go I.'

CJ scans the letter and drops it back into the fruit bowl. 'Paris seems a long time ago. Frankly, I'm glad I got out of it alive. I don't think my liver will ever be the same.'

The kettle whistles and Etta pours the boiling water into the teapot. 'I don't think Hollywood is the best place for livers either, darling.'

CJ nods as he lights a cigarette. 'Etta, hon. I've quit my job.'

Etta's head jolts up. 'You what?'

'I quit my job at the studio. I couldn't take it anymore. I'm just not the screenwriting type. Three years and not one script put into production. I've had enough.'

'But what are we going to do for money? That rat DuRose is squeezing us dry.'

CJ shakes his head. 'Money? Is that all you're concerned about?'

'Well, it's a valid concern, CJ. I barely make enough to keep me in silk stockings.'

CJ grabs a mug of tea and heads over to the sofa. 'So I've noticed.' He picks up a discarded newspaper and flips through to the sports pages.

Etta slams her hand onto the counter. 'CJ! Talk to me. What are we going to do?'

CJ looks up from the paper. 'We? I don't expect you'll be lining up for a job behind the lingerie counter at Bullock's.' He takes a gulp of tea. 'I spoke to the news editor at the *LA Tribune*. I know him from my Associated Press days. I'm starting there next Monday as a stringer. He said if it worked out, he'd be sure to put me up for a permanent job when one opens up.'

'You're going back to journalism? But, CJ, what about the pictures? If you're not working in motion pictures in LA, you're nobody.'

'Then I guess I'm a nobody. I'm done with the picture business.'

'But CJ, what am I going to do? If you leave the business, you won't know anyone at the movie premières. We'll walk up the red carpet and you'll be … you'll be a nobody.'

'Hon, I *am* a nobody.'

'But you're a nobody in the movie business. It's different. CJ, it won't look good for me.'

CJ tosses the newspaper down and jolts out of the sofa. 'Are you serious? Tell me you're not serious, Etta. Haven't you even noticed how frustrated and unhappy I've been seeing all my screenplays dumped? Three years, and not one single movie credit. I gave it a try, but I'm a journalist at heart. I miss it, Etta, and I'm over the moon that I've gotten a job on the *Trib*. Can't you just be happy for me, for once? Not everything has to revolve around you.'

'CJ, don't be like that. Maybe I can talk to someone. Maybe Groucho can get you a job on his latest picture—'

'Etta, I *liked* being a journalist. I *liked* covering the European beat. So many things are happening in the world now, and I'm missing the story. I felt like an idiot here trying to write crime thrillers and romantic comedies for the pictures. I felt like I was wasting my life. I thought I could do it, but I can't. And I don't want to.'

'But CJ—'

CJ grabs his fedora from the table and pushes past Etta. 'I'm going out.'

'Where are you going?'

'Out. Don't wait up.'

Chapter Thirty-Five

Etta

Hollywood, California – November 1935

Etta glances out of the window of the limousine at the animated crowd corralled behind a red rope barrier either side of the entrance to Grauman's Chinese Theatre.

'Looks like half of Los Angeles is out tonight,' CJ says.

'Of course they are. The Marx Brothers are gods. Everybody who's anybody has been trying to get an invitation to the première of *A Night at the Opera*, and here we are arriving in a limousine. Groucho is so thoughtful.' Etta squeezes CJ's arm. 'Isn't it exciting? I can't wait to see my scene in the stateroom. I'm featured, you know.'

'I know, hon. I've heard it a hundred times. Two lines and giving Groucho a manicure. It's star-making.'

Etta frowns into her compact as she checks her make-up. 'It's a shame they had to dye my hair brown for the movie. Irving Thalberg said I looked too glamorous with my blonde hair in the rushes so we had to film it all over again after they dyed my hair. How is anyone going to recognise me on the red carpet?'

'Honey, they'll scream because you look like a star. Believe me, if they think you're a star, you're a star.'

Etta favours CJ with her dimpled smile. 'I feel like this is the beginning of everything, CJ.'

'You said that about that Bing Crosby picture you were in, and 42nd Street, and Duck Soup before you were fired from that one. Why don't you go back to being an artist? You're great at that.'

Etta waves at him dismissively as the chauffeur pulls the car up to the red carpet. 'I'm done with that. Painting only brings back bad memories. Besides, I've got *lines* this time. I'm not an extra anymore. I'm a supporting player. I'll be able to get an agent now.'

'An agent? Is that a good idea? Look what happened with your art agent, DuRose. He's leeching us for every spare penny we have to keep quiet about you painting Carlo's pictures.'

'He's not leeching you. He's leeching me.'

CJ opens his door. 'Same difference.'

The chauffeur opens Etta's door and she steps out onto the red carpet, careful to let her gold satin gown slide enticingly over her exposed knee. The crowd erupts in a scream and cameras flash. CJ steps around the car and takes her hand.

'Told you. They think you're a star, so you're a star.'

Etta smiles graciously at the surging throng, pausing every few steps to pose for a photographer, as they make their way up the carpet to the entrance. 'I've always been a star, CJ. It's just that no one else knew it.' She blows a kiss to the crowd. 'But they're going to know it now.'

They are met at the threshold into the lobby by a burly tuxedo-clad doorman holding a clipboard. He eyes them with a face that has long lost the ability to be impressed. 'Names?'

'CJ Melton and Miss Etta Marine,' CJ says.

The doorman scans the list and shakes his head. 'No. Not here. Sorry, can't let ya in.'

Etta gasps. 'What?! No, that's impossible. I'm *in* the picture. I'm one of the stars.'

The man sweeps his gaze over her. 'Etta Marine?'

'Yes. Yes, that's right.'

'I never heard o' ya.'

CJ takes out a pack of cigarettes and a lighter. 'There's obviously a mistake. She *is* in the picture. We're totally legit.' He offers the doorman a cigarette. 'Help yourself.'

The doorman accepts the offer and sucks as CJ lights the cigarette. He blows out a stream of white smoke.

'No can do. I've got my orders. No invite, no entry.' He gestures to the queue of irritated thespians growing behind them. 'You're causin' a line here. Ya'd better move on. Can't have the real stars waitin'.'

Etta stamps her foot. 'I'm not going anywhere! I have every right to get in to watch *my* picture!'

The doorman grabs Etta's arm. 'Not on my watch, honey.'

CJ shoves the man against the doorway. 'Get your hands off her.'

The doorman holds up his hands and nods to the two policemen who are making their way down the red carpet. 'No problem. It's over to them now.'

'Oh, for heaven's sake!' Etta says as one of the policemen takes hold of her arm. 'Let me go! It's *my* picture! Groucho knows me. He sent the limo for us!'

'Great story, lady,' the policeman says as he pulls her down the red carpet. 'Tell it to the judge.'

'She's telling the truth,' CJ says as the other policeman strong-arms him away from the theatre.

The crowd erupts into a deafening roar as the door of a shining black Rolls Royce opens and Groucho Marx steps out onto the red carpet. His famous eyebrows shoot up as he takes in the scene before him.

'Well, well, you do know how to make an entrance, Miss Marine, if I do say so myself. Or should I say an exit?'

'Groucho! They don't believe I'm in the picture!'

Groucho slaps one of the policemen on the shoulder and stuffs his half-smoked cigar in the breast pocket of the man's uniform. 'What's this I see? Smoking on duty?'

The policeman laughs nervously and, removing the cigar, offers it back to Groucho. 'I couldn't take your cigar, Mr Marx.'

'You certainly can, my good man.' Groucho slides another cigar out of his tuxedo pocket. 'I got a regular cigar store in here.' He nods at Etta and CJ. 'Now if you release these two into my custody, I'll be sure they make the appropriate kind of ruckus at the picture show.'

CJ slams the apartment door and yanks at his bow tie. 'That was humiliating, Etta.'

Etta kicks off her gold shoes and heads over to the liquor cabinet. 'Don't be silly, CJ. We got noticed. That's what everyone in Hollywood wants more than anything. We're sure to be in the papers tomorrow. I can't wait.'

CJ slumps into the one threadbare armchair. 'You can't wait to see a picture of us being pulled down the red carpet by policemen?'

Etta pours out two glasses of bourbon and pads across the carpet. She hands a glass to CJ and, knocking the cushions onto the floor, curls up like a cat on the sagging sofa. 'As Oscar Wilde said, there's only one thing worse than being talked about, and that's not being talked about. I'd definitely rather be talked about.'

'Yes, well, you're good at that.'

Etta takes a sip of her drink. 'What do you mean by that?'

CJ laughs. 'Etta, you've been gossip fodder ever since I've known you. The woman Carlo Marinetti murdered his first wife for?'

'You know that's not true.'

'Doesn't matter if it's true or not. It's what people have believed for years.'

He takes a drink and scrutinises Etta over the rim of his glass. 'Then there was the sparkling Etta Marinetti of Paris, friend and muse of writers, artists and dubious photographers. And now, Miss Etta Marine, Hollywood starlet.'

He shakes his head. 'What happened to you, Etta? You're a fantastic artist. Those paintings you painted under Carlo's name were incredible. When I met you, you wanted nothing more than to be recognised for your talent. You were hungry for that, and I loved that about you. It was an honourable goal and I was sure you'd manage it one day if you kept at it.' He shrugs. 'Now you're twisting yourself in knots lying about your age just to get two lines in a movie. You're better than that, hon.'

'Don't talk about art! I'm fed up to the teeth with it. No one was interested in my own paintings, CJ. Do you remember the one exhibit François DuRose put on for me at his gallery? It was a disaster! He called my work "pernicious" and "a pale imitation of Carlo's work". I remember every word. I won't be treated like that.'

'So, you gave up painting.'

'Yes! Wouldn't you? It was humiliating.'

CJ rises from the armchair and retrieves the bourbon bottle from the liquor cabinet. He refills their glasses. 'That's exactly how I felt about not getting my screenplays made. Humiliated.'

Etta rubs her forehead. 'CJ, it's been a long night. I don't want us to fight.'

'I gave up journalism to write scripts in Hollywood, just like you gave up painting to become a star. That's what you want to be, isn't it, Etta? A star, not an actress.'

'I don't see anything wrong with being a star.'

'Well, I hope it happens. It'll pay better than the newspaper.'

'Darling, we'll be rolling in money before you know it. My time is coming. I feel it in my bones.' Etta sets down her glass and loops her arms around CJ's neck. 'Now, how about you meet me in the bedroom in five minutes.'

'I thought you said you were tired.'

Etta bends over and nibbles on his earlobe. 'I'm a very good actress.'

Chapter Thirty-Six

Jessie

Cairo, Egypt –November 14th, 1935

Mustapha inches the Aston Martin through the mass of student protestors, shouting uncharacteristically as they pound at the black paintwork he has so meticulously polished to a high sheen. Jessie peers out the window, wincing as a hand slaps against the glass.

'There are thousands, Mustapha. Twice as many as yesterday, I'm sure. We'll never get home through this.'

He presses on the horn, which only incites the students to pound harder on the car's bonnet. 'We will, *inshallah*. I will find a way.'

Jessie sits back against the leather seat behind Mustapha, cursing Layla for insisting on such an opulent car, when both she and Aziz had said a more modest vehicle would have served their needs just as well.

She flinches as someone pounds on the roof as Mustapha steers the vehicle down a side alley. It is far worse today, no question. Thousands more have joined the students from Giza University in the anti-British demonstrations.

Mustapha veers around a chicken and exits onto a narrow road toward Gezira Island, where he suddenly brakes. Jessie looks past his shoulder at a parade of Green Shirts marching their way.

'Back up, Mustapha.'

Mustapha shakes his head, the tassel on his dark red *tarbouche* swinging along the embroidered neck of his *jellabiya*. He points to the rearview mirror, which reflects a crowd of women and children gathering, drawn like flies to honey by the sight of the opulent car and the approaching 'soldiers'.

Her heart skips a beat. 'What should we do?'

'We wait.'

Jessie swallows, aware that her throat has gone dry. Her heart flutters against her ribcage, like a bird flapping in a cage. She sits back against the seat, willing herself invisible as the young men in their green uniforms part in front of the car and file silently by. Only one turns his gaze into the car. She is not surprised to see Isham this time.

'Mama!' Shani calls out, beckoning her mother to the dining table. 'Marta and I made *Hamam Mahshi*. I fried the onions and made the rice.'

Layla looks up from her dinner of stuffed pigeon and rice and draws her dark eyebrows together as she regards her daughter-in-law. 'Again, you are late. Even Aziz is here before you. It is not right for a wife to keep her husband waiting.'

Jessie pulls out a chair and sits beside her husband, Layla having usurped her place at the end of the table opposite Aziz.

'I'm sorry. It couldn't be helped. There's another student protest going on. There's barely room to move in town. There are thousands on the streets.'

Layla waves an elegant, long-fingered hand, setting her bracelets jangling. 'As long as they stay away from Gezira Island, I don't care what they do.'

Aziz sits back in his chair and sets his napkin on the table. 'You should care, Mama. The students are tired of British self-interest and a king who cares only for himself and his family.'

Jessie smiles at Marta as the housekeeper sets a hot plate of food in front of her. 'But the government is trying, isn't it, Aziz? You're out at meetings all the time.'

'Yes, but the young are impatient, and truthfully, I am impatient as well. It is all taking too long. They are like the waters of a reservoir swollen by a storm pushing at the barrier of a dam. Even the strongest dam can break under the pressure of a flood.'

Shani swallows a mouthful of rice. 'Auntie Zara says the Egyptians will rule one day soon and the king will have to listen to them.'

Layla laughs mirthlessly. 'And what a disaster that will be. The Egyptian people are sheep who require a shepherd. Without a protector, they will be swallowed up by someone else. Italy has just invaded Abyssinia. I have no doubt they would be happy to take over from the British in Egypt. A strong leader like Benito Mussolini is exactly whom the Egyptian people need.'

Jessie sets down her fork. 'Mussolini is a dictator, Layla. He jails anyone he objects to and his Blackshirt thugs use violence and intimidation against his opponents. Is that what you want for Egypt? Would you be happy with a dictator ruling Egypt?'

'What do I care who runs Egypt, as long as I am left alone to live as I wish?'

'That is the crux of the matter, Mama,' Aziz says. 'Dictators love rules, and they usually distrust the rich, unless, of course, the rich support them financially. As to women, well, they don't care much for those, either.'

'Is there going to be a war in Egypt, Baba?'

'Not if I can help it, Shani. This is why I go to so many

meetings.' He eyes Zara's empty place at the table. 'Where is Zara? She's not still working in the clinic, is she?'

Layla shrugs. 'She has no concept of time. She will come in when she is hungry. It is impossible to have a civilised meal in this house.'

Jessie bites her lip. If anything were to happen to Zara, she would never forgive herself. She clears her throat. 'I think ... I think I might know where she is. I think she'll be at the demonstration with the Green Shirts.'

'What?' Aziz pushes away from the table. 'Why didn't you say that when you came in?' Aziz runs his hand through his hair as he paces across the floor. 'I have to go find her.'

'Aziz, I'm sure she'll be fine. I saw Isham at the demonstration. Zara will be with him.'

'Isham! And you didn't tell me? I swear if anything happens to her, I will kill him.'

'Baba!' Shani cries. 'Baba, don't say that!'

The words spill out of Jessie before she can stop them. 'Aziz, Isham is her husband!'

'What?'

The room falls silent as all eyes turn to Jessie.

Layla rises from her chair, narrowing her eyes like a cobra about to strike. 'You knew about this disgrace, and yet you said nothing?'

'Zara insisted that I say nothing. She wanted to be the one to tell you when she felt the time was right.'

Layla huffs in disgust. 'Isham is nothing but a common street boy. I will not have another of my children ruined by a disastrous marriage.' She looks over at Aziz. 'Go find Zara. Bring her back home where she belongs. Then we will discuss your wife.'

Jessie slams the door of the Aston Martin and pushes through the jostling shoulders of the throng. She tries not to lose sight of Aziz, who had leapt out when Mustapha had been forced to stop because of the crowds. A whistle blows behind her to the left and then another and another as hundreds of police stream through the protestors like a dark river. They are met with a surge of students brandishing wooden staffs whose shouts drown out the shrill whistles. She strains her neck to look past the confusion of staffs and *tarbouches* to glimpse Aziz, but he has vanished into the melee like a ghost into a cloud.

A shot rings out over the tumult like a stone hitting tin. Then another. The crowd roars and surges toward the police like a flood. Someone screams. She sees blood on someone's hands as he waves above the protestors' heads. She elbows her way forward. '*I'm a doctor!*' she shouts in Arabic. '*I'm a doctor!*'

The wall of bodies part and she sees him lying on the street, a pool of blood collecting beneath his ear like a crimson puddle. She kneels beside him and cradles his head in her lap.

'Aziz!' she screams. 'Aziz!' She kneels beside her husband and cradles his head in her lap. But she is too late.

Zara pushes through the crowd. 'Aziz!'

Jessie looks up at her sister-in-law. When she speaks, her voice is eerily calm.

'You did this, Zara. You killed him. You killed Aziz.'

Part V

1936

Chapter Thirty-Seven

Jessie

Altumanina, Cairo, Egypt – April 1936

L ayla Khalid looks up from the copy of French *Vogue* she's been reading. 'To what do we owe the pleasure of your company so early in the day, Jessica? Shani is not even back from school yet. Have you offended yet another of the senior residents?'

Jessie sets her well-worn leather schoolbag onto the low brass table and flops into the plump chintz cushions of a wicker chair on the shaded terrace.

'I'm sorry to disappoint you, Layla, but I had some work to do in the clinic, so I left the hospital early today. If truth be told, I'm tired of being stuck in the obstetrics and paediatrics departments, but nothing I say to Dr Salah persuades him that I am capable of becoming part of the surgical team.'

Layla shudders and rings a small brass bell. 'A woman has no place practising medicine. I applaud Dr Salah.'

The sturdy figure of the housekeeper appears in the doorway, her dark brown hair tied back with a floral kerchief. 'Yes, Madame Khalid?'

'Tea, Marta.'

'I have just made *ghorayebah*. Shall I bring some before Shani eats them all when she's home?' Her blue eyes twinkle as she looks over at Jessie. 'My butter cookies are her favourite.'

Layla waves a slender hand dismissively. 'Not for me, but no doubt Jessica will indulge herself.'

When Marta has left, Layla directs her amber gaze on her daughter-in-law. 'Will you be joining us for dinner tonight, Jessica? I am rather fatigued of making conversation with a thirteen-year-old girl, although it appears that Shani is all the family you have left me with.'

Jessie sighs wearily. 'Layla, I'd rather not talk about Zara.'

Layla nods, setting her gold earrings swinging. 'On this, at least, we can agree. If it weren't for Zara's foolishness, my son would still be here. And to marry the son of a gardener! She is as good as dead to me. So, Jessica, now we are left with each other. I wonder every day what I did to deserve such a fate.'

'Layla—'

Layla holds up her hand. 'No. I wish to speak. Given we are so rarely alone, I will take this opportunity.'

Jessie folds her arms. 'Fine. What is it?'

'Jessica, Mohammed caught two men trying to break through the gate to the house yesterday.'

'What?'

'It is not the first time. We are being targeted because you are English. It is common knowledge that we are a house of women here. No one would have dared such things when my son was alive, but now … do you not understand that you have made us all a target for all the many people in Cairo who hate the British? Think of your daughter in that English school. It is not safe, Jessica. I was spat on outside of Cicurel last week because I emerged from a British car!'

Marta enters with a tray carrying two steaming glasses of black tea and a plate heaped with butter cookies. Layla sits back in her chair and, picking up her Spanish fan, fans her face until the housekeeper leaves.

Jessie picks up a glass of tea and stirs in several spoonfuls of sugar. 'I'm sorry, Layla, I had no idea. We can hire someone to watch the gate.'

Layla laughs, the sound hollow and humourless. 'And when the mob comes, this guard will protect us?'

Jessie sets down the glass. 'What do you want me to do?'

'Go back to Britain.'

'Go back to Britain? But this is my home.'

'Altumanina? Since my poor son's death, you do nothing more than sleep here. All you do is work. Marta is more of a mother to your daughter than you are. Do you think you will ease your guilt for your part in Aziz's death by burying yourself in work? I can assure you, you will not. Do you not think I have wept and cursed myself for sending Aziz to find Zara that day?' Layla's voice breaks. 'I killed my son. I sent him there. I killed him.'

'It was an accident, Layla. It was no one's fault.'

'It was everyone's fault!' Layla slams her hand down on the arm of her chair. 'Every time I look at you, I am reminded of my failings as well as yours!'

Jessie stares at her mother-in-law as the truth of Layla's words seeps into her numbed mind. Layla is right. She has anaesthetised herself from facing Aziz's death by filling every waking minute with work, at both the hospital and the clinic. She sleeps now on a cot in her study because she cannot bear the thought of lying in the bed that had been theirs. Every corner of Altumanina reminds her of Aziz. Every street in Cairo, every shop in the Khan-el-Khalili souk, the Gezira Sporting Club, Shepheard's Hotel … Aziz haunts it all. Worst of all, she has left Shani to Marta's care, because every time she looks at her daughter, she sees Aziz's face and the pain slices through her like a sword.

She has to stop it. She has a daughter to think of. She has to face their future. A future without Aziz.

She rises from the chair and picks up her schoolbag.

'Jessica, where are you going?'

'To find Mustapha. I'm going to pick up Shani from school.'

Chapter Thirty-Eight

Celie

West Lake, Alberta, Canada – May 1936

Celie leans her bicycle against a weather-worn fence post and takes her camera out of the wire basket. She removes it from its leather case, which she drops back into the basket beside her water bottle and the egg sandwich she has carefully wrapped in waxed paper, and loops the strap around her neck. She tightens her hat string under her chin to keep her straw hat from flying off across the dust-blown fields in the hot, dry wind. It is only the middle of May, but the temperature has been climbing day on day, and, even though it's still early, the heat penetrates the thin cotton of her flour sack dress and films her exposed skin with perspiration. She fans her face with her hand and squints across the withered and rotting stalks of last year's abandoned wheat at the peeling white paint and cracked windows of the Philbys' once-handsome farmhouse.

She looks down into the camera's viewfinder, and, after focusing the lens, snaps a black and white photograph. Letting the camera fall against her chest, she walks up the rock-hard dirt road with nothing but the howling wind and the buzz of grasshoppers breaking the silence.

Behind the house, the grey structure of the wooden barn, leaning like a tired old man against the onslaught of the prairie weather, creaks and groans as the wind whips through the cracks in its siding. Somewhere a board has come loose and beats against a wall like a ruler slapping a student's hand. The rusting skeleton of the Philbys' plough pokes through overgrown grass that is an unexpected green in the otherwise bleached-out scene.

She focuses the camera and takes several shots, pleased when a pair of crows land on the plough, adding to the atmosphere of death and decay.

'It seems we have the same idea.'

Celie gasps at the sound of the man's voice and spins around. He is walking toward her from behind the barn, but she is blinded by the sun and can't make out his face. She glances at the house to her right and the barn to her left, and takes a step back as she realises the vulnerability of her position. She holds out her hand and squints at the man's silhouette.

'Wait. Stop. Don't come any closer.'

The man stops abruptly. 'I'm sorry. I didn't mean to startle you.' He steps into the shade of the house and removes his fedora. 'We've met before. I recognised you as soon as I saw you. At the May Day parade in Edmonton last year? You were photographing Boy Scouts and Communists.'

She exhales in relief as she recognises the American photographer. 'Of course. Yes, I remember. I'm sorry, but you startled me. Mr McCrea, isn't it?'

He smiles, his teeth flashing white in his tanned, weather-beaten face. 'That's right. Robson McCrea. And you're Celie Jeffries. Celie's an unusual name. It was easy to remember.'

'It's short for Cecelia. My mother hates it, but everyone else calls me Celie.'

'It suits you.'

She glances around the deserted farmyard miles from the nearest neighbour. 'Yes, well, it was nice to see you again. I should be going.'

He shoves his hat back on his head. 'Don't leave on my account. I've got a car parked behind the barn. I'll get out of your hair. I know what it's like to try to capture images with someone breathing down your neck. Unfortunately, there are a lot of other places like this I can photograph.'

'Thank you. I do work best on my own.'

'Me too.'

Celie watches him head toward the rear of the barn. He is just about to turn the corner when she calls out.

'Wait!'

He turns around, once again a black silhouette in the sun's glare.

'You don't have to go. It's a big enough farm. I'm sure we can both do our work without bothering each other.'

'All right, if you're okay with that.' He steps toward her and holds out his hand. 'It's a deal.'

Celie takes hold of his hand, conscious of the firmness of his warm grip as they shake.

Celie tosses her apple core into the weeds that have taken over Emma Philby's kitchen garden and looks over at Robson McCrea, who is sitting beside her on the top step of the farmhouse's porch.

'So, you're travelling around North America taking photographs of the Great Depression?'

Robson bites into the half of the egg sandwich Celie has insisted he take, refusing his objections. He chews and swallows. 'That's right. *Life* liked the pictures I took up here in Canada last

May, so they sent me back to see how things have changed in a year.'

'And what have you noticed?'

He shrugs. 'Everything's worse. The weather hasn't let up, the crops are dying, banks are repossessing homes and farms, shantytowns and soup kitchens are springing up everywhere. Just like in the States. Our governments are spending millions on relief programmes, but dole rations are heavily policed and too small to live on if you're lucky enough to get them at all. Then, to pay for the spending, the governments are laying off employees, and making cuts to health care, education and social programmes. Don't even get me started about corruption among politicians and big business.'

Celie folds up the waxed paper into a neat square and slips it into her dress pocket.

'I know. I've been writing about this for the past four years, but my editor at the *West Lake News* won't publish any of it. He prefers articles on "Ten Ways to Use Flour Sacks in Home Decoration". He says it's unpatriotic to criticise the government, who are working in the country's best interests.' She harrumphs. 'Hopefully, the new Liberal government will make a real difference to this country and I'll be able to get some of my articles and pictures published.'

Robson whistles through his teeth. 'You're feisty, I'll give you that, Celie Jeffries. Were you always like this?'

Celie smiles as she brushes breadcrumbs off her skirt and laughs.

'I don't think my sisters have yet forgiven me for all the suffragist meetings I dragged them to when they'd much rather have gone to the local picture house. My sister Etta fancied herself the next Lillian Gish. In fact, she's living in Hollywood now trying to become an actress.'

'Is that right? I'll have to keep an eye out for her in the pictures.'

'Etta Marine. That's her stage name.'

'Catchy.'

'My other sister, Jessie, is a doctor in Cairo. She was married to an Egyptian surgeon she met during the war when she was there as an army nurse. He was killed in a riot there in November.'

'I'm sorry.'

She nods. 'It was a terrible tragedy. Jessie's decided to go back to London with her daughter. She's secured herself a good position as a surgeon at King's College Hospital. She said she couldn't stay in Cairo as everything reminded her too much of Aziz.'

The American gazes out toward the horizon line where the blue sky meets the desiccated earth. 'You're an adventurous family.'

She shrugs. 'My sisters are anyway. I'm just a farmer's wife.'

'You're not "just" anything, Celie.' He stands up and looks back at her. 'I'm looking for some other good places to take pictures around here. Do you have any suggestions?'

'Happy pictures or sad pictures?'

'Real pictures.'

Celie scrutinises the farmyard, with its withered plants and the old rubber tyre still swinging from a rope in the tall maple tree.

'There are a lot of places to take real pictures out here. We've been hit hard by the Depression.' She looks over at the American. 'How long are you here?'

'A week. I'm staying at the hotel. Rented a car from the guy at the garage.'

'Fred Wheatley?'

'Yeah, that's the one.'

Celie taps her shoe on the step, aware that he is watching her as she smooths out her dress over her knees. 'Would you like me to show you around?'

His stern expression softens as he smiles. 'I would, as long as you bring your camera. I'll pay you, of course.'

'Don't be ridiculous.'

'I'm never ridiculous. You'll be my guide, and I'll throw in some of my photography tips if you want.'

Celie scrutinises the American. Lulu's in school every day until three, and Frank is out in the field planting the new crop from eight in the morning till suppertime. She can use the money to pay for the film and processing fluids she'll need, and she'll be learning photography from Robson McCrea, award-winning photographer – she'd read his biography in the *Life Magazine* in Forbes's General Store. She will be no better nor worse off financially than she already is, but she will come out of the week a better photographer. Maybe she'll even manage to sell a few pictures to Rex Majors. It's a fair exchange of services.

She holds out her hand. 'It's a deal.'

Chapter Thirty-Nine

Celie

West Lake, Alberta, Canada – May 1936

Robson McCrea steers the old Ford he'd rented from Fred Wheatley down a freshly gravelled road that slices through a dense forest of towering jack pines punctuated by an occasional shivering aspen or the flash of a white-skinned birch. The crunch of the tyres on the gravel disturbs a deer that dashes out of the shadows and across the road in front of the car.

Robson slams on the brakes and the car skids to a halt. 'Jesus!'

Celie tuts. 'It's just a deer. Be thankful it wasn't a moose. Those are as big as a house. Or a grizzly. It's best to keep away from those. We're not likely to see a wolf during the day, and the cougars tend to stay in the forest. The hunters and fishermen have to watch out for those. They like to sit up in a tree and pounce on you when you're not looking.'

Robson shifts the gear and presses the accelerator with his foot. 'The day is young.' He glances over at Celie. 'Where exactly are you taking me?'

'Why? Don't you trust me? Haven't I been a good guide so far? I thought you might have had enough of the abandoned farms, the rusting cars and farm machinery, and the empty grain elevators. I'm bringing you somewhere different.'

'All right. Wherever we're going, at least there's a good road to it.'

'There is that.'

They continue along in silence for several minutes. Celie glances at the American in the rearview mirror, noting his frown of concentration as his eyes scan the shadowy forest for signs of an agitated animal. The past five days have been some of the best days she's had in Canada. Sharing her passion for photography with someone who loves it as much as she has been so uplifting. And learning about using shadows and form and simplicity to create images that evince a visceral response ... this is what her images had been lacking. She'd always been able to tell a story with her photographs, but the beauty of stark simplicity where the image and the story become one is a revelation. She has felt herself come alive, like she has awakened from a long hibernation. Even Frank had commented on her lightness of spirit, although he'd insinuated that she and Mavis might be indulging in Mavis's beer on the sly.

She points to a turnoff on the right which is barely visible through the trees. 'There. Turn here. We're not far.'

The car bounces down a rutted dirt lane that has not benefitted from the attention of the main road. The dense tree canopy thins to reveal a clearing where about fifty tar-paper shacks line the lane. A long queue of young men in dusty overalls and dungarees snakes down the road as they wait to enter a larger building with 'Food Hall' painted onto a wooden board affixed above the door. Another cluster of men carrying shovels and picks stamp down a path on a hill that has been denuded of trees.

Robson pulls the car up beside a large tree stump and parks. 'What is this place?'

'Welcome to one of the Canadian government's Unemployment Relief Camps, better known as a "Royal Twenty Centre".'

'Why are they called that?'

'Because the men here, if they're lucky, receive twenty cents a day for backbreaking work. When the Depression began, the Canadian government was concerned that all the unemployed single men in the cities might turn to communist ideas. So, the government came up with the idea of shipping them off to these work camps buried away in the wilderness to clear land and build roads in return for room, board and work clothes.'

'And twenty cents a day.'

'Six dollars a month, and a lot of them send half of that back to their families. They're basically stuck in these camps eating bad food, clearing the forests and building roads to towns that don't exist.'

Robson whistles through his teeth. 'That's tough. Still, they've got a roof over their heads and they're not starving. They're volunteers, aren't they? It's not like they're in prison here.'

'Theoretically, yes, but they're threatened with being arrested for vagrancy if they refuse to come. And, of course, they can leave, but how are they going to get out of here? We're miles from the closest farm, and if they did make it out, they wouldn't have enough money to live on. Then they'd be given the choice to "volunteer" again or be arrested for vagrancy. It's a vicious circle. In effect, it is a prison.'

'Right. I see.'

She grabs her camera. 'Shall we go?'

'Sure.'

'Why don't you have a wander around while I go speak to the men? I'm going to write an article about this place from the men's point of view. It's not something we read about in the papers. The government only wants us to read its side of the story.'

'Didn't you say your editor at the *West Lake News* only wants fluff pieces?'

'Who said I'm writing it for the *West Lake News*?' She nods toward the top of the denuded hill. 'I'll meet you up there in an hour.'

Celie steps into the shadow beside a bunkbed in one of the shacks and peers into the viewfinder at the face of the young man she has instructed to look out the window. The afternoon sunlight plays over the sharp contours of his face, which can't be more than twenty-three or twenty-four, but appears hardened by the years of backbreaking work and hopelessness he's endured in the camp. She presses the shutter and looks up.

'Thank you, John. Thank you very much.'

The young man nods and shrugs. 'Maybe somebody will do somethin' when they read your article in the paper. You heard about the Regina riot last summer?'

'Yes, I did. It was in all the papers. Lots of injuries. Two people dead.'

'A thousand of us camp workers comin' all the way from Vancouver aimin' to head to Ottawa to talk to the government about bein' paid a fair wage, first aid supplies and gettin' back our right to vote. You know we can't vote? We're citizens just like you. We're not criminals.'

'I agree with you. That's not right.'

'Yeah.' John traces his finger along the dirty window. 'We reached Regina and the Mounties wouldn't let us get on the train to Ottawa. Caused a riot. Beat us senseless. Nothin' left for us to do but go back to the camps.'

Celie nods. 'The camp workers had a lot of public sympathy after the riot. Bennett's government got voted out over that.'

John shrugs. 'One politician is pretty much the same as the

next. They stick us all up in these camps, out of sight, doing boondoggles.' He gestures out the window. 'Who's gonna use that road out there? You know where it goes? Nowhere, that's where. It's somethin' they make us do to keep us out of trouble. They stuck us here because they were afraid we'd turn into Commies in the city. Well, you wanna know somethin'? Don't give us girlie magazines, give us Marx and Lenin. That's what I say.'

'You feel like your own country has abandoned you.'

John laughs mirthlessly. 'Yeah, but it's not just us here. We've all been abandoned. Farmers, office workers, train conductors, teachers, nurses, you name it. It's workers they hate. We've all been abandoned by politicians and businessmen who only want to line their own pockets. I'd like to see any one of them manage on twenty cents a day for hard labour. Yup, that's a sight I'd sure like to see.'

Celie nods. 'That's a sight I'd like to see, too.'

'Hold it right there, Celie. Don't move.'

She looks up and smiles at the sight of Robson McCrea staring down the top of the Rolleiflex camera. She laughs as he takes several shots.

'I'm not used to being a model. That's more my sister Etta's domain.'

'You're a natural. It's a shame it's only in black and white. I'd love to capture you on colour film with that red hair of yours.'

'Colour film? Wouldn't that be something.'

'Oh, it will happen one day. Mark my words.'

Celie reaches the top of the hill and looks out over the camp. 'I only found out about this place a few months ago from Fred Wheatley. A camp manager drove into town to take him to the camp to fix one of their trucks.'

'There must be four hundred men here and no one knows about them?'

'Fred said the military brings them their supplies and post. I've never heard about the camp here near West Lake.' She brushes a loose strand of hair out of her eyes that the breeze has caught. 'Then again, we all have our own worries these days.'

'What are your worries, Celie?'

She looks at Robson and wrinkles her nose. 'It's nothing, really. Not compared to this.' She taps his camera. 'Did you get some good pictures?'

'I did. And you?'

'I did, too. I spoke to several of the men. It's an awful situation they're in. Did you know that they've had their right to vote taken away from them? It's shocking. They're being treated like they're criminals. I simply have to write about this. I think it will be a good article.'

'I have no doubt about that.' Robson reaches out and brushes the hair out of her eyes. He cups her face with his hand and kisses her, and for a brief moment, she remembers what it feels like to be desired, and to desire.

She turns her head away. 'I'm married, Robson.'

He drops his hand. 'I know.'

She brushes her fingers over her lips. 'But you still kissed me.'

'I did.'

'You shouldn't have.'

'That is conventional thinking.'

'I'm afraid I'm a conventional woman.'

The corners of Robson's green eyes wrinkle as he smiles. 'Just my luck.'

'It's not that I … that I don't—'

'There's nothing wrong with being a conventional woman, Celie.'

She nods. 'Being unconventional never seemed to hurt my sisters, but you're right. I'm a conventional woman.'

'Now that we've got that cleared up, how about we get back to town before we lose the light? I don't want to be bumping into any moose on the drive back.'

'Yes, of course.'

She follows him down the hill, fixated on the deep tan of his arms where he has rolled up the sleeves of his shirt. Her heart thumps in her chest, and she knows it has nothing to do with the exertions of the hill.

Just before they reach the bottom, he glances over his shoulder. 'For the record, I'm glad I kissed you.'

The following morning at breakfast, Frank sips at his cup of weak tea and sets the teacup back on its saucer. He digs his spoon into his porridge. 'I hear there's an American photographer in town.'

Celie's heart skips a beat. 'Is there? I wonder what he's doing in West Lake of all places?'

'He's rented a car off of Fred. He told Fred he was here to take pictures for an American magazine.'

Lulu grabs the teapot and splashes more tea into her cup. 'An American magazine? What's he look like?'

'Like an American, I expect, Lulu. Have you seen him in town, Celie?'

'I can't say that I have.'

'Looks like you've missed your chance, then. Fred said he's leaving for New York first thing in the morning.'

Celie swallows a spoonful of the oatmeal she has sweetened with the maple syrup Ol' Man Forbes has brought in from Québec. 'Oh, really? Well, life goes on.'

She'd promised to go with Robson to the lake today and she'd been racking her brain for a way to escape the house on a Sunday when both Frank and Lulu would be around. She had to see him, especially after the night she'd spent, with Robson's face invading her dreams, her arms reaching out for him, the feel of his lips on hers … and more than she can bring herself to remember. She hasn't felt this way since Max, but that is a dream that will never come true.

She feels her face flush and rises to open the window. 'Did I tell you I'm going to be out all day, Frank? Ursula Brandt has invited me to go over to their farm to teach me how to make her German plum cake.'

Frank frowns. 'On a Sunday? Can't you do that kind of thing during the week?'

'Normally, yes, Frank, but I bumped into Ursula in town yesterday. She'd just seen Klaus off on the train to Edmonton. I think she'd like the company.'

'What's he doing in Edmonton? The man can barely speak English.'

Celie sits down in her chair. 'I don't know. I didn't ask.' She sips at her tea. 'Ursula hasn't been that well since her fall last winter. It seems the neighbourly thing to do to go over and keep her company for the day.'

Frank grunts. 'So, you're off to bake cake and natter while I twiddle my thumbs and do without my Sunday lunch after a hard week of work on the farm.'

Lulu looks up from her bowl of oatmeal. 'I can cook Sunday lunch, Dad. I've helped Mom plenty of times.'

'It's your mother's job, Lulu.'

Celie pushes away her bowl of half-eaten porridge. 'Frank, I'm trying to do my Christian duty and be charitable to a lonely elderly woman.'

Frank huffs. 'What about church? You haven't missed a Sunday mass since we've moved here. A waste of time if you ask me. God hasn't got time for people like us.'

'I'll go to Monday prayers tomorrow morning.'

'How are you going to get there? Freedom's fifteen miles away.'

'I'll take my bike.'

Lulu laughs. 'That'll take you hours, Mom.'

'Ursula isn't expecting me till eleven. I have plenty of time, and I can use the exercise.'

'That's for sure,' Frank says. He gets up from the table and sits in his armchair. He picks up his pipe and *The Edmonton Journal* crossword he's been working on for the past week. 'You've put on a few pounds since we married.'

Celie bites her lip as anger wells up inside her. 'Yes, well, there are worse things than gaining a few pounds, aren't there, Frank? I could be an alcoholic or a drug addict, couldn't I?' She looks over at Lulu. 'Lulu, I've got tripe hanging in the cold store. Give it a good scrub with salt and vinegar and parboil it for twenty minutes. Cook it up with some onions and parsley and vegetables for Sunday lunch.'

Lulu nods. 'I will.' She reaches for her schoolbag and unloads a notebook and a battered biology book onto the table. 'It'll give me something to do when I get bored studying for my biology exam. Do you want me to save you some?'

'No, darling. I'll keep Mrs Brandt company for Sunday lunch today. I won't get home till later this afternoon. I think I'll come home the long way. It'll give me a chance to work off some of those pounds.'

Robson McCrea parks the car under a birch tree by the lake that had given the town its name. The inky water shimmers in the morning sunlight and green-headed mallards and golden-eyed buffleheads paddle around on the rippling waves.

'Are you sure coming here is a good idea, Robson? Plenty of people come to the lake to picnic and fish, especially on a Sunday.'

He reaches over the seat and grabs a paper bag packed with food. 'I know, Fred told me. He also told me about this spot where he said no one comes because the fish like the margins over by the weed beds on the north side. No one will see us here.'

Celie nods, thanking God that the demands of the farm have seen the end to Frank's short stint working in Fred's garage. 'Fred knows an awful lot.'

'Fred only knows that I'm taking pictures for *Life Magazine*,' Robson says as he gets out of the car.

'Mr Forbes didn't ask you about all the food you were buying?'

Robson laughs as he opens Celie's door. 'Of course he did. I said I was stocking up for my train journey back to New York. Told him the train food was terrible. He threw in a packet of chocolate bourbon cookies.'

She climbs out of the car. 'He must have taken a shine to you. Lulu's the only one I know who can wheedle anything free from him.'

'He said it was a gift from one American to another.'

Celie frowns. 'Where did you put my bicycle? You didn't leave it at Fred's, did you? He'll wonder why you had it.'

'It's behind the hotel's shed with the staff bikes. No one will be the wiser.' He jiggles her arm with his elbow. 'Come on, Celie. It's our last day and it looks like it's going to be hot. Let's have our picnic and enjoy a nice day off. I'd say we earned it.'

'All right. I haven't been to the lake in years. I think I'll stick my feet in the water and have a wade.'

———————————

Robson leans back against the rock rolling a cigarette as Celie wraps up the leftovers from their picnic in wax paper and packs them back into the paper bag. She folds down the top of the bag and sits beside him on a patch of grass.

'There, all done. You should have enough to keep you going on the train until Winnipeg if you ration it.'

'Thanks, but I told you that you didn't have to do that.'

'It was my pleasure. Besides, it would be a shame to see it go to waste.' She leans against the rock and, closing her eyes, raises her face to the sun and lets the heat penetrate her skin.

'Your cheeks are flushed.'

'I don't care.'

'Won't Frank wonder about how you caught the sun today?'

'He never notices anything about me, but if he does say anything, I'll just say it was from the bike ride to Ursula Brandt's.'

Robson lights the cigarette and sucks on it until the tip glows red. He blows out a puff of smoke. 'I've made you a liar. It's not something I feel good about.'

'I'm better at it than I thought I'd be.' She opens her eyes and looks at him. 'Don't worry. I chose to come here with you today. If I had to fib, so be it. Needs must. I'll go to church, say some Hail Marys and all will be right with the world.'

'You're quite the pragmatist.'

'I've had to learn to be. I used to be more of an idealist. I thought I might, in some small way, do something to make the world a better place. I told you I was a suffragist before the war. I wrote speeches and even organised a big march to London one summer. I wanted to play a part in getting women the right to vote.'

'I can imagine it.'

'Can you? I can barely remember that girl. Then, when the war came, my father gave me his Reflex camera and encouraged me to get out into London to take pictures.'

'That was very forward-thinking of him.'

'Papa always encouraged my sisters and me to follow our dreams. He never subscribed to the opinion that women are naturally intellectually limited by their biology. He and I were very close. I think I'm the most like him in my character.'

'What did you photograph?'

'Oh, anything that caught my eye. Papa told me to think about the story I wished to tell, and experiment to find out what subjects I preferred photographing.'

'What did you discover?'

'I discovered that I like to photograph people. I like to search for the world in a person's face.'

'Do you find it?'

The memory of the teacher carrying an injured girl as she staggered out of a bombed school in London's East End during the war, the two coated in a film of grey dust, their faces masks of shock, flashes into her mind. She'd seen the world in that teacher's face that day, in the face of the child struck dumb, but she hadn't taken the picture. Maybe she would have, if Milly Smith, who lost her brother and sister in the blast, hadn't shamed her. When does taking a picture become indecent? She'd always regretted not taking that picture. Celie shrugs. 'Sometimes. Not always.'

Robson nods. 'I prefer to photograph anything but people.'

'I've noticed. It's been a good lesson for me, watching you take pictures of the landscape and the abandoned farms with their foreclosure signs and rusting farm equipment. I've realised there are stories in those kinds of images, too. Powerful stories. You've helped me open my eyes.'

They sit in companionable silence for several minutes. Robson blows out a final stream of smoke and stubs out his cigarette on the rock.

'I think you're still an idealist under that pragmatic exterior.'

'Why do you think that?'

'The way you were so incensed at the treatment of the men in the work camp. How your eyes lit up when you spoke about writing an article about it. You still want to make a difference. I can see that. You're an idealist. You haven't lost that. It's still there.'

She shrugs. 'Maybe. Sometimes it's just been hard to do anything but … survive.'

Robson scrutinises Celie from under the rim of his brown fedora. 'Why did you come here with me today, Celie?'

'Because you're leaving tomorrow, and I … and I … I suppose I wanted to make this week with you last as long as possible.'

He reaches out and threads his fingers through hers. 'I'm glad you came.' He raises her hand to his lips and kisses each knuckle, one after the other, then he turns her hand over and kisses her palm.

Her heart jumps at each press of his lips on her skin, until she is powerless to do anything but reach for him and pull him into a kiss as a loon's whooping call resonates across the lake towards its mate.

The next morning, as soon as Frank has left for the fields and Lulu has left with Ben on their bikes for the school, Celie dries the last breakfast dish and walks into the bedroom she shares with Lulu.

She opens up the wardrobe and changes from her plain flour sack dress into the blue cotton dress she wears to church on Sundays and pins a white straw hat onto her head over hair she has made some effort to fix into finger waves. Examining her face in the mirror, she bites her lips and pinches her cheeks and grimaces at the lines that encircle her blue eyes.

She moves away from the mirror and picks up her handbag and Frank's old carpetbag, which she has filled with the clothes, toiletries and the few mementos she has chosen to keep. Removing a letter from the carpetbag, she places it on the dresser beside Lulu's biology book, where she is certain to find it. Then she shuts the door behind her.

She makes it as far as the front porch when she stops. She hears a car out on the main road. She hears it stop at the junction, though, from where she is standing, it is obscured by the maple tree. Robson is there, waiting for her. Waiting to drive with her to

Edmonton, from where he will call Fred to collect the car from the train station. Waiting to take her away from West Lake for good.

Robson McCrea is waiting for her. He said he loves her and she thinks she might love him, too. But then she wonders if it is love, or simply that he is her last chance to escape this life for one full of hope and opportunity.

The rough wool of the carpetbag brushes against her leg, threatening a run in her stockings. There is a scratch at the door, then a whine and a low 'woof'. She sets down the carpetbag and opens the door. Kip stands there with his crooked black and white ears and his soft brown eyes, and he looks at her like he knows what she is doing.

She bends down and hugs the dog, burying her face in his soft fur.

'Oh, Kip. Kip, I'm so sorry. I'm so sorry.'

She hugs the dog until she hears the car's motor engage. The car's tyres crunch on the gravel as it reverses and turns back toward the town. She hugs the dog until the sound of the life she never had with Robson McCrea fades away into the distance.

Chapter Forty

Jessie

Port Said, Egypt – July 1936

The gardener, Mohammed, in the sudden absence of Mustapha and the Aston Martin, unloads Jessie's and Shani's trunks from his new truck and negotiates the transfer of the luggage to the SS *Strathnaver* with the stevedores, while Jessie checks the rear passenger seats to ensure they've left nothing behind. She holds up the woven straw handbag that had been Marta's parting gift to her daughter.

'Shani? Were you intending to leave this behind?'

Shani, petite and pretty in an expensive white straw hat and blue floral dress made up under Layla's directives by one of the Parisian couturiers in Cairo's grand Cicurel department store, spins around on the paved dock from where she's been watching the parade of fashionable passengers embark onto the gleaming white ship.

'Sorry, Mama. I forgot.'

'Shani, you have to pay attention. You won't have Marta

picking up after you anymore. I can assure you Nana Christina isn't going to.'

Shani loops the handbag over her arm and looks up at the ship's three yellow smokestacks that glint like giant sticks of rock candy in the searing sun. 'Why is the middle smokestack the only one steaming?'

Jessie glances up at the ship. 'The other two are there just for show because passengers feel more secure if a ship has more than one smokestack.'

'Baba would have said that's ridiculous.'

Jessie smiles. 'He would, wouldn't he?'

'I wish he were with us.'

Jessie brushes a wayward dark curl out of Shani's eyes. 'Me too.'

Shani looks up at her mother, her large brown eyes troubled. 'What if I don't like England? What if the girls at the boarding school don't like me?'

'Don't worry, darling. You'll be absolutely fine. And you're not going to a boarding school, no matter what Nana Christina says. You'll be going to a good day school and live at Clover Bar with me and your grandmother, so we can spend more time together. You won't have Marta around anymore, remember?'

'Nana Layla says my hair is too curly and my skin is too brown and that no one will like me in England because I'm part Egyptian.'

'Well, Nana Layla is wrong. You've inherited your father's good looks, and furthermore, Nana Layla has never been to England, so she doesn't know what she's talking about.'

'You don't like Nana Layla, do you?'

Jessie raises an eyebrow. 'Why do you say that?'

Shani shrugs. 'Marta doesn't like her either, nor do I. She's mean to Marta and Mustapha and totally ignores Mohammed.'

'You notice a lot of things.'

'I guess so. Sister Evangeline at the convent school said I was too curious for my own good and that it would only get me into trouble one day. I don't think being curious is bad, do you, Mama?'

'No, darling. I don't think it's a bad thing at all.'

A familiar voice calls through the crowd waiting to board the ship. 'Jessica! Jessica! Wait! Wait, please!'

Jessie looks down the pier to see Zara jostling through the crowds of passengers and stevedores. She stiffens as she remembers the furious words they'd exchanged the night of Aziz's death, where she'd blamed Zara for drawing Aziz into the riot, and Zara had called her a colonialist traitor for revealing the secret of her marriage.

Zara pushes past a cluster of overdressed Englishwomen. 'Jessica, I could not let you leave Egypt without saying goodbye.'

'Zara? How did you get here? We're miles from Cairo.'

Jessie's sister-in-law glances over her shoulder and Jessie follows her gaze. Isham and Mustapha emerge from the crowd. Isham nods in her direction before being engulfed in his father Mohammed's emotional embrace.

'They brought you?'

'Yes. Mustapha drove us.'

Jessie frowns. 'How long has Mustapha known about the two of you?'

'He's known from the day we married. He was a witness. He supports what we are trying to achieve in the Egypt Youth Party. It amused us that Aziz had him follow me. It made things easier for us. He drove us wherever we needed to go.'

'Auntie Zara, why didn't you invite us to your wedding?' Shani asks. 'I could have worn one of my new dresses. Have you been away on your honeymoon?'

Zara leans over and kisses Shani on her cheeks. 'Isham and I did not have a wedding ceremony, *habibti*. We simply went to the judge and had our wedding certificate signed. Then' – Zara glances at Jessie – 'then we travelled around the country to visit Isham's relatives.'

'You didn't have a wedding? All brides need to have a wedding and a lovely dress, Auntie Zara.'

'I didn't have a wedding either, darling,' Jessie says. 'Your father and I got married in an office over a butcher shop. There was a goat involved. It wasn't terribly romantic.'

Shani's smooth forehead wrinkles. 'Well, *I* want to have a wedding and a big dress and lots of guests and food and music when I get married. I'm *not* getting married with a goat.'

Zara looks at Jessie. 'You will not have to worry about Shani in this life, I think. She is a girl who knows what she wants.'

Jessie nods stiffly. 'She has a bit of Layla in her, I'm afraid.' She points over at the three men who are waiting patiently by Mohammed's truck. 'Shani, why don't you go and say goodbye to Mustapha and the others? We have a few minutes yet before we have to board the ship.'

'May I ask Mustapha to buy us some peanuts?'

'Of course.' Jessie roots into her purse and fishes out a few coins. 'Ask him to buy some for everyone.'

Zara watches Shani head toward the men. 'I shall miss her. I shall miss you both.' She takes hold of Jessie's hand. 'Jessica, I am so sorry about what I said that night after Aziz was killed. I was devastated, and I felt so guilty. If I hadn't gone off with Isham, Aziz would have never been caught in the middle of the riots looking for me. You were right to blame me. It is my fault he was there when the police starting firing on the crowd. You have every reason to hate me.'

'There's no point apportioning blame, Zara. Aziz is gone. There's nothing for it but for us all to move on.'

'Jessica, you are permitted to grieve. You need not always be the strong one. You have lost your husband, just as I have lost my brother.'

Jessie sighs wearily. 'Zara, I don't hate you. And I don't hate

Isham, although I don't understand him. I was angry that night, absolutely I was. I was in shock. I said things I shouldn't have.'

'Jessica—'

'No, let me say my piece.' Jessie rubs her forehead. 'I wanted to blame someone and you and Isham were the logical ones to blame. I said horrible things. But I've had a great deal of time to think about what happened that night. There was no sense to it. My father was killed by a German bomb one night when he went to get something from his photography shop. He was in the wrong place at the wrong time. Aziz was in the wrong place at the wrong time. It's as simple and as complicated as that.'

'I am so sorry, Jessica.'

Jessie scrutinises Zara's despondent face, noticing the dark circles under her eyes and the fine lines like parentheses framing her lips. If Zara hadn't guided her through the complexities of Egyptian life, supported her in the clinic and given Shani the love of a doting aunt, she never would have managed all these years in Cairo without considerable disasters and misunderstandings. She loves Zara. Despite everything.

'I'll miss you, Zara. You've been a good friend to me.'

Zara shakes her head. 'No, not a friend. A sister.'

Jessica smiles weakly. 'That would make Layla my mother, and I'm not certain I'd like that.'

Zara smiles. 'Yes, this is true.'

'Have you spoken to Layla about your marriage?'

Zara exhales a deep sigh. 'No. She refuses to see me. She blames me for everything.'

'I'm sorry, Zara. I could almost feel sorry for her.'

Zara wipes at a tear swelling in her eye. 'I wish that day had never happened. I wish that Aziz … that Aziz—' Her voice breaks.

Jessie hesitates for a moment, then she pulls Zara into her embrace. 'I think your fortune-teller was half right.'

'What do you mean?'

'That first time we went to the fortune-teller, she told me I would come to a divide in a path. One direction would lead to great joy and the other one to great sorrow. I chose to marry Aziz when I could have gone back to London. My marriage gave me great joy, while his death has brought me great sorrow. My decision brought me both. Perhaps you can't have one without the other.'

'Do you think so?'

'Perhaps. Now I've had to choose between staying in Cairo or following a new path, and I don't know if I'm doing the right thing. What I do know is that if I'd stayed in Cairo, I would have been terribly unhappy. Everything would have reminded me of Aziz. So, I've chosen another path. Maybe there will be joys and maybe there will be sorrows. It's called living, and you can't let a fortune-teller's prophecy frighten you into inaction. I have loved and been loved by a wonderful man. I will always carry Aziz inside my heart, but I have to live my life, and it's no longer here in Egypt.'

'I understand.' Zara smiles, her amber eyes still shining from the earlier tears. 'I wish you and Shani great happiness.'

'And I wish you and Isham the same. I hope Layla comes to accept your marriage.'

Zara pats the gentle swelling of her belly under her *jellabiya*. 'She will need to if she wishes to meet our child.'

'You're expecting?' She envelopes Zara in a hug. 'Oh, Zara! Congratulations!'

'Thank you, my sister. I did not think it was possible at the age of forty-four, but Allah has sent us this gift. It is my new path.'

―――――――

Jessie leans on the white railing of the SS *Strathnaver* and holds her face up to the salty breeze as the ship steams through the turquoise sea past the sandy limestone cliffs of Crete. Out on the water, two fishermen haul a net of gleaming silver fish into their blue-painted boat. She holds up a hand to them as the ship sails by and they wave back. Just like the day she'd been on the HMHS *Letitia* back in the summer of 1915 as it steamed through the Mediterranean to Gallipoli. Twenty-one years ago, but even now she can remember every detail – the way the blue-green waves had rippled and crested as the hospital ship had steamed through the sea; the way the sun had played a game of shadow tag with the white limestone cliffs of the islands; the fishermen bobbing benignly along in their blue boats.

She runs her hands through her short brown hair. She must stop all these maudlin memories. The war is long over. Egypt is over. Aziz is dead. At almost forty-two, the life she'd thought she'd live for ever – the life she'd loved – is over.

Her mother is waiting for them in Gibraltar to take Shani back to England, while she takes the train to Barcelona to meet Ruth for a fortnight's holiday. Then she'll head to London and whatever the future holds.

Behind her she hears the shouts and laughter of Shani and the Australian girls she's befriended playing what sounds like a very competitive game of shuffleboard. Zara is right about that at least. Shani will be fine. Her daughter is as resilient as the reed in Aesop's fable.

Jessie presses her fingers over her eyes as a jab of grief threatens to form into tears. *Oh, Aziz.* A sob rises to her throat but she swallows it down. She grips the railing and takes a deep breath. *I miss you so much, Aziz. I can't believe you're gone. Why are you making me live without you?*

She watches a gull skim along the waves and plunge into the water after a fish. It emerges victorious, a fish flapping in its yellow beak. Straightening her back, she turns away from the sea and goes to join her daughter on the shuffleboard court.

Chapter Forty-One

Jessie

Barcelona, Spain - July 18th-19th, 1936

'Jessie! Jessie! Over here!'

Jessie cranes her neck to see past a surge of excited French athletes arriving on the Paris train. She spots Ruth waving at her from beneath the large clock above one of the sweeping neoclassical arches of the grand Estació de França in Barcelona. Tucking her handbag under her arm, she grips the handle of her suitcase and edges past the horde of well-dressed foreigners streaming onto the expansive star-patterned marble concourse from the various train platforms.

She kisses Ruth on her cheeks. 'Good heavens, Ruth. It looks like half of Europe is descending on Barcelona.'

'I know. They're all here for the People's Olympiad. The Opening Ceremony is tomorrow.'

'What exactly is the People's Olympiad?' Jessie asks as they exit through the arched doors out onto the street. 'I thought the Olympics were being held in Berlin next month.'

'They are. Blast, the taxi queue is miles long. We'll have to take the tram and the Metro. Follow me.' They dodge the taxis pulling away from the taxi rank and head toward a tram stop. A tram pulls up and they clamber on board and find seats beside a foursome of tall blond Norwegians.

'So, the Olympics,' Ruth says as she pays the conductor for her two tickets. 'The Berlin Olympics are nothing short of a propaganda project for Hitler and his Nazis. A lot of athletic groups and political organisations protested, but the IOC refused to relocate the Games. So, all the groups that refused to participate in the Berlin Olympics put their heads together to create an alternative here in Barcelona.' Ruth gestures to a large poster of male and female athletes under a banner proclaiming *Olimpiada Popular* plastered to the wall of a building as the tram trundles down the street. 'Ta-da! The People's Olympiad!'

'And here I thought you'd invited me to Barcelona for a holiday.'

'Well, it's a working holiday. It's a great way of meeting people. Wait till I introduce you to the Scottish Highland dancers I met in the hotel bar the other night. We drained the bar of their single malt scotches *and* I learned what Scottish men wear under their kilt.'

'And what is that?'

'Ha! That's for me to know and you to find out. There's quite a brawny red-bearded Scot called Hamish who I'm sure would oblige.'

'I think I'll pass.'

'Probably best. Pull the cord, will you? We'll change here for the Metro. Wait till you see our hotel. I called in a favour from Salvador Dalí, whom I used to play backgammon with on the terrace there back in the day.'

'Salvador Dalí? The artist?'

'Yeah. Long story involving a zebra and a red wig.'

'Really?'

Ruth smiles at Jessie. 'There's a lot you don't know about me, Jessie. Maybe one day you'll find out.'

Hotel Colón, Plaça de Catalunya

Jessie pulls aside the thick blue damask bedroom curtains and pushes open the glazed doors to a small balcony overlooking the large circular plaza of Plaça de Catalunya. Stepping out on the balcony, she looks out at the tents pitched amongst the plaza's baroque fountains and classical statues. Ruth joins her and lights up a cigarette.

'What did I tell you, Jessie? The Hotel Colón's the best hotel in Barcelona and the Plaça de Catalunya is Barcelona's beating heart.' She gestures to a tall building topped by a square tower fronted by windows across the plaza. 'That's the Telephone Exchange over there, and we've got the best restaurants and shops right at our feet.'

Jessie fans her face against the heat of the July afternoon. 'What are the tents for?'

Ruth blows out a puff of smoke. 'Tourists who can't afford hotel rooms. The Popular Front Government in France has given workers two weeks holiday and it seems a good bunch of them have taken the trains down from Montpellier and Perpignan. I'll bet it's the first time most of them have been out of France.'

'It looks like I've come to Barcelona at the right time.'

Ruth stubs out her cigarette on the stone balustrade and gazes out at the plaza, which hums with the voices of the tourists and strains of accordion music. 'I hope so.'

Jessie glances at Ruth. 'You hope so?'

'I went over to the Telephone Exchange to file a story while you were unpacking. I met a couple of journalists I know. There was a coup by the Spanish Army in Morocco yesterday against the

Spanish Republican government there. A couple hundred people were killed and the coup has spread into southern Spain. It looks like they've taken Seville.'

'Why the coup?'

'There's been a lot of labour unrest in Spain over the past few years and a leftist Popular Front government was voted into power in February. The right, made up of the church, landowners, businessmen and a large part of the military, opposes this left-wing government. Last week, a top right-wing politician was murdered in Madrid. It was the spark that started the coup.'

'I see. Well, hopefully things will calm down.'

'Sure. They probably will.'

Jessie looks down at the excited tourists in the plaza below, where several couples have begun dancing a tango to the strains of the accordion and a violin. 'What should we do?'

'It looks like everyone is in the mood for some fun down there. I suggest we join them.'

Late that night, after an evening wandering with Ruth down the long pedestrian street of La Rambla, past shops and buildings festooned with the red flags of the socialists, the red and black flags of the anarchists, and posters announcing the Olympiad, and chatting with tourists in the queues for the food stalls hawking golden *tortilla de patatas*, crunchy *croquettes* with creamy centres, or plates of crispy fried potatoes topped with spicy tomato sauce or garlic mayonnaise, Jessie stirs sleeplessly in the comfortable bed in her hotel room. She kicks off the sheet and wanders over to the glazed doors, which she has left open in the hope of catching a breeze to cool the oppressive heat.

The night is moonless, and stars glitter in the black sky. In the plaza below, there is silence, the tourists sleeping off the evening's beers, cavas, vermouths and sangrias. Despite the buzz of excitement in the air, she couldn't help but notice the way La Rambla split the city in two – the medieval Gothic Quarter on the east side, with its towering churches and elegant hotels, restaurants, shops and clubs; and the shacks and tenements of the working-class section of El Raval on the west side.

The tourists and athletes carried a thrum of excitement with them, but beyond that, leftist street-corner orators espoused their beliefs, while locals debated the reports and rumours filtering into the city from the south. She'd experienced that same nervous energy before on the streets of Cairo. It had always been the precursor to violence. That energy was like a *djinni* released from a magic lamp. Once it had escaped, there was no getting it back in.

The shrill whine of sirens jolts Jessie from a dreamless sleep. The whine resonates around her bedroom, rushing in through the open windows like a storm. She jumps out of bed and is half-way to the windows when someone hammers at her door.

'Jessie! It's Ruth!'

She unlocks the door and Ruth bursts in, dressed in trousers and a blue shirt, her short, curly hair unbrushed.

'Get dressed. Something's going on. They've set off all the factory sirens.'

'Who's they?'

'The left, the government, the workers … anyone who's against the coup. They must have heard something. I think there's going to be trouble.'

Jessie throws open the door of her wardrobe. 'Right. I'll only be a minute.'

Ruth shuts the bedroom door and rushes over to the balcony. Below, the camping tourists are running from the plaza like cockroaches scattering under a switched-on light, urged on by armed men and women in rough clothing and the red and black neckerchiefs of the anarchists.

Shots ring out from the balconies of the floor directly above them. Ruth jumps back into the room and slams the windows shut. 'Oh my God.'

Jessie looks up at her from the bed where she is tying her shoelaces. 'What's going on?'

A bullet crashes through the bedroom window, sending splinters of glass over the floral carpet. Ruth grabs Jessie's arm and pulls her down from the bed.

'People are shooting at the anarchist militia in the square from the balconies above us. They've got machine guns. The militia are shooting back.'

The room shakes as an explosion rocks the plaza, followed by another and another.

Jessie looks over at Ruth. 'Grenades.'

Ruth nods. 'It looks like we've found ourselves in the middle of a war.'

Chapter Forty-Two

Etta

Santa Rosa Apartments, Hollywood, California - July 1936

'CJ! Where are you?'

Etta bursts into the living room. CJ looks up from his old Remington typewriter and stubs out his cigarette in an ashtray some previous tenant had pilfered from the Beverly Hills Hotel.

'What's up?'

Etta thrusts a thick yellow-jacketed book at him along with a copy of the *Los Angeles Examiner*. 'This!'

'*Gone with the Wind?*'

'Yes! David O. Selznick of Selznick Pictures has just bought the movie rights! He's launching a search for the main character, Scarlett O'Hara. I'll simply *have* to read it now!'

CJ sets the book and the newspaper down on the card table he's using as a desk and picks up a pack of Camel cigarettes. He shakes out a cigarette and picks up his lighter.

'Looks like that book'll keep you out of trouble for a while,' he says as he lights the cigarette. 'It's thicker than the LA phone book.' He nods at an envelope on the sideboard. 'Telegram came for you.'

Etta's eyes light up. 'A telegram? Do you suppose it's a callback from MGM for *Marie Antoinette?*' She picks up the envelope. 'Oh, it's from Britain.' She drops it back on the sideboard.

'Aren't you going to open it?'

Etta walks over to CJ and, taking the cigarette out of his fingers, sucks in a long drag. She shakes her platinum-waved bob and blows out a stream of smoke.

'It'll just be Mama being Mama making my life difficult. I'll read it later.'

She takes another puff and hands him back the cigarette, oblivious to the red lipstick smudges around the filter. 'The important thing is *Gone with the Wind.* Don't you understand, silly? This is finally my big chance! *I'm* Scarlett O'Hara! I feel it in my bones.'

'What makes you think you're Scarlett O'Hara? Isn't she supposed to be a Southern belle?'

'How do you know that?'

'Baby, I sit next to the entertainment editor at the *Trib*. All I've heard about for the past two weeks is *Gone with the Wind.*'

Etta grabs the book and flops onto the saggy brown sofa. 'I can play a Southern belle. I can sound as American as the next girl, after all my elocution lessons. How difficult can it be?'

'If anyone can manage it, Etta, you can.' CJ stubs out the cigarette in the dregs of his coffee and picks up the newspaper.

'Oh, no! Oh, no, no, no!' Etta throws the book down onto a worn needlepoint cushion of a cowboy on a bucking horse.

CJ looks over at Etta. 'What's up?'

'She's sixteen!'

'Who?'

'Scarlett, you idiot! The silly girl is sixteen! I'll be forty-two next month. How am I meant to play a sixteen-year-old?'

'Ah, hon,' he says, turning back to the paper. 'Don't worry, something else'll come along.'

'CJ, you don't understand. *Everyone* wants to be Scarlett. I read in Louella Parsons's column just the other day that Katharine Hepburn begged RKO to buy the film rights for her, which made Bette Davis livid because she wants the role for herself. If Mr Selznick is throwing open the auditions to anyone, then he must want a new face. *I* want to be Scarlett, CJ. I'll simply have to use every trick in the book to get it. CJ, are you listening to me?'

CJ glances over at Etta. 'Sure, honey.' He taps the front page of the newspaper. 'It's just that it's hard to take all this *Gone with the Wind* stuff seriously with what's happening over in Europe right now. Dictators in Germany and Italy and now there's just been a military coup in Spain.'

'Who cares about Europe? I'm done with Europe.'

'You should care, Etta. Your mother and daughter are in England.'

'Nothing's going on in England. Besides, Mama and Adriana are quite capable of taking care of themselves.'

CJ folds the paper and lays it on the table beside the typewriter. 'Etta, I've been thinking a lot about Europe.'

'Why? What's all that nonsense to do with you or me, or any of us over here?'

He stands up and grabs the half-empty bottle of bourbon from the sideboard and pours himself a glass. He leans against the sideboard and observes Etta as he takes a drink.

'They've got me covering local council elections, petty theft and shop openings. I'm not allowed to go near anything that smells of corruption in Hollywood, even though I've got leads on a half dozen cases, not to mention sexual assaults. I used to be a real journalist, covering real stories. I miss it, Etta. I was good at it.'

'Things change, CJ. You're making decent money at the paper. Well, it would be decent if we didn't have to give half away to that

French extortionist every month. You're the one who wanted to be a newspaper reporter, remember? If you'd kept writing screenplays, you'd probably have an Oscar by now.'

'Sure.'

Etta picks up *Gone with the Wind*. 'Be happy, CJ. You've got me. Isn't that all you really need?'

CJ drains the glass and sets it down on the sideboard beside the unopened telegram. He picks up the newspaper and joins her on the sofa, pointing to an item at the bottom of the front page.

'Read that.'

'What? Why?'

'Just read it, please.'

Etta sighs and holds the newspaper closer to her face. '*A large-scale military revolt began in Spanish Morocco and several Spanish towns Friday night. The leftist government of the Spanish Second Republic still rules in Madrid, although it is reported that Barcelona has been bombed by the rebel faction of fascists and Nationalists —* CJ, what has this got to do with us?'

'Just read a little more.'

Etta rolls her eyes. '*The rebel-held wireless station in Seville broadcast yesterday a report stating that General Francisco Franco, who heads the rebel troops, has landed in Spain from Morocco and is marching on Madrid.*'

She hands CJ the paper. 'Why do I need to know this?'

'There's going to be a war.'

'In Spain? So?'

'Etta, the fascists have to be stopped. Haven't you paid any attention to what's happening in Italy and German, or in Britain with Oswald Mosley's Blackshirts? It's even spreading here in America.'

'I don't even know what fascism is, nor do I care. I've got enough on my mind.'

CJ shakes his head and heads back over to the sideboard. He pours himself another drink.

'Fascism is a form of far-right authoritarian nationalism, which rallies around a charismatic leader like a Hitler or a Mussolini. Fascists persecute anyone who disagrees with them. It's dangerous and it's happening all around us, Etta, and people need to know. And I'm here writing crap that no one reads.'

'All right, I get it, CJ. Fascism's bad, but, sweetie, life goes on.' She tosses the newspaper into a wastepaper basket. 'How about I make us some Gin Rickeys and we head out for some Chinese food? I could kill for some shrimp chop suey.' CJ downs the last of his bourbon. 'Sure. Sounds great.'

Etta claps her hands together. 'Wonderful! I'll put on that blue dress you like and you can tell me what a wonderful Scarlett O'Hara I'll make and we can forget all about this war nonsense.'

Chapter Forty-Three

Jessie

Bar El Pi, Barcelona, Spain – October 1936

Jessie glances at her watch and peers over the Bar El Pi's wrought-iron railing beside her table on the interior mezzanine, and scans the heads of the workers celebrating the arrival of the first Soviet ship bringing food supplies to the Republic. She spears her fork into a fried potato dribbled with tomato sauce and glances at her watch again; she'd been waiting for Ruth for over an hour. Even with all the turmoil still erupting in the city's streets, it wasn't like her to be so late. Then again, Ruth may have run into one of the idealistic Americans who'd begun arriving in Spain to join the Republican fight against the fascists. It wouldn't be the first time.

She takes Shani's letter out of her trouser pocket and smooths out the paper on the marble table. She has read it so many times that she could probably recite it from memory.

September 23rd, 1936

Dearest Mama,

I hope you are well. The weather here is terribly hot and we are all sweltering in our uniforms, though we are not permitted to take off our jackets and ties even though Erica Grafton-Armstrong keeled over in maths class yesterday. Mrs Traynor told us all we simply have to 'buck up and face unpleasantness with fortitude and grace'. Thankfully, I am used to the heat in Cairo, but our dormitory mistress is very displeased by the state of my hair in this humidity. I've broken every tooth on my comb. Marta used to rub olive oil into my hair to keep it manageable, but when I asked Cook for some, she looked at me as if I were asking her to fly to the moon! I don't think they know what olives are here.

Mama, will lye soap make my skin lighter? Becky Richardson said I could sit at her table in the dining hall if I could make myself look more English. She is trying to teach me how to speak like more of an English girl. Mrs Traynor says I speak English like a foreigner and it won't do. I miss Marta and Auntie Zara and my friends in Cairo. I miss Baba and you so much too. You promised we would go to the beach in Cornwall on holiday and go to the pictures together. You said I would go to a local school and you would help me with my science homework, which is so very hard. You said you were going to Spain for a holiday for a fortnight with Miss Bellico and then you would come straight to London, but then you said you had to stay to help in the war.

Nana Christina won't go to the beach and she won't buy me a prayer mat. She said that I am a Catholic and I will go to Catholic church only now. I played with Alice and took all the Nancy Drews out of the library and re-read them all. 'The Password to Larkspur Lane' is still my favourite. Hettie took me to the pictures a few times during the summer holiday, but it's not the same as going with you or Auntie Zara. Cousin Adriana was in Italy all summer so I still haven't met her.

Mama, you promised you would only be in Spain a little while, but it has been months and months. Nana rang me at the school last night and said you're finally coming home next week. I'm so, so happy! We can start being a proper family, like you said, even though it won't be the same as before. I have been ever so lonely.

Please be careful, Mama. I miss you.

Lots of love,

Shani

PS: Nobody here pays the war in Spain much notice. The girls at school are more interested in Clark Gable's next picture. Can we go see it when you're here?

Jessie folds the letter and tucks it back into her pocket as guilt floods over her like a rising tide. She'd never intended to stay in Spain this long. She'd thought everything would settle down and she'd be on her way to England within a few weeks, but then France closed its border with Spain and the cost of flights out of the airport, if you were lucky enough to get a seat, had become extortionate.

But it won't be long now. Things had calmed down in Barcelona, with the Republican government in control of the city, and she'd booked passage on the *Ciudad de Barcelona* for Marseille, where it was stopping to collect International Brigade volunteers. She'll take the train from there to Paris, and then travel from there to London. She made a promise to Shani to start afresh in London, and she means to keep it.

'Jessie!'

Jessie gasps at the sight of her friend leaning on the bar, supported by a young Spaniard. 'Ruth!' She rushes down the staircase and elbows her way through the men and women dressed in workers' blue overalls. Ruth's cheek is bloody and her left arm has been secured in a sling fashioned from an anarchist's red and black neck scarf.

'My God, Ruth. What happened?'

'It's not as bad as it looks, Jessie. I was just in the wrong place at the wrong time.'

'It was an argument between the Trotskyists and the Stalinists,' the Spaniard says in fluent, though heavily accented, English.

'They disagree who should be the leading Communists in the fight against the Nationalists.'

Ruth grimaces. 'This war is making some strange bedfellows, Jessie. I was down at the harbour trying to find out something about the Russian ship and things got heated. Antonio pulled me out of the thick of things and wrapped up my arm.'

Jessie glances at the young Spaniard. 'Thank you. You needn't stay. I can take it from here.' She turns back to Ruth. 'Let's get you back to the hotel and let me look at your arm.'

'Later, Jessie. I have one priority right now, and that's to have a very large glass of whisky.'

Antonio Rey, who looks no more than twenty-five in Jessie's estimation, returns from the bar with an uncorked bottle of red wine and three glasses and proceeds to pour out the dark ruby wine.

Jessie shakes her head. 'I shouldn't. I'm going over to the hospital tomorrow to help with their blood drive.'

Ruth pushes a glass across the table toward Jessie. 'All the more reason to fortify yourself, then we can go back to the hotel and you can patch me up. I'm sure Antonio would like his scarf back.'

The young Spaniard sits back in his chair as he takes a drink of wine. 'What brought you to Barcelona, Jessica? Do you like danger?'

She glances at Ruth. 'I blame Ruth. She persuaded me to have a holiday in Barcelona while I was on my way back to England from Egypt. My mother met me and my daughter in Gibraltar to take her back to London, and I hopped on the train to Barcelona. I was only meant to be here for a fortnight. We were staying in the Hotel Colón when the revolution started. I'm a doctor, so I stayed. I thought I'd be of more use here than in London.'

The barman approaches and places plates of sardines, bread and a shallow dish of olive oil on the table. Jessie tears off a corner of bread and dips it into the oil. Antonio leans forward and takes a piece of fish. 'I am afraid you are right.'

Ruth splashes more wine into her glass. 'Jessie ran a health clinic in Cairo with her husband.'

'Your husband is in England now?'

Jessie takes a drink of wine. 'He died. Last November.'

'I am sorry for that.'

'Thank you.'

'How old is your daughter?'

'Fourteen.'

'I have a sister the same age. Teresa. A brother as well, Luis. He is seventeen and has just joined the CNT anarchists. Just like me.'

Jessie watches him dip a slice of bread into the oil. 'What do you do, when you're not fighting for the anarchists?'

Antonio scrutinises at her as he chews the bread. 'I am an architect. I studied English at university because I thought it might be useful one day. It seems I was right.' He reaches for another sardine. 'I heard Ruth shout some very rude things in English at the Stalinists today, and I had to see what that was about. And now I have met an English woman doctor.' He tears off another piece of bread and dips it in the olive oil. 'It has been an interesting day.'

He swallows the oily bread and pushes away from the table. 'I must go.'

'Wait,' Jessie says. 'What about your neck scarf?'

'I will get another.'

She watches him as he stamps down the stairs and out past the bar.

'He's young, Jessie.'

Jessie laughs. 'Don't be silly, Ruth. That's the last thing on my mind. Besides, I'm leaving for London next week. I've booked passage on a boat to Marseille.'

'You're leaving? Now? But we need you here, Jessie. The situation's getting worse. Cities all over Spain are falling to Franco's Nationalist forces. Franco's marching on Madrid. It's only a matter of time before he heads north to Barcelona. We need trained doctors, and you've got war experience. You can't leave.'

'I promised Shani, Ruth.'

'Shani's resilient. She'll be fine. Isn't she away at boarding school? You won't even see her except on holidays. What are you going to do? Take out tonsils and patch up broken bones? Anyone can do that. Not everyone can be a field doctor. You can.'

'I know. It's just that I've missed out on so much of Shani's life already. She's growing up so fast, and I barely have a relationship with her.'

Ruth nods. 'Look, why don't you hold off going back till Christmas? It's only a couple of months away. Stay at least till then. It'll give Shani something to look forward to.' Jessie chews her lip. Maybe … maybe … no, she promised Shani.

'I can see the wheels turning in your head, Jessie. Look, it's entirely up to you. It's just that…' Ruth shakes her head. 'Never mind. I get it, I do. No one would think badly of you if you went home. You have another life to live.'

Jessie expels a heavy breath. Ruth's right. What's she going to do back at King's College Hospital in London? Surely Shani will understand when she explains it to her.'

'All right. I'll stay. Just till Christmas. I can help the hospital get set up in case the Nationalists attack the city at some point. Train them in war triage. Hopefully, it won't come to that with the International Brigades pouring into Spain to help the Republicans. I'll make it up to Shani.'

'That's more like it,' Ruth says as she downs the last of her wine. 'Let's get back. I seriously need a bath and proper arm sling.'

Jessie nods and helps Ruth down the stairs. She'll take the first train back to London for Christmas. She'll join the surgical staff at

King's College Hospital like she'd planned, buy a little house near her mother's as soon as Aziz's money is released from Egypt, and she and Shani will start their new lives properly. She'll make Shani her top priority, absolutely.

She'll make everything up to her daughter. Shani will understand.

Chapter Forty-Four

Christina

Clover Bar, Hither Green, London – December 1936

'Hettie, do stop your stomping around and settle down. The King's coming on the BBC any moment.'

'Cryin' shame, I say. Poor bloke can't choose 'is own wife in this day and age.'

'She's an American, Hettie,' Christina says as she turns up the volume knob on the wood-cased Steepletone wireless. 'A *divorced* American. She can't possibly be queen. It would be an abomination.'

Hettie tuts as she settles into Gerald's favourite armchair. 'Poor man, 'aving to put up wiff all this rubbish in the papers.'

'Ssh, Hettie! History is occurring and I can't hear a word the King is saying.'

'I'm just saying that 'e and she 'ave been treated like criminals, when all they've done is fall in love.'

Christina huffs. 'The King should have had more sense than to pursue a relationship with an American divorcée. It's all the WI have been talking about at our meetings. It's no wonder the Christmas tombola is in such a shambles. You have remembered to make cherry cake for my meeting with Ellen Jackson and Mildred Chadwick here tomorrow to sort out the mess? A Saturday morning, no less, when I have so much shopping still to do, what with both Adriana and Shani here for Christmas. I worry they won't get on. Adriana is so wilful and Shani so spoiled. I blame my own daughters, of course. Jessica and Etta are far too wrapped up in themselves for motherhood. That is the one thing they have in common. I had hoped that Jessica would be back from Spain by now, but she's just taken on a temporary position at a hospital in Barcelona. Shani is most upset about it, which is another thing I shall have to deal with at Christmas.' She frowns. 'Do you suppose this will be Shani's first Christmas? I can't imagine they had a Christmas tree and roast goose for Christmas in Cairo.'

Hettie points at the wireless. 'I 'aven't 'eard a word the poor bloke's been saying, with you rabbiting on.'

'I'm trying to envisage what our Christmas will be like this year, Hettie. Jessica is insisting I buy Shani a prayer mat. Where am I meant to buy something like that?'

'Liberty's 'as a good rug department.'

Alice rubs against Christina's leg and Christina leans over and places him on her lap. 'Adriana is quite keen to have me invite Mr Brandt for Boxing Day lunch. They did seem to get on when he came for dinner on Harvest Sunday. She rather ignored poor Shani, who'd been so looking forward to meeting her cousin. Still, I expect a fourteen-year-old girl holds little interest for a twenty-one-year-old woman. Certainly not as much interest as a handsome young German.'

'Sshhhh!'

Christina sighs. 'You remember Max Fischer, don't you, Hettie? I was terribly worried Cecelia was going to run off to Germany with him, but then the war and that nice Frank Jeffries came along. He was so much the better choice. She's doing awfully well out in Canada, you know. I had a lovely Christmas letter from her. Louisa is top of her class, Cecelia's writing for the local newspaper and Frank has become a dab hand at farming. Apparently, they haven't been affected by the Depression out there in the least.'

Hettie grimaces and leans closer to the wireless. Alice rolls over onto his back, purring as Christina rubs him under his chin.

'I haven't heard from Etta, of course. I'll likely receive a dashed-off note in the New Year. Do you think I should invite Hans Brandt to Boxing Day lunch? I'm of two minds about it. I mean, he is German, after all, and I shall never forgive them for Gerald's passing.'

Hettie shrugs. 'What can it 'urt? You'll 'ave more food than you'll know what to do wiff after Christmas lunch. I'm down at my sister's in Worving for Boxing Day, in case you're forgetting.'

'Oh, heavens, yes. I had forgotten. Well, the girls will have to make peace with each other and help with Boxing Day lunch. I was hoping Jessica might come home for Christmas at the very least, but she seems determined to stay out in Spain patching up soldiers. I simply can't get my head around the war in Spain. I've never understood why Jessica has always felt the need to be in the middle of such things. She had a perfectly good position lined up at King's College Hospital.'

A sob wrenches out of Hettie's throat.

'Hettie? Are you all right?'

The housekeeper dabs at her eyes with her apron. 'It's just so bleedin' sad. 'E would 'ave made a lovely king.'

Christina hands Hettie her handkerchief. 'Oh, and scones as well, Hettie. You will bake some scones in the morning for my WI meeting? They always go over terribly well.'

Part VI

1937

Chapter Forty-Five

Jessie

Hospital Clinic de Barcelona, Spain – May 1937

May 2nd, 1937

J essie sits down at a table in the hospital canteen with her tray
of the ubiquitous garlicky porridge called *gachas*, bread and
coffee, and takes Celie's letter out of her skirt pocket, still
amazed that it had found its way to her at the Hotel Oriente all the
way from Canada, even if it did, judging by the postmark, take
almost two months to arrive. She slits open the envelope with her
knife and slides out the letter.

Sweet Briar Farm,
*   West Lake, Alberta*
*   Canada*

March 15th, 1937

Dear Jessie,

How are you managing out in Spain? I read about it in The Edmonton Journal in the local library and hope you're keeping yourself safe. It sounds like an awful affair. Do be careful. You have always been one to get yourself into the thick of things, haven't you?

Jessie, my wonderful sister, you have no idea how grateful I am for your wire of £10 which I collected from Forbes's General Store this morning. Imagine my astonishment when Mr Forbes told me I had received an international money transfer through Western Union!

When Frank and I left Britain for Canada after the war, he was convinced we'd build a prosperous new life out here, but it seems that we jumped from the frying pan into the fire. I know I have unburdened myself to you over the years, and I do carry some guilt for that. It has been dreadful, that's the long and short of it, but I chose my destiny and I don't feel I have any right to complain or to tax you or Mama with my burdens.

Please don't worry about us out here. We will manage. I am a Fry sister, after all.

With love, affection and the deepest gratitude,

Celie

PS: Here's a photo of Lulu (and Kip, of course) and me with her friend Ben Wheatley and his mother, Mavis, my best friend out here. I know I've mentioned them often in my letters, and I thought you'd like to put some faces to their names.

Jessie slides the letter back in the envelope. She'd had a feeling that things weren't right with Celie out in Canada. She'd been reading in the foreign newspapers at the Gezira Sporting Club that the devastating North American drought combined with vicious heatwaves and the Depression were now contributing not only to homelessness and financial hardship, but to deaths as well. She'd felt certain that Celie and her family must be suffering, but Celie was rarely one to complain. Her sister is so stoic that she would march a thousand miles without mentioning once that she had worn through her shoe leather.

Aziz had left her and Shani well provided for in his will, though much of his money is still tied up in the knot of the Egyptian banking system, and proving virtually impossible to transfer out of the country. Her mother insisted on paying for Shani's tuition as a boarder at Woldingham until she got back to Britain, and with her share of her father's legacy, and her savings from her medical salary that she'd taken out of Egypt in cash, she had enough to help Celie out.

Etta, on the other hand … well, Etta is another story. Giving Etta money is like watching it sweep down a drain in a rainstorm. Another rainstorm, another pleading letter from Etta, and more money down the drain in an endless cycle of entitlement and waste. The best thing she can do for Etta is not to prop her up, though it is probably of no use. Etta will always find someone to lean on, like that American writer she lives with. Etta is one of life's users, and that is something Jessie finds difficult to accept, particularly from a twin sister.

May 3rd, 1937

The following afternoon, Jessie is half-way down La Rambla after visiting the food market, where she is pleased to have found goat's cheese, eggs and fresh bread, when she hears several rifle shots ahead of her. She ducks behind the thick grey trunk of a plane tree and spies several youths in anarchist neck scarves edging up a side street as they exchange fire with someone in a church tower. There is a lull, then shots fly from the tower, slamming into the cobblestones and sending a crowd of afternoon shoppers running down La Rambla away from the sniper.

Jessie hides behind the tree as the shopkeepers slam down

their steel shutters. At the entrance to the side street, the anarchists are joined by several others who collect at the street entrance, shouting at people not to cross the line of fire.

'What's happening?' she shouts in Catalan at a woman running by, carrying a dead rabbit by its ears, but the woman ignores her in her rush to reach the entrance to the Metro across the street.

Someone grabs her elbow. 'Come, you have to get out of here.'

She jerks her head around and sees the young Spanish architect she'd met the day Ruth had broken her arm. He is wearing the anarchist neck scarf and carrying a rifle.

'What's happening? Is it the Nationalists?'

'No. The government's Assault Guards are trying to take control of the Telephone Exchange from the anarchists. They claim our operators have been listening in on their conversations.'

'What does that matter? You're both on the same side.'

'Yes and no. The anarchists are fighting alongside the Republican government against the Nationalist fascists in the Civil War. But our ultimate goal is revolution. We do not see any reason to wait until the Civil War is over to pursue this fight against the Republican government if they seek to squash the gains we have achieved since last July.'

'You're talking about a war inside a war.'

'If necessary. The government cannot be allowed to take the control of the Telephone Exchange away from us. The workers of Barcelona, most of whom support us, will not permit it. Our presence there symbolises hope for people who have been oppressed for far too long.'

Another spate of shots rings out from the side street and Antonio grabs Jessie's hand.

'Come with me. It's not safe here. We must get you back to your hotel.'

Inside the Hotel Oriente, the lobby heaves with a motley collection of people – residents and others who have taken refuge from the escalating violence outside. A group of foreign journalists in fedoras huddles by the bar drinking whisky; a barrel-bodied Russian smokes a pungent cigar as he holds court with a pair of anxious Spanish Communists; a dark-haired young Spanish woman with a rifle slung across her shoulder pushes her way toward a group of anarchists who are clustered around a table in deep consultation; and two swarthy French lorry drivers, stranded in the city by the closure of the roads north to France, are selling oranges from their cargo at what appear to be eye-watering prices judging by the arguments and objections of their prospective customers. Jessie spies Ruth sitting at a table, writing and smoking.

'Ruth!' she shouts, waving. She turns to Antonio. 'Thank you for getting me here in one piece, though it really wasn't necessary. I'm perfectly capable of taking care of myself. I've been through a war and a revolution before.'

'So you've said.'

Ruth joins them by the telephone cubicle. 'It looks like things are kicking off. I've just been in Plaça de Catalunya. The Assault Guards are everywhere and there's a crowd gathering in the Plaça. They're building barricades from the cobblestones and the police are taking up positions on the rooftops.'

'*Hóstia!*' Antonio swears. 'I have to go. You should both stay here. It is not safe outside.'

Ruth grunts as they watch him push through the doors out into the street. 'Fat chance of that.' She stuffs her notebook and pencil into the canvas bag she has slung across her body. 'I'm a journalist. It's my job to go out and get the story.'

'I'm coming, too, Ruth. I'm a doctor. It's my job to go out and clean up the mess everyone else makes.'

May 5th, 1937

Jessie looks up from the reception desk she has commandeered in the lobby of an abandoned hotel in a side street near Plaça de Catalunya, and points to a box of bandages that a young anarchist has just delivered.

'Change the dressings on the girl with the head wound, would you, Ester?' she shouts in broken Catalan over the racket of gunfire echoing across the Plaça to one of the two nurses who have joined her from the Hospital Clinic de Barcelona. 'Be sure to clean it well with soap and water and use a little of the iodine Comrade Rey brought us.'

The nurse nods. 'I will do my best, but the poor girl will never find a husband now.'

'I think that is the least of her worries at the moment, Ester.'

Jessie looks over at the second nurse, who has just finished sponging the face of an injured Trotskyist of about sixty, and who has proven herself to be fearless in the search for supplies in the abandoned shops. 'Ginebra, see if you can find us more aspirin and iodine in the pharmacy down the street. Be careful. Don't go near the Plaça and stay by the buildings.'

'Don't worry about me. I am as careful as a cat in a fish shop.'

'Cats have nine lives, Ginebra,' Ester says to the younger nurse.

Ginebra grabs an empty flour sack from a stack on the floor. 'Then I have at least six left, Ester,' she says as she heads for the door. 'Meow.'

Jessie heads over to the cot where a young, red-haired communist who looks no more than eighteen lies shivering under the blanket despite the May heat. She wrings out a cloth and presses it against the boy's forehead.

'His fever is worse,' she says to Ester. 'We have to get him to the hospital.'

Ester winces as bullets ricochet off a cobblestone outside the hotel. 'Good luck with that. Haven't you noticed? There isn't a soul out on the streets, and I don't blame them. They'll only come out after sunset once the shooting stops.'

'Then we'll have to find someone to take him to the hospital. He's only going to get worse here. Aspirin isn't going to help him. An infection is setting into his wound, despite everything we've done.'

The hotel door slams open, and the din of the street fighting roars into the lobby. Antonio Rey and another young anarchist stagger inside carrying a girl of about fifteen dressed in the blue overalls of a revolutionary. The girl's blood-soaked left leg has been roughly splinted with a piece of wood and two belts.

'Jessica. Please, we need your help. It's my sister, Teresa.'

'Your sister?' Jessie waves them inside and points to an empty cot. 'Put her there.'

The two men lay the girl down and Ester joins Jessie beside the cot.

Antonio wipes his bloody hands on his trousers. 'My brother Luis was with her at the barricades on Carrer de Pelai. Someone was shot and part of the barricade collapsed on her when he fell. It is his blood, not hers.'

Jessie gently unstraps one of the belts as Teresa tries to stifle a moan. 'She should be in school, not fighting behind a barricade. This is madness.'

The girl grabs Antonio's hand. 'I'm sorry, Antonio. I didn't mean to get hurt. I only wanted to shoot the Assault Guards.'

'Teresa, you are not even out of school. It is not a fight for you.'

'But Luis is fighting and he's only seventeen.'

'Luis is a man.'

'He's not a man! He's a boy!'

'Oh, for heaven's sake,' Jessie says as she cuts though the leg of the girl's trousers. 'If you want to fight, Antonio, then go! If you're lucky, someone will bring you here when you get shot. Then you can join your sister and be a happy family together.'

May 7th, 1937

'It is over, Jessica.'

Jessie looks up from the reception desk where she sits alone, writing in a notebook, the two nurses having gone to the hospital in search of more plaster for casts. 'Good. I'm glad.'

Antonio shuts the hotel door. He takes off his black beret and runs his hands through his hair as he exhales a sigh of exhaustion. 'Good? We are overrun by Assault Guards the Republican government has sent from Valencia, and you are glad? Do you know what this means for the workers' revolution? It is a disaster.'

Jessie sets down her pencil. 'Antonio, I have seen more bloodshed and death in these past five days than I've seen since the Great War. And for what? I don't understand any of this infighting. The Nationalists must be rubbing their hands in glee to see you fight amongst each other.'

'We are not fighting for nothing, Jessica.' Antonio sets down his rifle beside the reception desk. 'I believe there are better ways we can live than by the fears and the restrictions put upon us by the church and by the capitalists.'

'What do you believe in, if not God?'

'I never said I do not believe in God. It is organised religion I do not believe in.'

'Well, that is something we can agree on. I feel the same way, although I was never able to express it to my Muslim husband or Catholic mother.'

She sits back in her chair and scrutinises Antonio, taking in his dirty clothes, his unshaven face, and the grime ground into his skin by the five days of street fighting. 'What do you think will happen now?'

He pulls a chair up to the desk. 'Now? Now we know that the

anarchists of the street like me who wish for revolution, and the anarchist ministers in the government who tell us to wait until after the war for the revolution, cannot act with a single voice. These last few days have shown that there are a great many cracks in the Republican side in the war against Franco's Nationalists. I do not know how the war will end, but I believe you are right. The Nationalists will take advantage of our divisions. It has been a failure on every level.'

'I believe all war is a failure, ultimately. I only wish we could find another way to solve our disputes and disagreements.'

Antonio reaches across the desk and takes hold of Jessie's hand. 'Thank you for taking care of my sister. I would never have forgiven myself if anything had happened to her. She is resting at home now. She is making my mother's life a misery and counts the days until she receives crutches. She is threatening to take her rifle and hobble over to a barricade to "fight against the oppressive bastards".' He smiles.

Jessie slips her hand away from his. 'It's what I do. Teresa will need to wear her leg cast for at least six weeks. If you let me know your address, I'll check on her every week.'

His dark eyes flick over Jessie's face. 'If I tell you my address, my mother will tell you everything about me.'

'You're young. There can't be much to tell.'

'I am twenty-six and I am an architect and an anarchist. Now you know everything you need to about me.' He leans across the desk and brushes his lips against hers. Jessie pulls away and stares at him in shock. Then, she reaches for him and kisses him fully on his lips.

She releases him and sits back abruptly, pressing her lips together in an effort to still the desire that has flared inside her. 'I'm sorry. I shouldn't have done that.'

'There is something else you should know about me, Jessica.'

'What's that?'

'That I am falling in love with you.'

'That isn't wise.'

'Call me a fool, then.'

'You're a fool, Antonio Rey.'

He presses his mouth against hers and Jessie pulls him into her embrace. They kiss until the memories of the past five days of bloodshed and violence dissolve into a passion that engulfs them both like a cleansing fire.

Chapter Forty-Six

Jessie & Etta

Hotel Oriente, Barcelona, Spain – June 1937

5, Santa Rosa Apartments,
  Hollywood, California

May 25th, 1937

Dear Jessie,

Let me tell you my news! I've just had a screen test for 'Gone with the Wind'! I expect you must have heard about the book, even in Egypt and Spain. It's all everybody's talking about here in the States. MGM are auditioning everyone, from salesgirls to movie legends. Of course, I jumped at the chance. I knew that with a wig and a juice diet I could play Scarlett O'Hara as well – no, better – than anyone.

Let me tell you what happened. I arrived at MGM Studios and was transformed into a blushing Southern belle by the hair and make-up department – they gave me a black wig which I felt washed me out *terribly but they said Scarlett would never have been a platinum blonde. Well, one has to suffer for one's craft, and I insisted on extra pancake make-up to hide the shadows it cast under my eyes. The make-up team were pleased with my hazel eyes which they said worked perfectly as Scarlett's green eyes.*

Then I was sent off to the costume department where I was pulled and tugged into a corset. After the juice diet, I'm the tiniest I've ever been since I was eighteen, but no amount of effort was going to squash my figure into Scarlett's seventeen-inch waist! They did their best, and, after dressing me in a lacy white gown, which made me look like one of Mama's lampshades, herded me off to the soundstage to a room set up to look like a sitting room in an elegant plantation house. Then Mr Cukor, a very famous director – he just made 'Camille' with Greta Garbo – came in to direct the scene with me and a handsome actor, whose name I quite forget. I was doing so well, then Mr Cukor started telling me, right in the middle of the scene, to: 'Do it more quietly, more gently, with more mood.' He quite threw me off my stride! I had to start all over, then, when I'd said the lines just as he wanted, he told me to do it again because my face was so hard! Honestly, Jessie, I don't believe he knew what he wanted.

Of course, being a professional, I kept smiling and did as I was told, and I have every reason to think that I will be one of the top contenders for Scarlett once they're done with all the screen tests. I expect to be called back any day for a scene with Clark Gable. Can you imagine?! I'm so glad I came to Hollywood! It is so much more thrilling than dull old Hither Green, London.

That's all my news for now. You'll be the first to know when I get the part (I believe in being positive!). Be careful out there in Spain, and come visit me in Hollywood when you're done with fixing up soldiers. We'll have such fun! I'll introduce you to Clark Gable!

All my love,

Your twin,

Etta

PS.: You couldn't see your way to loaning me $100 could you? I

could really use the money and CJ is being such an old pinchpenny. I'll
pay it back, don't worry!

'There we go,' Jessie says. 'I was waiting for her to ask me for money. Etta always does.'

Ruth tops up their glasses with the whisky one of the Irish members of the International Brigades had left behind before meeting his fate in the battle for control of the Barcelona Telephone Exchange the previous month.

'Bless Etta,' Ruth says as she hands Jessie back her glass. 'She does love living in her own little bubble.'

'Etta's always been like that. She used to swan about pretending to be Lillian Gish when we were younger. You should have seen the look on Mama's face when she wore harem pants and a *tarbouche* to Sunday dinner once.' Jessie makes a face of frozen horror at Ruth.

Ruth laughs. 'I'd advise you to do that if we're ever stopped by the Nationalists. They'd run a mile.' She takes a drink and scrutinises Jessie. 'I know I've said it before, but I can't believe you're twins. I've never met two more different people. You have absolutely nothing in common.'

Jessie sets down her half-empty glass on the card table which serves as her desk. 'I used to think that, but now I'm not so sure.'

'What do you mean?'

Jessie walks over to the tall, elegant French doors, which she has opened to air out the summer humidity, and steps out onto the small balcony. Below her, La Rambla runs through the city like an artery supplying blood to its heart. But now, instead of wealthy Catalans in the latest Paris fashions, the scene is of workers – women as well as men – in the white shirts, blue overalls and black berets of the anarchists and Republicans, going about their day in buildings draped with red communist flags or the black and red flags of the anarchists. She turns around and leans against the ornate iron railing, smiling at Ruth, who is stretched out on the double bed.

'Ruth, do you think I'm selfish?'

'What? You set up a health clinic in Cairo, and now you're here patching up people in the middle of a war. How can that be selfish?'

'I had a letter from Shani the other day. She's having a miserable time at the boarding school. She says the girls pick on her because she's dark. I thought it would stop once they got to know her, but she says it's only gotten worse.'

'Girls that age can be mean. I went through that, too. I still come up against it back in the States. It seems that women of colour aren't meant to have dreams and aspirations. I've had to fight every step of the way to get where I am now. I'm afraid Shani may have to do the same thing.'

'It's not easy being a woman in this world.'

'No, it isn't. Even harder if you're a Black woman.'

'Yes, I imagine that's true. Oh, Ruth, I worry about Shani. I'd promised her that we'd live together at Clover Bar with Mama, that she'd go to a local school and we'd spend more time together. I left her to be raised by Marta and Zara in Cairo and now she's being raised by Mama and Hettie in London. I'm a terrible mother. I wanted so much to make it up to her.'

'I'm sure Shani understands why you stayed in Spain. You're a doctor and you're needed here.'

'Shani said she hates England. She wants to go back to Cairo.'

'She'll come around, Jessie. Shani's tougher than you give her credit for. She had to put up with Layla, didn't she?' Ruth reaches for the whisky bottle and splashes the liquor into their glasses. She rises from the bed and, joining Jessie on the balcony, hands her a glass. Jessie takes a sip of the cheap whisky.

'She's accused me of abandoning her, Ruth.' She shakes her head. 'I don't know what to do. I can't go back to Cairo. But I can't go back to London right now, either. The truth is I'm dreading going back to London. I don't want an ordinary life there. I'm worried that the routine and the dullness will swallow me up. It's why I left in the first place. I love Shani and I want us to be together, but I want to stay here for as long as I can. I feel alive here. Does that make me a terrible mother?'

'Of course not. You'll have plenty of time to spend time with Shani when this is over.'

Jessie takes a larger gulp of the liquor, shuddering as it burns its way down her throat. 'It doesn't make me feel any better now.'

'Then go.'

Jessie stares at Ruth. 'Go?'

Ruth shrugs. 'If you feel so bad, just go. Go to London.'

Jessie looks out at the busy street below. 'There's a war on.'

'There are always wars on somewhere.'

'But I'm needed here. I feel useful.'

'You could be useful in a London hospital.'

'It's not the same.'

'What's different? You patch people up and send them on their way. You can do that here or in London.'

She looks over at Ruth. 'The truth is I enjoy it here. I know that must sound horrible, with this war going on. I like … I like the adventure. I live for the adventure. I know I have to go back to London, eventually. But not now, not yet, not when I'm needed here.'

'So why all this soul-searching?'

'Because as much as I love my daughter, I feel like I'm failing her.' A sob rasps against her throat. 'I'm an awful person. Selfish, selfish, selfish.'

Ruth takes Jessie into her arms. 'For God's sake, Jessie. You're not an awful person. You're meant to be here. Aziz would have understood that.'

Jessie wipes at her eyes. 'You're right. Aziz would have understood. I miss him so much.'

'He was the best of men.' Ruth reaches out to brush a strand of hair off Jessie's wet cheek. 'And you're the best of women.'

Jessie smiles. 'I think you've had enough whisky. You're getting hyperbolic.'

'I'm only saying what I've always thought, Jessie. From the very first time I met you. Do you remember? In Lord Carnarvon's tent at the Tutankhamun dig?'

'I remember. This woman with wild hair burst into the tent and sent Howard Carter running off to the safety of his mummies and then we all drank gin and tonics. Lady Evelyn certainly knew how to throw a dinner party in the desert.'

Ruth laughs. 'That was a fun time.'

'It was.' Jessie drinks the last of her whisky. Ruth takes the glass from her and licks at a drop of the whisky dripping down the side. She sets the two glasses down on the balcony. Reaching over to Jessie, she cups her face in her hands and kisses her.

Jessie feels the softness of Ruth's lips, so different from Aziz's warm, affectionate kisses, or Antonio's hungry, passionate kisses, or the revolting probing tongue of Archie Winter's assault all those years ago, and gives into the curious sensation for a brief moment before she pulls away.

'I'm sorry, Ruth. I … I'm not that way.'

Ruth looks at Jessie, her face etched with yearning. 'I love you, Jessie. I've always loved you.'

'I love you, too, Ruth. You're like a sister to me.'

'I was hoping for something more than that.'

'Ruth, I can't. I … I don't feel that way.'

Ruth's expression hardens. 'It's Antonio, isn't it?'

'I don't want to talk about Antonio. He's just a boy.'

'That's the thing, isn't it? He's a boy.' Ruth stomps back into the room. Grabbing the black beret she'd filched from a drunken mercenary in the International Brigades off the door hook, she slams it on her head.

'Ruth—'

'It's fine, Jessie. I understand. We'll just be friends, like we always were. Sisters, even, if you like. But I don't imagine Antonio will ever understand you or love you like I do. I don't think even Aziz ever did. I'm glad you're going to Madrid. It will be good not to see you for a while.'

Chapter Forty-Seven

Celie

Sweet Briar Farm, West Lake, Alberta, Canada - July 1937

Lulu takes a clothes peg out of her mouth and stabs it over a tea towel on the clothesline.

'Mom?'

'Yes, darling?'

'So, I was thinking that I'd like to apply for nursing school at the University of Alberta next year after I graduate from school. I mean, I know it'll cost money...' Her voice trails off as she squeezes excess water from the bottom of the quilt.

Celie throws a white sheet over the clothesline and pats down the damp wrinkles. 'That sounds like a wonderful plan, Lulu. We'll see what we can do.'

'Really? Are you sure?'

She smiles at her daughter. 'Don't worry, Lulu. We'll find a way.' Celie pegs up a wet towel. How can she tell Lulu they can't afford to send her to nursing college? That her dreams may just have to remain dreams? They're three months behind on their mortgage repayments with no foreseeable way to pay until the wheat is harvested and sold in the autumn, and the knowledge weighs on her like a sack of bricks.

She is too embarrassed to ask Jessie for more money after her sister had been so recently generous, and her mother has her hands full paying for Shani's boarding school and Adriana's postgraduate year studying sculpture and painting at Les Beaux-Arts de Paris. And Etta is definitely not an option, given her frequent begging letters.

Lulu surveys the bone-dry fields across the road, where the new wheat waves limply in the hot Chinook wind blowing down from the Rockies. 'I understand if I have to wait, Mom. I know how hard it's been for you and Dad. I've got myself a job as a maid at the hotel starting the beginning of August. I can do it on weekends and after school from September.'

'A maid? Are you sure you know what a feather duster looks like?'

'I know. I promise I'll do better. It's just that housework is so boring.' She sticks out her chin at the wheat fields and stamps her foot, stirring up a cloud of dust. 'Bloody, bloody, bloody stupid drought.'

'Lulu! Language.'

'Dad says it.'

'Your father is under a great deal of strain.'

'I can't wait to get out of this place. I want to see the world.'

Celie glances over at her daughter, who, at seventeen, is small and sturdy and sensible, choosing to eschew the popular marcel-waved hairdos for a practical pageboy that frames her heart-shaped face and highlights her striking blue eyes.

'You remind me of your Auntie Jessie. She was just like you at your age. She couldn't wait to get out of London.'

'I think Auntie Jessie is amazing. Imagine being a doctor out in Spain!'

'She's in the middle of a war, Lulu. I don't imagine it's terribly romantic.'

Lulu shrugs. 'I know. Anywhere seems better than here. I wish you and Dad had stayed in England. I wish you'd never come here.'

'You don't mean that.'

'I do.'

'Then you'd never have met Ben or Hans or' – Celie gestures to the old dog who is snoozing on the porch – 'Kip.'

'I guess.' Lulu jerks her head up at the sky, where grey clouds are sweeping in. 'Did you feel that?'

Celie pegs the last dress to the clothesline. 'Feel what?'

Lulu holds out her hand and a large raindrop splashes onto her palm. 'Mom! It's raining! It's raining, Mom!'

Celie looks up at the sky. The raindrops touch and slide against her face like soft kisses. She holds open her arms to the deluge and laughs.

'It's raining, Lulu!' She grabs Lulu's hands and swings her around in a dance.

'It's raining! It's raining!' they shout as the rain pelts onto the dusty earth around their dancing feet.

Six days later

Celie holds out the teapot to Frank, who is dipping a slice of unbuttered toast into a soft-boiled egg.

'More tea, Frank?'

He nods, watching as she fills his teacup. 'We'll be drinking Earl Grey again before long, Celie. Mark my words. Six inches of rain in three days and more to come. It's going to be a good wheat year. We'll be back on our feet before you know it.'

Lulu looks up from her boiled egg. 'Dad, do you think everything will be back to normal by next year?'

'Next year?' He rubs his finger and thumb together. 'Honey, we'll be cashing in a great harvest this autumn. I can feel it in my bones.'

Celie spreads honey from Ol' Man Forbes's new beehives on her toast. 'Best not to count our chickens, Frank.'

'That's just like you, isn't it, Celie? Throwing cold water on good news.'

'Frank, I—'

Kip lifts his head from his blanket by the stove and lets out a low 'woof' at the sound of feet stamping up the porch steps. The door rattles as someone knocks.

Frank frowns. 'You expecting someone? It's not even seven.'

Celie shakes her head. Frank pushes away from the table as the knocking grows more persistent. He opens the door and two rough-looking men push past him into the house.

'Hold on!' Frank shouts as he follows them into the house. 'What's going on? Who do you think you are?'

'Mr Jeffries?'

Frank spins around. A thin young man in an ill-fitting navy suit, grey fedora and horn-rimmed spectacles smiles awkwardly as he edges his way across the threshold.

'Harvey? Harvey Withers? What are you doing here?'

Harvey Withers, the bank clerk from the Merchant Bank, extends his hand. 'Mr Jeffries.'

Frank stares down at his hand, then he turns and gestures to the other men with his thumb. 'Who are they?'

'Lulu, make some more tea for these gentlemen, please,' Celie says. She joins Frank by the door. 'What's going on, Harvey?'

Harvey Withers removes his hat and runs his hand nervously through his oiled hair. 'I've been promoted, Mrs Jeffries. Marion is awfully pleased. I'm the new junior assistant manager of the West Lake Merchant Bank.'

'Bully for you, Harvey,' Frank says as he slams the door shut. 'What I want to know is what you and they are doing in my house at seven in the morning.'

Harvey frowns as he reaches into his jacket pocket and removes a letter. He hands it to Frank. 'I'm afraid it's not good news, Mr Jeffries.'

Frank tears open the envelope. He scans the document and thrusts it at Celie.

NOTICE OF FORECLOSURE

Mr Frank Jeffries
 Sweet Briar Farm
 West Lake, Alberta

This letter is a formal notification that you are in default of your obligations to make payments on your home loan and other loans related to farm equipment and livestock, account #546324 held at the West Lake, Alberta branch of The Merchant Bank.

You are in arrears $7,453.67 since April 1st, 1937 and you have ignored multiple requests to repay your debt. We are now issuing a foreclosure order on your property, Sweet Briar Farm, West Lake, Alberta, including all contents of value therein, effective today, July 20th, 1937.

We ask for your cooperation with the eviction process.

Harvey P. Withers P/P
 Graham Bosworth
 Branch Manager
 The Merchant Bank
 West Lake, Alberta

'What letters, Frank? You've had letters warning of foreclosure from the bank and you haven't told me?'

Frank slumps into a kitchen chair, ignoring Celie's question.

She turns to Harvey Withers. 'I had no idea it had gotten this bad, Harvey. If you can give us a couple of weeks, we'll see what we can do to find the money—'

Frank sighs wearily. 'Celie, it's no use. We've been living on a wish and a prayer for months.'

Lulu sets the teapot on the table. 'I've just got a job housekeeping at the hotel, Dad. I was afraid to tell you before in case you disapproved, but I'm sure I can extend my hours. That would be a help, wouldn't it?' She looks at the bank employee. 'Wouldn't it, Mr Withers? Can't you speak to Mr Bosworth?'

'It's too late, Lulu.' Frank's shoulders shake, setting off a coughing fit.

Celie points at the taller of the two men accompanying Harvey Withers. 'Get me some water. Quickly.'

The man brings Frank a glass of water. Harvey fidgets with the brim of his hat as Frank gulps it down. 'I'm sorry, Mrs Jeffries. We have our orders. This is the bank's property and you need to be out by noon today. You may take your clothes and personal possessions, but everything else has to stay for the auction.'

Lulu stares at her mother. 'Mom? What's he talking about? This is our home!' She grabs the bank employee's arm. 'You can't want us out on the street, Mr Withers. You know us. We've been to your house for dinners. I've babysat Sally. Please, Mr Withers—'

Celie rests her hand on Lulu's arm. 'That's enough, Lulu. Mr Withers is just doing his job. The trunks are in the shed. We have work to do.'

Fred and Ben Wheatley, who, at seventeen, is already taller and broader than his father, shove the final trunk onto the back of Fred's flatbed truck as Celie, Mavis and Lulu watch from the front porch. Kip leans against Lulu's legs, cocking his shaggy black and white head at the peculiar activity as Lulu scratches him behind his ears. Celie glances at Frank, who has escaped to the truck's cab, and sits in brooding silence in the passenger seat as their world crashes down around them.

Fred jumps down from the back of the truck and slaps his dirty hands on his trousers. 'Looks like that's the last of it, Celie.'

'Thank you, Fred. I don't know what we would have done without you and Mavis, and Ben, too, of course.'

Mavis loops her arm around Celie's waist. 'We're friends, Celie. You'd do the same for us.'

Celie looks over at Mavis, whose grey eyes are shadowed with sadness and compassion. 'Are you sure about us using Fred's shack by the railway? Where will he put all his tools and tyres?'

Fred leans on the porch railing. 'Don't ya be worryin' about that, Celie. It's more important ya have a roof over your head. It was a railworkers' cabin, so there's an old stove and a sink and an outside toilet. I'm warnin' ya, though. It's not the Ritz. I only wish I could do better by ya.'

'No, no, it's absolutely fine, Fred. We all appreciate it.'

Mavis squeezes Celie's waist. 'You'll stay with us for the next few days, of course. We'll need to clear the place out and give it a good clean. I'm sure I can find some old curtains and bits and bobs to furnish the place.'

'Mom?' Lulu points to a car turning down their road at the junction. 'They're coming back.'

Ben joins them by the porch and they watch in silence as the car bumps down the road. It pulls to a stop in front of the house, and Harvey Withers and the two men step out of the car. The gate squeaks as Harvey opens it.

'Are you all done, Mrs Jeffries?'

'We are, Mr Withers.'

'Good. You won't mind if my men take a look inside? We just need to check that you've only taken your personal effects. I mean,

I know you would have complied, but it's the bank's policy. There have been some … complications in the past.'

'You can hardly blame people, can you, Harvey?' Mavis interjects. 'Running hard-working people off their properties with hardly a moment's notice? I don't know how you can sleep at night.'

'It's all right, Mavis.' Celie turns to Harvey Withers. 'You'll find everything in order. Come on, Lulu, let's get in the back of the truck with Ben. We'll sit on the trunks. Mavis, you sit in the cab with Fred and Frank.'

Lulu scoops Kip up in her arms. 'Come on, Kippy. Time to go to our new home.'

Harvey Withers holds up his hand. 'I'm sorry, but you'll have to leave the dog. All livestock is to be confiscated.'

Lulu's eyes widen as she looks at her mother and back at the bank employee. 'Kip is my dog. He's not livestock. He's part of the family.'

'I'm sorry, Miss Jeffries. All animals are categorised as livestock. We have to take the dog. It's the rules.' He nods at one of the men who approaches Lulu and reaches out for the dog.

Lulu presses Kip against her body. 'You're not having my dog! I grew up with Kip! You're not having my dog!'

Celie glances over at Frank who is sitting staring fixedly at the fields across the road. She looks back at the bank employee. 'Mr Withers, surely an old dog is of no value to the bank. He's the family pet. He's our personal possession. You said we could take our personal possessions.'

Harvey Withers looks at the distressed girl and sighs. 'I'm just an employee, Mrs Jeffries. I have to do my job. I hope you understand. It's out of my control. Rules are rules.'

Celie bites her lips to keep her anger from exploding in words she is sure to regret. 'Lulu, give the man the dog.'

Ben Wheatley steps forward. 'No, Mrs Jeffries. You can't let them. Mr Withers, you can't take Kip. It's just wrong.'

'Mrs Jeffries, if you don't hand over the dog, I'm afraid I will need to call the police.'

Celie shuts her eyes and breathes. She opens her eyes. 'Give me Kip, darling.'

'But, Mommy!' Lulu bursts into tears. 'It's Kip!'

'I know, darling.'

Lulu emits a gut-wrenching sob as she relinquishes the dog to her mother. Celie hands Kip to one of the bailiffs and wraps her arms around Lulu as they watch the man take the dog to the car. Kip looks over the man's shoulder and barks as he tries to worm his way out of the man's grip.

'Kip!' Lulu screams. 'Kip!'

Celie looks at Frank. In the truck's cab, he sits as silent and rigid as a stone.

***

Three days later

Celie surveys the results of her and Mavis's cleaning and furnishing efforts in the old railway workers' cabin that Frank has uncharitably called the Chicken Coop. The thin wooden structure jiggles as a freight train rumbles by just a few feet from the back wall.

'It's looking so much better, Mavis. Thank you so much.'

'It wasn't just me, Celie. Mrs Forbes donated the sofa and the rug, and Rosita Majors had a call around to the Temperance ladies and that's where all the pots and pans came from, and the two old brass beds. Ben's got the stove working and the water's connected. And I'll bring you over a meatloaf and an apple pie later.'

'Mavis, honestly, I'll never be able to thank you enough for all this.'

Mavis swats away the compliment. 'I'm happy to do it.' She

glances over at Lulu, who sits in a chair with a book in her lap, staring out the back window overlooking the railway tracks. 'I feel awful about what happened. I mean, how can they take a person's dog? It's just not right.'

'Lulu's barely said a word since Tuesday. She won't eat and can't seem to muster the energy to do anything.'

'She's grieving, Celie. She'll get over it, eventually.'

'I don't know that you ever get over something like that.'

Mavis picks up the old kettle and fills it with water from the one tap over the kitchen sink. 'How's Frank doing?'

Celie shrugs. 'He's out standing in the yard. He's out there every day, just standing and looking at the ground. I've barely been able to get a word out of either of them.'

Mavis sets the kettle on top of the stove. 'They'll come around. It's been a shock. It's happening to so many people, Celie. It's not like Frank did anything wrong. He's a victim of circumstances.'

Celie grabs three mismatched mugs from the shelf Ben Wheatley has fixed onto the wall above the sink. 'He should never have poured our money into those stocks. If only I'd known about it.'

'A lot of men did, Celie.'

'It doesn't make me feel any better.'

Celie is about to pour the boiled water into the teapot when Ben shouts from the path at the front of the shack. 'Lulu! Lulu! Where are you?'

Mavis frowns. 'What's Ben hollering about?'

Celie looks over at her daughter. 'Lulu, Ben's calling you.'

Lulu shrugs as she half-heartedly flips a page. 'Not right now.'

Ben hammers on the front door. 'Lulu Jeffries! I need to speak to you.'

'Good heavens, what's that boy on about?' Mavis stomps over to the door and pulls it open. 'Ben Wheatley, where are your ma—'

The old border collie lopes into the kitchen, barking and

wagging his tail. Lulu springs out of the chair and throws open her arms. 'Kip!' She hugs the dog and buries her face in his fur. 'My baby! Kip, my darling boy!'

Ben steps into the shack. 'Glad to see he's home where he belongs.'

Celie hugs the gangly boy. 'Ben Wheatley, what have you done? You didn't break him out of the dog pound, did you?'

Ben smiles, his blue eyes lighting up at the sight of Lulu's joy. 'I had a little money set aside from helping Pop at the garage. I made Mr Withers an offer he couldn't refuse.'

Celie kisses Ben on his cheek, causing him to blush bright red. 'Thank you for bringing Kip home.'

Ben shrugs. 'No problem, Mrs Jeffries. Anything for Lulu.'

Chapter Forty-Eight

Etta

Hollywood, California - July 1937

Etta glances past F. Scott Fitzgerald, who, with age and the ravages of years of alcoholism and ill health, is softening at the edges like an out-of-focus portrait. An attractive sapphire-eyed blonde of around thirty in a blue satin dress of precisely the same shade as her eyes sits between him and the window in the back of the taxi. Etta catches the woman's eye, and she tilts her chin upwards in defiance.

'I can imagine what you're thinking, Miss Marine.'

'I wouldn't have thought so, Miss Graham.'

CJ glances at Etta in the rearview mirror. 'Play nice, Etta.'

'I always play nice, CJ.' She smiles at Scott, being sure to offer him the full effect of her dimpled cheek. 'So, tell me, Scott. How did you and Miss Graham meet? You only just arrived in Hollywood a few weeks ago.'

Scott looks over at the young woman and slides his fingers through hers. 'At Sheilah's engagement party to the Marquess of

Donegall last week. I took one look at her and whisked her off into the velvet night.'

Sheilah Graham smiles at Scott in the exclusionary way lovers do, and for a moment Etta thinks they may actually kiss. 'I took one look at Scott and that was it,' Sheilah says. 'A *coup de foudre*, as the French say.'

'A bolt of lightning.'

The woman looks at Etta. 'You know French?'

'I've spent a considerable amount of time in Paris. With Scott and his wife, Zelda, in fact. Isn't that right, Scott? How is darling Zelda, by the way?'

'As well as can be expected for someone who claims to be in direct contact with William the Conqueror, Mary Queen of Scots and Jesus Christ.'

Scott dabs at the perspiration collecting on his forehead with a starched white handkerchief. 'I may start thanking God myself after this writing contract at MGM came out of the blue last month,' he says in his soft Southern drawl. 'Six months at a thousand dollars a month will go some way to paying my debts and Zelda's upkeep in the hospital, not to mention Scottie's boarding school fees. I am trying to be a very good boy and only drink Coca-Cola. My liver is thanking me, even if my teeth aren't.' He squeezes Sheilah's hand. 'Sheilah's keeping me on the straight and narrow.'

Sheilah laughs. 'Well, as much as is possible considering we live in Sin City. Ah, here we are! The Garden of Allah.'

CJ jumps out of the taxi and walks around the side to open Sheilah's door. She thanks him and waits on the pavement in front of the modest terracotta-roofed bungalows on Sunset Boulevard as Scott clambers out of the back of the taxi.

'Are you sure we can't drop you home, Sheilah?' Etta asks pointedly as Scott takes hold of the woman's hand.

'I am home, darling,' Sheilah responds.

CJ climbs into the back of the taxi and slams the door. Etta watches the couple walk down a path to one of the bungalows as the taxi pulls out into the road.

'You do know who you've been insulting all night?' CJ asks as he lights up a cigarette.

'What are you talking about?'

'That's Sheilah Graham. *The* Sheilah Graham, writer of the *Hollywood Today* gossip column. I'd make friends if I was you, hon. Otherwise, you can kiss your dream of being Scarlett O'Hara goodbye.'

Santa Rosa Apartments, two weeks later

'Etta, there's something I need to speak to you about.'

Etta glances at CJ in the mirror on top of her vanity table as she brushes mascara onto her eyelashes.

'Can it wait till after the party? I don't want to miss my chance to catch Jack Warner's eye with this new gown I bought with the birthday money Jessie sent me. Edith Head did a wonderful job, don't you think?' Etta flutters her fingers through the white feathers sprouting around the neckline. 'I got the idea for the feathers from Ginger Rogers's dress in *Top Hat*.'

CJ nods absentmindedly. 'Sure, hon. You look great.'

Etta smiles into the mirror. The smile transforms into a grimace as she presses a finger against the wrinkle that has entrenched itself between her pencilled eyebrows. She should have bought surgical tape to pull back the skin behind her ears. *Stupid to have forgotten.*

'I'm going to show Mr Selznick that he's made the mistake of his life not choosing me to play Scarlett O'Hara. I would have been perfect, CJ. You know how hard I've been practising my Southern accent.' She turns around on the vanity stool. 'You don't suppose that Graham woman put him off me, do you? I did wonder if that column she wrote about ageing Scarletts was a dig at me.'

'Honey, I really need to talk to you. It's important.'

Etta looks back into the mirror and dabs at her lips with scarlet lipstick. 'Errol's been reading the script for *The Adventures of Robin Hood* at Warner Brothers and he told me that I'd make the perfect Maid Marian. For goodness sake, I already have the right accent. This party's my best chance to persuade Jack Warner to cast me. I'm tired of hovering in the background in all these pictures.'

'Etta, I'm leaving for Spain the day after tomorrow.'

Etta drops the tube of lipstick onto the vanity table and spins around on the stool. 'What!'

'The *Los Angeles Examiner* has hired me to cover the Civil War. It's a proper journalism job. I'll be a war correspondent for one of the biggest newspapers in America.'

'You're leaving me?'

CJ paces the width of the narrow room. 'Look, in Spain I've got a chance to do something real, something important. The world's changing, and not for the better, Etta. The fascist thugs are supporting the Spanish Nationalists who want a dictatorship under this Franco clown against the Republicans who want a social democracy. It's a class struggle. Any journalist worth his salt is going out there.' He runs his hand through his hair. 'I want to go, Etta. I *need* to go. I can't do this Hollywood thing anymore.'

Anger grows inside Etta like a sprouting weed. She grabs her powder puff and dabs at her face, sending a flurry of fine peach dust over the marble vanity top. 'Well, *I* don't want to go to Spain.'

CJ rests his hands on her shoulders as he watches her fuss at her face in the mirror. 'I wasn't asking you to, baby. Haven't you heard me? It's a war. There's going to be fighting. It's not a place for someone like you.'

'I'm supposed to stay here on my own? You know I make next to nothing doing these bit parts in the pictures. How am I supposed to pay for this apartment? What about the money for that vulture François DuRose?' She throws open her arms, setting the feathers on the chiffon sleeves flapping. 'How am I supposed to pay for my gowns?'

'I'll send back some money for you every month. When I get back, if you want, we can get married and live wherever you want.'

Etta twists around on the stool. 'Married? CJ, are you asking me to marry you?'

'Sure, why not? You know me. I know you. I get a feeling that we kinda like each other. There's a custom over here that when that happens, people get hitched.'

Etta springs up from the stool. 'Oh, CJ!'

'Hold on, I'm not finished,' he says, pushing her away. 'We gotta do this right.'

He gets down on one knee and takes her right hand in his. 'What do you say, Etta? Do you want to get hitched when I come back, if Errol Flynn hasn't run off with you by then?'

Etta throws her arms around him. 'Yes, of course I'll marry you, CJ, my darling man! I'll act my socks off and become a big star and I promise not to run off with Errol Flynn!'

Chapter Forty-Nine

Celie & Jessie

The Chicken Coop, West Lake, Alberta, Canada – August 1937

The Chicken Coop
Station Lane
West Lake, Alberta
Canada

August 6th, 1937

Dear Jessie,

I'm so sorry not to have answered your letter sooner, but quite a lot has been happening here, which I only now feel ready to write to you about. I certainly don't want to burden Mama with my troubles, so I'm afraid you are going to be my shoulder to cry on.

Jessie, our farm was repossessed last month. The bailiffs arrived one Saturday morning and gave us one hour to leave the house. The bank had sent them. We had to leave behind anything they felt could be resold – all

the farm equipment and animals, the piano, furniture. They even tried to
take Lulu's dog, Kip. It was heart-wrenching. I can't think about it now
without—

Celie sets down the pen and presses her fingers against her eyes, willing the tears back into her body. No matter how long she lives, she will never be able to erase the scene of that day. She takes a deep breath and picks up her pen and crosses out the unfinished sentence.

Lulu's friend Ben Wheatley rescued Kip and brought our little family
back together. I'll never be able to thank him enough.

Frank and I had been trying so hard to keep the farm going these past
few years, but we've had drought and grasshopper plagues and wheat
prices tumbling on what we have managed to harvest. Frank took a part-
time job in Fred Wheatley's garage, and I've been writing for the local
paper, taking in sewing and trying to twist Mr Forbes's arm in the local
store to buy my cakes, eggs and bread. I think he agrees more out of the
kindness of his heart than any great need. Lulu's just started working
part-time as a chambermaid in the hotel, too. Unfortunately, I've had to
give up my photography as the film and processing costs have become too
dear. I have a box of undeveloped film under my bed as it is!

Celie crumples up the letter and drops her head into her hands. How can she burden Jessie with all of this? Jessie, who lost her husband to a police bullet in a street riot, who is now in the middle of a civil war caring for the injured and the dying under heaven only knows what kind of horrifying circumstances.

Jessie is a saint and Etta is a sinner. Where does that leave her? The pathetic dutiful wretch who gets nowhere because she believes that hard work will be rewarded?

She walks over to the small window over the sink and looks out at the vegetable garden Frank has scratched out of the dirt in front of the old railway shack. The two chickens Mavis gave her squawk and flutter as they poke at invisible insects amongst the pebbles, and Kip lies snoozing in the shade of a maple tree as he does most days, oblivious to the turmoil that surrounds him.

Frank is out in the garden again, hoeing at imaginary weeds between the corn stalks and pumpkins. He has taken the loss of the farm hard. Where she and Lulu have knuckled down to find ways to bring in some money, Frank is like a man who has lost the will to fight. He is as accommodating and docile now as he was once stubborn and irascible, eating the endless eggs and drinking the bitter chicory coffee without complaint, saying nothing when she works late on her stack of sewing or on a newspaper article, spending endless hours tending the vegetables and leaning on his hoe, gazing sightlessly out across the railway track to the sparse wheat fields beyond. If Frank's behaviour wasn't so uncharacteristic, she might even begin to enjoy this new husband. But the change is so odd that it unsettles her.

If it weren't for Fred and Mavis, she doesn't know what they would have done. Frank had called the shack a chicken coop when they'd first laid eyes on the squat, square wooden building abutting the train tracks. Bless Ben Wheatley, an optimist if she'd ever met one. 'The Chicken Coop! What a great name!' he'd said. He'd even made them a sign to affix to their new mailbox. She smiles at the memory. Jessie would call it making lemonade out of lemons.

Celie surveys the chainlink fence surrounding the modest yard. All these years of backbreaking work, and they live in a chicken coop. God has a sense of humour.

She turns away from the window. She'll finish the letter. She needs someone to know the truth about what has been happening to her and her family out here in Alberta. She'll iron out the sheet of paper and it will be fine. At least she still has an iron. The bailiffs obviously didn't see any value in it.

Celie sets plates of fried kidneys and mashed potatoes on the table in front of Frank and Lulu. She goes back to the makeshift counter beside the oven and retrieves her own plate of food.

'Frank, have you seen my camera anywhere? I can't find it nor my tripod. I've looked everywhere.'

Frank chews at a kidney. 'I pawned them.'

Celie stares at her husband. 'You what?'

Frank looks away, unable to meet her gaze. 'I pawned them. They were of no use lying around gathering dust.'

Celie's face flushes with rising anger. 'Those were mine, Frank! My father gave them to me. They weren't yours to take!'

'Mom, I'm sure Dad didn't mean any harm.'

'Lulu, stay out of this. This is between me and your father.'

'Celie, calm down.'

Celie rises from her chair and slams her hand on the table. 'Don't you dare tell me to calm down, Frank. Where's the ticket?'

'The ticket?'

'The pawn ticket. Where is it?'

'In my coat pocket.'

Celie bolts over to where the coats hang on hooks beside the door. She stuffs her hand into the coat pocket and retrieves a crumbled piece of paper. She reads the expiration date on the ticket. 'Tomorrow? It expires tomorrow? How much did they loan you, Frank?'

'Ten dollars.'

'Ten dollars! Where are we going to get ten dollars from by tomorrow? What did you spend it on?'

Frank spears his fork into the mashed potato and remains silent.

'Mama, I'm going to go over to the Wheatleys for a while, okay?'

'That's fine, Lulu. Have Ben walk you home.'

Lulu pulls her coat and hat off a hook and, calling for Kip, hurries out of the shack with the dog at her heels.

The anger Celie has been fighting to suppress in front of Lulu boils over. 'Frank! What did you spend the money you got for my camera equipment on? Because it had better be more important than what those things meant to me.'

Frank shakes his head. 'It doesn't matter. It's gone.'

'It's gone? The money's gone and my camera's gone? Is that what you're saying?' She stomps into the lean-to that houses Frank's bed and a dresser.

'Celie! What are you doing?' Frank says as he follows her into the room.

She pulls open the drawers until she finds it: the brass tin of Frank's morphine supplies.

'Celie.'

She opens the lid and checks the six vials. All full but one. She snaps the lid shut. 'Morphine? You spent it on morphine?'

'Celie.'

The emotion drains out of her until she is left empty. 'You said you'd stop, Frank. You promised.'

'I know.' Frank rubs his forehead. 'It's not that easy.'

'And now you've stolen something precious from your own wife. You're an addict and a thief. Well done, Frank. Well done.'

Chapter Fifty

Etta

Santa Rosa Apartments, Hollywood, California – August 1937

Etta stuffs the apple into her mouth and shuffles though the post as she climbs the stairs to the apartment. Bills, bills, flyers, another bill. She pulls out a crumpled, dirt-stained letter and squints at the postmark: *Madrid, 28 July 1937*. She pushes open the door and drops the other post onto the Formica-topped table as she sits down on a dining chair. She sets the apple on top of the stack of post and turns the envelope over. A return address in Spain. From Dr J. Khalid.

Jessie. The only one from home who still answers her letters. She'll have to write her back and tell her to look out for CJ in Spain.

A pang of regret tweaks her conscience. She should never have let CJ leave that way. She hadn't meant to be so unreasonable at the train station, especially after he'd proposed. He'd called her selfish and self-centred for wanting him to stay in Hollywood. How could he blame her for being upset about him going off to cover a war in a country she has no interest in between people fighting about things she couldn't begin to understand? Who cares what happens in Spain? And he was so happy about it! How could he be so happy to leave her alone miles away from anyone she knows?

She taps the envelope against her fingers. Still, she was wrong to let him leave trailing her anger and recriminations. Surely, he knows how much she loves him. She'll make it right. She'll write him a lovely letter as soon as he lets her know his address in Madrid.

She takes a bite of the apple and tears open the envelope.

El Goloso
   Madrid
   Spain

July 28th, 1937

Dearest Etta,

   I don't know how to write you this letter so I shall simply get on with it. I am currently working in the English hospital just outside of Madrid. There has just been a terrible battle between the Republicans and Franco's Nationalists at Brunete, about fifteen miles west of here. My friend Ruth Bellico, whom you met in Paris some years ago, is here covering the war for a French newspaper. She was with the Republicans and she met CJ there. He'd told her that he had just arrived from the United States to cover the war for the Los Angeles Examiner, and she found out that you two were together. Ruth told him that she'd met you and knew me. He told her he was keen to meet Etta's twin sister.

   Etta, there was an accident two days ago on their way back to Madrid. Ruth told me that she and CJ had hopped onto the running boards of General Walter's car to get back to the city. The general was carrying wounded from the battle to the hospital. Just outside of Madrid, a tank backed into the side of the car and CJ was badly injured. They got

him to the hospital as quickly as they could. I operated on him as soon as
he arrived. It seemed ... I hoped...
   I don't know how to write this. Etta, CJ died last night.

Etta's foot slips on the rung of the ladder attached to the 'Hollywoodland' sign that stands on a hill overlooking the city. She clings to the wooden ladder and takes another drink of gin from the bottle she'd found in CJ's hidden liquor stash in his wardrobe. She has already polished off the last of the cheap wine and the half bottle of bourbon from the living room sideboard.

'Why did you die, CJ?' she cries as she crumbles in a heap at the foot of the ladder. 'Why did you leave me?' The sobs wrench out of her shaking body. 'Carlo! Why did you leave me too? Why!'

She sits up and gulps down another swig of gin. She rubs her wet eyes, leaving streaks of black mascara across her face. She looks up the ladder that clings precariously to the fifty-foot 'Y', secured only by a piece of rope. *'Y' for Why. Celie will probably figure it out. She's smart that way.*

Staggering to her feet, she re-ties the belt around her satin dressing gown and chucks her shoes into the hillside's scrub bushes. She grasps hold of the ladder and steps onto the lowest rung. Then she slowly makes her way up.

When she is half-way, she stops to rest and looks out at the sparkling city below. *La Land, Tinseltown, The Big Orange, Lotusland. Land of the Screen Sirens.*

She laughs. 'What a joke! You're a big joke!' She takes another swig of gin. 'I'm a big joke!' Etta begins to giggle and her body shakes until she gasps for breath.

A light flashes into her face and she reaches up to screen her eyes.

'Miss? What are you doing up there?'

She blinks at the two policemen at the foot of the sign. 'I'm climbing to Heaven, can't you see, officer?'

'Miss, we need you to come down,' the other policeman says. 'It's dangerous up there. You could get hurt and we wouldn't want that.'

'You wouldn't?' She laughs and drains the last of the gin. 'Here, catch.' She flings the bottle out into the darkness.

'Miss, please. You need to get down. You're trespassing.'

Etta swings against the 'Y'. 'Did you know I'm a real Siren? Not one of these Hollywood ones. Oh, no. I come from a long line of bona fide Sirens. Straight from Italy. It's true. You know how I know it's true?' She frowns down at the men when they don't respond. 'I said, do you know how I know it's true?'

'No, miss,' one of the officers says as the other begins to climb the ladder. 'How do you know it's true?'

'Because every man I love dies! It's the Sirens' curse. I'd stay away from me, if I were you.'

The police officer grabs hold of Etta's legs. 'I've got you, miss. Don't worry, everything will work out just fine.'

Chapter Fifty-One

Celie & Adriana

Forbes's General Store, West Lake, Alberta, Canada – August 1937

Celie presses the telephone receiver against her ear in the new phone cubicle Ol' Man Forbes has installed in his store, grimacing at the clicking and buzzing on the line.

'Adriana? Can you hear me all right?'

'Yes, Auntie Celie. It's good to speak to you.'

'The same here, Adriana,' she says as she absentmindedly twists the telephone cord around her fingers. 'What's going on with Etta? I received your telegram about you wanting to speak to me urgently this morning. I've had Mr Forbes here barring anyone from using the telephone because of your call coming through.'

'I need your help, Auntie Celie. You've heard about Mr Melton's death in Spain?'

'Yes, Jessie sent me a telegram. An awful thing.'

'Yes, well … Mama, she … she has had another breakdown.'

'Oh, no! What's happened?'

The line clicks as Adriana pauses. 'The police found Mama confused and drunk trying to climb the Hollywoodland sign. She said she wanted to die to be with Carlo and CJ. They said that she was screaming something about a Sirens' curse.'

Her poor sister.

'Where's Etta now?'

'Mama is in a mental hospital in Los Angeles. A friend of hers heard about it on the radio and visited the hospital to identify her. The police found *Nonna's* address in Mama's apartment and telegraphed us.'

The operator's voice interrupts the call. 'Further minutes will incur additional charges. Do you wish to continue?'

'Yes, yes!' Adriana shouts. 'Two minutes, please! Wait, wait! I will pay for it!'

'Thank you. The telephone call will terminate in two minutes.'

'Adriana, tell me quickly, what can I do?'

'Auntie Celie, will you go to California and bring Mama back to Canada with you? *Nonna* will send you money, don't worry about that. Whatever you need, she said.'

Celie's mind jumbles with images of Etta screaming at her rescuers at the foot of the Hollywoodland sign, and then sitting stupefied and dishevelled in a corner of a bleak hospital ward. There is no room in the Chicken Coop, and they barely have enough dole money to feed themselves, but she will make it work somehow.

'Of course. Anything.'

'Thank you so much. Mama needs to be with family. When she's better, *Nonna* will send money for you to take her on the train to Montréal. We will meet you there and bring her home to England by ship. I will send you the details of the hospital in Los Angeles where Mama is. Is that all right?'

Celie stares blindly at the numbers on the payphone dial. It won't be easy. They will need more food, more water. Etta will need winter clothes, a bed to sleep in. But that is all like dust on a dirty window; none of it is of any consequence. Etta needs help, that is all that matters.

'It's more than all right, Adriana. Etta needs her family. I will go and get her.'

Chapter Fifty-Two

Christina

Clover Bar, Hither Green, London – October 1937

Ellen Jackson, the president of the Hither Green & Lewisham branch of the Women's Institute, takes her customary three sips of milky Earl Grey tea from the delicate Royal Worcester teacup and sets the cup back on the saucer she holds in her hand.

'I'm afraid I can't agree with you in the least, Christina. The Duke and Duchess of Windsor's visit to visit Herr Hitler in Germany can only be seen as a benefit to Britain. Who is better suited to broker peace between Britain and Germany than our own dear fallen king? It was absolutely a travesty that he was made to feel that his only course of action last December was to abdicate the Crown in order to marry his love. I, for one, think Edward and Wallis are marvellous. Hitler and the Nazi generals obviously agree with me. Haven't you seen the newsreel footage in the cinema? Herr Hitler looked most charmed by the Duchess.'

Christina runs her hand behind her ear and pats at her marcelled waves as she struggles to suppress the irritation that threatens to undermine the progress she'd made convincing Ellen to replace the WI's Christmas jumble sale (which, to her mind, was nothing more than a glorified boot sale for the WI ladies to gouge extortionate sums of money out of the customers for tat rescued from garden sheds and attics) with a curated Christmas market of quality crafts and home-baked goods. However, Ellen's haughty condescension and her objectionable opinions were more than she could bear.

'Ellen, I don't care a fig if Herr Hitler was charmed by Mrs Simpson. The Nazis are using the Windsors' presence for their own propaganda. The two of them have no sense whatsoever.'

Ellen sets down her teacup and saucer, and, after brushing cannoli crumbs from her fingers with her napkin, focuses her hooded steel-blue gaze on Christina.

'It appears that, yet again, we must agree to disagree, Christina.'

She picks up her handbag and white leather gloves from the settee. 'I must be off. Mr Jackson is taking me to see *The Laughing Cavalier* at the Adelphi this evening. I don't much appreciate musical theatre, but Mr Jackson is an aficionado, so I must do my wifely duty.'

Christina pours herself another cup of tea as she hears the front door slam. Hettie appears in the sitting room doorway, a letter from the afternoon post in her hand.

'She's left, Hettie?'

Hettie nods, her customarily dour expression folded into lines of deep disapproval. 'Good riddance to 'er, I say. 'Ow can she be talking up them two characters prancing around wiff the Nazis in Germany when Edward's dumped the country on 'is poor brother George just to go off wiff an American floozy? Selfish, I call it. We're better off wiffout 'im and 'er.'

Christina picks up another chocolate cannoli from the cake stand and sets it on her plate. 'You've changed your tune. I thought you were all for the royal love affair.'

'Me and 'alf of Britain. If they'd only stayed in France minding their own business, I'd 'ave been all for it. But them traipsing off to Germany to 'obnob wiff Hitler? Nah, they lost me. Let the Americans 'ave 'em, I say.'

'I can't say I disagree with you for once, Hettie. Is that letter for me? Is it from one of the girls?'

Hettie squints at the stamp. ''Oo do you know in France?'

Christina holds out her hand. 'Just give me the letter, please. And you can take away the cannoli before I eat them all.'

When Hettie has gone, Christina slices open the envelope with her butter knife and removes the thick white sheet of paper that has been meticulously folded by some careful hand. Unfolding it, she reads.

Galerie DuRose,
  62 rue la Boétie,
  Paris

October 8th, 1937

Dear Madame Fry,
  You may remember me as the person who contacted you several years ago for your daughter, Mrs Etta Marinetti's, address in California. Permit me to re-introduce myself in the event you have forgotten. I am François DuRose, the owner of the prestigious Galerie DuRose in Paris. I deal in selling art of the highest quality to discerning patrons throughout Europe, and now, through my affiliates in London, and even America, although it must be said the Americans must be directed as to what is tasteful and what is, quite clearly to my mind, not. I had the honour of dealing with the sale of Carlo Marinetti's paintings while the poor man was, quite wrongfully, of course, incarcerated in that dreadful Italian prison during that terrible scandal.

  No doubt you have heard quite enough about all of that, being as you are the mother of the woman for which Carlo Marinetti left his wife.

However, it is my unfortunate task to inform you of some delicate developments in your daughter's financial obligations to me.

It came to my attention some years ago that the later paintings by Carlo Marinetti that were sent to me by your daughter when Mr Marinetti was in prison were, in fact, fake. I will not go into how this revelation came about; I have no doubt your daughter can apprise you of these details when she recovers from her latest unfortunate illness. Owing to this discovery, Mrs Marinetti entered into an agreement with me to refund me a significant amount to assuage any impugning of my reputation should the provenance of these paintings come to light in the future.

It is with great regret that I heard of Mrs Marinetti's most recent breakdown, which came to my attention after my latest letters to her were returned to me marked 'Moved – Address Unknown'. I had my assistant look into this and he discovered the circumstances of her rescue by police from the top of the Hollywoodland sign, which had appeared in several of the American newspapers. Mrs Marinetti was always so dramatic, wasn't she? It seems she hasn't changed.

With your daughter's incapacitation, it has fallen upon me to contact you, as her mother, and, I expect, her legal guardian given the circumstances, in order to pursue her outstanding debt to me. I calculate this to be, given the interest the debt has accrued owing to late payments, $2,757.00 US dollars. This amount is subject to increase on a monthly basis. Being of a generous disposition, and given your daughter's unfortunate circumstances, I have set this rate at only 10%.

I would be most appreciative of payment in full as this debt has been active since 1934, and I have been most accommodating of Mrs Marinetti's laxity in fulfilling her financial obligation to me. I have enclosed my bank details for ease of an international transfer of funds into my account. I am, of course, very happy to accept payment in pounds sterling.

I appreciate that this must be a shock to you, but I assure you that once this debt is paid in full, neither you nor your daughter will hear from me again, and her role in the provision of fraudulent paintings to my gallery will be conveniently forgotten. Of course, should the payment not be forthcoming (and, being the reasonable businessman I am, I am willing to discuss a payment plan to our mutual satisfaction), I will have no choice but to reveal the fraud to both the authorities and the press. This would only be detrimental to your daughter, as I am confident you are aware.

I look forward to receiving payment in full, or by a mutually agreed payment plan. Please telegram me upon receipt of this letter to acknowledge your agreement to my terms.

I remain your indebted servant,

François DuRose

Christina sets down the letter beside her teacup. Anger at the brazen impertinence of the man heats her body like a fire taking hold. Oh, she'll send him a telegram. The stalemate of her claim on the Bishop House, and Dorothy Adam's intransigence, have been ongoing frustrations to her. Now, she will have an entertaining outlet for these frustrations. She is ready for a fight, and this is one she is determined to win decisively.

Chapter Fifty-Three

Etta

The Chicken Coop, West Lake, Alberta, Canada - November 1937

Etta wraps her mink stole around the rough brown wool of her new winter coat – where Celie had bought it, she couldn't be certain, but its ill fit and the pilling on the elbows and the collar suggest that there had been a previous owner. She pulls on a red felt hat she'd pilfered from the MGM costume department. Glancing down at the flat-heeled brown leather boots Celie has loaned her for the winter, she wrinkles her nose and opts for the stylish white rubber overshoes she's brought from California, which she slips on over her patent leather pumps. She inspects her face in the mirror beside the door, pinching her cheeks and biting her lips to heighten her colour, and frowns at the frizzy curls of her overlong bleached hair. What she wouldn't give for a visit to a beauty salon and some lipstick and face powder! How Celie allows herself to go make-upless and submit to Mavis Wheatley's kitchen haircuts – which are hardly the height of fashion – and make no effort to hide the grey threading through her auburn hair is beyond her comprehension.

She is still confused as to how she ended up in West Lake, Alberta. In fact, the past few months are a muddle. She'd been living in Hollywood, acting, that much she remembers. And there'd been a man, she's fairly certain of that, though she can't quite conjure up his face, which is just as well as he's made no effort to contact her since she's been in Canada. She remembers a long, long train journey, then sleep, so much sleep, and dreams of her darling Carlo and their lovemaking in his little hut in the woods at Asheham House in Sussex before the war.

She'd been ill, Celie had said, and Lulu had made it her business to nurse her through the fevers and night sweats. She remembers a calm voice reading to her and cool compresses on her face, and the warm body of a dog who'd taken to sleeping on the bedcovers at the foot of her tiny bed behind the kitchen curtain.

At any rate, she is much better now, and will be going home to London in the new year, and then back to Capri and Carlo and Adriana, of course. It feels like ages since she's seen her daughter. She would have to find something nice in Forbes's General Store for Adriana's birthday in the spring. What did ten-year-old girls like? She'll speak to Lulu. Yes, Lulu would help her find just the right thing.

She smiles into the mirror, pleased that her dimples are still intact despite the weight she's lost. Carlo will be so pleased to see her. Her heart skips a beat as a memory of his dark hair under her hands and his warm lips on hers slides into her mind. *Carlo! My darling, darling man! I will be home soon.*

She opens the flimsy door and steps out into the ankle-deep snow. Pulling the fur stole closer around her shoulders, she wanders toward the kitchen garden where cornstalks stand in the snow like exhausted sentries. Overhead, the sky is a dead, flat white, and her footsteps disturb a crow that flaps away from the garden, emitting a raspy caw. She spies a movement behind the garden shed and steps through the crusty snow in that direction.

'Frank?'

Frank turns around. His face is waxy and gaunt, his cheeks and jaw shadowy with new-growth whiskers. He has an open metal flask in his hand.

'Etta? What are you doing here?'

Etta reaches for the flask and takes a drink. She hands it back to him. 'The same as you, apparently.'

'You drink whisky?'

Etta laughs. 'I drink anything.'

Frank takes a swig and slides the flask back into his coat pocket. 'Well, don't let Celie find out. She's in with the Temperance ladies. Alcohol is the Devil's water.'

'I did notice a dearth of alcohol in the house. Not even a bottle of claret for Sunday lunches. Papa definitely wouldn't have approved.'

'Celie didn't used to be that way. She's changed. It's my fault. I should never have brought her out here. She's had to give up a lot to be my wife.'

'I'm sure that's not true, Frank.'

Frank laughs, the sound hollow and joyless. He waves at the patch of snowy earth and the unpainted clapboard shack beside the railway track.

'Look at what I've given her. A shack we don't even own and an empty bank account. Oh, and don't forget the public humiliation of a bankruptcy.'

'There's Lulu.'

Frank nods. 'I think our daughter's been the glue that's held us together all these years.' He takes out the flask again and offers it to Etta. 'Lulu and her ruddy dog.'

'I won't hear a bad word about that dog, Frank. Kip keeps me warm at night.'

'That's something, I suppose.'

They stand behind the shed and share the whisky in silence for some moments.

'Frank, do you remember the first time you met our family? Your father was selling some furniture we'd inherited and you'd both come to dinner at Clover Bar.'

'How could I forget? I had no idea I'd be faced with three beautiful sisters and a mother with an eye to me being an eligible bachelor.'

Etta laughs. 'Celie spent the evening accosting you for your opinion on women's suffrage and Jessie ate two desserts while reading an anatomy textbook she'd hidden in her lap.'

'And you told me about painting "an explosion of daffodils" at your art college.'

'You said you were too busy to go to the moving pictures or theatre revues. I thought you were awfully dull.'

'Oh, really?'

Etta drains the last drop of whisky. 'I'm afraid so, much to Mama's disappointment. She was terribly keen on us getting together.'

Frank pockets the empty flask. 'Well, here we are, together at last.'

They look at each other and burst out laughing.

'What a pair we are, Frank! What a disaster we would have been together.'

A crunch of footsteps and Celie appears around the corner of the shed.

'Look at you two! I heard laughter out here and had to come and explore.' She raises her eyebrows at the sight of the unabashedly gleeful pair. 'What's so funny?'

'We were just reminiscing about the first time Frank came to dinner. Do you remember, Celie? You gave him a hard time about the Suffragettes, Jessie had her nose in a book, and Mama tried to marry him and me off, while Papa tried to do business with Frank's father.'

'It's a credit to you, Frank, that you ever came back,' Celie says.

'I had to, didn't I? You were there.'

Celie glances away, as though unsure how to react at the unexpected compliment.

'Come inside and have some tea. It's freezing out here.' She looks over at her sister as they walk back to the Chicken Coop. 'You're looking much better, Etta. You've got some colour in your cheeks.'

'No thanks to rouge, Celie. It's this freezing weather. I don't know how you bear it.'

'I drink a lot of hot tea.' Celie opens the door to the shack. 'Oh, what was it that you wanted to speak to me about yesterday? I'm sorry, I had to get the apple pies over to Mr Forbes before the store shut.'

Etta stamps the snow off her overshoes. 'What are you talking about?'

'Yesterday you said you had something very important that you wanted to talk to me about. You made me promise to remind you today.'

'Did I?' Etta shakes her head and giggles as she shrugs out of the old coat. 'I haven't a clue! It couldn't have been that important.' She hangs the coat and hat on a hook beside the door. 'No. Wait. I remember.' She looks back at Celie.

'What is it?'

Etta scrutinises her sister. *There'd been something. Something important. What was it? It had something to do with their mother. It was … it was …* But the thought drifts away, like a feather on the wind.

'Celie, I will simply expire if I can't paint my lips. Do you suppose you might buy me the "Snow White Red" lipstick I saw in Forbes's General Store? I would absolutely love you for ever if you did.'

'Ah, a true emergency, then. I'll let Santa know for Christmas, Etta. Now let's go and make some omelettes for supper. Mavis gave me a loaf of fresh bread this morning. Lulu will be home soon and she'll be fit to eat a bear.'

Chapter Fifty-Four

Christina

The Café Royal, Piccadilly, London – December 1937

Christina looks up from her seat at the table she has carefully chosen in the centre of the vast mirrored dining room of the Café Royal in the heart of Piccadilly, and inclines her head as the *maître d'* ushers her luncheon companion to his seat.

She extends her hand. 'Monsieur DuRose, I'm so pleased you were able to accept my invitation. I know how busy you must be on your visit here to London.'

François DuRose brushes his lips against the back of Christina's hand and nods in greeting. 'I couldn't very well refuse, could I, Madame Fry? I am certain you are as anxious to conclude our … negotiations as I am.'

Christina smiles as she takes in the slender, middle-aged Frenchman's slick, brilliantined – and, owing to its inky blackness, obviously dyed – hair, pencil-thin moustache and exquisitely tailored Savile Row suit.

'Oh, are you anxious? I confess, I am not in the least anxious. I

335

have been enjoying our spirited correspondence. It is a delight to have a worthy sparring partner. Most people are so very dull, wouldn't you agree?'

François DuRose takes his seat. Behind him, fashionable Londoners sit in metal-tubed cantilevered tub chairs at marble-topped tables, their reflections bouncing around the room with their conversations.

'The world has changed, has it not, Madame Fry? There was a time I could be assured of a vigorous exchange with everyone from my barber to the most elite of my clients.' He shrugs. 'Now, no one is interesting. Present company excepted, of course.'

Christina accepts the compliment with an inclination of her head. 'Ah, here's our waiter now. Shall we order? I should rather enjoy a glass of sweet champagne with lunch.'

'That sounds like a delightful suggestion. We can take it off your debt to me.'

Christina smiles, though her cool blue gaze turns even frostier. 'Let us eat, then we shall discuss business. I would prefer for neither of us to ruin our appetites. I recommend the chicken pie. It is quite delicious.'

Christina stirs milk into her tea and lays the teaspoon on the white china saucer. 'I understand you are doing business with the Parkhurst Gallery on Bond Street.'

François DuRose inclines his head as he takes the final forkful of his fig pudding and custard. 'That is right. I am gratified that the advertising appears to be effective. You would not credit the prices *The Times* charges for a modest advertisement.'

'What, may I ask, has prompted this expansion into the London art world?'

The Frenchman taps at his lips with his linen napkin and lays it on the table.

'Politics, and the situation in Europe. The Americans have deserted Paris and my European clients are more concerned with the events in Spain, Germany and Italy than they are with buying art. Going into business with Mr Beauchamp at the Parkhurst Gallery is simply a decision necessitated by the fact that art is still being bought and sold in London, particularly to the North American market. One must protect one's interests.'

'I couldn't agree more, Monsieur DuRose. Which is precisely why I invited you here today. I have every intention of protecting my interests.'

She nods at the waiter as he removes their dessert plates. 'I do not take kindly to blackmail.' She smiles. 'That is, if it is directed at me. I have found it to be rather useful myself.'

Monsieur DuRose raises a finely plucked eyebrow. 'Blackmail is a rather strong word, Madame Fry. I prefer … negotiation.'

'Oh, yes, negotiation is so much more civilised than blackmail or extortion or, perhaps, bribery. They are all such nasty words, wouldn't you agree? So beneath someone of your reputation.'

Monsieur DuRose sits back against the curved back of his chair and folds his hands in his lap. 'Madame Fry, I have not come here to be insulted. I have come to collect a cheque for what is owed to me through your daughter's folly. My reputation is at stake should anyone discover that I have sold fake Carlo Marinettis onto the market. I simply wish to ensure that this unfortunate episode remains … buried. I might remind you that, should the fraud perpetuated by your daughter be revealed, not only mine but Madame Marinetti's reputation would be destroyed.'

Christina sips at her tea and sets the teacup back on the saucer. She glances around the stylish room, whose earlier *fin de siècle* opulence has been transformed into an Art Deco marvel of etched mirror glass and hidden lighting.

'You may wonder why I chose to meet you in such a public place, and to select such an exposed table, when, perhaps, a more private meeting might have suited you better.'

The Frenchman shrugs. 'I appreciate good taste. I would have expected nothing less of a woman such as yourself.'

'That's very kind, Monsieur DuRose, however, I didn't choose the Café Royal for any other reason than that it will be difficult for you to express any level of … pique at what I am about to say. I don't imagine you are a man who believes in making a spectacle of himself in public. Particularly not in the middle of the Café Royal when he is about to engage in a business endeavour with a prestigious London art gallery.'

François DuRose stares at Christina. He reaches into the pocket of his fine charcoal grey suit and removes a silver cigarette case and a lighter. He opens the case and offers Christina a slender cigarette.

'Thank you. I have not developed the habit.'

'You do not mind if I indulge? I quite enjoy a smoke after lunch.'

'Be my guest.'

Christina watches as the art dealer lights a cigarette. He pockets the silver case and the lighter and exhales a discreet puff of smoke.

'Madame Fry, what is it exactly you wish to say to me? I am a very busy man and I do not have time for games. My patience in this matter is wearing thin.'

'Of course, Monsieur DuRose. I am a simple middle-class widow for whom a visit to the Café Royal is a rare treat. I'm sure you can indulge me a while longer while we resolve our differences.'

'As I said, Madame Fry, I am a busy man—'

'Of course. I understand.' Christina leans toward her luncheon guest. 'Monsieur DuRose, I have no intention of paying you one penny. No intention whatsoever.'

'Madame Fry, you are making a grave mistake.'

'No, no, Monsieur DuRose. It is you who are making the mistake by thinking you can extort money from Etta or me for a fraud in which you very happily complied in order to line your own pockets.'

The art dealer stubs out his cigarette in his empty champagne coupe. 'Madame Fry! I object to this … this impugning of my reputation—'

Christina smiles magnanimously. 'Now, now, Monsieur DuRose. There's no need to cause a scene. People are watching. Let me make this very clear. I have been a patron of several of the top London art galleries for some years now. Amongst others, I was introduced to the services of the highly respected Parkhurst Gallery by my dear friend Syrie Maugham when she decorated my Chelsea flat some years ago. In fact, I have two lovely Modiglianis in my sitting room and an exquisite Matisse in my bedroom there, all of which I purchased from our mutual friend, Mr Beauchamp, at the Parkhurst Gallery.'

'I fail to see what this has to do with anything.'

'Ah, yes, well. Owing to my connections as an art patron here in London, I made some enquiries about your gallery, and I was extraordinarily gratified to discover your impending partnership with the Parkhurst Gallery. It occurred to me that Mr Beauchamp would be entertaining a partnership only if his gallery required investment.'

She sits back and smiles at the waiter as he refreshes her tea. She stirs in some milk. 'Meet Mr Beauchamp's new silent partner.'

The art dealer's face freezes into an expression of horror. 'That cannot be true—'

'I assure you that it is. So, you see, your little enterprise to extort money from me has no future should you wish to partner with the Parkhurst Gallery. I can also assure you, that if you approach any other gallery in London, I will hear about it, and I will do everything in my power to keep you out of this city. Alternatively, I should be delighted to welcome you into the fold of the Parkhurst Gallery should you desist from this tawdry endeavour, which is, quite frankly, unbecoming a man of your obvious discernment and taste.'

François DuRose raises a groomed eyebrow. 'I must admit, I am most impressed by your tenacity, Madame Fry. I had thought this would be quite straightforward.'

'You are not the first man to underestimate me.'

He shakes his head as he reaches for his cigarette case. 'I suppose we should celebrate our new business relationship with a glass of champagne.'

Christina smiles. 'What a delightful suggestion. The sweet champagne here is excellent.'

Part VII

1938

Chapter Fifty-Five

Frank & Celie

Sweet Briar Farm, West Lake, Alberta – January 1938

F rank jumps down from the cab of Ol' Man Forbes's pickup truck into the fresh snow blanketing the ground around the farmhouse. He slams the door shut and leans into the open window.

'Thank you, Mr Forbes. Much obliged.'

Ol' Man Forbes leans on the steering wheel and eyes the farmhouse, taking in the floral curtains at the front room windows and the large sign nailed across the front door: 'Farm for Sale Owing to Foreclosure. Enquiries: Merchant Bank, West Lake.'

'You sure you don't want me to wait for you, Frank? It's mighty cold out there today. Evenin'll be drawing in soon.'

'Thanks, but I'm fine. It might take me a while to find it. You know women. Celie won't settle until I find the china she's left in the barn. It's in the hayloft somewhere. She didn't want the bank to get their hands on it. It was her grandmother's. Sentimental value, you understand. It's only an hour's walk to the Chicken

Coop from here. Besides,' Frank shakes his head and sighs heavily, 'I could use some time to clear my head.'

'Sure enough, Frank.' Ol' Man Forbes turns on the engine. 'You take care. It's hard times all around. Don't take it personal. All this is not your fault. You'll land on your feet, you'll see. Celie will see to that.'

'Sure. Celie sees to everything.'

Frank watches as the truck rattles through the ruts of the snow-covered road. At the crossroads, the pickup turns left toward town and disappears behind a bank of snow. He looks back at the farmhouse. His house. Celie's house. Lulu's house.

The Merchant Bank's house.

He stamps through the snow and climbs the steps to the porch. The bench is where they had left it. Not theirs anymore. The bank's bench now. He brushes off the snow and sits down. Before him, the flat white landscape spreads to the horizon, stopped abruptly where it abuts the dead grey afternoon sky. He reaches into his pocket and takes out his pipe and a packet of tobacco. After stuffing the pipe's bowl, he lights the tobacco. He inhales deeply, draws his scarf closer around his neck, and shuts his eyes.

How did it all come to this? Eighteen years of backbreaking work, not just him, but Celie too. Coaxing a living out of this brutal, implacable scrap of God's earth. All for nothing. *NOTHING! Did you hear that, God? NOTHING!*

He grinds his teeth and takes another puff on his pipe. His throat catches as a sob climbs up his throat, emerging as a choked judder. How could they take Lulu's dog? How could they be such bastards? Thank God for Ben Wheatley, but he should have been the one to rescue Kip. What kind of father is he? He never should have let them take Kip in the first place.

He drops the pipe and buries his head in his hands, giving into the grief, anger and humiliation of the past few months. Lulu's screams as the bailiff carried away her beloved Kip. Celie begging him to leave the dog. To take anything else, but to just leave the dog …

God! God! God! God! God!

He sucks in a deep breath of the cold, dry air and leans back against the clapboard wall of the house. He is a failure. Bankrupt. A man unable to support his family. A disappointment to Celie, who has done nothing but be stoic and kind through all these years of misery. Celie who has never loved him. Celie who deserved so much better out of life. And then to see Lulu like that … to know that, no matter what Ol' Man Forbes says, it *is* all his fault. Every bit of it.

He should have stayed in England. Should have made a life in London with Celie, running his family's auction business while she made a name for herself as a photographer and journalist. But he couldn't stomach it. Not after all the horrors he'd seen in the war. He'd thought Canada would be heaven after all he'd seen. Instead, he'd brought his family into the hell of drought and the Great Depression.

A gust of wind blows across the snow-buried fields, slapping him across his face. Shivering, he rises and stamps out the chill creeping into his feet. He bends down to pick up his pipe and knocks out the wet tobacco against a post. Then he launches it across the yard, until it falls like a stone into the snow.

He has reached the fence in the north field. The fence he and Fred had hammered into the earth all those years ago, when he still believed that the world could be good, despite all he had seen. All around him the evening sky is aflame with a curtain of pulsating colours – red, blue, green, purple. Like the aurora borealis he'd seen on winter camps with Fred, but more, so much more. Two great throbbing rainbows of colour spanning its length and breath.

It is beautiful, but at the same time terrible. Like some celestial warning of dangers ahead.

He removes his coat and jacket and lays them across the posts of the fence. He rests his elbow on a fence post and rolls up his sleeve. Reaching into the back pocket of his trousers, he takes out the tin. He removes the syringe and, after filling it with morphine, injects the clear liquid into his vein. He takes a deep breath as the narcotic slides into his bloodstream. Then he fills the syringe with a second vial.

He slides down into the snow, his back against the fence post, while all around him the sky throbs like a psychedelic pulse. The colours reflect off the snow and dance around him like formless fairies.

Red. Green. Purple. Blue. So beautiful. So beautiful. So—

———————

Celie opens the Chicken Coop's door to see Fred and Ol' Man Forbes standing on the compacted snow.

'Fred? Mr Forbes? I wasn't expecting you. Come in and I'll make you some tea. I don't know where Frank's gone off to, but I'm sure he'll be home soon—'

Fred takes off his hat. 'Celie…' He clears his throat. 'Celie, Frank's not coming home.'

'Not coming home? Fred, whatever do you mean?'

Ol' Man Forbes steps forward. 'Mizz Jeffries, Frank asked me to drive him out to your old farm 'bout an hour ago. He said he needed to find some of your china in the barn—'

'China in the barn? There's no china in the barn.'

The old man nods. 'I thought as much. He was actin' awful strange. Somethin' didn't sit right with me. I got Fred here and we drove back out there. We … we found him…'

'We found him out in the field, Celie,' Fred says. 'He … he's dead, Celie. Frank's dead.'

Celie clutches at the doorframe. 'That's impossible. We had supper. Lulu and Etta had baked an apple pie. He seemed ... happy.'

'I'm sorry, Celie. Don't worry about anythin'. Mr Forbes here and I will sort things out. I'll send Mavis around, okay?'

Celie nods, though Fred's words are muddled, like she is hearing them through water. She stands in the doorway and watches them leave, oblivious to Etta's complaints about the freezing draught. Frank's dead? How? How could he be—

She spins around and rushes into the house to Frank's room. She pulls open his dresser drawers, then searches under his bed. It's not there. It's not anywhere. He'd taken the tin of morphine.

She sits on the floor beside the bed as the anger and frustration she'd suppressed for almost twenty years bubble up inside her like a geyser about to explode.

How could you do it, Frank? How could you abandon Lulu and me here? You bring us out here and we follow your lead, no matter how obtuse it often was. You always knew better, didn't you, Frank? You knew how to farm better because of your bloody book of English farming methods. You ridiculed me for cautioning you about all the loans you'd taken out, the foolhardy investments you'd made. You resented my photography, and anything I tried to do for myself. Well, now, you've freed me, Frank. Freed me and Lulu.

Her fury suddenly calms as a realisation dawns. *You've freed us. That's why you did it, isn't it? You haven't abandoned us at all. You've set us free.*

Chapter Fifty-Six

Jessie

Hotel Oriente, La Rambla, Barcelona, Spain - February 1938

Jessie tosses her hat and coat onto her bed and pries off her shoes. She pads, in her stockinged feet, over to the French doors and, throwing them open, steps out onto the balcony. Below her, La Rambla is silent in the light of the waning moon, although it wouldn't be long before the queues of women hoping to buy bread, eggs and olive oil would begin to form in lines that would snake around the buildings and down into the side streets.

She shuts her eyes and breathes in the chilly air. Eighteen innocent people dead from the Italian bomb on the Passieg de Sant Joan, and over forty injured. Ordinary people just going about their business.

She rubs her arms against the cold, frowning as she recalls the ridiculous situation at the hospital with the orderlies and the anaesthesiologist. How could these men believe, with such absolute conviction, in the inherent inferiority of women and that they had no place in the world except to keep house and raise children?

It hadn't been the first time she'd been subjected to this chauvinism in Spain, nor seen it enacted in the streets and restaurants of Barcelona and Madrid. Despite all their utopian rhetoric and the images of gun-toting militia women – who mostly ended up cooking and nursing when they reached the front lines, or constructing barricades from the streets' cobblestones in the cities – most of the anti-fascist men she'd met seemed incapable of changing their traditional attitudes to women. It's been twenty-five years since she joined her sisters in suffragist marches supporting women's rights. On days like today, she feels like very little has improved. It's simply infuriating.

She steps back into the room and is undressing when there's a soft knock at the door.

'Yes? Who is it?'

'Antonio. I brought you something.'

She opens the door a crack, her heart thumping at the sound of his voice. His figure is shadowed in the unlit hallway. 'It's late.'

'It is not late, Jessica. It is early.'

'I should sleep. I'm just back from the hospital and I have to go back at noon.'

He leans toward her and the warmth emanating from his body seeps into her flesh. 'I won't stay. I will let you sleep. I just want to give you something first.'

She nods and opens the door. 'Just for a moment.'

He steps into the room, which is lit a soft grey in the moonlight. He holds out a small paper bag. 'Take it.'

'What is it?'

He smiles. 'Why should I ruin the surprise?'

She takes the bag and, as she unrolls the top, the scent of freshly ground coffee wafts into the room. She gasps. 'Coffee? You found coffee?'

'I did.'

She sniffs in the earthy, barky scent. 'Come in! Sit down. I have a kettle and a camp stove. I'll make us some.'

'This is not the only thing I brought.' He reaches behind his back and presents her with a fat loaf of bread.

'Fresh bread? It's still warm! Oh, my word, Antonio. I think I love you!'

His dark eyes glint in the moonlight. 'You only love me for the food.'

She laughs as she fills the kettle with water from her sink. 'You have me entirely figured out.'

He watches her as she lights the camp stove and sets the kettle on to boil. Setting down the loaf on the card table, he approaches her and runs his finger along her arm where she has rolled up her sleeve.

'Jessica.'

Jessie shuts her eyes as Antonio brushes his lips against her neck. She shouldn't do this. She'd gone to Madrid to get him out of her life, out of her mind. He's far too young. It is impossible. There is no future in it. It's too complicated.

'Jessica.' His lips are warm on the chilled skin of her jaw. Her heart flutters against her ribcage like a butterfly released from its chrysalis.

'Antonio, this isn't a good idea.'

He presses kisses on the soft skin under her ear. 'Why is that?'

She gasps for breath. 'I'm forty-three years old.'

He kisses her cheek. 'So?'

She pulls her face away. 'Doesn't that matter to you?'

He brushes his fingers along her cheek. 'No.'

She turns away from him. 'Oh Lord.'

He laughs and reaches for her hand. 'It does not matter, Jessica. Not in the least. The way I see it, we are here alone together on this earth on this February night in Barcelona, and I want to kiss you.'

Jessie looks at him, and the loneliness of the years since Aziz's death wells up inside her. 'I want to kiss you too.'

Antonio pulls her into his embrace and they kiss until the sound of the whistling kettle reminds them of the coffee, which goes unmade until much, much later.

Chapter Fifty-Seven

Celie & Etta

West Lake, Alberta, Canada - March 1938

Mavis Wheatley thrusts a flour sack stuffed with chicken sandwiches and slices of apple pie into Celie's hand.

'A little something to keep you going while you wait for your train connection in Edmonton.' She whispers in Celie's ear. 'There's also a couple of bottles of my beer in there for when you get thirsty on the train half-way to Winnipeg.'

Celie embraces her friend. 'Thank you, Mavis. I don't know what I would have done here without you. You and Fred must come out to England to visit me and Lulu. We'd love that.'

Mavis brushes her fringe of wild wheat blonde hair out of her eyes as a blast of icy wind whips across the West Lake station train platform.

'Wouldn't that be something? Me and Fred on the town in London waving at the King and Queen and the little princesses in front of Buckingham Palace.'

'Yes, wouldn't that be something?'

Celie glances out at the snowdrifts blanketing the barren wheat fields surrounding the station and the four towering red grain elevators, their paint now faded and peeling from years of neglect.

'I remember the day Frank and I arrived here back in 1920. It was steaming hot and I remember thinking that we'd landed in the middle of nowhere. We had nothing but a plot of virgin land waiting for us. Not even a house. I remember being very cross with Frank for not telling me that the Soldiers' Land Settlement Scheme didn't come with an actual house, but a loan for a house and a barn. When we got off the train that day, we were essentially homeless. Then Fred rescued us and you fed us, and eventually it all worked out. Well, it didn't exactly work out, did it?'

Mavis squeezes Celie's arm. 'You and Lulu are always welcome back here with us.'

'I know. Thank you, Mavis.' She frowns at the road into the town. 'Speaking of Lulu, what on earth is keeping her and Ben? The train will be here in fifteen minutes.'

'I imagine Mr Forbes is spoiling Lulu in the store.'

'She's going to miss him and his jellybeans. No doubt she's loading up on them for the trip.'

A dog barks and Mavis gestures to her tall, lanky son and the small, compact figure of Lulu heading down the road with the border collie.

'There they are. Looks like Kip's wheedled a bone out of Mr Forbes.'

'Looks like it. Thank Ben for taking Kip. Lulu's going to miss her dog terribly, but we know Ben loves Kip as much as Lulu does.'

'Kip's in good hands. Nothing to worry about there.'

The door to the stationmaster's office slams and Fred Wheatley steps out onto the platform holding three train tickets in his mittened hands. 'There you go, Celie. You're all set for Montréal. Change at Edmonton and then straight across the country.'

'Thanks, Fred. You and Mavis have been wonderful.' She looks at the door to the stationmaster's office. 'Where's Etta?'

'Oh, she's chattin' up the new stationmaster. Seems he's from Canmore up in the Rockies. Been transferred out here. Etta's got it sorted for him to come over to our place for supper next week. Mostly, I think she's in there 'cause it's warmer and she's got him to give her a cup o' tea.'

'That's Etta all over. Looking out for herself above all.'

Fred reaches into the pocket of his thick winter jacket and pulls out the money she'd given him for the tickets to Edmonton. He folds the bills into her gloved hand.

'The tickets are on me 'n' Mavis. You keep the money your mother sent you. Buy somethin' nice in Montréal. I hear they got a big Eaton's store there.'

Celie opens her mouth to object and Fred raises his mittened hand. 'Don't wanna hear it. Ya just gotta promise to keep in touch.'

'There's something else, Celie,' Mavis says, nodding to Ben. He retrieves a canvas sack and carries it over to Celie.

'What's this?'

'Open the drawstring,' Mavis says.

Celie unties the string and reaches into the sack. Her hand clasps around a familiar object and she gasps. She takes out the camera.

'It's my camera.' She looks into the sack. 'And my tripod. Where did you—'

Fred smiles. 'Don't you mind about that. Consider it our going away present.'

'I can't thank you enough. You have no idea what this means to me.' She reaches over and kisses Mavis and Fred on their cheeks.

Down the track, the train's whistle hoots. Celie swallows the knot that's formed in her throat. 'It looks like that's our signal.'

She gives Fred and Mavis a final hug and turns to her daughter, who has buried her tearful face in Kip's fur.

'Say goodbye to Ben and Kip, Lulu. It's time to go.'

Celie slams the ship's metal door and steps out onto the deck. The frigid March wind whips around her, and she clutches her coat closer to her body as she heads over to the railing.

Below her, the ship churns up white-crested waves in the dense green water, and the sky is a dead white to the horizon. But, despite the chill, and the wind, and the forbidding view, her stomach quivers with an excitement she hasn't felt since the brief few days she'd spent with Robson McCrea.

Robson McCrea, Frank Jeffries, her father Gerald, Max Fischer … their faces drift through her mind as she gazes out to the horizon. All the men who'd come and gone through her life. Men who had given her things or taken things away. Now, they were all gone, and she was on her own. Except for Lulu. At the very least, Frank had given her Lulu, and for that she would always be grateful.

The ship's door slams. 'Celie? What are you doing out here? It's freezing!'

Celie smiles over at Etta, who is wrapped in the thick fur of the muskrat coat she'd cadged from the steward in the ship's lost luggage hold.

'Nothing. Just needed some fresh air. Where's Lulu?'

'She's in the cabin reading *Gone with the Wind*. I told her that Mr Selznick had offered me the role of Scarlett O'Hara, but she didn't believe me.'

'Did he?'

'Well, he would have, if I'd stayed in Hollywood. I can't for the life of me remember why I left.' She joins Celie at the railing, shivering despite the thick fur. 'Heavens, I've never known the Mediterranean to be so cold.'

'The Mediterranean?'

Etta threads her arm through Celie's as she looks out at the choppy waves. 'Aren't you excited to visit Capri, Celie? It's your first time, isn't it? I mean, the first time since you were born.'

'Etta, I was born in London just like you and Jessie. It's Adriana who was born on Capri. But we're not going to Capri. We're on a ship in the Atlantic Ocean on our way to England.'

Etta rubs her gloved hand against her forehead. 'We are?'

'Yes, you've been visiting me in Canada and now we're moving back to live with Mama at Clover Bar.'

'Oh. Clover Bar?'

'Yes.'

'I was sure we were going to Capri. It's been ages since I've seen Carlo. He must miss me terribly.'

Celie brushes a bleached curl out of her sister's eyes. 'I'm sure he does.'

Etta frowns as she regards her sister. 'You don't look like Papa at all.'

'I know. I look more like Mama.'

Etta cocks her head. 'Yes, I suppose that's it.' She frowns and shakes her head. 'I'm sure there was something I was meant to tell you.' She shrugs. 'Ah well, I guess it wasn't that important.'

Celie nods. 'You'll remember if it is. Now, I think it's teatime. No doubt Lulu's been looking at her watch. What are you having today? Cucumber sandwiches or scones?'

'Oh, scones, always. Though they're not a patch on Hettie's.'

Chapter Fifty-Eight

Jessie

Barcelona, Spain – March 1938

Before dawn, March 16th

Jessie wakes abruptly – one moment deep in a dreamless sleep, the next fully awake – a habit she had acquired back in her days on the hospital ship at Gallipoli. It is still night, and the city outside her hotel window is silent. Even the street dogs are asleep. The light from the moon, one day off fullness, filters through the grid of tape on the balcony windows and the thin cotton curtains, casting a silver-grey light into the room. Beside her, she feels the warmth of Antonio's body as he sleeps.

She rises from the bed and, after grabbing a jumper from the back of a chair against the night chill, goes over to the balcony windows and eases them open. The leaves of the plane trees lining La Rambla rustle in a faint breeze, and, if it weren't for the taped windows, it could be any night on any street in any city. But this is Barcelona during a war, and something feels off.

Life in the city has returned to a facsimile of normality after the riots of the previous May. The barricades of cobblestones have come down; the flower stalls are bright and pretty along the promenade; the cafés are open, selling a sweet, fizzy orange drink and an unpalatable sherry; women wearing hats and dresses fashionable back in 1936 walk their tiny dogs or push carriages of infants; boys toss chunks of broken cobblestones at each other in an injury-prone game of catch, and girls play hopscotch on the promenade with discarded bullet casings.

Many of the men are away at the front, engaged in bloody fighting against General Franco's encroaching Nationalists; but here, in Barcelona, those who remain sit in the cafés reading newspapers and engage in endless debates about the benefits and defects of the various leftist Republican groups.

She leans against the hotel's cool, grey stone wall and folds her arms as she listens for the first sounds of the awakening city, even as the memory of Antonio's lovemaking wafts around her mind like a mist. She doesn't love him; certainly not the way she had loved Aziz. But she wants him and he wants her, and though vestiges of Catholic guilt threaten to cloud her enjoyment of their time together, she refuses to succumb to it. If there is anything that she has learned from nursing in a war, losing a husband in a volatile Egypt and, now, doing what little she can to keep as many people alive as possible in a civil war, it's that nothing is knowable. Tomorrow is not a given. The plans you make may change in an instant. The people you love may leave you, or die, or go somewhere where they are far beyond your reach. When she'd kissed Shani goodbye in July 1936, she'd planned to be in Spain only for a couple of weeks. Now she has no idea when she will see her daughter again. Nothing is knowable except the moment that currently exists.

She hears Antonio stir in the bed. He sits up against the pillows and leans on his elbow.

'*Querida*, what are you doing? You can't sleep?'

She shakes her head. 'No.' She pads barefoot across the cool terrazzo floor and sits on the bed beside Antonio. She traces a line along his nose with her fingertip. 'When do you go back to the Matallana line?'

Antonio kisses Jessie's fingers. 'Saturday. It is Luis's nineteenth birthday on Friday. He will come with me to the front. It was his decision. My mother is upset, of course, and Teresa is like a tigress in a cage, wanting to be a part of the fight.'

'What does your father think?'

'He understands that it is necessary that we fight for the freedom of Spain from the threat of a fascist dictator.'

'What a world we live in.'

Antonio pulls her down on top of him. 'A civil war is always a terrible thing. The worst, I think. Blood against blood. But it has done one thing I am happy about.'

'What is that?'

He cups her head in his hands. 'It has brought you to me.'

2:05pm, March 17th

Jessie is in the operating theatre at the Hospital Clinic de Barcelona working on a young girl who had been dug out of the rubble in the Gothic Quarter, when she hears a roar like a hundred freight trains crashing. The hospital, despite its solid foundations and thick stone walls, shakes like a leaf caught in a storm.

'*Santa Maria!*' Ester swears. 'What is that?'

Jessie, the nurses and the anaesthesiologist look up at the ceiling where the green industrial lights swing like pendulums as the roar thunders around them.

Jessie nods toward the doors with her chin. 'Ginebra, go see if you can find out what's happened.'

Ester crosses herself. 'What are the Italian monsters doing to us now? Two days of this, night and day, dropping bombs on women and children. It is murder.'

Jessie looks at the broken body of the girl, who can be no more than six or seven. How many of these children has she seen since the bombing started the previous morning? How many pregnant women have died on the operating table, their future children never to see this world? How many boys in their school uniforms, or tram conductors in theirs? Flower sellers? Fashionable women in their outdated hats? She has lost count.

She hasn't seen Antonio since that morning. He had left early to join the other militia men and women digging survivors from the steaming rubble and powdered glass that had once been the walls and windows of homes, shops, restaurants and cinemas, even as the bombs keep falling. But she can't think of him now. She hasn't had time to think of anything except the victim on the operating table, then the next, and the next. She has barely slept and has eaten only a few bowls of lentil soup in the past two days, washed down with weak coffee. The hunger pangs that growl in her stomach have become nothing but a minor irritation, which she assuages with glasses of water.

Ginebra bursts through the swing doors. 'It was a bomb, by the Coliseum cinema. They said that the planes flew down the Gran Via dropping bombs all along the road, on top of buses, and trams and everything. One hit a lorry of explosives in front of the Coliseum. It's destroyed half of the block.'

'*Hóstia!*' Ester curses. 'Those bastards.'

Jessie looks across the operating table at Ester. 'Scissors.'

'What?'

'Scissors. We have work to do. We are going to be busy.'

Jessie enters the lobby of the Hotel Oriente, her body aching with weariness. She heads toward the reception desk to collect her key, intent only on reaching her bed before she collapses.

'Jessie.'

Jessie turns around to see Ruth rise from a chair, a glass of whisky in her hand.

'Ruth? I'm sorry, were we meant to meet for supper tonight? I'm absolutely exhausted. I just want to—'

'Jessie.'

'What?'

Ruth shakes her head.

'What? What is it?'

'Antonio's dead. He was near the Coliseum cinema when the bomb dropped on a lorry of high explosives. He ... he wouldn't have felt anything.'

Jessie clutches at a chair to steady herself. 'I just saw him. This morning.'

'I'm sorry, Jessie.'

Jessie turns and wills her legs to steer her up the stairs. 'I need to go to bed. I'm working first thing.'

Chapter Fifty-Nine

Christina & Celie

Clover Bar, Hither Green, London – April 1938

Christina crosses the room and opens a drawer in the walnut secretary. She takes out a white envelope and hands it to Celie, who is sitting by the fire reading Etta's copy of *Gone with the Wind*.

'This came for you. A few years after you emigrated to Canada. I … I thought it best not to forward it to you.'

Celie scans the familiar handwriting and the German stamp postmarked September 15th, 1929. She looks up at her mother. 'It's from Max. Why on earth—'

'Cecelia, you were married. You had a child. What possible good would it have done to send it to you? Some things should be left in the past where they belong.'

Celie stares at the envelope lying in her lap like a fallen leaf. 'It was wrong of you to keep it from me.' She rises suddenly and hurries past her mother into the hall.

Christina listens to her daughter's footsteps on the staircase and the slam of her bedroom door. She sits in her armchair and picks up her needlepoint. She stabs the needle through the half-finished pansy's black eye.

'You'll be 'avin' some tea?'

Christina looks up into Hettie's solid, expressionless face. 'Tea would be ideal at this juncture, Hettie.'

Celie sits in her desk chair and slices open the envelope with her letter opener. Her heart beats a drum in her chest and she sucks in a deep breath.

> *Sandgasse, 10,*
> *Heidelberg,*
> *Germany*

> *September 15th, 1929*

> *My dearest Schatzi,*
> *You are surprised to hear from me, yes? It has been a very long time, I know this well, but, truly, I did not know what to say or how to say it.*
> *I have started this letter so many times, and each time the words were not the words I wished to say to you. You, who have always been, and who always will be, so special to me.*
> *So many times, I have looked at calendars and counted the days since we last met in your mother's house just after your marriage. I have missed you like the roses on the Philosopher's Walk, that I had so much wished to show you, miss the summer rain.*
> *For years I could not see how I could bear knowing that you were so far away from me, living your life with someone else. But, at the very least, when I looked at the moon, I knew it was the same moon you saw when you looked up into the night sky, and this gave me some small comfort. I have often wondered if you ever met my stepbrother, Hans*

Brandt, who lives with our aunt and uncle in Alberta. He has written me of his wonderful English teacher and I have often imagined her to be you. Isn't it strange that two of the people I have loved most in my life are both in Alberta? It is a sign, I think, that we were meant to know each other in this life.

You may have wondered why it took so long for me to contact you once the war ended. The fact is that I deserted from the army. I had been captured by the Russians when I was fighting on the Eastern Front and was a prisoner of war in Russia. I was working on laying new rail tracks near the Finnish border, and when the Russians left the war in March 1918, they had no more interest in us German prisoners, so I simply walked into the forest, determined to find my way back to you.

Schatzi, the Russian winter is something I never wish to experience again in this lifetime. This is to say that it took me a very long time to find my way back to England, and to you. I should have written you, but I had it in my head to surprise you, and to take you in my arms again. It seems I made a terrible mistake.

Now it is ten years since I last saw you. I have had to content myself with the photograph of us at your twenty-first birthday party at your parents' house. It is very worn and curled at the edges now, from all the handling I have given it.

I completed my legal studies at Humboldt University in Berlin and have been practising law back in Heidelberg since then. I have been living in my parents' house with other student lodgers. My parents – my mother and my stepfather, actually – have retired to the countryside outside of Munich, but Frau Knopfler has insisted she stay with us poor bachelors to ensure we have a steady supply of her plum cake.

I have a good position, and am very busy with clients in the courts, but the truth is that I buried myself in my studies and my work to suppress my memories of you and my great sadness. A year ago, I realised I could not live my life like that any longer. It was time for me to accept that we will never see each other again in this life, though it pained me beyond description…

So, here it is. I am marrying at Christmas, Schatzi. It is Anneliese

Schneider, whom I have known for many years. She has been a very kind and patient friend. I know we will have a good life together.

Now we can both be happy in the lives that the world has given us, though you will always remain to me my own dearest Schatzi.

Love always,

Max

PS: I hope you and Frank Jeffries are happy together. You of all people deserve happiness.

PPS: When you think of me, if you do, look up at the moon – you will always find me there.

Celie folds the letter and slips it into her skirt pocket. Rising, she walks over to the window and gazes out at the familiar view of the rowan tree, its budding branches heavy with rain, leaning over the greenhouse; the winter-flowering cherry tree with its burgundy leaves unfolding; the yellow daffodils bouncing under the raindrops, and the old rose on the arch sprouting green and red stems from where someone has pruned it earlier that spring.

She swallows and grits her teeth until the pain that tears her heart into pieces is tamed into a dull throb.

Chapter Sixty

Etta

Clover Bar, Hither Green, London – June 1938

'Mama?'

Adriana looks into the glass-walled conservatory, which is verdant with the plants Christina has nurtured from cuttings obtained from the WI's garden club members. In a corner, under the arching leaves of a banana tree, Etta is standing in front of an easel dabbing magenta paint onto the canvas.

'There you are. You're painting again.'

Etta turns around and smiles at Adriana, oblivious of the streak of yellow paint across her cheek. 'I am. I suddenly felt the urge.'

'*Nonna* will be pleased. She's spent a fortune at Green & Stone on paints for you.' Adriana fans her face with the envelope she's holding. 'I don't know how you can stand the heat in here. Don't you feel it?' She jams opens the garden door with a pot of peace lilies, then she skirts around the white wicker furniture to her mother.

'What are you painting?' she asks in Italian.

Etta cleans her brush absentmindedly on her skirt. 'Circe turning the crew of Odysseus's ship into pigs.' On the canvas, a blue-skinned goddess in flowing white robes and a mass of scarlet hair laughs from a cloud as the unfortunate sailors metamorphose into magenta pigs.

'It's good, Mama. You are a surrealist, like Dali. You could teach at the Slade.'

Etta laughs. 'I don't know about any of that. This is just how I see it in my head. I have to paint it before it disappears.'

'You are an artist, Mama. Like Papa, and me. Although I am not so fond of magenta.' She waves an envelope. 'Mario has sent me a letter. Shall I read it out loud?'

'Liliana's boy? That would be lovely.'

Adriana flops onto a chair and rips open the envelope. 'He's not a boy, Mama. He's thirty-five years old.'

Etta swirls dabs of Prussian Blue and Bismuth Yellow into a rich viridian on her palette and attacks the sea with sweeping brushstrokes. 'Don't tease, Adriana. I taught him sketching just last year in the garden of Villa Serenissima. I intend to have him start with oils when I'm back in Capri after my visit here.'

Adriana glances over at her mother. 'You haven't been back to Capri in years, Mama.'

Etta smiles indulgently at her daughter. 'You do enjoy teasing your mother, don't you? You and me and your papa and Aunt Stefania had a picnic at the Grotta di Matermania last summer on the Feast of the Assumption, don't you remember? Mario and Liliana came as well and brought cannoli from the bakery.'

Adriana slips the letter out of the envelope. Her mother wasn't getting any better. Only yesterday she'd told Auntie Celie that *Nonno* Gerald wasn't her father. The bouts of mania had subsided, and she was sleeping through the nights now, but her mother's mind seemed to be stuck in a world that had folded in on itself like a painted fan, with memories and time squashed together in a mix that only her mother could understand.

'*Allora, Mama.* Let's hear what Mario has to say.'

Dear Adriana,

I am sending you and your family a big welcome from Capri. Today it is sunny and hot and everywhere is the smell of lemons and rosemary in the air. My grandmother is in the kitchen cooking scialatielli con gamberoni with the shrimp I bought from a fisherman in the marina this morning. I am hungry just to think about it. She is singing about love as she cooks, and I have been fixing some broken tiles on the roof of the shed. She is happy when I come to Villa Serenissima. I will go to the church with her tomorrow morning. Father Izzo is coming for lunch and we will eat far too much of my Nonna's cooking. It is a nice tradition.

Now that the Accademia di Belle Arti is closed for the summer, I do not need to teach, so I will stay here at the villa with my grandmother and help with the vegetable garden and repairs. The villa needs to be repainted and the fountain has stopped working, so I will fix these things this summer.

How is your painting? Did you enjoy your year studying in Paris? I admit I was envious! And to have such a successful exhibition at the Galerie DuRose as well! My grandmother and I are so proud of you. When you come to Capri, we will all celebrate your success, but it is better for now for you to stay in England. Italy has changed very much since you were here two years ago.

We are so happy that you and Signora Etta are together again in Signora Fry's house. I remember what a happy time we all had when we were together in Capri, before the misunderstanding with your father. I hope you understand that he was justified to banish me from Villa Serenissima. I had thought I was helping your mother by posting her letters to your father from Capri when she was in Paris promoting his paintings, but it was wrong to deceive your father when he was helpless in prison, even with the best of intentions, and I am so sorry for it.

One thing I am not sorry for is that your half-brother, Paolo, is now too busy working for Mussolini's government in Rome to bother my grandmother with visits to the villa where he would strut around the property like a king surveying his castle while she berated him from the balcony. You can imagine it, I am certain! Paolo is still sending letters here, threatening to throw my grandmother off the property once he succeeds in having Signora Albertini's will overturned. He is claiming that she was not in her right mind when she made the will, and that he, as your elder half-brother, should inherit the house. But Signora Albertini was very clever in her will, and included instructions that the villa was never to be sold to, or inherited by, Paolo Marinetti under any circumstances, and that the rightful heir is Adriana.

We have just had to suffer through the spectacle of Adolf Hitler's visit to Il Duce last month, with Nazi swastikas and Italian flags flying in all the big cities. There were parades and celebrations and Hitler enjoyed the hospitality of our king in the Quirinal Palace. I was in Napoli the evening Hitler and Mussolini came to view the Italian navy in the harbour. The people lined the roads and crowded onto the roofs to cheer on the Fascist alliance. How can so many people be blinded to the evil that is before their eyes? Have they not seen the Slavs and Croats being beaten in our streets? The intellectuals herded into prisons or simply disappearing? Have they not noticed that any political opposition is suppressed, so that no voice is heard but that of Il Duce's? And now our government is becoming an aggressor, just like Hitler's. We have murdered hundreds of thousands of Ethiopian civilians in the Ethiopian War, and our bombs have killed thousands in support of the fascist Nationalists in the war in Spain. It is an ugly time here in Italy. I am ashamed for my country.

I am sorry for all this. The situation makes me angry, as you can see. I am angry for my country and I am angry for myself. I am an art teacher. What use is this when your country is growing a great cancer? I think of Paolo in Mussolini's offices in Rome, and I see that he is involved in what is happening in Italy. Then I think of myself in my studio classroom in the Accademia and I see that I am not. This does not feel right to me, and I must think about what I can do to have a voice in this situation.

Enough of this. I am sorry. You can see what is on my mind more than anything else. I promise to look out for your interests, Adriana. Villa Serenissima is yours and it will be here when it is safe for you to come, so long as I breathe.

Ciao Stellina,

Mario

Adriana folds the letter. 'Things sound bad in Italy. I worry for Lili and Mario.'

'Don't worry, *il mio angelo*. Your papa will take care of them,' Etta says as she meticulously adds a grimace to the face of a sailor/pig being eaten by a sea monster.

'Papa's gone, Mama.'

Etta stands back to appraise her work. 'Gone? Where's he gone? Oh, that's right, I'd forgotten. He has a flat in Naples. Is that where he is?'

Adriana joins her mother in front of the easel and rests her hand on Etta's shoulder. 'Papa died, Mama.'

Etta jerks her head around, her hazel eyes flashing with anger. 'That's not funny, Adriana. Where do you learn to joke about such things? At school? I'll have to speak to Sister Maria Benedicta. She must keep a closer watch on her pupils.'

'Mama, don't you remember? Papa—'

'Etta!' Christina says as she appears at the garden door. She exchanges a glance with Adriana as she enters the conservatory. 'How lovely, darling. You're painting! I'm so pleased. And such vivid colours.'

'I'm painting the story of Circe and Odysseus's sailors.'

'You always did have such a vivid imagination. It's much better for you to channel your imaginings into art rather than upsetting Cecelia with silly stories about her father.'

Etta frowns. 'What did I say?'

Christina takes the paintbrush from Etta's hand and dabs at the painting. 'You said Gerald wasn't her father. It quite upset her. You know how close they were.'

'Why would I have said that? I didn't mean to upset her. She and Lulu have been ever so good to me since I arrived.'

Christina hands Etta back the paintbrush and sits down on the wicker settee. 'It's not of any importance, my dear, although if it happens again, I may have to consider sending you back to the hospital for some treatment. You can't be saying things that upset other people.'

A vague memory of a gag being put into her mouth and her arms being strapped down flashes through Etta's mind. 'I'm so sorry, Mama. I'll be very careful.'

'Don't worry, darling. I'm certain you will be.' Christina glances over at her granddaughter. 'Adriana, would you go ask Hettie to make us all some tea? None of that Lapsang Souchong rubbish. Earl Grey. And some of the shortbread biscuits she baked yesterday.'

Adriana rises from the wicker chair and darts her eyes at her mother. 'She's confused, *Nonna*.'

'These things take time. She will be fine.'

'I hope so, *Nonna*.'

Christina listens until Adriana's footsteps fade away down the hallway. She turns to Etta. 'Darling, I need to ask you something important.'

Etta frowns as she focuses on painting scales on the sea monster. 'Yes?'

Christina rubs dust off an aspidistra leaf with her fingers and sits in the chair Adriana vacated. 'You haven't told Cecelia anything about … our secret, have you?'

Etta looks at her mother and raises her eyebrows. 'What secret?'

Christina frowns as she scrutinises the quizzical expression on her daughter's face. 'You spoke to your Cousin Stefania about it in

Capri. You don't remember?'

Etta laughs. 'You're talking in riddles, Mama.' She is about to refine the sea monster's scales when she gasps. 'Wait. I remember.'

Christina's heart flutters. 'You do?'

She drops her paintbrush into a glass. 'I never went back to Capri for Cousin Stefania's funeral.' She rushes over to her mother and throws her arms around her. 'Oh, Mama. I'm so sorry! It was awful of me not to come back for that.'

Christina pats Etta's back. 'It's all right, Etta. You're forgiven.'

Etta sits on the settee beside her mother. 'Adriana was furious with me, wasn't she?' She drops her head into her hands. 'I remember she sent me an awful telegram. She said I was a horrible, irresponsible, selfish woman and she never wanted to speak to me again.'

Etta sits up and wipes at her wet eyes, leaving a streak of Cadmium Orange on her right cheek. 'Where was I? If I wasn't at Villa Serenissima or here, where was I? I can't remember.'

Christina sits back against the cushions and feels the tension she has been carrying since Etta's revelation that she knew the truth about Cecelia's birth ease away, like a burden released after a long journey. *She doesn't remember! Etta doesn't remember that Harry was Cecelia's father!*

She reaches out to pat Etta's hand. 'You were in Paris, speaking to an art gallery about selling Carlo's paintings, don't you remember?'

Etta nods. 'Yes. Yes, I do. That's where I was.'

Christina takes Etta's hand into hers. 'Adriana is speaking to you now, isn't she?'

Etta nods as she sniffs. 'Yes.'

'Then, no harm done, my dear. No one blames you in the least for not going.'

'Lili wasn't angry? Or Mario?'

'No, darling. They understood.'

'And Carlo? He wasn't mad, either? He's terribly cross with CJ, you know. They had a fight in Paris.'

Christina shakes her head. 'Carlo wasn't mad either, darling. He simply said that he missed you and wished you would come home soon.'

Part VIII

1939

Chapter Sixty-One

Jessie

Barcelona, Spain - January 25th, 1939

J essie staggers over the mounds of charred wooden beams, which are still smoking from the earlier German air raid, her feet crunching on the shattered glass that covers the cobbles of La Rambla like salt. The tattered remains of posters urging the mobilisation of all men and women under fifty flutter in the sharp January wind, and pamphlets inciting resistance litter the pavements. Since the bloody defeat of the Republicans at Ebro in November, it had become clear that the Republic had been abandoned to its fate by the international community, and an all-encompassing fatalism had descended upon the population.

The street is deserted; she has seen barely a soul on her walk from the hospital through the devastated city. The Barcelona of hope, the Barcelona of 1936 full of the zeal of revolutionary change, is long gone, replaced by a cemetery of dead citizens and dead illusions.

Her stomach rumbles. She has eaten nothing but lentils and

slices of stale bread for the last month, like everyone else who hadn't yet fled the city for the French border. It's been twelve hours since she's eaten breakfast and the thought of the boiled lentils and the whisky Ruth had pilfered from the foreign journalists at the Hotel Majestic is one of the two things that had kept her ploughing forward through the ravaged city in the freezing winter night. That, and Ruth, whom she hasn't seen since the German Stukas started dropping bombs five days before.

Behind her, by the port, she hears another bomb explode, then another, then the belated mournful whine of the air raid sirens. She ducks into one of the makeshift shelters of sandbags and cobblestones that Barcelona's women and children have constructed throughout the city, and sits inside with an old man cradling a shivering dog in his arms. They exchange a brief greeting, then wait.

That evening, Jessie is in her room in the Hotel Oriente eating the last of her supper of boiled lentils when someone hammers on her door.

'Jessie! It's Ruth.'

She hurries to the door and throws it open. 'Thank God, Ruth. I've been worried sick.'

Ruth grabs Jessie's glass of whisky off the table and downs the liquor in one gulp. She pours out another glassful of whisky and drinks it down. 'Get your stuff. We're leaving.'

'Leaving? I've got to get to the hospital in the morning.'

'No, you won't. I've just been in the censor's office sending a dispatch. I saw Capa and some of the other reporters there. Franco's army has just crossed the river south of the city. They'll be here in a few hours and they're taking no prisoners. If they find you in the hospital tomorrow, there's every chance you'll be shot.'

'But I'm a doctor.'

'Doesn't matter. As far as they're concerned, you're the enemy. Jessie, I saw what they did to the Republicans in Ebro. Boys as young as seventeen hung from trees, women raped and killed, children—'

She shakes her head and picks up Jessie's leather suitcase. She begins stuffing it with clothes. 'I've got us a lift to the French border with Capa and some other reporters, but they're leaving in half an hour whether we're there or not.'

'But Ruth—'

Ruth drops the suitcase on the floor. 'Look, here's the deal. I'm only going to go if you go, too. Otherwise, I'll stay and we'll figure it out, but I'd really rather not stay. Jessie, think of Shani. She's already lost one parent. Don't make her an orphan.'

Jessie stares at Ruth, who has folded her arms and is regarding her with an air of stubborn exasperation. *Shani*. Yes, of course. She's a mother. She can't risk her life. What was she thinking?

'All right. Give me ten minutes, Ruth. There isn't much to pack.'

Jessie gazes out the car's window as it bumps over the bomb-rutted road toward the French border in the north. The night is still and dark, with the moon a waxing sliver amongst the stars in the black sky. Ruth is asleep beside her and the reporters' voices have subsided into murmurs about what they will do once they reach France.

It has all finished so suddenly. The frantic pace of her life in the hospital and amongst the anarchists had become the norm. Now, suddenly, it is over, and she's going home. Home to her mother and her sisters and her nieces. Home to Shani.

The letters from Shani had tailed off in the past year. There hadn't even been one at Christmas. How can she blame her daughter for being upset with her? Shani had accused her of abandoning her in the last letter she'd received back in August. She'd written Shani immediately, explaining how important her work was, how sometimes sacrifices had to be made for the greater good. Assuring her that she hadn't been abandoned. That she loved her. That she would make it all up to her when she got to London.

She'd waited for days, then weeks, then months for a reply, but there had been none.

Now, she is finally going to London, and she will have the opportunity to repair her relationship with her daughter, and start their new life together as they were meant to after Aziz's death. She hopes that she isn't too late.

Chapter Sixty-Two

The Fry Women

Clover Bar, Hither Green, London - April 1939

Christina looks up from her needlepoint and draws her auburn eyebrows together in irritation.

'Hettie? Hettie? Where is that woman? Can't she hear the doorbell?'

Lulu grimaces as she hits another wrong note on the piano. 'Shani's teaching Hettie how to make *qatayef* for Easter pudding tomorrow.' She flips the sheet music and stumbles into the next verse of *Jeepers Creepers*.

'*Qatayef*? What is wrong with bread and butter pudding?'

The doorbell rings again and Christina stuffs the needlepoint into her wicker sewing basket. 'It appears I'm expected to play housemaid yet again. I shall have to have a word with Hettie.'

A voice calls through the letterbox. 'Are you going to let me in or do I have to go back to Spain?'

Lulu yells in the direction of the kitchen. 'Shani! Auntie Jessie's here!'

'Please, Lulu, decorum,' Christina says as she heads toward the hallway. 'You are not calling pigs on a farm.' She opens the door to Jessie, who enfolds her mother in an effusive embrace.

'Mama!' Jessie kisses her mother on both her cheeks. 'It's so good to see you!'

Christina squirms as she submits to the unanticipated display of affection.

'Oh, 'ere we go, giving the neighbours a show,' Hettie says as she holds back the door curtain and ushers them into the house. ''And me your suitcase, Jessie. Trunk's coming later, I take it?'

Jessie relinquishes her battered leather suitcase to Hettie. 'No trunk, Hettie. I've discovered that one only needs a few things. Possessions can end up owning you and holding you back. You know me, I don't like restrictions.'

Christina scans Jessie's navy skirt, scuffed black lace-up shoes, plain white blouse and grey wool cardigan unravelling at the cuffs.

'Two months in France and you come home looking like a factory worker? Didn't you visit any of the lovely shops in Paris? You can't be going off to your new position at King's College Hospital looking like that, Jessie. What would your lovely husband have thought? He was always so nicely turned out. We'll head out to Selfridges next week and get you fixed up.'

'My clothes are perfectly functional, Mama. I was too busy in the refugee camp in France to go clothes shopping.'

A voice calls out from the staircase. 'Jessie, you may as well surrender. This is an argument you won't win.'

Jessie looks up to see Celie standing on the half-landing, a book in her hands and wire-rimmed glasses framing her striking blue eyes. Celie smiles, and Jessie sees the shadows that years of worry and stoicism have painted on her sister's face lift, like the sun breaking through a cloud.

'Jessie!' Etta runs down the hallway, oblivious to the yellow paint flying off the paintbrush she waves in her hand. She throws her arms around her sister and, kissing her on her cheek, grabs her hand. 'Come with me. I'm painting Medusa beheading Perseus.'

Celie leans across the banister. 'It was the other way around, Etta.'

Etta laughs. 'Not in my painting, Celie.' She yanks at Jessie's hand.

Jessie pulls her hand out of Etta's grasp. 'Wait, Etta. Where's Shani?'

Hettie pushes through the cluster of women. 'It's like bleedin' Covent Garden in 'ere. She's in the kitchen. I'll get 'er.'

Lulu emerges from the sitting room and waves shyly at the aunt she has come to idolise. 'Hello, Auntie Jessie, I'm Lulu. Do you want to hear me play "Jeepers Creepers"? I've been practising all week.'

'What a good idea, Lulu,' Christina says as she hands Jessie's coat to Celie. 'Then you can start on a new song next week for which, I am certain, we shall all be grateful.'

They have just made themselves comfortable in the sitting room when Shani appears in the doorway.

'Hello, Mama.'

'Shani!' Jessie blinks at the slender young sixteen-year-old in a fashionable cap-sleeved blue dress and black patent leather shoes. She jumps out of her chair and throws open her arms. 'Come here, *habibti!* I've missed you so much.'

Shani looks at her mother, her face devoid of expression. 'Have you?'

Jessie drops her arms. 'Of course. There wasn't a moment that you weren't in my mind.'

Shani shakes her head, her dark curly hair bouncing on her shoulders. 'Don't lie, Mama.' She turns to Christina. 'I'm going out to the pictures with Sibyl Chadwick. I'll be home in time for tea.'

Jessie sits down in the chair. For the first time, she realises that her decision to stay in Spain has cost her something that may be very difficult to recoup: Shani's trust.

The following day, Easter Sunday

Christina sets down her teacup on a side table and glances at her wristwatch. Behind her, Lulu sits at the piano working her way through a catalogue of Cole Porter songs.

'Whatever could be taking Etta and Adriana? They were meant to have been here half an hour ago. The lamb will be burnt to a crisp. I shall go and see how Hettie is faring. No doubt she is fuming at the delay.'

'She's not,' Shani says without looking up from the *Vogue* magazine article she is reading. 'She's eating biscuits and doing *The Times* crossword.'

'So that's where my crossword went. I shall have to have a word.'

Lulu is two shaky bars into 'Anything Goes' when the front door bangs against the hallway coat rack followed by Etta's 'Oops! Oh, dear!'

Jessie looks over her teacup at Celie. 'She's here.'

Etta appears in the doorway, resplendent in a black silk crepe dress with a white organdie collar and cuffs, and high-heeled patent leather shoes.

Christina frowns. 'Etta, you've been into my wardrobe again.'

Etta spins around and laughs. 'You can hardly blame me, Mama. You have all these lovely dresses hanging up in the wardrobe in your Chelsea flat simply calling out to be worn.'

'Where's Adriana?' Celie asks. 'I thought that's why you stayed with her in Chelsea last night. To make sure she got here on time. Mama's fretting about the roast lamb.'

Etta settles down on Christina's chair. 'She won't be a minute. We had to wait for Hans at Sloane Square Station.'

'Anything Goes' stops mid-note. Lulu looks over at Etta. 'Hans is coming? *My* Hans from Canada?'

'Yes,' Etta says. 'Didn't Mama tell you?'

'No, she didn't!' Lulu leaps up from the piano stool and runs over to look into the mirror over the fireplace mantel.

The teacup rattles on its saucer in Celie's hand. She sets it on the table beside her chair. She'd only seen Hans once since she'd arrived back in London. It was for Christmas lunch and Adriana and Etta had fought for his attention. Poor Lulu had been so upset to miss him as she'd been in the hospital recuperating from a tonsillectomy. There had been no opportunity to speak to Hans privately, and he hadn't alluded to any knowledge of her relationship with Max, but there had been a moment over the Christmas pudding when she'd caught him regarding her oddly before he'd looked away to laugh at some silly comment from Etta.

'Hans Brandt is coming for Easter lunch?'

Etta helps herself to a shortbread biscuit. 'Yes. It will be lovely to have a man here. What a shame our wonderful husbands couldn't be here for Easter, too. But, then, they are all such busy men. I've no doubt that Liliana is cooking up a wonderful feast for Carlo and Cousin Stefania at Villa Serenissima. Easter is quite the event on Capri.'

Jessie glances at Celie, who shakes her head.

Out in the hallway, the front door opens and heels click on the tiled floor. Adriana and Hans appear in the doorway.

'Sorry we're late,' Adriana says. Her face is flushed and her blonde curls are doing their best to escape the restriction of her navy hat. She smiles at Hans. 'We were unavoidably detained.'

'Hans!' Lulu runs across the room and throws her arms around him. 'I've missed you! No one told me you were coming or I would have worn my best dress!'

Hans laughs as he pats Lulu on her back. 'I've missed you, too,' he says as he extricates himself. 'My goodness, I barely recognise you. You're not a little girl anymore.'

'I've just turned nineteen. I'm training to be a nurse. I'm going back to residence at King's College Hospital tomorrow.'

'A nurse? I remember how you would patch up poor Ben Wheatley when you wanted to practise bandaging with your mother's old sheets. I'm glad to see you put all that to good use.'

He extends his hand to Celie as she joins them. 'I'm so happy to see you again, Mrs Jeffries.'

Celie brushes away his hand and gives him a hug. 'I am too, Hans. You're looking very well. I told you at Christmas to call me Celie. You're not my student anymore.'

Lulu grabs Hans's hand. 'Come and tell me all about everything, Hans. Do you like London? Have you seen *Algiers* yet? I love Charles Boyer. Perhaps you can take me.'

Adriana taps her fingers on Hans's shoulder, the diamond on her ring finger flashing. 'Perhaps Hans can take both of us, Lulu.'

Shani gasps and jumps out of her chair. 'Adriana! Are you engaged?'

Lulu's face falls. 'You're engaged? To Adriana?'

Adriana kisses Hans on his cheek. 'I am! We are!' She wiggles her fingers, the diamond throwing off sparks as it catches the light. 'Hans asked his stepbrother to send him his grandmother's engagement ring. Now it's mine!'

Hans smiles at his fiancée. 'As soon as I received it, I couldn't wait. I proposed to Adriana in the middle of Sloane Square.'

'He got down on his knees and everything!' Adriana says.

Celie rises from her chair and kisses Adriana on her cheek. 'Congratulations, my dear. I had no idea you even knew each other.'

'We met very briefly when I was here for tea with your mother after I'd come to London. You made me promise to ring her, remember? Then we bumped into each other several months later in Terroni's buying cannoli and she invited me to Sunday lunch. One thing led to another, as they say.'

Adriana pouts petulantly. 'You make it sound so unromantic, Hans. We fell in love and now I am going to become Mrs Hans Brandt.' She frowns. 'Or is it Mrs Henry Brand? Which is it here in the UK, darling?'

'I never understood why a woman has to give up her own name when she gets married,' Lulu grumbles. 'I'm never going to do that. I'm Louisa Jeffries till the day I die.'

'Spoken like a true suffragist, Lulu,' Celie says.

Shani pushes past Lulu. 'Let me see your ring. Oh, Adriana, it's lovely.'

Christina's heels click on the hallway tiles and she enters the room. 'What on earth is going on? I've no doubt Father Murphy can hear you all the way to St. Saviour's in Lewisham.'

'Adriana and Hans have just gotten engaged,' Shani says.

'Have you, really?' Christina smiles tightly as Adriana flashes the ring at her. 'Are you certain about this, Adriana? I thought you were taking up a position at the Central School of Arts and Crafts in September.'

'I can still do that, *Nonna*. This isn't the nineteenth century. Married women can work, in some places, at least.'

'Until you have children.'

'*Nonna*, please be happy for me.' Adriana looks over at Hans. 'I'm so happy.'

Shani returns to her chair and picks up the magazine. 'I thought you were in love with Mario.'

Jessie frowns at her daughter. 'Shani, really. Be polite.'

Shani glares at her mother. 'Who are you to tell me anything?'

'I'm your mother, Shani.'

Shani grunts as she flips a page. 'Barely.'

A bell rings and Christina gestures toward the dining room. 'Thank goodness for that. Let's all be happy, shall we? Hettie has cooked up a delicious Easter ham. Let us enjoy our lunch and give thanks for the risen Lord.'

Shani grimaces at her grandmother. 'Ham, Nana? I can't eat ham. I'm Muslim.'

Christina ushers Shani ahead of her into the hall. 'Don't be ridiculous, Shani. You were baptised a Catholic.'

Jessie joins them as they make their way down the hall to the dining room. 'Shani is both a Catholic and a Muslim, Mama. We must respect her wishes if they are contrary to her religious beliefs. I'm certain there's still some chicken leftover from yesterday. Shani can have that.'

Celie smiles as the voices of the others drift away. She collects the empty teacups and sets them on a silver tray.

'Can I be of any help, Mrs Jef— Celie?'

Celie looks up, startled. 'No, thank you, Hans. I can manage. Where's Adriana?'

'I believe the polite term is "powdering her nose".'

Celie nods. 'Yes, of course.' She picks up the tray and moves toward the doorway.

Hans holds out his hands. 'Please, I insist. Just tell me where to take it.'

'All right. I give up. Follow me to the kitchen. Hettie will love you for it.'

He follows her down the hallway. 'I meant to say earlier. Max sends his regards.'

Celie stops short. She stares straight ahead, though she feels like she is falling through a vast void. 'Max?'

'My stepbrother. I was in Bavaria skiing with him last month. It seems your name always comes up somehow when I'm with him.'

'Does it? How strange.'

'Not so very strange. When did you realise that Max was my stepbrother? When you stole the picture of Max and me from Uncle Klaus's house?'

Celie spins around. 'I never did such a thing!'

Hans smiles. 'It is all right. I never liked that picture anyway. I had such knobbly knees in that lederhosen!'

'Hans...' She sighs. 'As you evidently already know, Max was my German tutor before the war. That's all. There seemed to be no reason to tell you. It was a simple coincidence, nothing more.'

'Really? Nothing more? That is not the impression I was given by Max.'

Chapter Sixty-Three

Jessie & Celie

Clover Bar, Hither Green, London – May 1939

Celie opens the door of the greenhouse and steps inside. She offers a steaming mug of tea to her sister. 'So, here's where you're hiding, Jessie. Escaping from Mama or Etta?'

Jessie looks up from the potting trays where she's been planting garlic cloves in the compost. 'How about all of the above?' She brushes her dirty hands on her skirt and takes the mug of tea. 'Shani's missing garlic. I managed to get some bulbs from Terroni's and I'm trying to propagate them. I'll have to teach Hettie some Egyptian recipes. I'm trying my best to make up with Shani for being such a bad mother.'

Celie leans against the potting shelf. 'You're not a bad mother. You're just a different kind of mother. Shani will come around.'

'I hope so.' Jessie takes a sip of the tea. 'Sometimes I think I should never have stayed in Spain. That it was a selfish thing to do.'

'Jessie, you helped a lot of people there. Shani will understand that someday, and she'll be proud of you.'

Jessie grunts. 'Do you think so? She barely says two words to me at the moment. She's even said she wants to stay at Woldingham for her final year instead of living with me here at Clover Bar and going to a local school.'

'Don't take it personally. She's made friends there. It's not easy to start over.'

Jessie laughs. 'Don't take it personally? Of course I take it personally, Celie. The plan was for us go live together in London. She'll be eighteen when she graduates next year, and I will have missed my chance with her. I wish I knew how to fix it, but I don't.'

'Just be you, Jessie. It will be fine.'

'Sure.' She takes another sip of tea. 'How are you? I heard from Hettie that Mama has roped you into organising the WI's summer tombola.'

Celie shrugs. 'Yes. It's something. It keeps me busy.'

Jessie sets down her mug. 'No luck with any of the newspapers?'

'No. It seems no one wants a middle-aged woman journalist.'

'So that's it then? You're going to take up needlepoint and work for the WI for the rest of your days? Come on, Celie. Where's your old spirit? You used to have your fingers in so many pies. What's happened?'

'Life happened.' Celie picks up another handful of garlic cloves and resumes poking them into the potting tray. 'Canada was hard. The Depression was hard. My marriage was hard.'

'I know. But that's all behind you now. You're only forty-six. You've got a wonderful daughter who actually wants to spend time with you. You can write, you're a brilliant photographer, you can speak German, you've got a social conscience like no one else I know. You have a lot to offer, Celie. Look at being back here in

London as a chance to start over and do something for yourself instead of for Frank and the farm.'

Celie nods. 'Maybe you're right. I've felt quite lost.'

'I know. This is all new for me too. For Etta as well. We're all starting over. Three very different peas from the same pod.'

Celie smiles. 'The three Fry sisters.'

'The three Fry sisters.'

Chapter Sixty-Four

Celie & Christina

Selfridges Department Store, London – June 1939

Etta twirls around in front of the mirrors in the ladies' changing room, the emerald-green satin skirt of the drop-shoulder dress spinning around her.

'I love it, Celie! This is the one.'

'You look like a spinning top, Etta, and you can't wear that to Adriana's wedding. It's bad luck to wear green at weddings.'

'Says who? I think I look divine.'

'Something to do with jealous fairies. I read about it once when I was researching wedding traditions for my column in the *West Lake News*.'

Etta wrinkles her nose. 'Oh, pooh. Let me try on the mauve again.' She disappears behind one of the dressing room curtains.

Celie sets down her shopping bags and glances at her watch. 'It's almost five, Etta. We have to catch the bus in twenty minutes. We won't hear the end of it from Hettie if we're late for dinner.'

'I won't be a minute!'

Celie sighs and sits down on an empty stool. She tries unsuccessfully to stifle a yawn. She and Etta had been all over central London shopping for outfits for Adriana's wedding, funded by their mother, who had insisted her daughters and granddaughters look 'presentable' for Father Murphy at St Saviour's Church. Jessie had outright refused to join them, saying she had better things to do with her time, before leaving with Shani and Lulu to spend the day at Brighton Beach. Poor Jessie was running herself ragged between her new position as a surgeon at King's College Hospital and spending every moment of her spare time trying to make up to Shani for her long absence in Spain.

It had been good to talk to Jessie about how lost she'd been feeling since she'd come back to London with Lulu and Etta. She'd tried to find work with the *Daily Mirror*, but her contacts there had long departed, and she'd had no luck with any of the other newspapers or magazines she'd approached. She'd converted the attic into a small photography studio and dark room and had taken to experimenting with the solarisation techniques popularised by Man Ray and Lee Miller, using Etta as her model. But it was nothing more than a hobby, and Celie needed work. The relentless idleness of the endless unproductive months since she'd returned home had begun to weigh down on her, and it took all her will to force a cheerfulness that she didn't feel.

Jessie had noticed, of course. She'd always been able to read Celie like a book. She'd been right, too. Doing something, anything, was better than dragging herself through the oppressively empty days. So she'd taken Jessie's advice, and started to apply for positions teaching German. She'd even applied to the government for translation work in the hope that her sex would no longer be considered a liability, as it had when she'd applied to work for the Home Office Translation Bureau during the Great War. The world had changed a great deal since then.

'Etta? You collected the post this morning, didn't you? Did you see anything for me from the government's translation bureau?'

'No. Wait, there was something for you from a solicitor's office.'

'A solicitor's office? Are you certain? Why would I receive a letter like that?'

'Don't ask me. Ask Mama. She took it.'

'Mama took it? Why would she take my letter?'

Etta throws open the curtain, resplendent in a mauve silk dress. 'This is definitely the one. Mauve is absolutely my colour.'

Clover Bar, the following day

Christina taps her shoe on the hallway's encaustic tiles as she twists the telephone cord around her finger.

'… really, Dorothy, this is an egregious error on the part of your solicitors. It has caused me no end of problems with Ce— With my housekeeper who possesses far more curiosity than is advisable. Servants talk and I do not wish for this contentious issue to become idle gossip in London households. Your solicitors have very clear instructions to send any correspondence relating to the Bishop House matter to my solicitors in Lincoln's Inn Fields. It is not to come to my home address again, do I make myself clear?'

'My word, Christina,' Dorothy Adam says down the phone line. 'You're making a quite a mountain out of a molehill. It's almost like you have something to hide. *Do* you have something to hide, Christina?'

Christina runs her hand over her ear and tucks at her hair in irritation. 'I will not dignify that question with an answer,

Dorothy. This is a legal matter. We agreed that all correspondence should go through our solicitors in the first instance. I am merely pointing out this error. Please assure me that you will instruct your solicitors to rectify this for the future.'

'I honestly don't know why you're getting into such a huff, Christina. It was a simple oversight. But, since we're speaking, how is your lovely daughter Cecelia? Will she be returning to England any time soon, or has she become a Canadian?'

'Cecelia is fine. She is very happy in Canada, but she has no desire to relinquish her share of Bishop House. She and her husband have been discussing returning to London in the near future and would be looking to relocate to Bishop House. I have no doubt you and your son would find them to be delightful company.'

'Christina, we cannot live our lives based on speculation. Bishop House is mine and Christopher's, make no mistake. It has been our home since Harry's death. Pieces of paper are not going to change anything.'

Christina laughs coldly. 'That is where you are quite wrong, Dorothy. Pieces of paper, particularly if they are bequests in a will, change everything. Now, I really must go. I am extraordinarily busy.'

———————

Lulu steps back from the half-open door to the study as she listens to her grandmother ring off and stomp up the stairs. She runs the telephone conversation through her mind, examining her grandmother's responses as forensically as she scrutinises objects under her treasured microscope.

Why had Nana lied about her mother still being in Canada? And what was all that business about her mother and her late father moving to this Bishop House in London? What has Bishop House got to do with her mother? Who is Dorothy? Does her mother know anything about this? What's going on?

She screws up her mouth and rubs her forehead as she ponders her options. She won't say anything just yet. But she will keep her eyes and ears open. Something's going on, and she will make a point of finding out what it is.

Chapter Sixty-Five

The Fry Women

Clover Bar, Hither Green, London – September 3rd, 1939

Jessie fiddles with the knob on the sitting room wireless. 'It would be today of all days that the wireless chooses to give us bother. The Prime Minister's coming on in five minutes to tell us if we're at war or not.'

Celie looks up from her hand of cards. 'Stand it on top of Papa's *Complete Works of Alfred, Lord Tennyson*. That always works for me.'

'Put in your pennies, Mama,' Lulu says. 'We're all waiting for you.'

Etta sifts through her playing cards. 'I don't know how we're meant to play Whist when the Prime Minister's about to come on the wireless.'

Jessie joins the group at the table. 'It's something to do while we wait, isn't it? I expect everyone's glued to their sets this morning to hear if Germany is going to retreat from Poland. Remind me, what's trumps?'

'Spades,' Celie says. 'Everyone except our mother is glued to the wireless. She said the Prime Minister is irreligious for setting his ultimatum to Germany on a Sunday morning, and that she wasn't going to miss Mass to listen to him drone on about politics again.'

Lulu takes a trick with a two of spades, prompting a groan from Shani, who has lost her ace of diamonds. 'What happens to Hans if we go to war with Germany? Will you still get married, Adriana?'

'Of course we'll get married. The church is booked for Boxing Day, and we're going to Paris to stay at the George V Hotel for our honeymoon. I've already had my second fitting for my dress with Norman Hartnell and Hans is having his morning suit made in Savile Row. We were in Holland & Sherry choosing his suit fabric just the other day.'

'But Hans is German. He might be arrested if he stays here. Maybe he'll go back to Alberta. Would you go to Alberta with him, Adriana? I can teach you how to build an igloo.'

Celie flicks her gaze over at her daughter. 'Lulu, really.'

'Hans and I are not going anywhere, Lulu. Nobody knows Hans is German but us. Everyone else knows him as Henry Brand. That doesn't sound in the least German to me, so don't make a problem where there isn't one.'

Shani takes Lulu's king of hearts with her ace. 'Lulu's just jealous, Adriana. She has a crush on Hans.'

'Shani, don't stir the pot,' Jessie chides.

'Don't tell me what I can and can't do, Mama.'

Lulu tosses her cards on the table. 'I'm tired of this game.' She glares at Shani. 'And I don't have a crush on Hans, Little Miss Perfect.'

'Lulu, pick up your cards,' Celie admonishes. 'That's not very sportswoman-like behaviour.'

'What's the point? Everyone knows what I have now.'

The wireless crackles and the voice of the BBC's Alvar Liddell comes on. *'This is London. You will now hear a statement from the Prime Minister.'*

'Hettie!' Jessie shouts. 'Hettie, it's on!'

Christina enters the room, taking off her gloves. 'Really, Jessica. There's no need to holler like a banshee.' She looks at her family. 'If you must know, Father Murphy gave a very short sermon, which allowed us all to get home in time for the broadcast.'

Hettie stamps down the hallway and joins them in the sitting room just as Neville Chamberlain begins his announcement.

'This morning the British Ambassador in Berlin handed the German government a final note stating that unless we heard from them by eleven o'clock that they were prepared at once to withdraw their troops from Poland, a state of war would exist between us. I have to tell you now that no such undertaking has been received, and that, consequently, this country is at war with Germany…'

When the broadcast concludes, Christina turns off the wireless. The others sit in silence, the card game abandoned. Suddenly the shrieking whine of the air raid sirens penetrates through the streets of Hither Green, prompting the suburb's dogs to join in with howls and wails.

'Sirens!' Hettie shouts as she waves her arms in the direction of the garden. 'Get out to the shelter, quick!'

'The shelter?' Christina picks up her needlepoint from its basket. 'It's only just been finished. There's nothing in it yet. Surely the Germans won't be flying over London within seconds of the broadcast. It's scaremongering. I intend to stay right where I am.'

Hettie stomps across the Persian carpet and grabs the needlepoint out of Christina's hands.

'We're at flippin' war, didn't you 'ear? I don't fancy 'aving a bomb drop on me 'ead on account of you being an idiot, Christina Fry. I'm 'eading out to the shelter. Anyone else wiff a shred of sense will join me. We'd best get used to it. Nuffing is going to be the same again.'

Chapter Sixty-Six

Lulu & Christina

Central London Employment Exchange, London - October 1939

Lulu sets a mug of milky tea and a plate of chocolate digestive biscuits down on the table in the medical examinations room at the Central London Employment Exchange.

'Milk and two sugars, is that right, Betty?'

Her fellow nursing colleague, Betty Edwards, looks up from the medical assessment forms she is arranging in alphabetical order and smiles broadly. 'You are a doll, Lulu. I'm absolutely parched.' She pushes her chair away from the table. 'I swear if I have to fend off one more randy conscript's offer of marriage, I'll join the Catholics and become a nun.'

Lulu slides into the vacated chair, careful not to spill her own tea on her pristine white apron.

'There's something about a nurse's uniform that seems to make men's minds go funny. Even I've had a chat-up line or two, and I'm no Olivia de Havilland.'

'You've got that wholesome "girl next door" look that men love, Lulu.'

Lulu laughs as she eyes her voluptuous blonde friend. 'You mean the girl who's the loyal friend of the pretty girl who gets the boy?'

'You know that's not what I meant.'

Lulu shoos Betty away. 'Go on. Have your tea and get back to the hospital. I'll see you at supper at the residence once I've done my shift. Save some treacle pudding for me.'

'I will.'

Lulu watches the gazes of the young male conscripts follow Betty as she walks toward the lobby.

'And custard!'

Lulu picks up a biscuit. She takes a bite and chews as she shuffles through the stack of forms, correcting the placement of the 'F's Betty has filed after the 'G's. Someone clears his throat and she looks up to see a dark-haired young man, with eyes the exact bright blue of the delphiniums in her grandmother's summer garden, smiling at her.

'Sorry to disturb your tea break.'

She swallows the biscuit and rubs the crumbs off her lips. 'I'm not supposed to eat or drink at the table, but' – she shrugs – 'what are they going to do? Fire a volunteer?'

'I entirely agree. Sacking a nurse for eating a chocolate digestive with her tea is positively unBritish.' He hands her his medical form. 'It appears I've passed.'

She takes the form and scans the doctor's assessment. 'A1, Mr Adam. Very good. Looks like you'll be off to training camp. The Air Force, I see.'

'That's if the RAF will have me.'

She rubber-stamps the form and adds it to the top of her stack. 'I imagine they'll be thrilled to have you. I hope you're not afraid of heights.'

He laughs and leans across the table conspiratorially. 'I best not tell them about the time I got stuck in the oak tree in the garden when I climbed it to rescue our cat. There we were, the two of us, happy to go up, not so happy to come down.'

Lulu laughs. 'You would never have managed out in Alberta. Climbing trees was an absolute requirement when I was growing up.'

'Ah, Alberta. A Canadian. I knew you weren't English.' He holds out his hand. 'Christopher Adam.'

Lulu shakes his hand. 'Very nice to meet you, Mr Adam. I'm Louisa Jeffries. Everyone calls me Lulu.'

Someone taps Christopher on his shoulder. 'Ay, mate. We ain't got all day. Stop chattin' up the nurse.'

'It looks like you've been caught out, Mr Adam.'

'It looks like I have. Enjoy your tea and biscuits.' He taps the form. 'You've got my address. Look me up in six weeks when I've finished my training. I know a great place for tea.'

'And cake?'

'Of course, cake.'

Lulu smiles. 'That sounds like an offer I can't refuse.'

Several weeks later

The telephone in the hallway in Clover Bar rings. Christina looks up from her needlepoint.

'Hettie! The phone is ringing!'

The telephone's rings cut through the silent house.

'Hettie!' Christina sets down her needlepoint and rises from her chair with a huff. 'I suppose I shall answer it then!' She stamps into the hallway and lifts up the receiver. 'Gilmore 9721.'

'Hello. May I speak with Mrs Fry, please.'

Christina stiffens as she recognises the voice. 'This is she.'

'Good. This is Dorothy Adam.'

'I know. How may I help you, Dorothy?'

'I shall keep this short, Christina.'

'That would be ideal.' Christina smiles as the woman on the other end of the line huffs irritably.

'I have just had the pleasure of hosting my son and a young Canadian nurse he's quite taken with for tea.'

'Have you? How nice. What has this to do with me?'

'It has everything to do with you, Christina. The young lady's name is Louisa Jeffries, although she insisted upon being called Lulu.'

Christina's heart jolts. 'Is that so?'

'Yes. Of course I found it most interesting that she shared a surname with your daughter Cecelia. I couldn't help but dig a little deeper.'

Christina runs her hand over her ear. 'Did you?'

'Oh, do stop playing the fool, Christina. You and I both know that this Lulu Jeffries is your granddaughter. I understand that Cecelia is back in London and has been for over a year. It begs the question as to why you still have been acting as her legal representation in the matter of her claim on Bishop House.'

'Dorothy, I…' She clears her throat. 'I think this would be best discussed in person.'

'I couldn't agree more, Christina.' There is a pause on the line. 'There's something which concerns me as much as I believe it will concern you.'

'I couldn't possibly imagine what that could be, Dorothy.'

'Have you not put it together? As I said, my son, Christopher – Harry's son, Christopher – appears to be enamoured of Harry's granddaughter, Louisa.'

Christina gasps.

'Yes, Christina, I was as shocked as you are.'

'It can't be permitted, Dorothy. We have to stop them.'

'I am entirely in agreement, Christina. The sooner we meet, the better.'

Acknowledgments

I have in my possession an old black and white photograph of my grandmother, Edith Fry Chinn, holding the hands of my two-year-old father and four-year-old Auntie Betty on Capilano Suspension Bridge in Vancouver in the winter of 1922. They are bundled up against the Canadian cold and smile into the lens of my grandfather Frank's camera. They'd just arrived in Canada from England, and would soon head out to Westlock, Alberta to the piece of virgin land granted to my grandfather by the Soldiers' Land Settlement Scheme.

The story of the struggle they, and many others like them, faced over the next twenty years is one I wanted to explore in this book. My father did indeed have a border collie named Kip, and the Chinns did eventually find themselves living in the 'Chicken Coop' by the Westlock rail tracks after their farm was repossessed during the Depression. This book is my acknowledgement of the sacrifices my grandparents made in the hope of creating a better life for their family. Their children, grandchildren and great-grandchildren have reaped the benefit of their courage and fortitude.

I have always been a history buff and, through Jessie, chose to develop her story against the backdrop of the political unrest in Egypt and the fight between the left-wing Republicans and fascist Nationalists during the Spanish Civil War. I could never have come anywhere near to achieving this without the insights and information on offer in George Orwell's *Homage to Catalonia*, *Orwell in Spain* edited by Peter Davison, and Nick Lloyd's

Forgotten Places: Barcelona and the Spanish Civil War. I was most fortunate to join the Spanish Civil War tour, devised by Nick, during a research trip to Barcelona with my sister, Carolyn, where we were guided through the city's experience of the war by the immensely knowledgeable historian Catherine Howley.

And then, of course, there's Etta's life in Hollywood. I'm an immense film buff, and where else could I put Etta in the 1930s but Hollywood in the Golden Age? I can't tell you how much I enjoyed re-watching old Marx Brothers movies and the numerous auditions of seasoned actresses and starlets during the search for Scarlett O'Hara that can be found on YouTube.

Thanks, as always, must go to my sister and trusted beta reader, Carolyn Chinn, who is always there as a sounding board when I reach tangles in the stories that need to be unknotted. Thanks go as well to my brother-in-law, James Dodson, for his support, which is greatly appreciated, and to my nephew, Henry, and his speagle, Hugo, who always brighten my day. Thank you to my friends who have offered me so much encouragement during the year of this book's creation: Vicky Seton, Margo Savitskaya, Melvyn Fickling (thank you for the title!) and my sister Judith Chinn, in particular.

My colleagues at KLC School of Design/West Dean College and Holland & Sherry London (especially Dudley Beckwith) help me balance the solitude of writing with social days of teaching and engaging with interior design clients, and my fellow thespians at the Burgess Hill Theatre Club bring fun into my life (with thanks to Robson Ternouth for giving me such a great name for Robson McCrea).

As for my editor, Charlotte Ledger, at One More Chapter, I couldn't ask for a better champion of my work. I am forever appreciative of the insights she brings to my early drafts, and know my books are greatly improved by her perceptive input.

There are many people who come together to create a book. This book would not exist without the work of the wonderful copyeditor Laura Burge, eagle-eyed proofreader Tony Russell, editor Bonnie Macleod, designer Lucy Bennett who created the eye-catching cover, and the continued support of my agent, Joanna Swainson.

I hope you enjoy the stories of the three Fry sisters and their mother Christina as much as I enjoy writing them.

ONE MORE CHAPTER

YOUR NUMBER ONE STOP

FOR PAGETURNING BOOKS

The author and One More Chapter would like to thank everyone who contributed to the publication of this story...

Analytics
Abigail Fryer
Maria Osa

Audio
Fionnuala Barrett
Ciara Briggs

Contracts
Sasha Duszynska Lewis
Florence Shepherd

Design
Lucy Bennett
Fiona Greenway
Holly Macdonald
Liane Payne
Dean Russell

Digital Sales
Lydia Grainge
Emily Scorer
Georgina Ugen

Editorial
Laura Burge
Kate Elton
Arsalan Isa
Charlotte Ledger
Bonnie Macleod
Jennie Rothwell
Tony Russell

International Sales
Bethan Moore

Marketing & Publicity
Chloe Cummings
Emma Petfield

Operations
Melissa Okusanya
Hannah Stamp

Production
Emily Chan
Denis Manson
Francesca Tuzzeo

Rights
Lana Beckwith
Rachel McCarron
Agnes Rigou
Hany Sheikh Mohamed
Zoe Shine
Aisling Smyth

The HarperCollins Distribution Team

The HarperCollins Finance & Royalties Team

The HarperCollins Legal Team

The HarperCollins Technology Team

Trade Marketing
Ben Hurd
Eleanor Slater

UK Sales
Laura Carpenter
Isabel Coburn
Jay Cochrane
Tom Dunstan
Sabina Lewis
Holly Martin
Erin White
Harriet Williams
Leah Woods

And every other essential link in the chain from delivery drivers to booksellers to librarians and beyond!

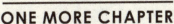

ONE MORE CHAPTER

One More Chapter is an
award-winning global
division of HarperCollins.

Sign up to our newsletter to get our
latest eBook deals and stay up to date
with our weekly Book Club!
<u>Subscribe here.</u>

Meet the team at
<u>www.onemorechapter.com</u>

Follow us!

 @OneMoreChapter_
 @OneMoreChapter
 @onemorechapterhc

Do you write unputdownable fiction?
We love to hear from new voices.
Find out how to submit your novel at
<u>www.onemorechapter.com/submissions</u>